D1082779

DIVISIBLE MAN™
ENGINE OUT
&
OTHER SHORT FLIGHTS

by

Howard Seaborne

ALSO BY HOWARD SEABORNE

DIVISIBLE MAN
A Novel – September 2017
DIVISIBLE MAN: THE SIXTH PAWN
A Novel – June 2018
DIVISIBLE MAN: THE SECOND GHOST
A Novel – September 2018
ANGEL FLIGHT
A Story – September 2018
DIVISIBLE MAN: THE SEVENTH STAR
A Novel – June 2019
ENGINE OUT
A Story – September 2019
WHEN IT MATTERS
A Story – October 2019
A SNOWBALL'S CHANCE
A Story – November 2019
DIVISIBLE MAN: TEN MAN CREW
A Novel – November 2019
DIVISIBLE MAN: THE THIRD LIE
A Novel – May 2020
DIVISIBLE MAN: THREE NINES FINE
A Novel – November 2020
DIVISIBLE MAN: EIGHT BALL
A Novel – September 2021
DIVISIBLE MAN: ENGINE OUT
AND OTHER SHORT FLIGHTS
A Story Collection – June 2022
DIVISIBLE MAN: NINE LIVES LOST
A Novel – June 2022

PRAISE FOR HOWARD SEABORNE

"This book is a strong start to a series…Well-written and engaging, with memorable characters and an intriguing hero."
—Kirkus Reviews
DIVISIBLE MAN [DM1]

"Seaborne's crisp prose, playful dialogue, and mastery of technical details of flight distinguish the story…this is a striking and original start to a series, buoyed by fresh and vivid depictions of extra-human powers and a clutch of memorably drawn characters…"
—BookLife
DIVISIBLE MAN [DM1]

"Even more than flight, (Will's relationship with Andy)—and that crack prose—powers this thriller to a satisfying climax that sets up more to come."
—BookLife
DIVISIBLE MAN [DM1]

"Seaborne, a former flight instructor and charter pilot, once again gives readers a crisply written thriller. Self-powered flight is a potent fantasy, and Seaborne explores its joys and difficulties engagingly. Will's narrative voice is amusing, intelligent and humane; he draws readers in with his wit, appreciation for his wife, and his flight-drunk joy…Even more entertaining than its predecessor—a great read."
—Kirkus Reviews
DIVISIBLE MAN: THE SIXTH PAWN [DM2]

"Seaborne, a former flight instructor and pilot, delivers a solid, well-written tale that taps into the near-universal dream of personal flight. Will's narrative voice is engaging and crisp, clearly explaining technical matters while never losing sight of humane, emotional concerns. The environments he describes...feel absolutely real. Another intelligent and exciting superpowered thriller."

—*Kirkus Reviews*
DIVISIBLE MAN: THE SECOND GHOST [DM3]

"As in this series' three previous books, Seaborne...proves he's a natural born storyteller, serving up an exciting, well-written thriller. He makes even minor moments in the story memorable with his sharp, evocative prose...Will's smart, humane and humorous narrative voice is appealing, as is his sincere appreciation for Andy—not just for her considerable beauty, but also for her dedication and intelligence...Seaborne does a fine job making side characters and locales believable. It's deeply gratifying to see Will deliver righteous justice to some very bad people. An intensely satisfying thriller—another winner from Seaborne."

—*Kirkus Reviews*
DIVISIBLE MAN: THE SECOND GHOST [DM4]

"Seaborne...continues his winning streak in this series, offering another page-turner. By having Will's knowledge of and control over his powers continue to expand while the questions over how he should best deploy his abilities grow, Seaborne keeps the concept fresh and readers guessing...Will's enemies are becoming aware of him and perhaps developing techniques to detect him, which makes the question of how he can protect himself while doing the most good a thorny one. The conspiracy is highly dramatic yet not implausible given today's political events, and the action sequences are excitingly cinematic...Another compelling and hugely fun adventure that delivers a thrill ride."

"Any reader of this series knows that they're in good hands with Seaborne, who's a natural storyteller. His descriptions and dialogue are crisp, and his characters deftly sketched...The book keeps readers tied into its complex and exciting thriller plot with lucid and graceful exposition, laying out clues with cleverness and subtlety...Also, although Will's abilities are powerful, they have reasonable limitations, and the protagonist is always a relatable character with plenty of humanity and humor...Another riveting, taut, and timely adventure with engaging characters and a great premise."

— *Kirkus Reviews*
DIVISIBLE MAN: EIGHT BALL [DM8]

"Seaborne's latest series entry packs a good deal of mystery. Everything Will stumbles on, it seems, dredges up more questions...All this shady stuff in Montana and unrest in Wisconsin make for a tense narrative...Will's periodic sarcasm is welcome, as it's good-natured and never overwhelming...A smart, diverting tale of an audacious aviator with an extraordinary ability."

— *Kirkus Reviews*
DIVISIBLE MAN: NINE LIVES LOST [DM9]

"This engaging compendium will surely pique new readers' interest in earlier series installments. A captivating, altruistic hero and appealing cast propel this enjoyable collection of supernatural-flavored tales."

— *Kirkus Reviews*
DIVISIBLE MAN: ENGINE OUT & OTHER SHORT FLIGHTS

THE SERIES

While each DIVISIBLE MAN ^{TM} novel tells its own tale, many elements carry forward and the novels are best enjoyed in sequence. The short story "Angel Flight" is a bridge between the third and fourth novels and is included with the third novel, DIVISIBLE MAN - THE SECOND GHOST.

DIVISIBLE MAN ^{TM} is available in print, digital and audio.

DIVISIBLE MAN ^{TM} is available at or can be ordered from your local independent bookseller.

For advance notice of new releases and exclusive material available only to Email Members, join the DIVISIBLE MAN ^{TM} Email List at **HowardSeaborne.com**.

Sign up today and get a FREE DOWNLOAD.

CONTENTS

HHDPU - Hand Held Directable Power Unit

SCUZ - Self-Contained Unit for Zooming

ZIPPY - Zoom Implementing Personal Propulsion in the Yard

FLUB - Flight Launching Unit - B-Model

SCRAM - Special Creation Rendering Aerial Maneuverability

DOLT - Discrete Operational Lift Transmitter

FLOP - Flight Launching Operational Propulsion

BLASTER - Basic Linear Aerial System for Transport, Electric Rechargeable

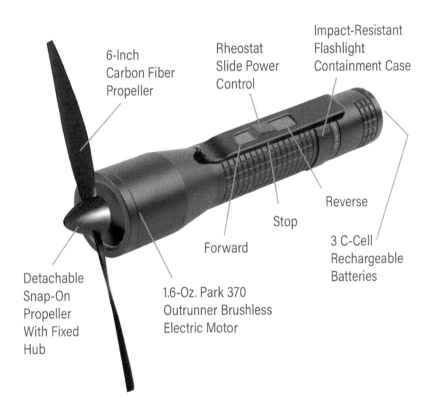

6-Inch
Carbon Fiber
Propeller

Rheostat
Slide Power
Control

Impact-Resistant
Flashlight
Containment Case

Reverse

Stop

Forward

3 C-Cell
Rechargeable
Batteries

Detachable
Snap-On
Propeller
With Fixed
Hub

1.6-Oz. Park 370
Outrunner Brushless
Electric Motor

ACKNOWLEDGMENTS

This pilot is blessed with a crew that deserves recognition for their patience, dedication, expertise and collaboration. My wife, for the "read and write" evenings spent in connected silence. My dear friends and family for invaluable help with big events like the EAA Airventure (thank you, Robin, Ariana, Rich and Chryste!) My incomparable editor, Stephen Parolini, for his unflinching assessment of these characters and their motivations. The team at TWD, David, Carol, April, Claire, Kristie, Rebecca and Steve, for operating the machinery that makes this possible. My medical expert, Stacey, for making right what I got wrong. My dear friend, cheerleader, challenger, beta reader and trivia champ, Rich. The indispensable Robin Ann, my incredible beta reader and re-reader and re-re-reader, the Copy Editor who can spot a typo on the manifest of a passing airliner. This collection is the Divisible Man's tenth mission. Like all before it, and many more to come, it would never have left the ground without such willing and supportive hands. Thank you.

For Ariana and Isabella
because you let me begin with
"Once upon a time…"

PREFACE

THE OTHER THING

It's like this: I wake up nearly every morning in the bed I share with my wife. After devoting a religious moment to appreciating the stunning, loving woman beside me, I ease off the mattress and pick my way across the minefield of creaks and groans in the old farmhouse's wooden floor. I slip into the hall and head for the guest bathroom two doors down—the one with the quietest toilet flush. I take care of essential business, then pull up to the mirror. The face offers no surprises. I give it a moment, then picture a set of levers in my head—part of the throttle-prop-mixture quadrant on a twin-engine Piper Navajo. The levers I imagine are to the right, a fourth set not found on any airplane, topped with classic round balls. I see them fully retracted, pulled toward me, the pilot. My eyes are open —it makes no difference—I can see the levers either way. I close my hand on them. I push. They move smoothly and swiftly. Balls to the wall.

For a split second I wonder, as I did the day before, and the day before that, if this trick will work again. Then—

Fwooomp!

—I hear it. A deep and breathy sound—like the air being sucked out of a room. The sound is audible only in my head, if that can be considered audible.

A cool sensation flashes over my skin. The first dip in a farm pond after a hot, dusty day. The shift of an evening breeze after sunset.

I vanish.

Bleary eyes and tossed hair wink out and the shower curtain behind me—the one with the frogs on it—fills in where my head had been. My feet leave the cold tile floor. My body remains solid, but gravity and I are no longer on speaking terms. I begin to float. A stiff breeze will send me on my way if I don't hang on to something.

The routine never varies. I've tested it nearly every morning since I piloted an air charter flight down the RNAV 31 Approach to Essex County Airport but never made the field. I have no memory of the crash. The running theory is that I collided with something in midair. I have dreams of hitting something, but I'm not sure if the dreams come from the event or were suggested afterward. In the dreams, everything is peachy until something—it's just a hole in the sky—tears the airplane apart under me. Evidence suggests I fell more than five hundred feet and landed in a marsh, sitting in the pilot's seat. That's where the Essex Volunteer Fire Department found me.

Since the night of the crash, whenever I picture that set of levers in my mind and I push them fully forward, I vanish. Pull them back, and I reappear.

Now you know as much as I do about *the other thing.*

Andy

1

ANDY

My wife likes to tell people we met when she pulled me over for driving while full of myself. She insists such a law exists on the books in Essex County. That she pulled me over in full uniform while on patrol in a City of Essex squad car is not a lie, but she employs a bit of creative license in our origin story. With good reason.

The first time I saw her, the *actual* first time, she walked into the fixed base operation offices at Essex County Airport on the arm of a man named Carl Lofton. I was in my second year working as a pilot for Essex County Air Services, wearing the multiple hats of flight instructor, charter pilot, and—when the weather or slow business meant no bookings—would-be mechanic wearing coveralls in the hangar, assisting with annual inspections and such repairs as Doc, our certified Airframe and Powerplant mechanic, would allow. Doc, thankfully, is about as good-natured a wrench-turner as the cold war Air Force ever minted, a fixture at Essex County Air Service since Bush Senior was president. I can follow directions and handle a set of tools, but I also ask a lot of questions, which Doc answers with endless patience. I think it has something to do with the fact that when I put on a set of coveralls, he hands off the dirtiest, most monotonous jobs to me.

The day Andrea Katherine Taylor walked through our tinted glass office doors, I was not, thankfully, wearing greasy coveralls. I stood looking my professional pilot best in a clean white shirt with a black tie and epaulets denoting my Captainly Authority, having just returned from an afternoon charter run to the upper peninsula of Michigan. I leaned on the counter, adding to my aura of great aviation prowess by holding a clipboard in one hand and a pen in the other.

Men are men, and when we see a woman like Andrea Taylor, we stop and look. Married men do it from behind sunglasses and with furtive glances. Single guys do it with tongues hanging out. We all do it. And we all run instant calculations, measuring ourselves against the dumb but lucky schmuck the woman is with. From those calculations, we project a flight path into a happily-ever-after future with such a woman. It's a fallacy that men don't want to commit. We do it all the time, all day long, with dozens of women we see on the street and in our minds.

Andrea Taylor could (and still can) stop a clock. Thick waves of auburn hair, taking and shooting back sheens of sunlight. A slender waist my hands instantly imagined gripping, blossoming into hips that signaled procreation to some lizard part of my brain. And legs. Oh, God bless the designer of that summer dress she wore, which shared most of her sculpted legs on one end and hung tastefully yet tantalizingly cut above the bosom at the other end, where she had just slightly more than most women her size and weight carry. Ever so slightly more.

Men stop and look, and some women collect those looks like Spanish gold, but a woman like Andrea will make you meet her at the eyes. They're too bright, too alert, too alive and they will hunt you down and demand direct contact, and once connected, she's the one doing the appraising, with little mercy. Her lips partnered with her eyes, pursed slightly, equally appraising. Their deep color seemed all her own and the smile they could conjure flashed like a magic spell. Her skin had just enough creamy caramel color to suggest what she took from the summer sun didn't burn and needed no enhancement.

She had the magazine looks, but it was immediately apparent she wasn't a two-dimensional beauty.

My first impression of Andrea Taylor was of a woman who knows when men are looking. When she chooses to look back, she will make you feel like the little boy you are.

My second impression was that she may have been on Carl Lofton's arm, but she flew in formation; she was nobody's cargo.

I didn't like Carl. Hadn't for as long as I'd known him.

Now I hated him.

Aviation is a family of like-minded people with a strong sense of dedication and purpose. The pilots I know, those I learned from, those I taught, and those I met along the way, are sharp, intelligent, precise, and humble before the forces of nature we challenge. Then there are the Carl Loftons. They don't fly because a childhood passion sent balsa wood airplanes zooming around the back yard. They fly because an airplane is another notch in the belt, like the boat, the SL Mercedes or Corvette, or the place on the lake. They fly because money is no object, and yet it is the sole object. So, Carl Lofton, an arrogant ass who made his money being an arrogant ass in real estate or an arrogant ass practicing law or perhaps as an arrogant ass stealing social security checks, added a pilot's license to his hundred-dollar haircuts and single-malt scotch collection.

Carl had passed his Private Pilot Checkride a few months before, and we all knew he would be buying his own airplane too soon. It's an old saw, but a pilot who earns his license—who has passed a difficult written exam and flown a practical test under the severe eye of an FAA examiner—has only earned a license to learn.

Except for the Carl Loftons of the world. They already know it all. Instead of continuing to learn, the Carl Loftons go out and buy more airplane than they should, usually a little too fast and a little too complex. And trouble follows.

Standing there, watching Carl and his new girlfriend sweep into the flight office, I faced a choice. Stay, and enjoy the view of the woman, or duck into the inner office and avoid Carl's smug, over-loud baritone. I caught a glance from Rosemary, the white-haired goddess of our front desk (ever since the Wright Brothers, she liked to claim). Her sharp look warned me not to run like the coward she knew I was, and she rolled her eyes when I did just that. Besides, I could still enjoy a view of the woman walking out to the flight line from the inner office, all the less obtrusively. A nice afternoon breeze swept the flight line, and that summer dress—lemonade and roses—looked delightfully light.

Carl rented one of the Cessna 172s he had trained in, and a short while later I watched the airplane wiggle a little in the cross-wind as they climbed out into the late afternoon, summer-hot sky.

* * * * *

"That girl is going to be sick," Rosemary announced a little over an hour later, looking out the office windows.

Leaning on the customer side of the counter, updating my logbook as a means of killing the last duty hour of the day, I had watched Carl's landing with clinical interest. We had a decent crosswind, ten to fifteen knots about forty degrees off the nose of the airplane. A Cessna 172 is a high-wing airplane, light in a wind, and a little slab sided. I grudgingly gave Carl points for holding a crab angle into the flare on landing yet kicking the rudder enough to line up the wheels on touchdown. He came in hot, though. I marked that against him. He rolled it off the runway and taxied to the gas pumps on the main ramp and shut down.

The woman let herself out of the passenger side without waiting for Carl to open the door. She stepped confidently onto the landing gear strut and down to the apron. She moved with sharp intent. The way she left Carl behind and immediately headed for the office suggested trouble between the dating couple. But Rosemary read people well, and as this dark-haired beauty stepped purposefully up the sidewalk toward the office, I saw what Rosemary saw. The woman's hands extended at her side with her fingers stretched out, the way someone might reach for balance walking on a beam. Her steps were measured and urgent. Her eyes hid behind a set of Ray Ban aviators, good pilot sunglasses though I later learned they were cop's sunglasses, but it was easy to see that her focus fixed on the next ten feet of pavement. She hurried.

"Here," Rosemary said. She handed me the plastic wastebasket from behind the counter. "She ain't gonna make it."

The woman's right hand swept up toward her lips. It was coming.

I pushed through the inner doors to the office, shoved open the outer doors and met her one pace beyond. She might have looked at me in horror, wishing no one was there to witness what was about to happen, but sharp appraisal kicked in; the wastebasket offered salvation.

I handed her the wastebasket. Took her by the elbow and pushed through the doors. She closed a two-handed grip on the wastebasket. Her pace doubled. With my hand on her elbow, I pulled her across the hall to the empty pilot's lounge. Her scent broke through the standard aviation office cologne of grease, fuel, and what traces of tobacco lingered in the ceiling tiles from the days when everybody smoked, and for a moment I caught a whiff of something like fresh fruit at a summer breakfast. She rushed the last few paces to the leather couch and dropped in a flutter of summer dress, doubling over.

I had her hair in my hands as the first retching shook her shoulders. My own stomach announced its intentions to go aerobatic, but I barked back at it in my head. *Stand down.*

It came fast, in body-shaking heaves, then spits and coughs. I continued to hold her hair but extended one leg behind me and kicked the door to the pilot lounge shut.

She gulped some air and vomited again. The first round had been productive. This, not so much. A sheen of sweat broke out on her slender neck and the fine slope where it met her shoulders. A few errant strands of her rich hair curled in glossy moisture forming mysterious glyphs. God help me, the woman was vomiting into a wastebasket, yet for an instant I imagined that sheen of sweat and that dark hair against a pillow.

She tried to rise, but I bunched her hair in one hand and put the other on her shoulder.

"Eyes shut, stay still, just breathe," I said.

I got a nod. She pushed the basket away from her face to escape the smell before it induced another round. I took it from her and set it aside. She nodded again.

"'M okay," she whispered.

"No, you're not. This will take a while." I didn't want to let go of her hair, but she turned her head slightly, signaling that the moment was over. "You're going to want to lie down for a bit."

"No, I really—" She started to rise.

"Lasagna," I said.

She dropped onto the leather cushions and her hands shot out, groping. I put the wastebasket in her fingers. She yanked it beneath her face. Her body heaved. More coughing. More spitting. Then gulps of air.

"Bastard."

I had my hands wrapped around her hair again, figuring that gave me temporary immunity.

Her lungs settled into a rhythm of short, strong breaths.

"I'm Will," I said.

"I'm deeply embarrassed," she said into the top of the waste-basket, this time enduring the swill at the bottom, knowing how close she was to launching again.

"Nice to meet you, Deeply," I said. "Been there. Done that."

She didn't speak for a moment. She drew herself upright, and God help me again, but the view improved dramatically from where I stood above her. The light sheen of sweat condensed and traced glistening lines down the center of her chest. Her breathing continued in short, choppy in-outs, with a pause between each to see if the vomiting would be triggered again. After a cautious assessment, she pushed away the wastebasket once more. I took it.

"Lie down. Let the room stop spinning. I'll get rid of this."

Still not looking up, eyes still shut, breathing still quick, she slid across the leather sofa, feeling its dimensions, then she eased herself down.

I stole another long look before I left.

I dumped the wastebasket in the Men's Room toilet and gave it a quick rinse. I left it there.

Carl Lofton walked up the sidewalk toward the office. I took up a casual stance beside the office counter. A light electric sensation eased down the back of my neck. I felt the nerves in my arms answer. I flexed my fingers the way I do when I'm coming up on the final approach fix on an instrument approach, about to drop the landing gear and nail the glide slope needle. All focus. Everything clear and in its place. Something in the look on my face made Rosemary say, "Uh-oh." She rose from the rolling office chair behind the counter and found something to do in the inner office.

"Hey, Carl," I said flatly when he pushed through the doors.

"Will! My man!" The handshake was over-strong. Playing the alpha dog. I grinned at him, and he grinned back, too stupid to see that my grin didn't go any farther than my lips.

I said, "What a great day to fly! A little bumpy, but wow. Did you show her some stuff?" I flexed my eyebrows, like we were buddies, like I wanted to hear him boast. His shit-eating grin widened. Boasting is what he did best.

"You know it!"

"Yeah? Crankin' and bankin'? Makin' big holes in the sky?"

"If you know what you're doing, even a 172 can sing, am I right?"

Except you don't know what you're doing, asshole.

"You know it, man! You know it!" I punched his shoulder.

Carl glanced around and adopted a theatrical expression of conspiracy between brother aviators. "I showed her. Rolled that baby." He puffed himself up like I was supposed to give him a high five. I wanted to punch his greasy nose through the back of his skull, but I kept up the grin, and he bought it like cheap land.

"No shit three-sixty rolled it? Up and over?"

His head bobbed. Idiot. "You know it. She loved it, man."

I stood there staring at him. Grin fixed. Eyes cold. I saw a flicker of dawning realization.

"Say, where is she?"

"You rolled it?"

More dawning. "Well, yeah. A nice barrel roll, you know. Pretty much just one gee."

"Carl, what category aircraft is a 172?"

"Huh? A 172? Say, did you see where she went? Is she in the can?" He gestured down the hall. "It was kinda bumpy out there today. I think she was getting a little green toward the end. Maybe I should check on her—"

"Carl, what category aircraft is a 172?"

I got a hesitant look from him. Somewhere in his smug self-confidence, a that's-not-right moment intruded on his lordly command of Carl's World. It's the moment when a pilot hears an engine misfire. When a landing gear light doesn't turn green. When the oil pressure needle wavers. Men like Carl generally don't recognize such moments. They don't listen when tiny voices whisper at them. But he looked at me now. My grin evaporated. Ice formed in my eyes.

"A 172 is not an aerobatic category aircraft, Carl."

"I know, but I can keep the gees well within limits. A barrel roll, that's just—that's easy, one gee if you do it ri—"

"You fucking barrel rolled one of our aircraft?"

"Look, I, uh—"

"Scared the shit out of some poor passenger?"

"C'mon, man, I know what—"

"You know what you're doing? Really?" My tone was smooth, even. Ice on a still pond. "You've had aerobatic training? You were in an aircraft rated for aerobatics?"

He stared.

"Hey, I was careful."

"You're done here, Carl. You're never renting another aircraft from us. Do you understand me?"

"You can't—"

"Oh, yes I can. And I'm going to e-mail every other FBO in the state, so you can forget about taking your shit show on the road. You're an arrogant prick who doesn't belong in the cockpit."

"Fuck you!" Red streaks rose in his cheeks. Carl probably had twenty pounds on me, most of it billowing over his belt, but I had an inch of height. This wasn't going anywhere. "You can't do that!"

"Take your shit and go."

I think he was close to jittering, like an old car with a bad clutch trying to take a hill it shouldn't. Nobody talks to Carl Lofton like that. But I just did.

"Fine," he said, like it was suddenly his idea. "Where's the broad?"

'The broad?' Are you fucking kidding me?

"She left. She said to tell you never to call her again."

The red ran from his cheeks down into his neck. A vein

throbbed above his right eye. I noticed for the first time that his hair was thinning badly. *Gonna need plugs soon, buddy.*

He still had the flight board in hand, with the aircraft key and the timecard showing how much rental time had been logged on the flight. He tossed it onto the counter. It slid across and dropped to the floor with a flat slap.

"I ain't fucking paying for this!" He started to turn.

My left hand clamped on his bicep, just above the elbow. He tried to jerk free, but I had it at the bone. With my right hand, I pulled my cell phone out of my pocket. I held it up in front of his face with the screen toward me.

"You're going to pull out your fucking Gold MasterCard and give it to Rosemary, and you're going to pay for this rental and anything else you have on your account. Because if you don't, the recording I just made of this conversation where you admitted violating several Federal Aviation Regulations and admitted to careless and reckless operation of an aircraft is going directly to the Feds, where it, and my testimony, and the testimony of that woman will guarantee your license is suspended, do you copy?"

Rosemary emerged from the inner office, her face aimed at the floor, probably to suppress a cheer. She picked up the flight board and began to work the keyboard on the front desk computer. I released my grip on Carl's arm.

Rosemary took her sweet time. She tallied up Carl's account. Today's rental. Two from earlier in the month. She ran his card while he stood staring, silent. His signature scratched through the slip. He threw down the pen.

"Fuck you," he muttered as he walked out of the office.

Rosemary squeezed her lips together, holding her tongue, watching him go.

After a moment, I jogged out the front doors after him. The sun hung low in the west, but a steady early-evening breeze pushed out the windsock. It may have been a beautiful summer day, but such days produce sharp thermals over the farmland and forests of Wisconsin, and the ride in a light plane can be rough, hot, and uncomfortable. Between that and Carl's bad judgment, I understood how the flight had spun the woman's head.

"Carl!" I called after him. He was on a march to his car, the inevitable Corvette. "Hey, man! Wait up a second!" I let a little softness ease into my tone, a little brother-to-brother.

He hesitated. He looked over his shoulder at me.

"Wait up a second, man," I said with a mild shrug, the kind he read as the signal an apology would follow. He was wrong. I let my eyes fall to his shoes for a second. Let him be the alpha dog. He waited for me.

"Listen, I want to ask you one thing, okay?"

"Okay."

"Don't take anyone with you."

He stood still, ready for the apology, but those weren't the words he expected.

"What?"

"Don't take anyone with you."

"What's that supposed to mean?"

I heaved a sigh. "You're an arrogant prick. You think you know it all. That makes you a dangerous pilot. So, don't take anyone with you. When you fuck up and kill yourself. Don't take anyone with you. A girl. A wife. Kids. Don't kill them, too. Please."

He took a thousand miles off the tires of his Corvette when he peeled out of the parking lot.

* * * * *

Rosemary waved her keys at me when I walked back into the office. The wall clock said closing time. The door to the pilot lounge stood open.

"She come out?"

Rosemary nodded. "She went down to the Ladies. Are you going to take her home?"

I shrugged with all the Casual I was able to muster up, but it didn't fool her. Her cheeks balled up over a knowing smile that, unlike my grin for Carl, rode high into her pale eyes and lit them up like landing lights. She laughed and started to leave.

At the door, she stopped and looked at me.

"That girl is going to marry you."

* * * * *

I didn't think so after I drove the woman home.

Except for curt directions, she hardly spoke. She didn't tell me her name. It wasn't a cold ride, but it was solitary. She directed me to an apartment building on the west side of Essex. I considered asking how she was feeling, but decided the question invited too much review of what had happened.

For some reason, I felt acutely aware that my car was an eleven-year-old Toyota Corolla that hadn't seen a car wash, well, ever. I wanted to reach over and scoop up the litter on the passenger-side floor, but I didn't want her thinking I was reaching for those beautiful bare legs. Except for shifting, I kept my hands at ten and two on the wheel.

Pulling into the parking space she indicated, I let the engine run.

To my surprise, she turned and looked frankly at me, eyes squeezed down slightly, like someone searching for a landmark on a distant horizon.

"I heard what you said. To Carl. Outside."

I suddenly wondered if she'd also heard me lie to the bastard, telling him she'd gone and never to call her again. The pilot's lounge door was closed, but it's not soundproof. She probably thought me an opportunistic ass.

"Did you mean it?"

"Mean what?"

"Will he kill someone?"

"I hope not."

She got out of the car without another word.

Rosemary was full of shit.

* * * * *

Two weeks later, as I turned onto the narrow blacktop about a quarter mile from the driveway to the farmhouse I'd been renting, a City of Essex squad car rolled up behind me with its light bar exploding blue and red against a high summer twilight. I felt a cold anchor drop in my stomach, the one everyone feels when the blazing cop car lights fill up the rearview mirror. I pulled over and fished my wallet out of my back pocket and held it in my hand. No sense reaching for something in the near-dark, something a cop can't see. Shit, was I speeding? I hadn't paid attention, but the default answer to that is approximately twelve over the limit. *Shit.*

The officer strolled up, filling my side-view mirror with utility belt and a black semi-automatic service weapon. I already had the window open. The air conditioning on the Corolla died long before I bought it used.

I looked up at the face beneath the peaked cap and the anchor in my stomach turned to a cloud of butterflies, like some sappy Disney animation.

She wore her hair in an official-looking bun. I had a split second to feel disappointed that she wouldn't need me to hold it.

"Hello, Will Stewart," she said. Dummy that I am, I wondered how she knew my last name.

"Hello, Deeply Embarrassed," I said, instantly wishing I hadn't, and just as instantly feeling better when it brought a smile. She let the smile linger.

"Yes, well, do you blame me?"

"I told you. Been there, done that. And I was the pilot."

"You were airsick?"

"Blew my breakfast out the side window."

"That's not exactly reassuring to the passengers." The smile stayed. It seemed to dance on her face, lit like a party by the blue and red lights from her squad car.

"Is there a problem, officer?" Stupid, stupid question.

"It's Sergeant. Andrea Taylor," she said. Her hand came out. I took it. We shook warmly, curtly, professionally. I wanted to hold that hand. "And yes, there is a problem if you ever tell my chief why I stopped you."

"Okay. I won't tell. Why did you stop me?"

"I want you to take me flying."

She could have been speaking a foreign language, it was so utterly beyond what I expected her to say. I looked at her for a long moment, to see if some joke lay beneath the surface. She gave no hint of anything but sincerity.

"No."

Surprise flashed in her eyes, then doubt, and maybe embarrassment, the genuine kind that follows when a sure-fire plan flops.

"No? You're the pilot."

"Why?"

"Because you have the license." Cute. The joke sparkled in her eyes. I liked those eyes.

"Why?" I repeated. "Why do you want me to take you flying?"

She hesitated.

"I don't like being defeated. I never flew in a small plane before, and I felt defeated afterward. I don't like that."

"Okay. Still No."

She rocked back on one foot. Her eyes darkened. "You won't take me flying?"

I shook my head. "You take me."

"Um, again. You're the pilot."

"Yes. But you do the flying. You take the controls. You'll be hands on. You'll be in control. You'll feel the aircraft and know what it's doing. I'll get you onto the runway, but you'll push the throttle up. You'll do the takeoff, and you'll do the flying."

"Me? Takeoff?"

"Little known secret. Airplanes fly nicely without us. The airplane will take off practically by itself."

She drew a breath and considered the idea.

"I'll be there, right there, the whole time. But no stunts. No bullshit. Not like—"

"That asshole?"

"I didn't know if the two of you, um, were…"

"It was the second date. My mind was made up after the first date, but he offered to take me flying and it's something I always wanted to do. And I got sick and that took it away from me. I want it back."

This had nothing to do with saving face or showing me something. This was between her and her expectations, between her and the sky.

"Then take me flying," I said.

And she did.

I knew before I showed her how to start the engine I was in love.

ANDY
June 2017

ANGEL FLIGHT

2

ANGEL FLIGHT

"Mistletoe?"

Andy looked up at me. I watched her sleepy eyes squeeze, attempting to focus on the sprig of leaf and berry I had taped to my forehead.

Her hair spread on the pillow, framing her face in sweet symmetry.

"Damn, how did that get there?" I asked.

She let a pair of dimples peek from the corners of her mouth.

"Bring it in, Pilot," she said, almost purring. "But we're going to have to be quick. I'm taking a patrol shift today."

"I don't think I can do quick." I lifted the covers and slid into the warm bed beside her.

"Right. You just keep on believing that."

Challenge accepted.

I made a point of not being quick. She did not protest.

* * * * *

Andy did that thing she does, the one where she rushes around the house performing half a dozen tasks simultaneously. She worked her hair into a bun, put on her belt, poured coffee into a thermos, holstered her weapon, and located her patrol uniform hat after asking me where she put it. I sat in the kitchen at the counter-height table and sipped my own coffee, feeling a certain pride in the fact she was running late.

"Are you going to the airport?" she asked on the move from somewhere in the living room.

"Thought I'd play Santa," I called back. "Although I don't know if anyone will be there in this weather. If they shut everything down, I may have to deliver house to house. Santa old school."

I glanced out the kitchen window. Still couldn't see the barn. People who don't fly often ask me what it's like being in a cloud. Stand outside on a foggy day. That's what it's like.

"Don't take Lane's gift, okay?" Andy blew into the kitchen in full uniform. Despite her promotion to detective, the scheduling needs of the department still required her to take an occasional shift as patrol sergeant. Especially around the Christmas holiday. "And don't take Rosemary II's. I want to drop them off on the way to Lydia's tonight."

"That's the opposite direction," I pointed out. "Maybe we should just go hang out with Lane and Rosemary II tonight instead."

The idea got no traction.

I didn't hide my trepidation about Christmas Eve at Lydia's recently rented lake house. Had it been simply Andy and Lydia and I, sipping wine (in Lydia's pregnant case, grape juice) and watching Lydia's little girls jumping out of their skin in anticipation of Santa's visit—that I would have loved.

Such was not the plan.

Lydia, flush with the success of reuniting with her sister Andy, had plunged ahead on the path of restoring peace in the family. She invited her parents and her brother and his wife for a family Christmas. Holidays bear a stress load all their own without attempting to implement an armistice in a six-year war—The Shitstorm, as Andy and I called it. Six years of Andy rejecting her father's wishes, and he in turn rejecting her.

Lydia decided the time had come to end it.

I did not foresee this going well.

"We have to give this a chance," Andy said, slipping into her Essex PD jacket. "We'll have Lane and her mom over for dinner this week. But tonight—tonight will be tonight."

Well, that makes it all better.

I'd been pulling for Lydia. But my opinion, which is as weightless as I am when I vanish, was that Lydia had campaigned a bridge too far. I was surprised by Andy's willingness to participate in Lydia's peacemaking. I thought she might want to firm up her new alliance with her older sister before taking on their father. I chalked it up to holiday spirit. And maybe Lydia's recent near-death experience.

Andy scooped up her keys and pulled me into a kiss.

"Thanks for the mistletoe," she hummed in my ear.

"There's more on the vine."

"Good."

I followed her to the door.

"Be safe out there. It's zero-zero."

"Roger that."

* * * * *

After Andy left, I finished the last-minute Christmas wrapping I traditionally save for Christmas Eve (and sometimes Christmas morning). In other words, Andy's gift.

This year, Andy's gift was easy. She strongly hinted for a rail-mounted laser sight compatible with her Beretta Model 92A—as in she e-mailed me a link to the item on the manufacturer's website. The compact box proved easy to wrap, but before I did so, I removed the laser sight and replaced it with a small, velvet-lined box containing a thin chain and a single tiny diamond framed in a stylized heart. I caught Andy admiring the necklace at Shinamon's Jewelers the night of the Essex Winter Festival. We had been walking from shop to shop under city-hung Christmas lights when Andy stopped at the window. I asked if she wanted to try it on, but she declined. Not in the family budget, she claimed. I protested that you only adhere to a budget if you have actual money. She claimed that I just proved her point. Of course, she didn't know I'd been salting away a few dollars here and there all year for precisely this sort of emergency. Now I looked forward to scoring extra points not only for the gift, but for the frugal foresight and the whole noticing-that-she-liked-it thing.

I planned to give her the gift tonight before we set off for Lydia's. I wasn't about to jeopardize my shot at Hero Husband status by waiting until the holiday lay in ruins.

Andy managed the rest of the gift wrapping, which I deemed only fair since she's the one who did all the shopping. There were gifts for Lydia and her two little girls. Gifts for Pidge and Dave Peterson, fellow pilots at Essex County Air Services. Something for Andy's boss, Tom Ceeves. Andy found something for Rosemary II—I'll be honest, I didn't pay attention when Andy described it to me. We purchased a Bluetooth speaker for Lane. Andy bought something for our friend, Sandy Stone—and again, I have no clue what. (It's a condition I call Girl Gift Blindness, and I insist it's a real thing.)

My second-favorite gift was a framed photo of Earl Jackson standing in front of his newly acquired King Air 90. Andy snapped the picture surreptitiously, catching my boss in a rare moment of introspection in the shadow of a beautiful airplane. Honestly, the intimacy of the photo stuns me. Earl is a human built on a gargoyle mold, with a head as bald as a boulder and a perpetual scowl on his face. The intimidating exterior makes perfect camouflage for a heart so big it requires a solid fireplug body to contain it. Yet the photo reveals a man connected to a machine and the sky beyond it in ways that perhaps only a pilot would understand.

Despite Earl's secret heart, I argued that Andy should be the one to give him the photo. I reasoned there would be less chance Earl would throw it back at her. Earl doesn't like gifts, but he has a giant soft spot for my wife.

I slipped into the afternoon by spending time reloading and fine-tuning the latest version of my flashlight-battery-powered propulsion units. The newest editions had detachable propellers, making them easier to carry in my flight jacket. The propellers simply snapped on and locked in place. I've learned to keep at least one of the compact power units at my fingertips at all times.

"Ladies and gentlemen, I give you the FLOP!" I announced to a capacity crowd cheering in my head. "Flight Launching Operational Propulsion!" I couldn't wait to tell Andy the new name. Maybe when I give her the diamond.

A little after two p.m. I loaded the Christmas packages in my car and edged my way into the fog.

Early December brought several icy Alberta Clippers through Wisconsin—fast-moving low-pressure systems followed by giant masses of frigid Canadian air. Starting the first weekend of the month, we had snowfall after snowfall, almost guaranteeing a white Christmas. Two days before the holiday, a warm air mass crept into the state, drawn by a broad low-pressure system that trudged east in no particular hurry. Temperatures rose above freezing. Snow melted by day, then refroze in the night as sheets of ice. Warm air flowed across a snow-covered landscape, which caused moisture in the air to condense as fog. Dense fog stretched from central Illinois all the way to the Canadian border. Holiday travelers at every major airport in the Midwest found themselves stranded as the airlines cancelled flights in record numbers.

Exiting our driveway, I glanced back. I couldn't see the house. There was no question in my mind. Nobody but Santa Claus would be flying today. I felt sure I'd find the offices at Essex County Air Service empty.

Wrong.

* * * * *

"What's the Mojave doing on the ramp?" I asked Rosemary II the moment I cleared the tinted glass doors.

She held up her just-a-minute hand and then touched the earpiece on her headset to send me her on-the-phone gesture.

She wore a grim expression.

I deposited the cardboard box containing Christmas gifts on the floor under the artificial tree in the corner. Colored tree lights along with the scent of fresh coffee warmed the flying service office. Rosemary II makes superb coffee. I helped myself to a cup while she carried on her largely silent side of what seemed to be a troubling conversation.

I finished a third of the heavenly brew before Rosemary II ended the call.

"Oh, dear," she said. She's not much older than me but she projects a potent mothering influence on everyone at Essex Air. We love her for it.

"What's going on?"

"That was Earl. He's been trying to work out an Angel Flight all morning, and it's going badly."

Earl Jackson donates his airplanes and pilots to Angel Flight, an organization that provides private aircraft transportation to families needing to travel long distances for medical treatment. I've flown a few Angel Flights for him. The missions are both fulfilling and heartbreaking, especially when transporting children.

"Jesus, nothing's flying in this," I said, but I had a bad feeling, noting again that the Piper Mojave had been pulled out of the hangar. Even from the office, just a few hundred feet away, fog softened the outline of the airplane.

"That's the problem," Rosemary II said. She suddenly remembered something and hurried through the inner office and out the door which put her on my side of the front counter. Almost spilling my coffee, she threw a big hug around me.

"Merry Christmas, Will," she whispered in my ear. "And thank you again."

She squeezed me in a deep and appreciative embrace, then backed away, leaving the scent of her perfume between us.

"Merry Christmas to you, too," I fumbled, feeling awkward.

She gave me a long look with dark brown eyes, then nodded and went back the way she came.

Six months ago, I had a hand in saving her daughter's life. One Thank-You would have long-since covered it, but I guess the holiday spirit reignites memories of the episode for Rosemary II.

"You were saying?" I sought a quick change of subject.

Rosemary II returned to her station behind the counter.

"Earl had an Angel Flight scheduled for this morning. Pick up at Milwaukee Mitchell, then up to Marshfield." Angel Flights to Marshfield and its world-famous research clinic were not uncommon.

"Well, that's not happening," I said, feeling grateful that someone employed sound decision-making.

Rosemary II drew a long breath and tipped her head from side to side.

"Tell me that's not happening."

"Oh, it's fucking happening!" Pidge marched out of the pilot briefing office with her flight bag in one hand and an iPad in the other. She wore her work uniform, which made her look like a teenaged girl dressed up as a pilot. At twenty-three she holds every rating including Airline Transport Pilot, and she flies everything Earl owns. She and Earl get along like fire and gasoline vapor, but the one thing they can both agree on is that she's the best pilot either of them knows.

"You can't be serious," I said. "Marshfield has to be as low as we are."

"Two hundred and a quarter, last hour," Pidge informed me. "Icing in the clouds."

"So, this is not happening," I said again, making it sound more like a command. I had been Earl's chief pilot before the FAA suspended my license. I still carried some authority.

Rosemary II issued one of her motherly sighs.

"There's a little girl," she said. And like the cold, heartless sonofabitch I can be, I thought *of course, it had to be a little girl*. "She has a blood disease. She was supposed to be treated two days ago, but she couldn't travel. She's taken a turn. Now it's a matter of life—"

"Don't say life or death," I warned Rosemary II. "Not when pilots have to make a go or no-go decision."

"Oh, that decision's already been made," Pidge said.

"What do you mean?"

Both women looked at me, leaving the question hanging. Rosemary II finally answered.

"Earl set up the flight for this morning, but the fog cancelled it. They decided to transport her by ambulance."

"Sounds like the right idea to me," I said.

"Twenty minutes ago, they called Earl, and Earl called Andy, and now they're coming here," Rosemary II said.

"Wait. What?"

"They called Earl because they got as far as Essex County, but there's a huge pile-up and the highway is closed. They thought maybe a helicopter could meet them on the highway and make the rest of the trip. But of course, that's impossible. So, Earl called Andy and got her to go out to the highway and find them and bring them here."

"Why here?" I didn't like where this was going.

"Because Earl told them I'd fucking fly them to Marshfield," Pidge said. Pidge drops F-bombs on everything, but even so, I knew from her tone she didn't like the idea. Not one bit.

"You can't. This is very bad shit."

"I can," she said, matter-of-factly. "I agree with you. It's very bad shit. But I can. And you know I can."

"Where's Earl?" If he was orchestrating all this, I wanted to speak to him.

"Once it looked like the flight wouldn't go, he hopped in his car and drove to Milwaukee. I think he planned on driving the family to Marshfield himself, but the girl is so bad off they need an ambulance and an attending nurse."

"Jesus," I said. "Does he know this family?"

Rosemary II gave me a look meant to shame me. "It's Christmas, Will. Everybody knows everybody."

"What about a detour? Can't they get around the pile-up?"

"It's Christmas, Will," Pidge said, piling on. "Granny and all the fucking uncles are taking the detour. It's a knot. That's why Earl called Andy for a police escort."

I turned to Pidge.

"You know the rules, Pidge. Angel Flight or not, the pilot cannot allow the need to infect his judgment."

"*Her* judgment, dumbass," she punched at my shoulder. "Yeah, I know the fucking rules."

But you're doing this anyway, I thought. *This is not good.*

Pidge busied herself with her flight kit, but it was a ploy. The way she had everything organized told me she had already filed a flight plan and finished the preflight.

"How much gas are you taking?" I asked.

"All of it," she said.

"Well," I said grimly. "You will need it. Because when you can't get into Marshfield, you may have to fly to Nebraska to find a place to land."

* * * * *

I didn't want anything to do with this.

My holiday delivery had been made. My work here was done. I didn't want to be around to see this emergency unfold. A big part of me feared Pidge was about to do something monumentally stupid.

I decided to finish my coffee and get out of the way.

Just as soon as I helped Pidge load her things in the plane.

"What are you doing?" she asked when I joined her on the walk to the ramp.

"Helping you load up."

"Then why am I fucking carrying all this shit?"

"Because you're pilot-in-command of this dumbass idea."

We walked to the airplane without continuing the conversation. Shining and damp, the Mojave sat on the ramp looking the way all airplanes look to me—like a glorious creature restrained. Like its landing gear and wheels represented chains locking her sleek body to the earth.

Pidge pulled down the door which served as a stair and climbed in. I waited on the ramp. While she thumped through the cabin toward the cockpit, I pressed my hand against the aluminum skin of the airplane. I closed my eyes and tried to feel something mean-ingful while my hand traded heat for cold with the airplane. I tried to feel the future—as if a touch could join me to this flying machine and tell me everything would be okay. Or tell me it would not.

I strained to hear machine whispers. I searched the insides of my eyelids for a vision of wheels touching down on damp pavement after a challenging but safe flight. The airplane protected its mysteries and revealed no prescient secrets to me. I broke the bonding touch, leaving the question unanswered.

I was about to take up the weather argument with Pidge when the distant sound of sirens cut through the fog. I recognized the warble of an Essex PD cruiser, but it harmonized with off-key notes from a second unit. Both grew louder, and the fog on the other side of the hangar soon throbbed with flashing heartbeats of blue and red.

The sirens abruptly stopped, and the lights grew brighter, eventually rounding the buildings. Andy nosed her cruiser up against the hangar. A large, square rescue squad ambulance pulled up behind the airplane.

An EMT hopped out and hurried to the back of the unit. The driver, another EMT, rounded the front fender and walked toward me. Andy came up close behind him.

"Are you the pilot?" the driver asked.

I thumbed toward the cabin and said, "She is. In the cockpit."

The driver glanced back at his unit, at the drama unfolding behind the rear doors. Then he leaned toward the aircraft door to look for Pidge.

"She's not really going to do this, is she?"

"She won't do anything unsafe, if that's your question," I answered a bit defensively. Andy correctly read my tone as unhappy and bounced a worried look in my direction.

The first EMT hustled up with a heavy case in hand. "This goes in the cabin with the kid."

"How much does it weigh?" I asked.

"About seventy pounds," he said. He strained against the weight. I leaned into it and grabbed one side of the case. Together we heaved it up into the cabin.

"I got it," I said, and I pushed it behind the last seat. I automatically estimated its effect on the aircraft weight and balance, considering that Pidge had loaded full fuel. The calculation grew more critical when the co-driver produced two more heavy, hardshell cases. I helped load them. I leaned in the cabin and called up to Pidge to give her the numbers for a revised weight-and-balance estimate.

By the time I stepped back onto the ramp, both EMTs had gone to the rear of the ambulance. I watched them help a nurse pull a gurney with folding legs from the back of the unit. An IV bag hung above the figure on the gurney.

So small.

The child had been wrapped in blankets for protection against the cold. She lay almost entirely hidden. Even with the blanket bulk, she looked tiny. A lock of brown hair peeked from her wrap. Someone, a civilian, a woman with worry etched deep in her skin, hurried to tuck the blankets around the child and over her face as the gurney rolled.

Andy looked at me with pain shading her green eyes.

"Oh, this is not good," I muttered to the only person listening. Me.

The cluster of attendants rolled the gurney up to the Mojave.

"That won't fit," I said of the stretcher on wheels. People think all airplanes have the interior dimensions of an airliner. "She'll have to be carried up and she'll have to be in a seat. We can recline it, but she'll have to be strapped in."

After a split second of hesitation, they set about untangling the child. The nurse detached the IV bag and readied herself to carry it alongside the girl. The EMTs rearranged the blankets, then slid their hands under the girl and effortlessly lifted her. One tucked the girl's head against the other's shoulder to ensure she would not be bumped against the door frame.

"Take the back seat on the left," I instructed them. I hurried up into the cabin ahead of them and positioned myself in the seat across the aisle.

The EMT carried the child up the steps embedded in the door. Hunched over, he squeezed into the cabin and swung her into the seat. I leaned over and grabbed the seatback mechanism, reclining it two notches. Any farther and it would interfere with the door.

The nurse entered the cabin with the IV bag. She looked around for somewhere to hang it. The smooth moldings in the cabin roof offered no anchor points.

"Andy!" I called out. "Go get a wire coat hanger from Rosemary II!"

A minute later Andy handed a coat hanger through the open cabin door. The nurse passed it to me. I did a little bending, then jammed it into the plastic molding above the seat. The nurse fixed the IV bag in place, then set about unpacking portable monitors from the hardshell cases. She meticulously unwound leads and made connections. After several minutes, two of the complex devices beeped and filled their screens with data.

After ensuring that the IV tubes were not pinched or obstructed, the nurse backed out of the cabin to let the co-driver and me out. The mother barely allowed us to clear before she hurried up into the cabin to be with her daughter.

I touched the nurse on the sleeve and beckoned her toward the tail of the airplane.

"This looks bad," I said in the lowest possible voice. It was a question. The expression on the nurse's face telegraphed her answer.

"She should have been at the clinic three days ago," she said. "Her condition has become…aggressive. We agreed to drive her but to be honest, especially in this fog…" she shook her head. "Can the pilot really get us there?"

I looked at the mist floating all around us. "If it's like this in Marshfield, no. And she can't bring you back here. She's going to have to fly on to find someplace above minimums to land. This is a very bad idea."

"This is the only idea," the nurse said. "I hate to put it that way. I know how these things work. If I were you, I wouldn't make the flight."

"And what's her outcome if we call it off?"

"I refuse to answer that."

"Okay."

I gave her a pat on the shoulder, and she hurried back to the stairs to take her place in the cabin. I backed away with Andy.

Pidge appeared in the cabin doorway. She reached down for the straps on the door.

"Wait!" I called out. I turned to Andy.

Her eyes told me she saw this coming.

"I guess this proves I'll do anything to avoid the big dinner tonight," I said.

She put her hands on either side of my face and planted a kiss.

"I know."

I broke away from wanting another kiss and hurried to the cabin door.

"You're going to need a hand," I told Pidge. I expected a smart-ass reply, but she simply nodded, then worked her way up to the pilot's seat.

I hunched my way into the cabin and took a knee beside the mother, who sat directly across the aisle from the child. The nurse had taken the seat behind the pilot's seat, facing aft toward her patient.

I put a hand on the mother's arm.

"Ma'am," I said. "You need her to arrive in Marshfield quickly and safely."

She nodded at me. Her eyes were wet.

"That pilot up front may not look like it, but she's the best there is. But this flight is going to be tough, and as good as she is, she's going to need help. We also need all the fuel we can carry. We're loaded up and we're going to pick up ice. You have a tough choice. You can go along, which means I have to get off. Or I can take the co-pilot's seat and increase the chances of getting her there. But if I do that, it has to be without you. Because we can't both go. We'll be overloaded."

It was a flat-out lie.

The woman's face quivered and wrinkled. Tears spilled. "But— but she's my—*she's my baby!*"

I took her hand. She had more to say but couldn't get the words out. She knew the potential dark side of this decision, of leaving her child. I knew it, too. I knew I might be stealing a mother from her child's final moments. But I also knew there was little chance we were going to land this flight in Marshfield.

"Let us do this for her. Like she was our own," I said.

* * * * *

Pidge ignited the right engine while I secured the door. On the way back up the aisle I gave the nurse a reassuring nod, entirely false. By the time I strapped in the co-pilot's seat, Pidge had the left engine running. She let the Mojave roll at once. We wheeled around on the ramp and rolled for a departure on Runway 13. As we taxied, I saw Andy standing beside her cruiser, holding the mother by the shoulder as the woman shook, sobbing.

I gave Andy an apologetic thumbs-up while working the radios to copy our IFR clearance. ATC cleared us direct and added the latest weather from Marshfield, as if to make a point. I read back their instructions and received an immediate release, with a request to report airborne on Center frequency.

You can know an airport intimately, but when low visibility steals your orientation, even the most familiar taxiways and runways become alien environments. Pidge and I strained to see the yellow taxi line that took us toward the runway. At the Hold Short line, I worked through the pre-takeoff checklist while Pidge performed each check. During the run-up, she took an extra minute to listen to the engines with her eyes closed.

"Zero-zero takeoff," I said through the intercom. We'd been through this before, recently, in a snowstorm, but this time our roles were reversed. This time Pidge sat in the command seat. She would fix her attention on the instruments while I maintained a visual orientation to the runway, holding us on the centerline with the rudder pedals until I called for her to rotate.

We finished the pre-takeoff checklist. Pidge back-taxied into position on the runway. I made the departure announcement over the silent radio frequency for Essex County. Pidge lined us up and slowly worked the throttles forward while holding the brakes. The engines sang. The airframe shuddered. When the manifold pressure reached twenty inches, she let the brakes go and pushed the throttles to the stops. The Mojave surged forward.

We both held the control yoke. I firmly worked the pedals, guiding the nosewheel down the runway centerline.

"Power check," Pidge called out.

"Suction," Pidge called out.

I fixed my eyes on the runway ahead. I barely saw the white lines below the nose as we raced forward into the blinding mist.

"Airspeed's alive," Pidge called out.

The runway lights ticked past us, ever faster. I watched the needle swing on the airspeed indicator.

"Rotate!" I called, giving us an extra five knots for comfort.

Pidge pulled the yoke and the Mojave leaped free of the runway. My world, the world over the nose, went white. Pidge glued her eyes to the instruments.

"Blue line. Gear up," she said. I pulled the handle and monitored until the light said all three wheels were tucked in.

"Positive rate," I reported as the airspeed indicator needle marked our climb speed.

I switched to the air traffic control frequency. "Chicago Center, Angel Flight One One Kilo with you, climbing to six thousand."

* * * * *

The cruise portion of the flight unfolded uneventfully. It may have been the Angel Flight call sign, or it may have been the utter absence of other aircraft on the frequency, but we seemed to get priority treatment from air traffic control. Direct routing put us close to Marshfield in less than an hour, far faster than an ambulance.

Not fast enough.

Just as we began our descent, the nurse touched my shoulder. I turned around and she met my eyes with a dark expression.

"She's not doing well. Not at all. How much longer?"

Pidge had accepted vectors for an instrument approach into Marshfield. We chose runway 16, which is fifteen hundred feet longer than the only other option. The best instrument approach into Marshfield could only lower us to within 400 feet of the ground. I didn't think the visibility in any direction was much more than 400 feet. On top of everything, we were accumulating ice. The surface temperature at Marshfield hovered above freezing, putting the freezing level just above the ground. If we were lucky, we might shed ice once we reached minimum descent altitude, but we'd be collecting it throughout the approach.

I looked back at the nurse. She didn't have headphones on, so I pulled mine off to avoid shouting over the intercom into Pidge's ears.

"Close. Another ten minutes," I said. She shook her head as if that might not do. I found myself trying hard not to look at the bundle wrapped up in the rear seat. As the nurse drew a deep breath and started to turn away, I caught her arm. "That's if we break out. It doesn't look good."

"Then what?"

"We try again," I said. "But it means picking up a lot of ice. We can't keep trying indefinitely."

She let it sink in.

"It might not matter," she said. She delivered a pointed look, then turned back to her charge.

I put the headphones back on.

"What's the story?" Pidge asked.

"Not your concern," I said.

"Fuck that," Pidge answered. "I'm taking us down to two hundred. Fourteen forty MSL."

Instrument pilots flying a blind approach follow strict procedures. The ironclad rule is to descend to the prescribed altitude. If you do not see the runway environment or find yourself in a position from which you can land safely, you execute the missed approach procedure. You don't descend one inch below the prescribed Minimums. Period. No other option exists.

Except the very dangerous practice of busting Minimums. Pidge just announced her intention to do exactly that, cutting our safety margin in half.

"I'll put us there. Needles crossed. You find our way out of this fucking muck," Pidge added.

"Affirmative."

* * * * *

We tracked inbound on the approach course. The one blessing hidden in this mass of stagnant, cold, wet air was an absence of turbulence. Except for the steady song of the engines, we might have been sitting in someone's living room. The Mojave rode through the air like a skater on glass.

I called out the final approach fix and dropped the landing gear. Pidge configured for the descent, adjusting speed, trim and attitude. The moving map display showed us dead center on course. The crossed needles on the navigation instruments told us we were aligned precisely on the glide path. Shades of darkness in the fog indicated the day had grown old.

"Five hundred above Minimums," I called out to Pidge.

Her hands moved the controls microscopically.

"Four hundred above Minimums."

Nothing but white in every direction.

"Three hundred."

Airspeed nailed.

"Two hundred. Final gear check. Three green."

"One hundred."

Steady. On course. Needles perfectly crossed.

"Minimums."

My eyes darted between the windshield and the altimeter.

"Minus one hundred."

Nothing. Nothing but white. Not even the hint of a light.

"Minus two hundred!"

"Anything?" Pidge demanded. I felt her flinch on the yoke to arrest the descent.

"Nothing! Missed approach!"

She powered up slightly but held the altitude for a second. Any other time, I would have criticized her. Instead, I grabbed the extra second and frantically searched ahead and directly below. For an instant, I thought I saw a runway light. Then another. But it did us no good.

Pidge went to full throttle for the Missed Approach climb. I retracted the gear and called out the speed. I contacted Minneapolis Center and reported the bad news. They asked our intentions. I said we would try again.

"She's starting to handle like a pig," Pidge said. I glanced at the ice building on our windshield frame and on the wings. Pidge hit the deicing boots. Pieces flew into the slipstream, but not all of them.

"One more and we're done," I said. "We stay down here too long, and we won't be able to climb out of it." I double-checked to ensure that the prop and windshield de-icing systems remained on.

I glanced back at the cabin. The nurse had unstrapped and now knelt in the aisle beside the child. She had the seat fully reclined and leaned over her patient, working frantically with what I took for a syringe. She must have felt my gaze, because she turned to me and shook her head sharply.

Center called. "One One Kilo, we have a request from Marshfield for you to contact them on CTAF. Frequency change approved. Report back on."

I acknowledged and switched over to the Marshfield frequency.

"Marshfield Unicom, Mojave One One Kilo."

"One One Kilo, this is Marshfield. We heard you go over. You need to know, we're down to zero-zero. Repeat. Down to zero-zero."

My heart sank.

"Roger, Marshfield. Thanks."

"Will," Pidge spoke in my head, the way headphones do.

I turned in my seat and looked at Pidge. She looked at me.

"We're not going to get this thing down," she said.

I said nothing.

"I'm willing to try," Pidge said. "But I can tell you how it's going to go."

"Affirmative."

I fought the urge to look at the bundle in the back.

I didn't know this child. I didn't know her story, her illness, her family. I didn't know what she wanted for Christmas except maybe just to wake up on Christmas morning. What I really needed to know, however, was if that was *just too God damned much to ask?*

Just to wake up one more day? Just to wake up on Christmas morning?

I surrendered to the urge and looked back, but I couldn't see the girl. The nurse had flipped up the seat armrest and worked herself into a position in the aisle, so she could hold the child in her arms. She had nothing else to give her but the touch of another human.

It's Christmas, Will. Everybody knows everybody.

"Pidge, level off. Right here. Hold eighteen hundred!" I commanded.

Pidge didn't question. She had configured for a climb back to three thousand, but she cut the power and leveled the aircraft at one-thousand-eight-hundred feet.

I grabbed the iPad from the flight bag.

"Where's the Marshfield clinic? The pediatric hospital?"

"The fuck should I know!"

I worked the iPad, stabbed at the screen, did a quick search on the non-aviation map page and found the prestigious and utterly useless—to us at this moment—clinic. I memorized the location and switched over to the ForeFlight navigation application. In a moment, switching to aerial view, I located and marked the building. Then I backed out to see where we were in relation to the clinic.

On the screen, the small airplane icon tracked northwest. Pidge had reversed our course for another attempt at the approach. The clinic, located near the center of town, lay ahead and to our left beneath the blanket of fog, almost directly under the approach course for runway 23.

"Pidge line up for the RNAV Two Three. Stay at this altitude. We've got towers all over hell here, but the highest is seventeen-oh-nine. Don't go below eighteen hundred."

I unstrapped.

"Sure. Ninety feet. No problem. What the fuck are you doing?"

I paused. She looked sharply at me.

"I'm going to take the kid and bail out."

Pidge gave me as much blank stare as she could afford while throwing her attention between me and the instrument panel.

"Oh," she said. "I was afraid you were going to do something fucking stupid."

I levered my way out of the cockpit, taking my headphones and the iPad with me. To get around the nurse, still occupying the thin aisle, I had to climb over the seat opposite the girl. I positioned myself at the rear of the cabin and hooked up the intercom again.

"Pidge hold the reciprocal course for the RNAV Two Three Approach. I'll call out when you should turn inbound."

"Got it."

I pulled off the headset and laid it aside. By now the nurse was looking at me, so I gestured for her to come close.

"How is she?" I asked, speaking up over the engines.

She shook her head. "She doesn't have long. Can we get down?"

Now I shook my head. She clutched her lips together, fighting tears. I waved them away.

"Listen to me," I said, taking her shoulders in my hands. "Do you believe in Christmas miracles?"

Her eyes grew wetter. She gave a helpless shrug.

"I'm going to do something you will find impossible to believe. I don't have time to explain it, but it may help her make it. I may be able to get her down there. Are you willing?"

She nodded emphatically.

"What's your name?" I asked.

"Christie," she said.

"Christie, I'm Will. There's only one catch to this. But it's a deal-breaker. You can't tell anyone what happens here tonight. No matter who it is, no matter how they ask. You can't tell anyone what you're about to see. Ever. Can you do that?"

I think she thought we were about to do something as prosaic as breaking a regulation because she nodded quickly.

"No, I'm serious. This is going to shake you up. You have to promise me, swear to me, on the life of this child!"

"I swear!" she said quickly. "Anything we can do to get her there, please."

"Okay. I'm going to show you something now. You won't believe it."

I made sure I had her eyes locked on me.

Fwooomp! I vanished.

It gave her a jolt, a small one. She blinked.

"You can't see me," I told her. "But I'm still here."

Fwooomp! Reappearing startled her, and now it sank in. Her eyes went wide.

"Listen to me!" I took her shoulders again before she became absorbed in a tangle of impossible thoughts. "I can do that. And I can also fly. Like freakin' Tinkerbell. Don't ask how. I can fly, and I want to take that girl with me and jump out of this perfectly good airplane right over the clinic and deliver her. It's the only way we can get her down. There's no way to land the plane."

Her mouth worked open and closed. Nothing came out.

"You have to swear to me, you will never tell anyone what happens here. Swear to me!" I gently shook her shoulders. "On the life of this child!"

"Uh! I swear! How—?"

"Secret government experiment gone bad," I said quickly. "This is going to work. Get her ready! Go!" I shook her shoulders again and she snapped out of her gawking. She turned quickly and busied herself with the patient.

I put on the headset.

"Pidge!"

"Right here."

"Turn us inbound. Line up on the Two Three approach course."

"Roger that. Are you seriously fucking doing this?"

"Slow us down, as slow as you can. And if you can throttle back the left engine, that will help. I'm going to open the door and that's going to create some serious yaw. Be ready. When I say so, I want you to cut the left engine for a count of five. Don't try to hold altitude. After I go out, power up and take it up a few thousand and put it on autopilot—slow but not too slow. You'll have to come back here and close the door. Get the nurse to sit up front for balance or you'll be way out of C.G."

"Fuck!"

I pulled up the iPad and checked the track. Pidge had gone about ten miles northeast of Marshfield. The tiny airplane icon turned to intercept the inbound course for the RNAV 23 approach. I wondered what in the world ATC was thinking of all this. Probably getting ready to call us a crash. I had no doubt they were already pitching altitude warnings at Pidge.

Christie gestured at me to indicate that the safety belts around the girl had been released. She removed the IV connection and disconnected the myriad electronic leads, setting off monitor warnings. She moved out of the aisle. I took her place.

I collected my first close look at our passenger.

"Jesus Christ," I said aloud.

The girl seemed impossibly small. I couldn't guess her age. She seemed smaller than Lydia's five-year-old. But this girl had older-girl features. Her face wore thin, almost translucent skin. Her closed eyes lay slightly sunken, and her forehead ran high. She seemed to glow in serene defiance of whatever ruthless killer she carried in her body. I felt a stab in the heart, seeing this beautiful child in such a state. I couldn't tell whether she slept peacefully or had simply begun to let go of life.

I tore my gaze away and checked the map. Pidge had aligned us with the RNAV 23 inbound approach course. We were just five miles from the center of town where my waypoint marked the clinic.

"Slow us down, Pidge. I'm opening the door."

I felt the change in pitch. The engine song changed. A vibration shuddered through the airframe as Pidge lowered the flaps. I felt the asymmetrical thrust and Pidge's counter pressure on the rudder as she reduced power on the left engine. The unsynchronized props sent a throbbing vibration through the airframe.

I scrambled back to the door and released the interior latch.

A door opening in flight is an emergency, but not a fatal emergency. Pilots tend to make door-release incidents fatal by failing to fly the airplane first and dealing with the door second. I knew of doors for this type of aircraft that had come open, and in one case of a small boy who had nearly fallen out. The airplane would continue to fly—at low speed, with skewed thrust, and burdened by ice on the wings—as long as Pidge maintained her deft touch.

Any pilot other than Pidge and I would have had doubts.

I threw the latch. The door blew open and nearly pulled me out. I grabbed the door frame. The wind roared, blinding and cold.

Christie's expression turned to horror. She had to be rethinking this. Someone was about to jump out of the airplane with her little patient and this mad act did not hold up to scrutiny in her logical mind.

I scrambled back up the aisle and looked directly at her.

"I can do this!" I shouted at her. I forgot about the intercom.

"Jesus, Will! Not in my ears!" Pidge scolded me. "Holding Vmc plus five. If you're going to do it, fucking do it!"

Christie nodded at me, clutching the seat's armrests.

I glanced at the iPad. Three miles.

I knelt beside the girl and slid my arms under her body. When I lifted, I nearly threw her. She had no body weight. I folded the blanket around her and felt extra hands helping. Christie leaned forward and tucked the blanket tightly in place as I positioned the child against my shoulder.

I gave her an appreciative nod. She sat back in her seat, put her hand across her mouth and began to cry.

Not much I could do about that.

The iPad indicated less than two miles to go.

"Five degrees left, Pidge."

Pidge didn't answer over the intercom, but I felt the airplane yaw.

I edged my way back to where the door hung open. The white fog had gone dark. Night seeped into the endless mist. Wind screamed past the cabin door at over a hundred miles per hour.

I held the girl tightly against my shoulder with my left arm. I took one last look at the iPad, at the aerial imagery showing the location of the pediatric hospital. I noted the large space identified as a cemetery across the street from my destination. That space would be an unlighted void among the city lights. It was the best available beacon, since I couldn't take the iPad with me. If I made the tablet vanish with me, I couldn't see it. If I made it reappear, it would have weight, and that weight would take us down at terminal velocity. Either way, it was useless to me.

I set the device on the rear right-side seat.

A low glow seeped into the cabin from below. The city lights of Marshfield radiated up through the fog.

"In ten seconds cut the left engine, Pidge! Then I'm out. Good luck!"

"Merry fucking Christmas!"

I threw off the headset, turned and dropped on my butt. I scooted toward the door with my legs out. The instant I extended my feet out the door the hundred-mile-per-hour wind pressure tried to tear them away.

My plan had been to vanish and fly out the door, but I couldn't hold the child and pull myself with my hands. In any case, the moment I vanished, wind blowing into the cabin would have pushed me against the opposite side of the airframe. Weightless, I'd never get out the door.

I would have to jump first, then vanish.

I suddenly realized I needed one more thing and almost blew the whole operation by nearly forgetting it.

I fixed a right-handed grip on the girl. Her legs dangled on either side of my thighs. With my left, I groped in my jacket for a FLOP unit. One-handed, I struggled to fix the propeller in place. In the gale-force wind I nearly fumbled the whole works out the door. This was not a well-thought-out plan.

Snap! The prop seated itself. I tested the power. It worked.

I glanced back at the iPad on the seat cushion.

Over the target. Pidge cut the left engine. The slipstream weakened.

Shit!

I heaved myself out the door, clutching the tiny child against my chest as the force of the wind tore us away from the airplane.

FWOOOMP! I put all I had into snapping *the other thing* around us.

Things happened fast.

The initial blast of wind roared like an angry sky creature and ripped us away from the door. Almost instantly, the gale died to nearly nothing, as if the beast lost its breath.

The Mojave engines thundered as Pidge restored the power to climb away.

We fell into a featureless gray void. I slid the FLOP power control to full forward thrust and held it opposite the wind generated by our fall. The FLOP sang its angry wasp song and arrested our descent. When the relative wind dropped to nothing, I eased the power to neutral. We floated in silence, wrapped in the cool sensation that comes with disappearing. Mist encircled us, but I had no problem with orientation. The Marshfield city lights radiated up from below. Dark night sky hung above us.

I angled my wrist and gently powered up the FLOP. A breeze stroked us as we descended into the glowing mist.

Streetlights emerged from the fog below like luminous bugs floating to the top of a creamy liquid. Bright Christmas lights added color to the fog, like sprinkles melted into white pastry frosting. Icicle lights traced the outlines of houses. Holiday lights turned trees into beacons.

Ahead and to my right, a dark patch nestled in the surrounding light. I aimed the power unit toward that darkness, the cemetery across from the clinic. Shapes and structures took form through the fog. Residential homes gave way to a campus of large buildings. I'd never seen the Pediatric Hospital wing of the expansive Marshfield clinic but felt reasonably certain I was on target.

We crossed a parking lot. Evenly spaced lamps all around us cast down cones of lighted mist, creating a magical misty forest of transparent Christmas trees. I felt the girl move. Her small arms around my neck applied a weak but steady embrace. Her head rose from my shoulder. She looked around. I wondered if somehow her vanished and weightless state gave her strength.

I aimed for what looked like an emergency entrance.

I eased us onto the concrete outside broad glass doors. A final pulse of the FLOP stabilized and stopped us. In the distance, I heard the airplane high above the fog. Engine song faded into the silent night.

Fwooomp! Gravity reacquired us. I settled onto my feet.

I looked down at the bundle in my arms. Wide, bright eyes stared up at me from an expression so serene, so at peace, it took my breath away.

"Are you an angel?" she asked.

"No, honey." I smiled down at her. "That's all you."

ANGEL FLIGHT
February 23, 2018

A SNOWBALL'S CHANCE

3

A SNOWBALL'S CHANCE

"You don't have a snowball's chance in hell."

Matt Lindor picked up his martini and tipped it toward the woman catching every male eye in the bar. She moved on long legs, high heels, and a form of physics no scientist could ever quantify or explain. She paid no attention to the eyes chasing her, navigating effortlessly through the minglers in a cocoon of self-confidence. Midway down the bar she slid smoothly onto a stool and brought her forearms to rest on the mahogany. An attentive bartender quickly accepted both her order and her smile.

"Watch and learn," I slugged down my Corona and pushed away the empty with its ship-in-a-bottle lime wedge.

"Hang on!" Matt pulled out his phone. "This is so I can call the fire department when you crash and burn."

I slid off the stool and gave myself a quick preflight inspection in the bar mirror. Leather jacket. White shirt. Slim blue-black tie with a Hap Arnold Air Corps pin. Pilot sunglasses tucked in my shirt pocket. Slipping them on in the dark bar might be a bit much, but I had it going on. My pilot thing.

"Better take off that wedding ring," Matt said.

I shook my head. "A woman like that...she thinks she can knock any man's wife off the board."

"Not happening."

I checked the competition. A few other men around the room, the ones not with a woman (and a few with) assessed her, gauging their chances. I dismissed each in turn. None of them had a pair of Ray Bans in their pocket or a pilot's license in their wallet.

"Tell you what, let's make this interesting, Matt," I leaned on the bar. "I make it through one drink with her and you buy me dinner tonight. I get her up to my room and you let me in on whatever it is you're doing here."

The bro-friendly grin on his face remained in place but the light behind it faded.

Matt Lindor, ten years my senior, had insisted on scheduling me as pilot for the charter flight he hired from Essex County Air Services. Twice before, I had flown him from Essex to Chicago's Midway Airport. A little shorter than me, he moved like a man made of tightly wound wire. He had handsome features, perfectly cropped black hair, enough tan to tell me that he didn't spend his winters in Wisconsin, and he wore his bank balance on his wrist and around his neck. Quick with a joke and a smile, he warmed up to me from the start. On the first trip, he had me wait in the pilot's lounge at Signature Aviation. On the second trip, he invited me along for the cab ride and had me wait in the bar at the Four Seasons Hotel, then bought dinner after he conducted his business. This time, he told me to pack an overnight bag. He implied he was closing a big deal and suggested we might make a night of it. Buddies, out on the town in The Windy City. Ladies beware.

The few times I inquired about his business in Chicago, he brushed the questions off. Consulting. Engineering. Something to do with his tool and die business. He shifted the subject to his many successes in life. As for the hard-shell cases he loaded into the cabin, he simply referred to them as "instruments."

He stared at me. His expression suggested I had overstepped.

"Now, why would I do that, Will? Are you suddenly an engineer?"

I dropped my eyes long enough to make sure he knew he was the alpha dog here, then came back up to meet his gaze.

"You've been hinting that these trips are the start of something big. That you might need a lot more air travel if things go well. Do I look like a guy who wants to play taxi driver for Earl Jackson for the rest of my life? I already told you the airlines will never take me because I don't have a college degree. And who wants to drive a glorified bus anyway?"

Matt maintained the cold stare.

"C'mon man, give me a chance. I'm a quick study. If you're expanding your business, private flight is the way to go. No check-in hassles. No security bullshit. *No TSA inspections.*"

"Well, don't you have a big brass pair."

"Just asking for the interview, that's all. I hook up with that babe down the bar and you give me that shot. I can talk my way in and out of just about anything."

He mulled it over for a five-count, suggesting my forward proposition pushed his limits. It didn't matter. I had him on the hook. He drew slowly from his martini. He struck a pose, jaw jutting, grin spreading.

"You hook up with her and I'll give you that shot. Get her to hook up with me and you're hired!" He laughed.

I forced a laugh along with him. He punched my shoulder and I pushed away from the bar.

It was a long walk, all of ten paces. I'm a married man and a few years out of practice, and it felt like climbing gallows steps. Men around the bar watched me make my move, ready to snicker when the trap door dropped.

The bartender delivered a martini glass filled with sparking crimson just as I arrived.

"Any chance you would let me pay for that?" I slid between her and the stool beside her and propped an elbow on the bar.

"Do I look like I can't afford it?" With scarcely a glance my way, she lifted the drink—I guessed Cosmopolitan—and sipped. I felt the first anti-aircraft hit go into my left engine.

"Honestly? You look like a woman who would never have to pay for a drink in her life."

"Really? That's your line? Suggesting I'm some sort of bar fly?" She blew the left engine right off the wing. She looked me up and down. In her smooth appraisal I saw strength and a dagger-sharp awareness that a potential suitor would ignore at his peril. "Are you on your way to a costume party?"

"I'm a pilot. Want me to put on my sunglasses? They're Ray Ban Aviators." I patted my shirt pocket.

She doled out a thin hint of smile. Then she said, "Show me your wrist."

I held up my hand.

"The other one. Let me see your watch."

I pulled back the leather cuff of my flight jacket. She studied my wristwatch. "Do you have enough dials and numbers? You can't tell me you actually use all of that."

"I can calculate density altitude, convert knots to miles per hour, and tell you how much fuel we need. And no, I never use it. It's completely impractical. Any pilot will tell you that."

"It looks like something you got for credit card reward points."

"Good eye."

I felt the rapport warming up.

"Well," she said, turning to me and putting her hand on my forearm; her touch ignited a thrill in me, "mister pilot with the free watch, why don't you go back down the bar and ask your friend with the Rolex to come over here and pay for my drink?" She gave me a warm, friendly not-if-you-were-the-last-man-on-Earth smile and then tipped a gesture toward Matt, who watched this unfolding disaster from behind a smug expression.

"This is what I get for being out of practice," I muttered. Her smile nearly broadened, but she tightened the corners of her mouth to fight it off. Dimples appeared. I reluctantly backed away from the bar. I could almost hear jeers from the men watching my retreat.

Matt laughed out loud when I sat down beside him and relayed the message. He stood up, downed the last of his drink, then peeled three twenties off a wad of cash and dropped them on the bar.

"I told you, Will," he said, clapping a hand on my shoulder. "See you in the morning!"

Matt's bar cash left room for one more drink. Pride didn't outweigh a second Corona. I helped myself. I watched him slide onto the stool beside her and after a few minutes they were chatting amiably. She repeated the watch routine, casting me a final pitying glance after admiring his Rolex, then warmed up to Matt's conversational repartee and obviously superior financial standing.

I didn't stay beyond the last drops of the second beer. By now he had her laughing and most of the witnesses to my flaming wreck had moved on. I slipped away in the opposite direction. I knew Matt's schedule. He told me dinner would be delayed because his clients were due at the hotel for a meeting a seven PM. I left him chatting up the woman at the bar at six-forty. The timing gave him a choice—either persuade her to wait while he conducted his business or invite her along. Matt didn't strike me as a man who would risk leaving a woman like that alone in a bar.

I took the elevator to the sixth floor and strolled past my room. I continued down the hall and stopped at the last door on the left. A glance at my overachieving watch told me I had a few minutes to wait. I checked for security cameras adjacent to the expensive Lakeview Suite Matt had booked. I found none. All clear.

Fwooomp!

I vanished. Gravity released me. I considered floating up to the ceiling to ensure no one would run into me, but traffic at the end of the hall was unlikely. I fixed an anchor grip on the brushed gold door handle of the suite across from Matt's, gambling that no one would suddenly emerge. If they did, I could easily push off to clear the space in front of the door.

When the elevator chimed, Matt, the woman and two men stepped out of the sixth-floor alcove. The men looked like a mismatched pair of investment bankers. One was tall and over-weight, with too much belly pushing his white shirt over the belt of his suit pants. The other was short, bone thin and nervous-looking. Both were well-dressed and well-heeled. Matt led with the woman beside him. If they were wary of him bringing a guest, they paid off their concerns with long looks at her legs as she walked ahead of them. I kindled an immediate dislike for all of them.

At the door, Matt stroked his key card in the lock, opened the door and stepped in, waving the entourage in after him. The woman suddenly created a log jam when she put one hand to her right ear and stopped in the doorway.

"My earring!" She patted her ear, then spun around searching the floor. "I dropped my earring!"

Matt's guests half-heartedly checked the carpet at their feet, then moved past Matt into the suite. She hurried into the hallway, searching.

"I found it!" she announced. She stepped to the far side of the hall and plucked something from the floor. I used the opportunity to slip through the door that Matt held open. She took her time to work the earring back into place while he held the door. Satisfied with her effort, she tossed Matt a smile and rejoined the group. Matt closed the door behind us.

I maneuvered ahead of them, through a short entry, into a broad sitting room with a high-priced view of Lake Michigan, at least in daylight.

"I've got a little plumbing supply business to conduct," he told her. "Very boring. Why don't you wait for me in the other room."

She glanced through the door he indicated. A bedroom.

"Let's not get ahead of ourselves," she told him. "You go ahead with your business. I'll see what the minibar has to offer."

She stepped past Matt, not waiting for his answer. He shifted his posture and moved his free left hand to pat her backside. She saw it coming and locked a withering look on him. He froze. For a moment I thought she might give him a fist to the face. Instead, she forced a disarming smile. He stayed his hand and bowed politely. She nodded acceptance of his better judgment and moved toward the miniature fridge located behind a small bar.

"A drink, gentlemen?" Matt offered.

"From a fuckin' minibar?" The small man dismissed the idea. "Let's get this done."

Matt lifted one of the hardshell cases off the floor and laid it on a low glass coffee table. He snapped the latches and split the case open like a book, laying both halves on the glass. Playing the proud salesman, Matt stepped aside to let his customers examine the contents of the case. From where I floated at the periphery of the room, I couldn't see around the big man, who leaned over the open case.

"Fifteen units as ordered," Matt said. He tapped the second case at his feet with his shoe. "Fifteen more in here. Ten of each sample you saw last time." He lifted the second case and handed it to the small man.

The big man lifted a black tube and examined it. After a moment he pushed the tube back into place and tapped his fingers across the rows of similar tubes held by the foam lining of the case. Satisfied with the count, he nodded at his companion who reached into his breast pocket and pulled out an envelope. The small man handed the envelope to Matt, who cracked it open and fanned through what I assumed to be cash.

At that moment, the woman closed the minibar door and walked over to the table inserting herself into Matt's presentation.

Matt's expression darkened. "Hey! Do you mind?"

"Not at all," she replied airily. She picked up one of the slim black tubes in the case. "Nice suppressors! Baffle stack design—no. From the weight, I'd say monocore. User serviceable. Looks like they're all nine mil." She lifted a smaller tube out of the case. It had a threaded end, which she twisted into the larger tube. "This one—let me see—I'd say Kimber 1911. Machining the barrel, too—good way to make it untraceable."

Matt stood in mid-count with his mouth hanging open.

"What the fuck, Lindor!" The big man took a step back.

The woman put down the first set of tubes and picked up a second. She examined them appreciatively. "Glock 26! What a coincidence!"

She snapped open the small purse she carried and stabbed her hand in. She extracted her hand with her slender fingers wrapped around the grip of a black handgun.

"I happen to have one of those right here!" she exclaimed with a smile. She lifted the handgun and pointed it in the general direction of the three men in the room.

The smile evaporated. The undercurrent of intensity that Matt opted to ignore at the bar now surfaced, transforming her.

Your mistake, buddy, I thought.

Acting on either instinct or idiocy, the big man brought his right hand up to reach into his coat. The woman reacted instantly, shifting her aim.

"If that hand disappears, so does your face." Her icy tone cut the air between them. He stopped.

"Who the fuck *are* you?" Matt demanded.

"I'm sorry. Did I forget to introduce myself? Detective Andrea Stewart, City of Essex Police Department." Andy used her free hand to pull her badge from a pocket in her shoulder strap handbag.

Matt's face went white. The big man turned on him. "You brought a fucking cop up here?"

"Miss," the small man said with a dismissive tone that I thought might get him killed, "I don't know who you think you are or where the City of Essex is, but last time I checked, this is Chicago." He reached out and snatched the envelope from Matt's fingers. "Furthermore, we just met this fellow and were under the impression he wanted to discuss an investment opportunity. Since you have no jurisdiction here, my friend and I are leaving."

"You're right about the jurisdiction. That would be a problem if I cared. But it's not a problem for my friends from the Chicago Police Department and the Bureau of Alcohol, Tobacco and Firearms who are about to take you into custody."

The small man lowered the case to the carpet. He moved away from it, as if distance might reduce incrimination. His move put the big man between him and Andy. As he slid sideways his right hand swung behind his back and lifted his coat tail. He closed his fingers around the grip of a gun holstered at the small of his back.

I pushed off the wall and shot across the short space between us. My outstretched hands made contact simultaneously. I closed one hand around his wrist. He struggled to pull his arm away. I planted my feet on the floor and lifted, forcing his wrist up the line of his spine. With the same motion, I twisted, counter-rotating his wrist and the gun. I heard a muted snap from his index finger, caught in the trigger guard. He cried out and doubled over. The gun slid free of his grip.

I grabbed the weapon and tossed it across the table to a sofa behind Andy. She scarcely gave it a glance, holding her Glock on the big man, who shifted a confused expression between the gun on the sofa cushion and his gasping bent-over companion.

"What the fuck!"

Matt stared at the scene wide-eyed.

I gave the wrist one more twist and felt something give. The small man released a girlish squeal and I let him go. Despite his pain, he spun around, searching for his attacker. Seeing none he fixed a rabid look on Matt, who put his hands up. "That wasn't me, man!"

I tapped my toes on the floor and floated to the suite's high ceiling. Gently pushing off a fire suppression nozzle, I maneuvered back down again and grabbed the corner of the suite's small dining table, ready to assist Andy if she needed me.

"Why don't you all take a step back," Andy suggested. "Hands where I can see them, please."

All three complied. The small man had to work at it, but managed to get both hands to chest height, cradling his right wrist in his left hand. The blood drained from his face and his skin glistened with sweat. He divided searing glances between Lindor and Andy.

The suite's door lock snapped. The door flew open. Men in dark tactical gear with weapons up hurried through the doorway. I maneuvered to stay out of the traffic flow. One of the tactical officers wedged the door open.

A distinguished senior officer in a gray suit strolled in wearing an expression of placid pleasure.

"Oooh! Look at all that!" Assistant Chief David Schultz said grandly, spotting the open case. "Illegal suppressors. And so many of them!"

In minutes the tactical officers handcuffed and escorted Matt and his clients from the room.

"Nicely done, Detective Stewart," Chief Schultz said. "A pleasure working with you again."

"Thank you, sir," Andy replied. A faint glow seeped into her light caramel complexion.

"Not at all! Thank *you* for letting us roll up the buyers. I'd say you can go ahead and call your chief and let him know he can serve his Essex warrants."

I didn't have a chance to see or hear Andy's response. A momentary gap in traffic offered the opportunity to slip away. Andy would revel in the chance to seal the arrest with Chief Schultz. His brother Don, a senior officer with the Milwaukee Police Department, fostered an open job offer for my wife. It would not surprise me if Andy came home with a similar offer from Chicago.

I pulled myself toward and through the doorway, hooked my hand on the jamb and heaved myself upward, into the hall. Over the heads of more arriving officers, including one carrying a video camera, I performed a slow glide away from the crime scene.

My single king-bed room was just five doors down the hall from Matt's suite. Cameras and police traffic in the hallway gave me no chance to drop down and reappear. The elevator alcove wasn't an option. Andy had warned me about video surveillance covering the hallway and the elevator alcove. She told me that once the arrests were made, Chicago PD would secure the suite as well as my room and any evidence therein. She warned me the process might take a while. She refused to estimate how long she might be tied up giving her statement and coordinating with the Essex PD raids on Matt's tool and die company and his home. It had been her investigation in Essex that tipped her to the fact that Lindor was selling illegal handgun silencers in Chicago. I'd like to think I played a role when I told my wife in passing that Essex County Air Services had a new client. Letting Lindor buddy up to me had been her idea, along with the charades in the bar. Backing her play in the room had been my idea.

Gliding down the hallway, I felt no pressing need to reappear.

I drifted past the elevator alcove to the stairwell access door. I checked for police and cameras, then propped myself against the wall and pulled the door open. I slipped out, went over the railing, and lowered myself down the center of the stairwell, six floors to ground level. I found a surveillance camera on the ground floor, another in the hallway outside the stairwell, and more in the lobby. Not until I managed to maneuver into a men's room stall was I able to reappear without some camera catching it. Before leaving the stall, I called Rosemary II and told her to run Matt's credit card ASAP for the cost of the charter flight. When she asked why, I simply said he had elected to extend his stay in Chicago.

Three hours, one cheeseburger and two Coronas later, I sat on a stool in the bar chatting with a lumber salesman from Louisiana. I saw his and the eyes of several other men shift to the entrance before I saw her enter. By the time I caught sight of her, most of the men in the bar were watching.

She threaded through a thinning but still energetic crowd and slid onto a seat three stools to my left. The bartender moved quickly. I heard him ask for her order.

"Same as before? Something that looks like a Cosmo, but without alcohol?"

"Not this time. A regular Cosmo, with Belvedere, please."

The lumber salesman hunched a little forward in his seat, giving himself a better view. Like most of the men around us, he studied her with quick glances, most of them stolen through the bar mirror. She paid no attention, lending her green eyes and friendly smile only to the bartender. I leaned toward the lumber salesman and spoke softly.

"I bet you think I have a snowball's chance in hell with a woman like that."

He glanced at her, then me. "You got that right."

I leaned back and took a casual slug of Corona.

"Watch and learn."

A SNOWBALL'S CHANCE
November 9, 2018

ENGINE OUT

4

ENGINE OUT

"I need a hand with something."

Earl Jackson doesn't ask for help. Between the look on his face and the choose-your-last-words-wisely tone of voice, I recognized it wasn't a request.

"Pidge can take your trip tomorrow. I need you with me."

Rosemary II pretended not to pay attention behind the front counter at Essex County Air Services. I looked up from penciling the day's flight time on the manifest sheet attached to the clipboard in my hand.

"Sure thing, Boss," I said. "What's up?"

"We are. Oh-five hundred. We'll take six one nine." If there was more, the back of his head wasn't sharing as he stomped down the hall to his office. The door closed solidly. Some might have said it slammed, but they haven't heard Earl Jackson slam a door.

"What's all that about?" I asked Rosemary II, who, if the CIA and NSA didn't have intel, usually had the answer. She rolled her dark eyes telling me she had no clue. "And isn't Pidge off tomorrow?"

"Uh-huh," she said.

"Are you going to call her and tell her?"

"Not me."

* * * * *

Oh-five hundred, to Earl Jackson, meant wheels up at oh-five hundred and not a second past. That meant crawling out of my warm bed at oh-Hell hundred to dress, beg my car to start, get to the airport, preflight the twin-engine Beechcraft Baron, and pull it out of the hangar in time for Earl to board so the two of us could taxi for takeoff on Runway 13 at precisely oh-five hundred. I probably should have just stayed up.

We were most of the way across northern Wisconsin before the first hint of dawn started chasing us. On the upside, the April air was clear and smooth, and now that the calendar said it was so, I imagined the scent of spring in the air, even if the temperature hadn't cracked freezing in two weeks.

Earl and I, veterans of the air charter business, packed light. In addition to our overnight bags, Earl loaded three toolboxes into the Baron. This had the feel of a maintenance rescue mission, but I knew from a glance at the schedule that all the Essex Air birds were in the nest.

Earl doesn't do chitchat, so for most of the trip the only voice in my headphones came from sector controllers. I relaxed and enjoyed the ride, knowing Earl would fill me in when he felt the need.

The flight plan was filed for Foxtrot Oscar Zulu, or Bigfork Municipal, which is an extravagant name for a one-runway airport outside the tiny Minnesota town of the same name. Coming up on the approach, with dawn catching up to us, the automated weather told us we had an overcast cloud deck twelve hundred feet above ground level. Earl told me to ask for the RNAV 33 approach despite a light wind out of the east. The choice of approach gave us a tailwind on final. I didn't question.

We broke out of the clouds at twelve hundred as predicted with the runway dead ahead. The landscape resembled the wooded Lakes Region in the northeast corner of Essex County. Highways cut thin lines between tracts of trees which stretched to the Canadian border not far away. The town of Bigfork lay behind me on the left side of the approach track, about four miles from the airport.

"Hold fifteen hundred and fly up the centerline," Earl commanded.

I leveled us and put the runway under the nose.

"Over the numbers for one five, gimme a left turn to two eight five and gimme one-twenty."

Earl held his watch up in front of his face. I adjusted the throttles and let the airspeed settle on one hundred and twenty knots.

"Now."

I turned to a course of two hundred eighty-five degrees.

Empty Minnesota winter forest, broken only by one last narrow road leading nowhere, created a moving carpet five hundred feet below us.

I locked the nose on course and held the speed. Old school dead reckoning, that's what Earl was doing. Just about the time I wondered if we were sightseeing Earl dropped his hands to the co-pilot's control yoke.

"My airplane," he called out, "gear down, flaps ten."

I reached for the gear and flaps as he landed his left hand on the throttle quadrant and pulled the power for both engines. He dropped the nose abruptly.

"Three green!" I called out, confirming the landing gear position.

"Flaps full," he commanded.

I hit the flap lever and looked over the nose. Nothing but forest.

We were dropping fast. Airspeed one zero five. Flaps and gear down. Earl fixed his eyes on the trees racing toward us over the nose.

"I gotta ask, Boss—"

"Hang on!" He cranked the yoke to the right. A knob of hill swept past our right wing.

Just as we swung around to a northerly heading a cut in the trees appeared, not much wider than our wingspan. Earl deftly dropped the airplane into the lane and our wheels touched rough frozen ground that had been recently snowplowed. Snow piles raced past both wingtips. The airplane rattled and shook.

Earl pulled both mixture levers full back and the rumbling engines stopped. We rolled toward a wall of trees. Both props ticked to a halt. Earl pumped the brakes, holding a perfect line on the narrow path. We eased to a stop in silence.

Earl cracked a grin in my direction and reached for the door handle.

"Gotta say, Boss, you haven't lost your touch. You still know how to scare the shit outta the passengers."

* * * * *

Earl hopped off the wing and opened the aft cabin doors. I paused for a moment to look back at our runway. It was straight. It was reasonably flat. Beyond that, it bore little resemblance to a runway. Trees stood tall on both sides. The knob hill we passed served as a marker at the other end, which looked a lot closer than I would have liked. I hoped Earl had no plans to carry any kind of load on takeoff, because getting out of here would be tight. At least the airplane was light on fuel.

"Um, I didn't bring any survival gear," I ventured after noting an absence of civilization.

"You shouldn't need any." A woman's voice surprised me from

behind. Earl popped his head out of the cabin and before I turned around to look for the source of the voice, I could have sworn I saw a look of excitement in the cracks and crevasses on his face.

She stepped out of the tree line wearing a faded blaze orange hunter's jacket, making me wonder how in the world I missed her on my first look around. She had a dark knit cap over gray-blonde hair that spilled on her shoulders. In knee-length rubber boots, she crunched across the snow toward the nose of the Baron, leaning to one side to see past me to where Earl stood.

"Is that you, Jackson? Lemme see you."

Earl stopped what he was doing and stepped up behind the wing. She looked him over. She had a handsome face and cream skin. Tiny lines formed at the corners of each eye when she worked up a pretty smile. She looked like she might be in the neighborhood of Earl's age but wore it much younger.

"Jesus, Jackson, what happened to your hair?"

"Burnt it all off in a pileup in Belize. Decided it was easier not to grow it back. You look the same, though."

Did I just hear Earl Jackson pay someone something resembling a compliment? I looked at the two of them. The way they studied each other, I had the distinct feeling they were peeling away years, seeing each other the way they had been, once.

A sweet expression settled on her face. "Who's the kid?"

"That's Will. Shitty pilot, but I keep him around to carry my bags. And speaking of..." He turned back to off-loading the bags and toolboxes.

"You're not going to introduce me, Boss?"

She lifted her eyebrows in Earl's direction.

"That's one of my wives. Now get down here and grab some of this!"

* * * * *

"Candice Hammond Stubowsky Day Jackson O'Connor Thorpe," she extended a hand after I lowered my overnight bag and two toolboxes to the rug of the lodge lobby. "Jackson was number three of five." I took her hand and we traded firm, friendly grips.

"Top of the bell curve," Earl sang out. "Everything was downhill after me."

"I see your ego hasn't shrunk." She moved behind a rustic stand-up counter serving as a check-in desk.

The building—or buildings—materialized out of nowhere after a jolting jeep ride through the woods. Individual cabins scattered around a main lodge sitting on one of Minnesota's ten thousand lakes. These were not the contemporary log homes you find on display in tourist towns. Someone hand cut the trees for these buildings more than a hundred years ago. The plaque beside the main lodge door read Renelle Lodge, Est. 1907.

"Ain't nothing else shrunk. Don't know why my ego would," Earl growled. He poked around the small lobby, taking in the furnishings, the trophy wildlife on the walls, and the view of the small frozen lake. "So, this was Tommy's dream."

Candice pulled off layers. The heavy coat. A scarf. A fleece hoodie. She had half a dozen warm layers to spare. "This is it. This is the place he talked about."

Day. The name rang a bell. Husband number two. I opened my mouth to ask, then thought better of it.

Tommy Day was Earl's backseater when he flew F-4 Phantoms out of Udorn Air Base in Thailand during the Vietnam war. After my accident, when I was strapped to a hospital bed with a broken pelvis and no memory of what happened, Earl told me the story. How a golden round fired by some enemy ground pounder hit the ejection system in his Phantom and blew him out of the aircraft. How his backseater, Tommy Day, didn't make it, and was never found. And how Earl, like me, had no memory of his airplane coming apart.

Son of a bitch. Earl married his Weapon Systems Officer's widow.

I must have worn the realization on my face. Earl shot me a look that suggested he didn't need to be told a story he already knew.

"How long you been here?" Earl asked.

"I bought it with the money from our divorce," Candice said. "First few years were rough. That's what retired O'Connor. He couldn't stand the winters. Then Thorpe came along, and we fixed it up pretty good. I handled the lodge business. He...dabbled."

"I heard," Earl said. "I s'pose we better take a look at it."

"I thought you might want to warm up a bit first. I've got coffee on. Will, can I offer you a mug?"

"Yes, ma'am!"

The coffee wasn't Rosemary II's delicate blend, but it wasn't bad. Candice served it in a well-worn mug that had a Grateful Dead logo on the side. She invited us to sit on equally well-worn furniture near a bank of windows that watched over the small lake. More of a pond, really.

"Have you explained any of this to your young friend here?" Candice asked Earl.

"Can't explain what I don't know."

Candice shook her head at Earl, a loving and patient gesture. "I'm starting to remember why we only lasted three weeks." Earl didn't answer. I hoped he would. I wanted to hear the counterpoint. "My final husband, Captain Thorpe, flew for North Central Airlines, as did your employer, Will."

"That part of the history, I know."

"Captain Thorpe also flew extensively between Canada and the United States in a variety of private aircraft, on a variety of private missions, in and out of a variety of private airstrips, like the one you just landed on. Runways that are not listed on any aeronautical charts."

"Oh."

"It was the eighties. Business was good. Most of that type of flying happened in the Caribbean, of course. But Captain Thorpe blazed new trails here in the north. He was what some called the Northwoods Barry Seal. Do you know the name?"

"I do." I had heard of the drug smuggler who did most of his work for the CIA. There was a movie not long ago. Andy wanted to see it, but I played the pilot card. I don't take her to movies about cops and she doesn't take me to movies where the plot involves airplanes. In both cases, something always comes off the screen reeking of stupid.

"Unlike Mr. Seal, my husband knew when to call it quits. One day I came home from spending Christmas in the twin cities with my sister and he was here. And he told me he was done. He also told me he had locked up the boathouse and I was never to go in it."

"The boathouse?"

She pointed out the windows at a low structure sitting at the edge of the lake, tucked off to the left, almost enveloped by the woods. Except for the angles marking the corners of the buildings, it was all but hidden under a blanket of snow. What remained visible suggested it was one big mother of a boathouse.

"He made me promise. Never go in. He also made me promise I wouldn't open it until five years after he died." She chuckled. "I remember asking him what was going to happen if I passed before him. He told me God's punishment waited for him in the next life, not this one. He would go first."

"Always was a pompous ass," Earl muttered.

"When was that? When did he lock it up?"

"That was nineteen eighty-seven. Twenty-two years ago. The Captain passed five years ago. Today."

She let the point settle. Earl seemed up to speed, but I needed a minute to catch up.

"You mean—this is the day? You're opening it up for the first time in twenty-two years?" Visions of drug runner treasure danced in my head. Or crates full of bootleg ABBA eight tracks. Then it hit me. I looked at Earl. "But you already know what's in there."

He poked his tongue at his cheek and said nothing.

"Which means," I turned to Candice, "you already know what's in there. Or you wouldn't have called Earl."

She shrugged. "You're married, Will." She nodded at my left hand. "A wife doesn't like secrets. I slept a lot better knowing, even though I respected his wishes. I never opened it up. And I waited the five years. But now it's time."

"Finish yer coffee," Earl ordered, standing up. "Let's go have a look."

* * * * *

The steps down to the half-hidden boathouse were snow-covered. Candice handed Earl a shovel to bring along, but it wasn't meant for the steps. At the back of the boathouse, a three-foot snowdrift had to be cleared to make room for the door to swing open. The glass in the door remained intact, but plywood had been nailed over the window's interior.

I offered to shovel, but Earl made quick work of it. I wondered if he felt a need to prove something to his once-wife. Candice stepped up with a heavy ring of keys. She worked old keys in three different deadbolt locks, then a fourth in the door-knob. She pulled. It stuck. Earl nudged her aside and put both hands on the knob. The door broke open with one swift yank. He swung it up against the remaining snow, then took a gentlemanly step aside.

Candice moved into the dark opening. She reached inside the frame and groped for a moment, then found a light switch. One bare bulb, out of four that I could see on the rafters, lit up.

"Wow," I said, sticking my head in after her. "That's not what you expect to see in a boathouse."

The bare bulb lit up her lines and surfaces, which wore a satin finish thanks to layers of dust. Tarps had been thrown over her engines. She sat on sheets of plywood that had been put down on what I took to be a dirt floor. I was surprised to see that none of the tires were flat.

"Queen Air," Earl said, stepping in behind Candice. "Sixty-five. Straight tail."

The big Beechcraft, a middle sister between the Baron I flew this morning and the King Air that Dave Peters had out on a charter, sat with her tail high and her broad wingtips all but scraping the walls. The paint job hadn't been good when it was parked, but twenty years in storage didn't do much additional harm. The white finish was flat. Slim blue lines ran down her sides. She wore Canadian registry, all letters instead of a combination of numbers and letters like the U.S.

"How does someone get a Queen Air into a boathouse?" I asked.

"The lake was frozen," Candice replied. "I'm not sure what he used to push it in."

I ducked under the wing and lifted the tarp on the right engine nacelle. "Do you think it belonged to somebody…you know, who might have wondered where it went?"

"I have no doubt. Somebody who didn't feel inclined to report it stolen." Candice turned to Earl, who ran his eyes over the big airplane like a horse trader about to ask to see the prospect's teeth. "Can you do what I asked?"

Earl didn't answer. I gave the question as much silence as I could, then had to ask, "What's that?"

Candice turned around and started to speak when Earl interrupted her. "She doesn't have the title. No paperwork. No Airworthiness Certificate. The registration is a fake. No idea who this thing belonged to. Or what kind of trouble it's been in." Earl stepped over some lumber on the boathouse floor and ducked under the tail. I moved around the nose to join him on the boarding side of the airplane as he reached for the cabin door. "Thing is, Candy, he left it here for a reason. You think there might be something inside? Something he wanted you to have that maybe he wanted somebody else to forget existed?"

She stepped up next to him and they both looked at the door. She gave him a nod and he pulled the latch. The door swung down. First Earl, then Candice poked their heads into the cabin.

I hurried around to look in after them as Earl climbed aboard and she followed.

"Anything interesting?" I asked, thinking of garbage bags filled with drug runner cash.

"Nope." Earl bumped his way up the center aisle and slid into the pilot's seat. Candice took a seat in the cabin. I stepped halfway in and leaned on the rearmost seat.

Dry old blue upholstery with original Beechcraft logos adorned three rows of seats. The Queen Air had piston engines that rarely provided enough power to allow owners to load up all the seats plus full fuel and baggage. The interior smelled of avgas, oil, and leather, with perhaps a hint of sweat and fear. Old airplanes wear an unmistakable cologne.

"Why would he have seats in here?" I asked. "I mean, if he was running 'cargo' across the border, these seats would all be rusting in some airport junk heap."

Neither of them offered an answer.

"Can you do it, Jackson?" Candice asked.

Earl looked around the cockpit. He grabbed the controls and wiggled them. He put one calloused claw on the top of the instrument panel like a doctor putting a stethoscope to a patient's chest.

"Didja get what I asked for?"

"Battery and fifty gallons of one hundred low lead."

"And how's the ice?"

"About eight inches. Ten in some spots. But another couple days and this cold is supposed to break."

"Alright," Earl said, pounding one fist on the top of the panel. "Let's get this bird in the air." He looked back at me. "Better call your wife and tell her you won't be home tonight."

* * * * *

I don't care how much clothing you put on, working on an airplane out in the cold is never anything but cold. Gloves on, you can't feel the tools. Gloves off, your fingers turn to inexplicably burning red sticks. If you crank a wrench too vigorously, you swim in your own sweat. Take off a layer and that sweat turns icy. There's nothing good about working on an airplane outside, let alone in a cold, poorly lit boathouse beside a frozen lake.

Earl attended to the engines. I drained ancient fuel from the tanks. Candice appeared at the wheel of a small Bombardier snowcat pulling a ski-cart with a fifty-five-gallon drum, a hand pump rig, a gas heater, the toolboxes that Earl and I brought along, and two cases of oil. From the drums, I pumped new fuel into the main tanks, then drained a couple gallons to try and flush any remaining sludge. I opened and cleared the fuel filter screens, drenching my fingers in frigid avgas. Then I pumped a little more fuel aboard until Earl snapped at me to wait with the fuel. He didn't want to pull this beast out onto the ice any heavier than it had to be.

The gas heater wasn't meant to bring any kind of comfort to our workspace. Earl set it up to heat the engine nacelles so that the old oil could be drained. Candice had fresh oil, but no new oil filters. We removed the old ones, drained them the best we could, sloshed a little gas around in them, and let them drip dry before putting them back on.

Sometime in the middle of the process, Candice brought soup in Thermos bottles. I don't know what was better. Hot soup on my insides or holding the warm bottle in my hands.

By mid-afternoon we had the engine oil replaced and the spark plugs cleaned. New would have been better, but the nearest maintenance shop was a long way from our boathouse hangar. Earl inspected the fuel and hydraulic lines. He declared the brake lines capable of an aneurism at any moment and suggested not using the brakes. It was his first hint that I might be flying this old Queen.

Candice had gone back up to the house. She had a pretty good sense of when men don't want a woman around, however capable she may be.

"Just what is it she wants done with this?" I asked. Earl answered from where he had his head stuck up in the gear well on the left nacelle.

"She wants it gone. She can't sell it. It's not worth much, anyway. She just wants it gone. She wants her boathouse back."

"Then why the mystery? Why wait twenty years, then tack on five for good measure?"

"I give up. Why?"

"C'mon, Boss. You know the woman. And you knew her last husband, too, didn't you? At Blue Goose?" North Central Airlines flew with a stylized blue Canada goose logo on the tail of their aircraft. "Aren't you just a little bit convinced that he left something for her? Something in this airplane?"

I saw Earl's hand drop and grope around the boathouse floor for a hammer. He found it, raised it into the gear well and gave her a pair of solid whacks.

"Yeah," he said emerging and working his way upright. "That's what worries her. That's why she wants it gone."

I looked at the Queen Air. Not a whole lot larger than the Mojave we flew, but bigger in the sense of having broad shoulders and solid 1960's construction. If Captain Thorpe hid something in this airplane, it might not be all that easy to find.

"Want me to pull some inspection covers? See if there's anything stashed?"

"Hell no. We're gonna get this thing outta here. Fly it to the nearest unattended airport, park it and let someone else wonder where it came from."

"We? You or me?"

"I ain't decided yet. Now let's lay some plywood and see if we can tow this thing out onto the ice. The bitch'll prob'ly break through and then we're all screwed."

* * * * *

The bitch didn't break through. It took us another hour to put down a track of plywood from the boathouse floor across a narrow gravel beach and onto the lake ice. Ice along the shore was less trustworthy, so we reinforced the three wood tracks, one for the nose gear and two for the main gear. I took a hammer out and hacked a hole in the ice to double-check Candice's estimate. She wasn't wrong. The lake had about nine inches of ice where I dug the hole.

While Earl and I worked, Candice made runs across the small lake with the snowcat, using a blade to plow a runway. The runway started directly in front of the boathouse and ended on the other side of the lake where cattails marked the edge of a marsh. An optimist might call it fifteen hundred feet of runway. A pessimist might call it the scene of the crash.

Once the plywood was in place, we flagged down Candice and got her to line up the snowcat so we could attach a nylon tow strap to the airplane's nose gear. The transition from boathouse to ice runway included a slight incline, a drop of maybe two feet over twenty feet. Just enough to worry us that the Queen, once she started rolling, might overrun her tow. Earl told me to mount up and work the brakes from the pilot's seat. The whole operation nearly ended before it started when Candice got a little too enthusiastic on the first pull, and the brakes on the left main proved frozen.

After some cursing and a few carefully applied whacks with the hammer by Earl, the brakes loosened and she began to roll, bumping and jolting. The plywood slid and shifted as the wheels moved forward. I couldn't tell if the brakes worked or not as the Queen Air picked up speed on the incline. Just about the time the tow strap went slack, and I thought the airplane would drive its nose through the engine cover of the snowcat, Candice gave the machine a shot of power and scooted ahead to prevent a collision.

Rocking and bouncing, I came to a stop on the ice.

Earl shouted for Candice to hold up. He ducked under the nose and pulled the strap, coiling it up on his arm and dumping it in the toolbox mounted at the back of the snowcat.

After a moment I felt his heavy footfalls on the airstair. He thumped into the cabin behind me and put a hand on my shoulder.

"Go get a fire bottle and then let's see if these old Lycomings still have spark."

* * * * *

Earl coaxed the twenty-years-dormant engines to life one by one. The left engine fired, popped, farted and backfired, then struggled into a ragged idle one cylinder at a time. The right engine lit up like a fearless lion. Like it had only been shut down for a twenty-minute fuel stop. Earl let them rumble while I watched for signs of fire. He tried to run them up, but as soon as he advanced the throttles, the whole airplane began to slide on the ice, despite locked wheels. I was in the middle of figuring a way to tie the tow line to a tree to hold the airplane in place when Earl shut them down.

"I would have bet against them starting up," Candice spoke up from where she stood framed in the empty boathouse doorway.

Earl popped his head out of the cabin and the expression of merely mild fury on his face told me he was happy. He looked at me and said, "Dump the rest of the fuel in her and we'll see if she falls through the ice. If not, we'll fly her outta here in the morning." He looked at Candice. "Whaddya got for dinner?"

* * * * *

Climbing the stairs to the lodge, Candice described a venison stew she'd been working on. My stomach rumbled in anticipation. Hot stew, a warm fire, a beer, and a bed after a long day of cold work and fresh air—I was ready for it.

"Let me show you your room," Candice offered, picking up my overnight bag. We climbed a set of stairs that overlooked the lodge great room. "You can warm up and wash up while I put dinner on."

I liked the place. I thought Andy might like it, too. We're not hunters, but we both like a comfortable getaway in a natural setting. A few days here might be fun. The room was small, with a single bed, a closet, and a dresser. The communal bathroom, Candice said, was the last door on the left. Light a match if you do any heavy lifting.

"Is that his? Captain Thorpe's?" I pointed at a plastic bag in the closet where a blue uniform with four cuff stripes hung. Through the plastic I saw dry-cleaning tags. A peaked cap in clear plastic sat on the shelf above.

"All my men were men in uniform of one kind or another," she said, fixing a gaze on the closet. "I can't seem to come up with a reason to get rid of that one."

I know when to keep my mouth shut. I gave her a moment.

Then she dropped my bag on the foot of the bed and said, "Dinner in half an hour."

* * * * *

Two shots, a double tap. The sound carried upstairs and into my room. Intentional and unmistakable. The gunshots were fired in the building, not outside.

I waited, listening. I had just finished peeling off the last extra layer and was about to head for the communal bathroom. I stopped cold. Near silence followed the two shots. Not return fire. Not shouting. Not cries of pain. I could hear conversational voices coming from the lodge great room.

Not a firefight, then. Maybe that's how they announce dinner up here in the woods.

I reached into my head, closed an imagined hand on a set of imagined levers and pushed.

Fwooomp!

I vanished. Gravity ceased to pester me. I lost touch with the floor. I leaned forward and pushed with my toes. The energy launched me toward the top of the doorframe. I put both hands on the wood and pulled myself into the hall.

The wood panel construction on the walls and ceilings didn't offer much for handholds. I fixed my eye on the stairway railing at the end of the hall and pushed. A gentle glide took me to the rail. I closed a grip on the polished wood and stopped overlooking the lodge great room.

A rugged man with a large handgun pointed his weapon at Earl and Candice, who stood side by side near a half-bar on the far side of the room. A shorter man, better dressed and considerably less fierce than the first, stood with his hands jammed in the pockets of an expensive-looking leather coat.

"A fuckin' airplane? That's it? A goddamned piece-of-shit

airplane?" The big man with the gun waved it back and forth between Earl and Candice, swapping aim with every other angry word. "I listened to that old man's shit for sixteen years and it's just an airplane?"

Earl's scowl wasn't much different from his have-a-nice-day look, but I could see heat in the glower he fixed on the big man. It worried me.

The smaller man didn't seem to appreciate his compatriot's commentary. "My father knew what he was talking about. Thorpe took something from him worth a lot more than an airplane. Sit down. Both of you."

Earl and Candice dropped onto a sofa. The big man held his position. The small man opened his coat and sat across from Earl and Candice, lifting one leg onto the other knee.

"Did you know my dad?" he asked.

"I don't know you. Don't know how I would know your old man. Did you know him?" Earl growled.

"Your dad was Peter Nevin," Candice said, not taking her eyes off the man. "And you would be his boy, Charlie. Your dad brought you here once. What were you? Eight? Nine?"

"Six," Nevin said. "Never forgot this place. I always hated fishing after that trip. So, you knew him."

"I knew what he was. I knew what he was doing with my husband. And I knew that after my husband stopped doing…what he was doing…your dad was arrested. They put him away for a long time."

"For life, it turns out. A heart attack in prison will do that. Puts that Life Without Parole stamp on your sentence."

"What do you want here?" Earl demanded. Candice laid a gentle hand on Earl's thigh. She saw what I saw. Earl coiled.

"What's mine," Nevin said. "God, that sounds villainous. Fact is, I knew nothing about this mysterious treasure until I met Roger. Roger spent a lot more time with my dad than I did, being cellmates and all. Oh, don't let that sound like a sob story. I hated my old man. Never spoke to him after he went in. Turned the knife when I took over the family business, so to speak." He laughed. "I never even sent the son of a bitch commissary cash."

"You're one of these guys who won't shut up, aren't you."

Nevin ignored Earl. "Roger had a tale to tell me. About a double-cross by a guy named Thorpe that ended up putting my dad in prison, and how my dad knew that Thorpe held onto something. Something big. Something he was gonna get back after he got out. I did some digging. Found out about Captain Thorpe. This place. I sent a couple friends up here last fall to check it out. They came back with a story about a locked-up boathouse. And how it wasn't supposed to be opened until, well, today, if Thorpe's death certificate is accurate. And here we are. Thought we'd join you for the big unveiling."

"Al Capone's vault," Earl muttered. "Nothin' there."

Nevin shook his head. "I think it deserves more examination."

"Well, you better examine quick," Earl said, "because that lake is thawing and pretty soon that airplane is going to be at the bottom."

"Not if you fly it out of here," Nevin said.

"Me?" Earl chuckled "Shit, I'm just an auto mechanic from over at the Subaru dealership in Belvin. I don't know nothin' about flying an airplane."

"I think you're lying. I think you're planning to fly it out of here tomorrow on that runway that somehow got plowed out there. And I think, why wait? I think you're going to fly me out of here tonight in that airplane and take me somewhere so that I can recover whatever it was my father had stolen from him."

"He's not a pilot," Candice said. "He's just here to get it ready. A pilot from the Sheriff's Department is coming in tomorrow to fly it out and impound it. You should get out of here now while you have a chance."

I hated to leave the conversation, but I had an idea. I pushed myself backward, down the hall. I snagged my room door and—

Fwooomp! I reappeared and pulled my clothes off.

* * * * *

They were still talking when I walked back down the hall and started down the steps.

"Nobody's taking my airplane unless I'm in the captain's seat," I said, slipping on the peaked cap and stopping on the mid-flight landing so everyone could look at me.

Candice's face blanched and her eyes went wide.

Earl took one look and clenched his jaw. His expression suggested what the surface of the ocean must look like with a school of sharks skimming below.

"Who the fuck are you?" Roger swung his arm to point his big pistol in my direction.

"I'm your captain," I said. I straightened my blue tie and tugged at the four-stripe cuffs of the neat blue jacket. The pants were a little loose and a little short, but otherwise Captain Thorpe's North Central Airlines uniform fit snugly. "And we have about ten minutes of dusk left before this unlighted airport closes for the night. I suggest we board and be on our way."

Nevin and Roger traded glances. Nevin, a man with a narrow face and a little too much forehead, reached a decision and stood up.

"Alright. Roger stays here with these two until we're safely in the air. A little insurance."

"I don't know if you're familiar with the term 'pilot in command' but that's me. Which means Roger is going to hand that pistol over to you, and then he's going to drive away to whatever rendezvous you two care to set up. Then you can point that gun at me all you want, and I'll fly you out of here." I tried to lower the register on my voice. Give it a good airline captain growl. I pointed at Earl and Candice. "They stay put."

Nevin considered it, but Roger wasn't at all comfortable with being commanded. "Fuck you!"

"Okay. Fuck me. Shoot me. Shoot them. Now you have a triple murder instead of a simple collection of property that she doesn't want in the first place. I'm sure you can work out a way to get that airplane off the ice before the cops get here in the morning."

For a moment, Roger appeared ready to proceed with my suggestion.

"Rog, there's no reason to escalate this," Nevin said. "It's like he said, we're just here to collect. They don't want it. Now we have a pilot. Let's keep this simple, okay?"

Roger gave it a dramatic moment, like he wanted me to know that he could kill me if he felt like it. He struck a pose, turned the handgun on its side and made a *Pow* sound with his mouth.

Nevin walked over to him and put his hand out. "Give me the gun. I'll meet you in St. Paul. Meet me at the airport there. Not the big one. The one in St. Paul."

"You better fuckin' be there," Roger said. He didn't seem like the trusting type. Nevin took the gun from him. Roger pulled keys from his pocket. He stomped to the door, giving me the stink-eye as he passed. "Fuck with him and I'll track you down."

"Affirmative," I said.

Nevin, now holding a gun that looked a little too big for his hand, gestured at the door. "You said we were running out of light. Let's go."

Earl gave me a dirty look and started to rise, but Candice clamped her hand on his thigh and locked him in place. She sent one more astonished glance in my direction as I headed out the door behind Roger.

"You kids don't wait up," I said.

* * * * *

She was cold and stiff, but the engines fired quickly, still warm from Earl's brief runup. I sat for a moment watching the oil pressure and letting the temperature needle crawl away from the stop. A little heat in the cabin would be nice, but I had no idea where to find the heater controls. I looked for and found light switches. Red instrument post lights added glow to the panel. The wingtip red nav light on the left side lit up, but the green on the right was out, and I had no way of seeing the white light on the tail. Flashing red on the landscape around me told me the beacon was working. I found the landing light switch and flipped it. Nothing happened. In a few minutes, that would be a real problem, but for now I had enough lingering dusk to see the narrow shaved ice runway. It looked short. Stupid short.

Everything about this was stupid. No inspection. No preflight. No idea if these engines would keep running or if a twenty-year-dormant control cable would snap or freeze up. On top of it all, I glanced at the fuel gauges. Neither worked.

"Are those gas tanks empty?" Nevin pointed at the gauges as if reading my mind. He had strapped himself uncomfortably in the co-pilot's seat.

"Hell no," I said. "Plenty of fuel! The gauges just don't work."

A little under twenty-five gallons in each tank wasn't plenty of fuel. I had no idea what the performance numbers for this airplane and these engines were, but I could guess that this flight was not going to last much past an hour. I could point us at Minneapolis but didn't have complete confidence we would arrive.

I picked up the old-school mic and spoke. "Ladies and gentlemen, this is your captain speaking. Thank you for flying North Central Airlines Fight 666 to Minneapolis tonight." I put the mic back on its holder and then turned on the radios. Why not? They might work.

Nevin looked at me with growing trepidation.

I didn't know if we were going to get off the ground, or if this airplane would stay in the air, but I knew one thing for certain.

If the shit hits the fan, I'm out of here. I voluntarily left a perfectly good airplane in flight once before. I could do it again. They could scrape Nevin out of the wreckage by himself.

"Pre-takeoff check complete," I shouted over the engine noise. "Rolling!"

There wasn't much to it. I pushed the throttle, prop and mixture balls to the wall. The engines thundered on either side of us. At least nothing quit or blew. Of course, shit like that usually happens two hundred feet up with nothing ahead but trees.

The old girl lumbered forward. I expected the ice to crack and drop the nose gear. I expected one engine to fail us at the worst possible moment, cartwheeling us into a heap. I expected the controls, which I worked vigorously now to ascertain that they were fully functional, to lock up.

What I didn't expect was the slow acceleration. I tapped the brakes to be sure they were working, but not locked up. Last I checked there was air in the tires. I'd never flown a Queen Air before. Was it always this anemic?

We crawled forward, consuming precious runway. Both power needles on the manifold pressure looked good. Both RPM needles looked good. What the hell?

The airspeed needle wiggled. Snow piles on either side accelerated.

"C'mon, you sweet old girl!" I muttered under my breath, trying hard not to pull on the yoke too soon out of wishful thinking. "C'mon!"

I wasn't used to flying without noise-cancelling headphones. The thundering engine noise felt disorienting. It had grown darker now, and only the carved path on the lake remained visible. Thirty knots. We were covering a lot of ground. Forty knots. Those cattails were coming for me, and with them, less stable ice. Forty-five knots. I felt myself pushing harder on the throttle levers, not that it made any difference. Fifty knots. The ice was far from smooth. The entire airplane rattled and thudded. Sixty knots. The needle on the airspeed indicator had yet to reach the bottom of the white arc—stall speed with flaps. And we weren't using any flaps. The bottom of the green arc—flying speed—looked like a distant dream.

In the windshield, black trees divided the near-black lake from the near-black sky. Falling night took away anything resembling depth perception.

"Fuck this!" I shouted. Nevin looked at me in a panic. I think he expected me to cut the power. Instead, I dropped my hand to the flap lever and pushed it down. I had no idea if they were hydraulic or electric. I moved the lever to the ten-degree mark.

She abruptly ballooned. I pushed the nose down to prevent us from clawing into the sky without enough speed. There's a cushion of air between the wings and the ground called Ground Effect. It makes airplanes fly when they shouldn't. I used every bit of it now. The wheels had stopped pounding on the ice. The engines screamed at me, claiming they were doing everything they were built to do.

The black tree line swept toward us. We skimmed the tops of cattails. I grabbed the gear handle and pulled it up. Something whined. Something shifted. Something thumped into place. On the panel, three green lights winked out and a single red lit. Gear up. If we came down now, it would be on the belly.

The airspeed needle wiggled in the white arc, then touched the green.

Jesus, she feels heavy!

I had a strangle hold on the yoke but moved it with a tender-ness I reserve for my wife. I let the nose dip back into the tops of the cattails streaming past us. It was probably a good thing the landing lights didn't work. Illumination might have scared us to death.

"PULL UP!" Nevin screamed. He grabbed the yoke but before he could kill us both I slammed a fist into his groin. He lost his grip and all the air in his lungs.

At the instant the trees arrived to take us I asked the old girl for fifty feet. She answered.

Above the trees, the urge to climb was overwhelming, but at this moment it was airspeed, not altitude, that meant life. We raced over the black as the needle crawled higher. Eighty knots. Eighty-five knots. I reached for the flaps and tapped them slowly upward. The ship wanted to drop, and the compensating back pressure I applied to hold her level stole away a few precious knots, but once clean, she regained them. Ninety knots. I pulled. We eased up and away from the trees.

After a few moments I stopped strangling the yoke and began contemplating the next emergency.

I had no navigation equipment, no maps, no iPad with GPS.

Minneapolis. Specifically, St. Paul. Something like a hundred and seventy miles away. My guess was that this old girl cruised around a hundred and seventy and the engines sucked in fuel around twenty gallons per hour. The math suggested we might make it into some of the busiest airspace in the country. I eased the power back to what I guesstimated to be sixty percent. Easier on the engines and the fuel consumption.

"Ladies and gentlemen, you may now move about the cabin," I sang out.

Nevin glared at me, his face red and glistening with sweat. He angrily held the gun up again.

"Or you can shoot me."

I think if he could have talked, he would have agreed. It took him a while to get his voice working.

* * * * *

"What's your name?"

We were forty-seven minutes into the flight, level at fifty-five hundred feet, flying on a one seven five heading. Roughly south. The cloud layer Earl and I flew through on the way into the Renelle Lodge had long since broken up, rendering an almost clear but moonless night. Small towns passed beneath us like glittering puddles on vast black asphalt. Not far ahead, on the horizon, I could see the glow I was looking for.

"Your name. I asked your name."

This was a moment I had been thinking about since slipping into the airline uniform. The cabin lights were off. We sat in the spooky red glow of the instrument post lights. I could have provided more cabin light, but the post lights were all I needed, and I wanted the crimson ambiance.

I turned in the seat and gave Nevin a long, unblinking stare.

"You know my name," I said, trying to sound eerie. I then rotated my head back and resumed working. The broad expanse of surface city light crawled toward us.

"Dude I don't know your name. And what's with the getup?"

I said nothing. I stared straight ahead. I let this go on for a few minutes. He could always point the gun at me again, but even he seemed to have figured out that it had no real power here.

Rivers of highway light flowed into the greater glitter of Minneapolis. I decided it was time. The engines hadn't quit yet, so now was as good a time as any. I surreptitiously reached down to the fuel control panel beside me and switched the right-side lever to Crossfeed. Fuel from the right tank now diverted to the left engine.

"What's wrong with you man? I just want to know your name!"

I rotated my head again slowly to stare at him. I never partici-pated in any kind of theater in my school days, but I must have given it a pretty good effort because he twitched nervously in his seat.

"You know my name," I said flatly. "I'm Captain Thorpe."

He blinked.

"What? Fuck, he's dead. You're not—"

Two things happened at once. First, the right engine surged, stabilized, surged again, and then lost power.

Second—

Fwooomp!

I vanished.

I kept my left hand on the yoke but worked my right hand on the power quadrant as I went through the engine-out procedure.

Everything forward. Everything up. Dead foot. Dead engine. Identify. Feather.

I pulled the right throttle and detected no change in the power, which now surged in the left engine and demanded almost full left rudder to remain on course. I pulled the prop control into Feather to diminish the drag caused by a windmilling prop. I glanced over at Nevin whose eyes could have served as landing lights. He stared at the empty space where I sat, at the control yoke still working with no hand upon it, at the prop and throttle levers moving by themselves. He looked like a man about to wet himself.

I leaned in his direction and locked my face on his. My blazing eyes would be the first thing he saw when I reappeared.

Fwooomp! He jolted against the window.

In the loudest unhinged voice I could muster, I shouted, "I AM CAPTAIN THORPE. WELCOME ABOARD NORTH CENTRAL FLIGHT 666!"

Nevin screamed. I sat back and relaxed as if nothing had happened. I focused on the work of flying an engine-out airplane. We were now well within the Minneapolis Class B airspace and busting all kinds of regulations. In the black sky I could see airliner landing lights all around us.

I glanced at the airspeed. Down to one hundred ten knots. I wasn't sure what Best Rate Single Engine speed was—the airspeed indicator had no blue line—so I settled on one hundred knots. It felt right. That speed should have given us the best climb performance for single engine operations.

I checked the vertical speed indicator. At full power, we were losing four hundred feet per minute.

Christ, this beast is heavy! It made no sense. We were light on fuel and had an almost empty cabin. What the hell?

I glanced over at the one-man audience for my horror show. He couldn't take his eyes off me. His jaw worked up and down and I think he was trying to talk, but nothing came out. The gun in his hand was pointed roughly in my direction and that had me worried. If I scared him too badly, he might decide that shooting was the better option.

I reached over and closed my hand over the long rectangular slide of the semi-automatic. With one finger, I found and flicked the safety on, then twisted the weapon from his shaking hands. He didn't resist. I lowered my hand between the seats and tossed the gun to the rear of the cabin.

Things were about to get busy, so I put in one last performance for him.

"Sure thing, son! I knew your dad! Me and him—we did some shit, for sure! Hauled a lot of product. Things just got too dicey. They were closing in on us. I knew I could quit, but he couldn't. That's what got me out—and got him twenty-five to life!" I grinned at him. "You gotta know when to quit!"

I had no idea how much of that was on the mark. He gaped at me, so I gave it the grand finish.

Fwooomp! I vanished right before his eyes.

"And then he died! And I died! And this old airplane, Lord Almighty, she keeps calling me back!"

Fwooomp! I reappeared.

He pressed himself against the cabin window, shaking. Too much more of this and his heart was going to stop.

We dropped faster than I hoped. I looked at the radio stack but couldn't for the life of me remember the frequency for Minneapolis Approach control. I remembered the tower frequency, however, and dialed it in. One two six point seven. I cranked the volume and started hearing chatter on the frequency through the overhead speakers.

This is going to piss off a lot of people.

Busting into Class B airspace at any of the dozen or so major airports that are so designated is perhaps second only to busting into Presidential Temporary Flight Restriction airspace. A damned good way to earn a license suspension. Not only does it upset a highly organized flow of air traffic, but lately it tends to ignite fears of a terrorist act. The flip side of that is that people who worry most about terrorists have the best resources for what I needed. Landing at any other airport, we would have been met by a lonely lineman asking if we wanted fuel. And that's only if the airport FBO wasn't closed. I wanted to land where Nevin could get the attention he deserved.

I waited for the chatter to die down on the tower frequency, then picked up the microphone.

"Mayday! Mayday! Mayday! North Central Flight 666, we are engine out! Repeat! Engine out! Unable to hold altitude, landing Minneapolis!"

This might have been the first realization Nevin had that one of our engines had quit. He spun his head and looked out the window at the prop on the right side, which had stopped turning.

"Aircraft calling Minneapolis, say again your Mayday." The controller did not sound happy.

I repeated the call along with a claim that I was a Convair 580, the old prop job that North Central once flew.

"North Central...uh, Flight 666, say your position."

"We are fifteen miles north, out of four thousand nine hundred. We are engine out, one soul on board, minimal fuel, descending at four hundred feet per minute."

"666, contact Minneapolis approach on one one nine point three."

"Unable!"

"666, squawk code seven seven zero zero."

"Unable!" I had already tried the transponder. It was as dead as I pretended to be.

"Uh, okay, 666, stand by." The controller ran through rapid-fire clearances for other aircraft, some of which were suddenly told to hold position on the ground or contact approach control on their last frequency. Another controller voice came up on the frequency. The change in voice told me they had the full fire drill going.

"666, say your heading."

"One seven five."

"666, turn right to heading two four zero for radar identification."

"Unable! Son, we have one engine gone and the other one threatening to go on strike. We're coming in on Runway One Two Right. Request you roll everything you have."

"666, radar contact, turn right two seven zero for Crystal Airport at your three o'clock and six miles."

"Unable!"

He couldn't argue with me. The pilot in command tops air traffic control.

"666, do you have Minneapolis in sight?"

"Praise the Lord, I do! Out of four thousand one hundred!"

He hesitated, knowing he was about to commit to a massive mess for a major airport jammed with back-to-back arrivals and departures.

"666, understand you are requesting Runway One Two Right?"

"Ahh-firmative!"

My left leg, stomped down on the rudder against the asymmetrical power of the remaining engine, started to shiver. I moved my right foot over to join the effort.

"All aircraft! All aircraft on tower frequency! The airport is now closed! All landing clearances are rescinded. Contact approach control on your last frequency!" Part of me felt bad about that. Part of me was grinning. I flashed that grin at Nevin. He had good reason to see it as insane. "666, you are cleared to land on Runway One Two Right at Minneapolis. We are rolling the emergency equipment." I know he wanted to help, but since I'd been a bit of a dick about each of the controller's requests, he said it with a hint of backlash.

"666, cleared to land!" I replied cheerfully.

Now I just had to find the airport. In a sea of urban lights, the airport is usually the dark spot. I had a couple dark spots in sight. I knew the Minneapolis area from countless flights and knew how the Mississippi River ran south through the city, then hooked north around West St. Paul. The dark spot I wanted was adjacent to where the river made its left turn.

There.

At something like ten thousand feet, Runway One Two Right wasn't the longest at Minneapolis, but it aligned with the wind, which I preferred. It also ran past the fire station, which I thought might be a good idea.

Landing a twin-engine airplane on a single engine is an exercise in commitment. Once you go down, there's no going back up, especially in this heavy old beast. The weight of this airplane nagged at me. We should have been able to get off that lake easily. We should have been able to hold altitude on one engine, yet we sank like an anchor. I decided to keep us as high as possible before lowering the gear.

I angled to join the final approach course about four miles from the threshold. My altitude checked in just under three thousand and dropping when I turned final. The runway lights stretched out in the distance.

I had all but forgotten about Nevin. A glance told me he was trying to decide whether to be terrified by the loss of an engine or the fact that a phantom was driving the airplane. I flashed him another crazy grin and then went back to work.

Even with full power on the good engine, we sank fast. I wanted to cross the threshold high, fully configured with lots of room to spare for the landing on a runway nearly two miles long. It wasn't working out that way.

A train of flashing red emergency lights emerged from the mid-field fire station. They lined up on the taxiway that ran parallel to Runway 4/22.

A mile to go. Too low to drop the gear. I knew once I threw down the gear lever, the old Queen would sink like an anchor. I had no idea how quickly the gear would fall in place and lock, however. So, I couldn't wait forever.

Half a mile to go. I kept full power on the left engine and marveled that it ran as well as it did. Airspeed ninety knots. Nearly Minimum Controllable Airspeed, Single Engine. If the speed dropped, I would have no choice but to cut the power on the good engine. Without sufficient airspeed, the rudder becomes ineffective, and the asymmetrical thrust overpowers all control, flipping the airplane into a fatal dive.

"North Central 666, good luck." The tower controller said it with heart.

"Thanks."

Now or never. I dropped the gear lever. Something whined. Something thumped. None of the gear lights lit up. Nor did I feel a sharp change in the aerodynamics of the airplane.

Shit!

Complete gear failure.

Of course.

The good news, I was going to make the runway with altitude to spare now that I didn't have the gear hanging out to drag me down.

The bad news, I now had to deal with belly-landing the airplane.

Five hundred feet. Four hundred feet.

Racing sequential strobe lights called The Rabbit passed under the nose, guiding me toward the runway. I could see the runway number painted on the concrete.

I pushed the nose down and moved fast. Fuel selectors off. Master switch off. We dove for the numbers. I caught a glimpse of the airspeed needle. One ten. Good.

The runway came up quickly and I heard a new sound. It momentarily amazed me that the old airplane could come up with something else at a time like this, until I realized it was Nevin, both hands braced on the instrument panel, screaming.

The huge runway numbers filled the windscreen. I jerked all remaining power levers back to the stops. The left engine wound down and died almost unnoticed under Nevin's girlish scream.

I eased back on the stick but once again misjudged the weight of the airplane. Momentum threatened to overpower me and drive us into the runway. I pulled harder and the nose came up. I wanted to get a reasonable flare out of it, and ease the airplane onto the concrete, but for the third and final time I misjudged the weight. Airspeed bled off at an alarming rate and it caught me high in the flare. Without warning, she stopped flying and dropped hard. We fell the last fifteen feet, still moving at seventy knots.

She hit like thunder and screamed. Her aluminum skin fought the concrete. Impact forces rippled up through my seat into my spine and knocked my teeth together. Sparks danced across my vision. The left prop didn't have time to stop turning. When it hit the concrete, the blades curled back like leaf fronds in a wind.

The fuselage tracked remarkably straight, and out of habit or instinct, I worked the rudder pedals to keep it that way, even though they had no effect.

The noise went on and on until it simply stopped. Except for Nevin. He sat next to me howling with his eyes closed until I tapped him on the shoulder.

"Hey!" It took a few taps. The man's composure was shattered. "HEY!"

Wild eyes found me. I unstrapped my belt. I slid out of the seat and worked my way backward, half out of the cockpit.

"Listen to me! For safety, I need you to slide over here! Over here!" I pointed at the pilot's seat. "They'll evacuate you from over here!" He bobbed his head senselessly and tried to move over into the pilot's seat without taking off his seatbelt. I reached down and released it. "That's right! Good! Slide over! Good! Now stay there!"

I patted him on the shoulder.

"Shouldn't we get out?" he asked weakly. "Are we on fire?"

"Oh hell, no! There's no fire. We don't have any fuel left. Just stay there. Someone will come and get you."

I ducked into the cabin and found the door latch only to realize the door was already partially open. The impact had broken the latch. For a moment, I worried it might be stuck, but a good kick dropped the door to the concrete. It was eerie, being this low in a cabin that I was accustomed to entering and exiting by a set of steps. I grabbed the North Central captain's hat from the back seat where I had placed it. I put it on. Out of habit, I tapped my left breast for my sunglasses. Surprisingly, I felt a pair in the old airline jacket. I pulled out a fine pair of Ray Bans and slipped them on, completing the look.

A phalanx of police and fire vehicles raced toward me. It looked like the old Queen Air made it most of the way to mid-field, so the trip was a short one.

I stepped out onto the concrete, adjusted the hat, straightened my tie, and tugged my cuffs. I looked at the trail we left between the runway lights.

"Son of a bitch…"

A light wind blew a storm of white powder into the air along the path we had scribed on the runway. I looked over the old Queen. Her body lay on the runway, her belly cracked and broken. The hot engine ticked as it cooled. From split aluminum belly seams, white powder and bricks wrapped in plastic spilled onto the pavement. White powder bled from the airplane and swirled away on the breeze.

Under her skin, she had been loaded with cocaine. Probably overweight. Still carrying the last shipment consigned to her nefarious career. The cocaine leaked and spilled—and once liberated, danced in the light breeze.

"Oh boy, Nevin," I said to myself. "You're in some deep shit now."

I waited until the first emergency vehicle swept its headlights across me—the dapper pilot wearing the uniform of a long-gone airline. I made sure the light caught my stripes and cool hat.

Then I vanished.

ENGINE OUT
October 26, 2018

Supervised Solo

5

SUPERVISED SOLO

M y phone rang. I reflexively slapped my shirt pocket despite knowing the device lay on the old desk in the Foundation hangar; the desk I use for flight planning.

"Never fails," I muttered, zipping my pants. I fumbled with my belt on the run, ducked out of the office restroom and hurried through the open door in the glass wall that separates the lounge from the hangar.

Counting off the ringtones and knowing I was about to miss the call I stabbed the green screen button without lifting the phone from the scarred desktop. The display read Essex County Air. I finished fastening my belt and picked up the phone.

"…you there, Will?" Rosemary II's voice rose to meet my ear.

"I don't know how you and my wife always know when I'm in the bathroom."

"No greater mystery than woman."

"What's up?"

"Are you available to take a student?"

"Sure," I said. "Who is it?"

"Ray Portman. You don't know him. He started a few weeks ago. One of Pidge's victims."

"Scheduling problem?" Pidge is the best pilot I know, but as an instructor, she can be a bit abrasive. Rosemary II carefully pairs her with students who display confidence and a thick skin.

"Uh-huh. Ray just soloed on Sunday. He's booked for his second supervised solo today, but Miss Page is out on a charter, and she's delayed, and I don't have anyone else on today." Use of Pidge's real name and a slight change in tone told me the student was standing across the counter from Rosemary II.

"Second solo, huh? He's got a good day for it." The weather promised to hold until late evening. A warm mid-afternoon breeze flowed lightly past the open hangar door. I checked the airport windsock. It waved in tidy alignment with runway 13. Good conditions for a student flexing new wings. I approve of students following up a first solo quickly. Muscle memory and confidence diminish with time.

"Shall I have him preflight?"

"Sure. I'll meet him on the ramp."

"He's taking Eight Zero Zero."

* * * * *

Earl's oldest Cessna Skyhawk betrayed nothing of her age. Her paint kicked back glints of afternoon sunshine. Her lines remained sleek, accented by a swept vertical fin. Her landing gear showed no sign of sagging under the weight of thousands of landings. If I had once known the year the airplane was manufactured, I've since forgotten. It had to be in the 1970s, before Cessna had been driven out of the aircraft manufacturing business by lawyers and the cost of liability insurance. Age didn't matter. New Skyhawks coming off Cessna's reawakened production line looked no different, save their trendy swept-stroke paint schemes. Old Eight Zero Zero soldiered on in good form.

Few students choose the 172 Skyhawk for training. Most primary training utilizes the smaller two-passenger Cessna 152. Newly certified private pilots often transition to the four-place 172 after getting their certificate. It's faster, more comfortable and offers a back seat for the kids. Students that opt for the more expensive 172 rental in training often do so because of personal physical size. It gets tight in a 152 for anyone over six feet tall.

I expected to find a tall or stout man pre-flighting the airplane, but the student pilot had already boarded, which struck me as unusual. Most students wait by the nose for the instructor, anticipating a question about the conduct of the preflight or the condition of the aircraft.

This student sat with his head down, a posture I recognized as a pilot reading a checklist. I picked up my pace across the ramp.

My urgency flared to a full-blown emergency when the student opened his side window and shouted out, "Clear!"

"Whoa! Hold up! Hold up!" I shouted, breaking into a jog across the nose of the airplane and waving my arms.

Ray Portman looked at me through dark plastic sunglasses. I curved well clear of the prop in case he hit the starter. I ducked under the left-wing strut and pulled open the pilot's door, prepared to grab the mixture control if he carried through his startup procedure.

"What are you doing?" I asked.

He turned his head, hands still on the yoke and the ignition.

"Uh...I was going to go fly."

"Solo?"

"Yeah." He looked surprised. "I soloed on Sunday. Are you Will? Rosemary said you would be supervising."

"Yeah."

"I thought she meant you'd be watching, you know, from the ground."

I shook my head, still assessing how much of this was misunderstanding and how much might be arrogance—a student thinking he knows it all and can just go bounding off into the sky with one solo under his belt.

"So, you were just going to go and fly?"

"I thought I was."

"Yeah...that's not how this works. This is your second supervised solo, which means you and I will go a couple circuits in the pattern, then if things look good, I'll turn you loose on the unsuspecting atmosphere."

He glanced at his watch.

"I thought I would just be able to go. You know. Since I soloed."

I backed away and hiked around the tail to the passenger side where I pulled the door open and slid into the instructor's seat.

"Like I said, not how it works. Why don't you start from the top of the checklist and we'll see how it goes." I sounded a bit stiff, but I didn't like the assumption he had made and the lack of humility that potentially lurked within. Confidence or arrogance—I had yet to decide.

He checked his watch again. "Uh, okay."

He cycled through the startup checklist. After another shout out the side window to clear the area, he cranked over the engine until it fired and hummed energetically. He sent me a glance to see if I approved, but I offered no feedback. I slipped on and adjusted my headset.

Pidge taught him well. I found no fault in his taxi and pre-takeoff procedures. He seemed tense, which I chalked up to performing with a new instructor in the right seat, and to having made a major error at the outset. Tension isn't good for a freshly soloed student pilot, so I laid plans to relax the situation with some friendly conversation after his first landing.

He visually cleared the final and base legs of the approach to the runway and announced that "Cessna Eight Zero Zero is back taxiing for departure on Runway 13, Essex County." His radio call demonstrated confidence. Back taxiing is a requirement for departure from Runway 13 at Essex County. The taxiway connecting the runway to the ramp doesn't join at the end of the runway. Utilizing the full available runway means rolling onto the runway itself, taxiing to the end and turning around for takeoff.

"I like to keep to the edge of the runway when I back taxi," I commented as he rolled onto the runway. "If something unexpected appears, you're out of the line of landing traffic and you can make a quick exit. And if you screw up completely, at least you won't get hit dead center."

He obediently steered the airplane away from the runway centerline. At the end, he swung to the right into the turnaround, then left in a tight reversal.

"Also double-check final when you make that turnaround. Treat it just like you would if you were taxiing onto an active runway from a taxiway."

He nodded. He touched the mic button and spoke. "Essex County Traffic, Cessna Eight Zero Zero departing runway 13, Essex County."

"Remaining in the pattern," I added via intercom.

"Oh, yeah." He transmitted my reminder.

I let a little of my stiffness evaporate. "Alright," I said. "Let's see if this bird can fly."

He lined up the nose with the broad dashed centerline markings and steadily pushed the throttle to the stop. The engine responded with power that seemed mild compared to the big engines on the Piper Navajo I regularly fly, but a quick check of the tachometer reported full takeoff power.

He danced on the rudder pedals to keep the airplane straight. We accelerated until the speed needle gave no reason to remain earthbound. He lifted the nose later than I would have liked. The instant the nose went light the main gear shed contact with the runway.

"Callouts?" Pidge would have taught him to call out power, suction and airspeed checks on the roll.

"Oh, yeah. Sorry." Another error, albeit minor. He might not have committed it had Pidge been in the right seat prompting familiar routine. My presence introduced a new variable.

He set up a climb and checked over his shoulder to see that his departure aligned with the runway. At five hundred feet, he cleared the air to our left and made the first turn in the rectangular traffic pattern that would take us back to the runway. My initial assessment of his skills suggested that unless his landing resulted in disaster, no more than three trips around the pattern would suffice. Then I would release him for an hour on his own.

"Would you take it for me?" he asked. "Just for a sec?"

I put my right hand on the yoke and my left on the throttle.

"My airplane."

He twisted and reached his right hand behind my seat. He fumbled with a flight bag, then turned to face forward.

"Keep your hands on the controls. Head northeast."

His face offered no explanation for the abruptly commanding tone, but the slab-sided Glock handgun he pointed at me made the point.

"Are you kidding me?"

"Hardly."

I swept the airplane into a turn as directed.

"Where are we going?"

Portman didn't answer. He reached up and switched the transponder from ALT to OFF.

I could not help but consider vanishing. Disappearing wouldn't take me out of the line of fire, but it would create confusion—perhaps enough to let me twist the weapon out of his grip. On the other hand, grabbed weapons go off.

I ruled out disappearing.

Portman reached under his seat and lifted an iPad from the floor. He flipped open the cover. The screen came to life. He touched the ForeFlight icon and a moment later the screen rendered the FAA sectional chart representing the earth beneath us. A magenta line stretched from Essex County Airport to the northeast.

"You figured you were going to solo today and go on a cross-country?"

"Go a little to the right."

I adjusted the heading.

Portman wasn't tall. Nor heavy. His choice of the 172 over the 152 wasn't a matter of size or comfort. I wondered if he had planned to take just enough lessons to steal the airplane. But why pull the gun? Why not wait until I released him for his supervised solo?

If this was about stealing an airplane, taking me along made no sense. After a few takeoffs and landings, I would have hopped out at the ramp. In another fifteen or twenty minutes, he would have had the airplane and his plans to himself.

The watch.

He couldn't wait.

He needed to be somewhere. He answered to a tight schedule.

"You know, it's practically impossible to get these doors open in flight," I pointed out.

"What?"

"If you're thinking about shooting me and pushing me out. Almost impossible." On the other hand, opening the door and heaving myself out fit entirely in my realm of the possible. But lacking a handheld power unit and propeller to get me to the ground safely, exiting the airplane in flight posed more problems than solutions.

"Just fly the airplane."

"Where? Escanaba? Menominee?" I pointed at his iPad screen. The blue aircraft icon merged with the magenta course line.

"We're going to Freeland Airport."

"Freeland?" I know most of the airports in Wisconsin and the UP. I'd heard the name, but never had reason to pinpoint its location.

"We're landing at Freeland, where you will get out and I will pick up passengers and then you'll never see me or this airplane again. Just do what you're told and you'll live to wonder what it was all about."

"What's the weather at Freeland?"

"What?"

His face, a plain affair with no facial hair, no scars and thin, reddish eyebrows that matched his near-shaved hair, betrayed a flash of uncertainty.

"Did you take a ground school course?"

He shook his head.

"So, you haven't done any cross-country planning. Weather analysis? Prog charts? MOS? Any of that?"

"Just fly the airplane."

"Where's Freeland?"

"The Upper Peninsula. East of Schoolcraft. Why?"

"Because this morning, the southern edge of a stationery front pushed down from Canada into the Great Lakes."

"So?"

"So, look at the weather for Freeland. On that." I dipped my head toward his iPad. "Do you know how?"

"Shut up. I know how." I noted the first demarcation line in his patience.

He shoved the iPad toward me. "You do it."

I switched hands to hold the yoke with my left and handle the iPad with my right. Placing the tablet on a knee and against the instrument panel, I swiped the screen to follow his magenta course line. It crossed the edge of Green Bay and caught up with the southern shore of Upper Michigan about 10 miles east of School-craft. Freeland was a single-runway airport attached to a small coastal town by the same name. I touched the airport icon and held my finger down until the data box appeared, then selected Details and Fullscreen.

I immediately saw what I needed to see.

I held up the screen and pointed at the pink lettering beside the caption for Latest Weather.

"IFR," I said. "Ceiling is 400 overcast, visibility is less than a mile. You were never going to get in there."

His expression told me this wasn't part of his plan.

"Look, Ray. You've had enough training to get in an airplane and fly it around a traffic pattern and land in one piece. And on a sunny day, you might have found your way to Freeland. But in about sixty miles we're going to be in the soup, and you're not trained for it. Statistics show that roughly one hundred and eighty seconds after losing visual reference an untrained pilot loses control of the airplane."

"I may be untrained, but you're not. You're going to get us there."

"And then what? I can get us in…maybe. But you said you were going to fly out again. How? Same scenario. You'd lose it as soon as you pop into the clouds."

He squirmed in his seat. For an instant, I hoped he might put away the weapon and tell me to head for home.

"Just get us there."

"Ray, I'm qualified, but we're not equipped. This is a VFR trainer."

He pointed at the radio stack. "That GPS can do blind approaches. Miss Page showed me."

Crap. I had hoped to bluff him. The Garmin 430 on the panel was a basic unit, but it could, in fact, do the job if Freeland had a published instrument approach procedure.

I touched the Procedures tab for Freeland.

"This airport doesn't have an instrument approach procedure. Look." I held up the device.

"The GPS can get us there and you can get us down. So that's what we'll do."

He wasn't wrong. It would be dangerous. But it could be done.

"But you—"

"Enough talk! Just fly." There it was again. The demarcation line.

I settled in for the ride.

* * * * *

We encountered the first low clouds before sighting the waters of Green Bay. I estimated the bases at eight hundred and tops at fifteen hundred. Ten minutes later, the next layer met us and made my point. We slipped into gray mist behind our droning engine. My eyes instantly fell from the windshield to the instrument panel. I tensed.

Instrument flying is nothing new to me. But the panel of a VFR training plane is a far cry from a fully equipped cockpit in a big, stable twin-engine aircraft that lightens the load with a three-axis autopilot. The controls of the Skyhawk suddenly felt loose, the platform unstable. My heading wandered and it took me a few minutes to find a good set of cues in the attitude indicator, given the parallax view of the flight instruments from the right seat. I didn't mess with the power, and I didn't pay much attention to my sloppy altitude control.

Portman wasn't wrong. I could get us down. I could do it in a way that might break us out of the low clouds in time to see the runway and possibly land. But without a published instrument approach procedure, there were no guarantees we wouldn't wrap ourselves up in a set of power lines. Or take off a wing with a radio tower. Or plow into a hill short of the field. To minimize the hazard, I planned my approach from over the waters of Lake Michigan. Nobody plants radio towers or tall trees in a lake. The downside was that my strategy made this a "black hole" approach. The water would provide no definition, no depth perception—and would probably be as gray below as the overcast above. We might slice into it before we knew what happened.

I briefly plotted duping Portman into thinking we were landing at Freeland, and instead flying a published approach into School-craft. My scheme was dashed when Portman took back the iPad and followed our progress on the moving map.

* * * * *

"The field elevation is 677," Portman said in answer to my question.

"Alright. We're turning inbound and starting descent. I'm slowing us down to give us a fighting chance if we hit anything."

I pulled the knob that sent heat to the carburetor, then adjusted the power. Holding the nose level, the airspeed decayed to seventy-five, at which point I assumed a slight nose-down attitude. A glance at the vertical speed indicator told me this configuration rendered a stable five-hundred-foot per minute descent. The GPS course needle held steady.

So far so good.

"I'm taking us down to 850," I said, "but I need you to call it out. Every hundred feet until we get to one thousand, then every fifty feet. Got it?"

I tapped the altimeter for emphasis.

"Right."

"Hold the iPad so I can see it."

Gray nothingness painted the windshield and side windows. Our track took us to a waypoint eight miles south of the Upper Michigan coastline. My inbound turn at the waypoint aligned us with the north-south runway at Freeland Airport. The airport lay several miles from the water's edge. With luck, we would break out over the lake and navigate visually to the runway.

If we broke out.

The automated weather broadcast for Schoolcraft, ten miles to the west, reported the ceiling at three hundred feet above the surface. Freeland offered no automated weather.

"You do know you'd be dead if you tried to fly in this."

"It doesn't look that hard."

"Then you're welcome to try. Just let me out first. Altitude?"

"Twenty-six hundred."

He counted us off as we dropped. I forced my arms and legs to relax. I flexed my fingers on the yoke. Strangling the controls only makes flying choppy and tense. The airplane was perfectly capable of holding a steady glide without me.

Portman called out the altitude. The cabin darkened. We descended. The clouds thickened above us. We'd seen the last of the sun back in Wisconsin.

"Fifteen hundred…fourteen hundred…"

A glance at the altimeter confirmed Portman's steady count-down. The navigation needle remained rock solid. Somewhere ahead, the waters of Lake Michigan slapped a pebbled beach. I reminded myself not to look for waves on the lake. The winds reported on Schoolcraft's automated weather had been dead calm, which more than likely translated to a smooth and dangerously undefined lake surface, a hazard seaplane pilots described with respect.

"Eleven hundred…one thousand…nine-fifty…"

I fought the impulse to pull back on the yoke and halt our descent.

"…nine hundred…"

Come on!

I locked my eyes on the instruments. Peripheral vision told me nothing outside the window had changed.

"Eight-fifty!"

I tugged the nose up and added power. Wings level. Attitude indicator dot planted on the instrument's artificial horizon. Vertical speed at zero.

"See anything?"

"I see water! Below us!"

"Right where it should be," I said, "but look out the front."

My attention remained locked on the instruments and the delicate game of holding the airplane less than two hundred feet from hitting the earth. Portman leaned forward. He peered ahead.

"Trees! I got trees!"

I broke my scan from the instruments and looked over the nose. A dim sketch of shoreline materialized. Wisps of hanging mist skimmed above us, close enough to reach out and touch. I let the airplane drop a few feet and the world sharpened. Water spread to either side of us. The shoreline swept below us. Trees reached up, straining for a piece of our landing gear. I added power.

Trees surrendered to open meadow. A ribbon of runway appeared with a faded 36 painted on narrow gray asphalt.

I cut the power and skidded the airplane to our right until the runway lined up under the nose. A new worry flourished. There hadn't been time to reduce speed and I had not lowered the flaps. Dumping the flaps now might balloon us into the mist or cause us to float down the runway. On the other hand, landing fast and clean might take us beyond the point of stopping.

I fought the impulse to flare out and hold the airplane off, bleeding away speed until she would stall and settle onto her wheels. Instead, I let it drop and plant hard. We were still flying when the tire rubber squeaked beneath us.

I pressed the toe brakes and eased backpressure into the yoke.

The end of the runway appeared far too soon.

Brakes. More backpressure. More brakes.

When feel told me the wings no longer produced lift, I heaved the yoke all the way back and stood on the brakes.

We rolled to a near stop in time to turn off the runway at the end. A narrow taxiway took us to a small, empty ramp beside a single airport office shack. Portman directed me to park on a spot directly in front of the building. Two men with rifles stood beside a beat-up sedan on the ramp.

* * * * *

"Who the fuck is this?" The size-wise junior of the two men pointed his rifle at me. I ducked under the wing strut. Portman jogged around the nose. He switched the Glock from his left to his right hand. The man with the rifle made up for his diminutive height with the meanest looking black military-style weapon money could buy. He had oily skin and oily black hair. The fringes of unidentifiable tattoos peeked from the frayed crew neck of a faded black t-shirt promoting a seventies hair band.

"He's an instructor," Portman said.

"I thought you knew how to fly this thing!"

The larger man, looking boyish behind a fleshy face and a well-fed beer gut, let Junior do the talking.

"I know how to fly it. They wouldn't let me just take the airplane like I expected. He was gonna ride around the pattern with me for half an hour. I had to bring him or I would'a been late. Turns out for the best because of this shit weather." Portman pointed at the sky.

"What are we supposed to do with him?"

Portman looked past the two men.

"Where's Naomi?"

"She wouldn't come," Junior said. "Told you she wouldn't."

"Dammit! You were supposed to bring her. Eddie'll go right for her!"

"Dude. She dumped you. Didja think this was gonna get her back? She wanted nothing to do with this. Get over her." Junior switched his attention to me. "What are we supposed to do with this guy?"

"I'm not taking off without Naomi," Portman declared.

I wondered who he planned to leave behind.

"Get it through your head, Ray. The bitch dumped you. Now answer my question. What the fuck are we supposed to do with this guy?" Junior waved a hand in the air. "You know what? Forget it. You. Instructor guy. Take a fucking hike. That way." He pointed across the single runway at the opposite side of the airport, where cut grass met the tree line. "And don't turn around or I'll put a round through your face. Go!"

I would have been happy to comply, but Portman interceded.

"No. He stays."

"Are you outta your mind?"

"He stays. Because he flies us out of here. I can fly this thing in the clear, but not in this cloudy shit. He stays."

"You said you could do this, Ray."

"I don't have the fucking training to fly blind. *He does.*"

Junior shifted his rifle toward Portman. Cords tightened in his skinny arms. A knot formed between shaggy black eyebrows. Portman ignored the threat.

"Did you get it?" he asked.

Junior tipped his head at Big Boy, who trotted to the rattletrap Chevy sedan. The trunk squeaked open. Big Boy extracted two duffle bags, one slightly larger than the other.

I glanced at Portman. Instead of satisfaction, his expression and posture said things had slipped from bad to worse. Big Boy laid the two bags at Portman's feet.

"What did you do? What is that?" He pointed at the smaller bag.

Junior grinned.

"We took it all. Gotta be three hundred K more than we planned."

Portman closed his eyes. "Christ, Jimmy, that shit is poison. We talked about this. Only Eddie's fucking cash. Nothing else."

"It's easy money, man," Junior pleaded.

"It's fucking full of die packs and RF chips, you idiot! It's poison. Every one of the serial numbers is recorded by the bank. That's the fastest way for them to find us. I told you!"

I edged toward the nose of the aircraft contemplating a dash to the pilot's side. For anyone but me, it would be a pointless move. I planned to duck below the cabin windows and vanish. This had the advantage of causing confusion as well as giving me time to grab the high wing and lift myself where no one would accidentally collide with me.

Junior snatched the smaller bag off the ramp surface. "I'm getting pretty sick of you bitching all the time. If you don't want it, fine. I'll take it."

"Jimmy, you don't get it," Portman pleaded. I took another step. "I not only don't want it—I don't want it anywhere near us. And I want to know what Naomi said."

"She said go fuck yourself," Junior snapped. "Let's load this up and get the hell out of here." Junior pointed his rifle at me. I froze. "Can you fly us out of here in this shit?"

"Yes." I surveyed the low hanging clouds and distant trees veiled in mist. "He can't. But I can. Where to?"

"Canada," Big Boy spoke for the first time. He had a high-pitched voice that fit his juvenile looks. I wondered how old he was.

I shook my head.

"What?" Junior demanded.

"Die packs? RF chips?" I pointed at the duffle bags. "You guys hit a bank?"

"None of your fucking business."

"Okay. But Ray here is right. That money points directly at you. And there's no way I can get you into Canada."

"What are you talking about? Just fly us to a little strip up north. I done it plenty of times to go fishing."

"Ever hear of an Air Defense Identification Zone? Because it stretches the full length of the border," I lied. "Your fishing charter was on a flight plan, and before that it was vetted and after landing it cleared Customs. If we go diddling our way across the border in an unidentified aircraft without clearance, you might as well send a written invitation to the RCMP to track us and meet us wherever we land—assuming an F-16 doesn't light us up."

Junior's grip on the rifle tightened. His finger slipped into the trigger guard.

"Bullshit."

"No," Portman said. "It's not bullshit."

"Are you telling us the truth?" Junior demanded of me.

"Like my life depends on it."

Junior threw down the bag. "Well, now what?"

"This still works," Portman said. "The airplane still makes a good getaway. It's been done before. Just not to Canada."

"Then where?"

I kept my mouth shut, but Portman knew more than I hoped he would. "There are ten thousand little airports like this all over the country. Pick one. Lots of 'em have a car you can drive off in. No paperwork. No questions. No witnesses. Point at a map and he'll get us there. Right?"

"You're right about that money," I said. "It will lead the FBI directly to you."

"God dammit," Junior muttered. He turned and kicked the smaller of the two bags.

"What about the other one?" I asked.

"Shut the fuck up."

Portman paced and stared at the ramp under his feet. "I don't want to leave Naomi like this. He'll know it was her."

"Screw her," Junior said. "She just works there. She doesn't know nothing." He picked up the larger duffle, swung it at his side, then heaved it at me. I grabbed. He grinned. "Bet you never had a million bucks in your hands before."

The lumpy contents could have been packs of money or old sneakers.

"Let's load that up and get the fuck outta here," Junior said.

"We need gas," I told Portman. "We're down to half tanks." I pointed at a self-serve gas pump near the unattended airport office.

"Not here," Portman said. "Somewhere else. Figure it out."

His tone signaled resignation on the issue of Naomi.

"Load it up, instructor dude!" Junior jerked his rifle at the Skyhawk.

"Okay. This feels like about thirty pounds. It'll fit in the baggage compartment." I gestured for permission from Portman to load it. He nodded. As I stuffed the duffle bag behind the rear seats, I added, "If you want me to fly in this weather, I get the pilot's seat."

"You're giving a lot of orders for an expendable asshole," Junior said.

"Well, here's another one. No more baggage." I tapped the fuselage for emphasis. "As it is, we're easily over gross weight and out of the center of gravity."

"What does that mean?"

"Fiery death shortly after takeoff."

"What the hell? We got bags in the car. We're not coming back here."

I looked at Jimmy, then at Big Boy. My mental weight and balance calculation of Big Boy topped two-twenty. Not good.

"How much can we carry?" Portman asked me.

"Don't shoot me for the truth, but I'd leave him here." I pointed at Big Boy.

"No way!" Junior exclaimed.

"I didn't expect this weather," Portman said. He jerked a thumb in my direction. "We need him."

"Hell no!"

"Then we don't fly. It's that simple." Portman sighed. "Nothing personal, Teddy."

"Can he drive? Does he have a license?" I asked.

"I can drive," Big Boy said.

"Then have him take the car and your bags and go. Meet up somewhere."

"Why are you being so fucking helpful?" Junior asked.

"It seems to be in my best interest."

"Did they see the car?" Portman asked. "Did you swap like I said to?"

"We used the van and ditched it for this piece of shit Chevy."

"Then that will work," Portman said. "Sorry, man. But you're gonna have to drive. We'll hook up. Gimme your rifle."

Big Boy awkwardly surrendered the weapon along with an extra magazine he produced from a jacket pocket. Portman placed it on the back seat of the Skyhawk. He walked to Big Boy and put a hand on his shoulder.

"As soon as you hit the highway, throw that bag as far as you can into the woods. Then drive. Stay off U.S. 2. Use back roads. And drive two or three over the limit, but no more and not under. Got it?"

Big Boy nodded.

"They'll be looking for two men in a van. Without the money and with no weapon, you'll be fine, even if you're stopped. If you do get stopped, say you're going to Green Bay to visit your grandmother."

"Don't do that," I said. "Tell 'em you're looking for a job."

"Why am I looking for a job?"

"You're not. But if you say you're going to visit your aunt or grandmother, they'll ask for names and addresses. See?"

Big Boy grinned. "Oh. Smart."

I pictured him encountering a cop like Andy and gave him no chance, but scoring a few points in my favor didn't hurt.

"I need some money, Ray," Big Boy said like a kid asking for allowance. "For gas."

Portman pulled a wallet from the back pocket of his pants and plucked out three twenties. He handed the cash to Big Boy. "I want you to go to Rochester. In Minnesota."

"What's in Rochester?"

"That's where my dad went to that clinic. We'll meet you there, buddy. Okay? Keep your phone charged and use it for a map. Stay off the interstate. Don't stop except for gas and food. And if you need to sleep, do it in the car. Don't buy anything you don't have to."

Junior fished keys from his pants pocket and tossed them to Big Boy.

Portman pointed at the bag on the ground.

"Toss that bank money as far as you can, Teddy. I mean it. Like it was burning your hands, okay?"

Big Boy hesitated.

"*I mean it. Get rid of that bank shit!*"

A reluctant nod signaled obedience if not understanding.

Portman's phone rang.

"Hold up," he said. He looked at the screen. "It's Naomi."

"Put it on speaker." Junior and Big Boy huddled closer.

Portman touched the screen and held up the phone. A woman's voice erupted in ragged panic from the tiny speaker.

"Ray? Ray, it's Naomi! Are you—" A flap slap cut her off. She shrieked. Something thumped and clattered.

"Naomi? Naomi?"

After a moment of jostling sounds, a man's voice joined the call.

"She's with me, Ray."

Junior silently mouthed *Eddie.*

"Are you there, asshole?"

Portman didn't respond.

"Because I've got your ex-girlfriend here with me. You and I need to discuss a few things. Like the effect a sledgehammer will have on every bone in her body, you feel me?"

"Leave her alone, Eddie. She had nothing to do with this."

"Like I care. Oh, I won't let her die, pal. You can count on that. Where's my money? And if you say you don't have it, I start hammering her pretty painted toes."

"It's here. I have it."

Junior stomped his feet and shook his head. He waved frantically at Portman, who ignored him.

"Did you think I wouldn't figure it out? Your ex- working at my bank. And those two stooges hitting it at just the right time on just the right day? Jesus, Ray, you used to be smart."

Portman squeezed his eyes shut.

"What do you want?"

"I want it back. All of it. Before the cops get to it."

Junior stomped and spun on the asphalt. He unleashed a panicky pantomime, which Portman ignored.

"Don't hurt her."

"That's up to you."

"I'm at the airport," Portman said. He jerked his free hand up in

Junior's face. The gesture brought him to a standstill. "Bring Naomi unharmed and I'll give it back."

The speaker fell silent. Portman slowly closed the screen.

* * * * *

We stood a few paces off the nose of Eight Zero Zero. A heated argument between Portman and Junior had ended with Portman declaring that if Junior didn't like the plan, he could start walking. He told Junior to choose.

Junior took one last look at the duffle full of money like it was the bike he never got for Christmas, then stomped off toward a cluster of dogwood bushes at the side of the empty airport office exactly as Portman had instructed him.

"Where do you want me, Ray?" Big Boy asked.

"Park over there. By those hangars."

"Can I have my gun?"

"No, you can't have your fucking gun! Jesus, you're more likely to shoot me than anything useful. Park and keep your head down and out of sight. He's never seen this car. I'll signal if I need you, okay?"

Big Boy obeyed. The Chevy rolled to the end of the ramp and stopped, then backed into a space between a single hangar and a row of t-hangars. It wasn't a horrible plan. The car looked like it belonged to an aircraft owner who had flown the family plane out for the day.

"She works at his bank?" I asked Portman. "Your friend, Naomi?"

"Yeah."

"And this guy Eddie, he's laundering money?"

Portman nodded.

"Money from what?"

"Meth."

I waited a minute before asking the question that would determine my next move.

"Is she involved?"

He paced back and forth past the duffle bag. "No. No…she didn't know shit. We were…we broke up a while ago. I did some business with her boss. She told me he kept uncounted cash in the vault. She said she intended to report it to state regulators. I told her to wait. I didn't tell her…I didn't tell her any of this. She never would have gone along. Jimmy was supposed to bring her…"

"What? Like a hostage? Jesus. And this was your getaway plan?"

Portman shifted his gaze to Eight Zero Zero. "I read a story once. About a guy who flew around the country robbing banks. I like it, you know. The flying. I'm going to finish and get my license. Miss Page is a riot, but she's a really good teacher."

I doubted Portman would see Pidge again.

He nodded at the highway.

"He's here."

The inevitable black SUV whispered down the mist-faded highway and slowed for the turn into the airport driveway. The vehicle disappeared briefly, blocked from view by the building. A moment later the SUV—a Cadillac—crunched across the gravel parking lot and rounded the office. It rolled onto the ramp, drove past us, performed a U-turn and parked between the airplane and the small building. The driver stepped out.

Eddie wore a gray suit and pinkish tie over expensive-looking shoes. He sported a tan and a precise haircut. He looked the part of the banker he pretended to be, a perennial officer in the Rotary Club, a glad-handing donor to the PTA—cash only, not his precious time. The gun in his hand suited the hard edges in his face.

He used the weapon to gesture at his passenger. "Care to join us?"

The woman climbed down from the SUV and walked around the front. When she stopped several feet away, Eddie stepped up beside her and grasped her elbow. She recoiled, but he held on.

"Goddammit, Eddie, she has nothing to do with this!" Portman snapped.

"Fuck you. Where's the rest?"

"That's yours. Teddy took the bank shit. He's on the road. I told him to get rid of it."

Eddie smirked. "He won't. I'll find him. And this is mine?"

"It's all there. Let her go."

"Who's this guy?" Once again, someone pointed a gun at me. It was getting tiresome.

"Pilot I hired to fly us outta here. We're done here. Sorry for the trouble."

"Hijacked," I said.

"What?"

"I wasn't hired. I was hijacked. Do you mind if I just take off?"

"What are you…a fucking comedian?"

"Eddie, let Naomi go."

"Sure, Ray. No problem." Eddie flashed a set of overly whitened teeth. No one mistook it for a smile. He shoved Naomi forward. She staggered to Portman. He gathered her with the arm that wasn't holding his gun at his side and hustled her behind him. I considered that scant protection, given that Portman and Eddie faced each other armed.

"You've got what you came for."

Eddie stepped forward and lifted the bag. He hefted it, gauging its weight.

"It's all there except for a couple hundred we gave Teddy. I'll mail it to you. There's no need for this to get—"

Sharp gunfire made everyone flinch and duck. Naomi shrieked and ducked backward, waving her hands around her head as if splayed fingers might shield her from bullets.

A figure broke from the dogwood shrubs, firing.

Junior.

I heard shots that didn't synchronize with the flashes from Junior's weapon, nor were they the sharp supersonic cracks generated by an AR-15. Red mist puffed from the side of Junior's face. He turned and ran, comically lifting his weapon over his shoulder and blasting away backward.

Junior's desperate flight took him toward a second row of hangars. Firing wildly backward, he pumped out rounds as fast as his finger could flex the trigger. Bullets struck the airport office shack. Sparks flashed on the ramp. I crouched and cringed.

Eddie backed away, clutching the bag. He shouted toward the airport office. "Riley! Riley are you there?"

Naomi shrieked and bolted past the nose of the Skyhawk.

"Riley!"

I took Riley to be Eddie's backup plan, dispatched from the vehicle when he drove into the parking lot behind the office. Riley apparently did his job of flushing Junior.

Bullets split the air. Bullets smacked into the airport office. I heard glass shatter. Feeling naked on the open ramp beside the airplane, I threw myself flat on the asphalt, then crawled and rolled under the aircraft's belly. The thin aluminum skin meant nothing to flying bullets, but the illusion of cover helped. I lifted myself and crouched forward, placing the engine between my upper body and the lunatics with guns.

"Fuck!" Portman dropped and covered his head with his arms.

Eddie swept his gun toward Junior. He squeezed off four shots. The explosive reports hammered my eardrums. Junior, now more than a hundred yards away and rapidly building distance, paid no attention. He sprinted, firing wildly backward in the general direction of the parking lot and office.

Portman rolled to his knees and pointed his weapon at Eddie.

Eddie, still clutching the bag, backed away and aimed his weapon at Portman.

"Drop it!"

"You drop it!"

"I'll fucking shoot you! I will!"

Neither man fired. At less than twenty paces, serious harm seemed certain, if not mutually assured destruction.

Junior ceased firing. He threw his weapon to the ground and kept on running. More shots popped from the other side of the airport shack. They served only to accelerate Junior.

An engine revved. Big Boy and the rattletrap Chevy lunged from its concealment.

Eddie swung his weapon at the car, then back at Portman. The Chevy bore down on him. He switched again and pointed the gun at the driver. I saw his hand jerk, but the weapon failed to fire. Eddie fumbled with the weapon.

I kicked myself out of my protective crouch and dashed after Naomi. She hobbled awkwardly away from the airplane. One high-heeled shoe had gone missing. I caught up to her and threw myself at her back. We collided. The instant we hit—

Fwooomp!

—I vanished, taking her with me.

More shots. Close now. I couldn't tell if Portman or Eddie fired, or both. The roaring Chevy grew louder. Screeching tires ended with a thudding impact. Eddie let out a scream.

"NAOMI!" Ray shouted.

Big Boy's high-pitched voice shouted, "Get in, Ray! Get in!"

Naomi twisted and struggled. I turned her. She threw her arms around me and dug her fingers into my back. She buried her head against my chest, and shivered against me, flinching with each gunshot.

The instant we vanished, I broke contact with the pavement, but thankfully didn't launch upward. My impact with Naomi propelled us horizontally over the edge of the ramp, across a span of grass, toward the runway. I didn't care where we went, provided we expanded the distance between us and the gunfire.

Portman cried out for Naomi.

Big Boy begged Portman to get in the car.

Naomi buried a scream in my chest.

More gunfire popped. I had no idea who shot, or in what direction. Every hair on my body seemed to feel bullets flying past.

I could not—nor did I want to—stop our glide. I rotated to gain a view of the battlefield. Eddie lay prone on the ramp near the Chevy's bumper looking like he had been hit by the car or shot by Portman. He clutched one knee and writhed in pain with one arm hooked through the duffle bag strap. On the other side of the car, Portman searched the ramp for Naomi, calling out to her.

Eddie crabbed backward, away from the car, dragging the bag. He picked his weapon up off the ramp, aimed and tried to fire. The gun failed again. He worked the slide, then fired at the car and Portman beyond. Portman ducked. Big Boy shouted. Portman jumped in the back seat of the Chevy. Big Boy stomped on it.

Eddie aimed at the windshield, but the car lunged at him. He dropped the gun and rolled clear. The Chevy leaned sharply as Big Boy cut in front of the black SUV and shot past the airport shack. Clearing the building, the Chevy drew gunfire from Eddie's hidden man, but the shots did nothing to stop the car. The old sedan bounced through a sharp turn onto the highway, skidding and screeching before accelerating.

Eddie heaved himself to his feet and picked up his handgun. He emptied the magazine at the distant Chevy to no apparent effect.

"FUCK!" He clutched the bag and hobbled to his black SUV, dragging one injured leg. He threw the bag inside and climbed aboard. The engine roared to life and jerked the vehicle forward, swinging the driver's door shut.

The SUV raced past the airport office. In the parking lot, Eddie stomped on the brakes. The brake lights skidded out of my line of sight. I heard a door slam. Gravel ground and sprayed from the tires. A moment later, the vehicle reappeared. Eddie launched onto the highway in pursuit of the Chevy.

I wondered why he bothered—until I remembered that the money laundering banker had recovered only one of his duffle bags and believed that Big Boy had the other.

As abruptly as it began, the chaos ended.

I pulled one hand free and patted myself, searching for torn flesh or pain. Nothing. I was either in shock or hadn't been hit.

Of the fifty or sixty rounds of ammunition expended, none found me, or apparently anyone else. I wondered if the Skyhawk remained untouched. If so, it was a miracle.

We floated to the center of the runway before I pulled the levers in my head. Naomi and I reappeared awkwardly. We staggered and fell.

Silence fell with us.

* * * * *

"Are you okay?"

The young woman sat on the steps of the airport office. She lifted one glazed eye at me. The bruise on her face gained color. Her other eye had swollen to a slit.

She looked drained and bewildered. And angry. And hurt. I relied on her stew of raw emotion and blind terror to confuse and obscure the fact that I made her vanish and float fifty yards across the airport. She must have closed her good eye because it seemed to work. After reappearing, picking ourselves up off the runway, Naomi trembled and cringed as if she feared the air around her might fill with bullets again. She didn't ask how we arrived on the runway. We cautiously marched back to the airport office without speaking.

When we found the office door locked, Naomi seated herself on the front steps of the building, holding her knees to her chest and shivering. I sat down beside her.

"I don't like your friends," I said.

"God!" Anger burst to the surface. "Have you ever met bigger idiots?"

"Idiots with guns."

Naomi mustered a trembling sigh. "I quit. I *hated* working at that fucking bank."

She glared one-eyed at a point roughly a thousand yards beyond the gravel airport parking lot. Distant warbling sound cut through the mist. I recognized a patrol car siren. The siren song stopped, replaced by chirping the cops use to gain the attention of a driver or pedestrian.

"I think they just picked up Junior."

"Who?"

"I think his name is Jimmy."

Naomi startled me with a venomous glance and whispered a vow through clenched teeth. "I will never let my daughter take a job like that. For a man like that. Never. Eddie was a pig."

"You have a daughter?"

She nodded but didn't elaborate.

The cloud-dimmed late afternoon light faded. The air cooled. Naomi wore no jacket. She clutched herself against the chill—or the shock—I couldn't be sure. I suppressed a potent impulse to share my light flight jacket because a fresh thought crossed my mind.

"I don't have a phone. Do you suppose anyone heard all the shooting and called the cops?"

"Around here?" She laughed without humor. "We're kinda remote here. People shoot off guns up here all the time."

"Like World War Three?"

She shrugged.

"Listen, uh…wait here."

I jogged around the building and back onto the ramp. When I returned, I dropped the larger duffle bag—the one that had been in the airplane—onto the grass beside the wooden steps. She watched me use one foot to shove the bag out of sight under the steps. Not satisfied, I kneeled and pushed the bag farther until black shadow swallowed it.

I rocked back and stood. She looked up at me.

"Eddie took the bank's money."

She blinked, bewildered for a moment. Then she dropped her gaze to the steps.

"I was thinking I'd go," I said.

"No! You can't leave me here. You have to stay."

"I could…certainly." I sat down beside her. "Here's the thing. Your friend Ray—"

"He's not my friend."

"Right. Anyway, he hijacked me and my plane. I never met the man until today. I didn't know anything about his plan. Frankly, you know more about all this than I do. Just tell the cops what happened."

"I just—all I did was tell Ray about Eddie's money—and that I wanted to report him. Ray said not to. I didn't know they were going to—that they…" She closed a grip on my arm. "You have to stay. You're a witness."

"And I have no problem giving a statement. In detail. How I got hijacked. How a bunch of crazy shitheads started shooting and Junior nearly killed all of us." I rapped on the wooden step between us. "And, of course, I'd have to tell the police there's a bag of uncounted, unregistered, unmarked money under these steps…if I stay, that is."

She looked at me.

"You, on the other hand, you're a victim. Kidnapping. Assault. You make a better witness than me. You know everyone involved and everything they did. Don't get me wrong. I'll stay if you want me to. But if I stay…"

Naomi said nothing.

"You can handle this. You can tell the police everything. *Everything.*"

I rapped on the step.

"Or not *everything.*"

She looked down.

I added, "It seems to me that Ray and his pals are going away for a long time. Sounds like you're quitting your job. You might want to have a chat with the state bank examiner as part of your exit interview."

"Oh, you can fucking count on it." Her outburst caught us both by surprise. "Oh. Sorry."

"Don't be. Either way, Eddie won't be a problem once the cops catch up to him."

She laughed weakly. "I could tell them things…"

"Funny thing about little airports like this…half the time there's no one around. That bag could sit under there for days… weeks…months. There's never anyone around. If someone were to come back for that bag, they'd have this place to themselves."

"Are you…are you coming back? For…?" She pointed.

"Me? No. Did I mention my wife is a cop? What's in that bag…" I tapped the step "…wouldn't pay for the divorce. Do something good with it. Put your kid through college so someday she owns the bank instead of working at it."

She took a long, hard look at me. Her hesitation counted for something. Maybe she'd keep the money. Maybe she'd turn it in. Either way, leaving it in her hands felt right.

"Eddie will still think the guy with the airplane took it. He'll come after you."

I shrugged. "He'll be in jail. The bank will recover their money.

And if he comes after me—did I mention my wife is a cop?" I put my hand on hers. "I think you can handle this."

Her good eye stayed on me.

"Months and months. You understand? Months."

She nodded.

"You'll be fine. More than fine."

She looked down at the steps, then back at me.

I shrugged.

* * * * *

Ten minutes later the mist swallowed Eight Zero Zero. I trimmed for a steady climb and turned for home.

SUPERVISED SOLO
February 5-6, 2021

6

NAKED GUY

I f you drive west from the farmhouse Andy and I rent, then turn right and go north for half a mile, there's a narrow track descending off the side of the road; just two depressions in the grass made by farm equipment belonging to my landlord and the owner of the county's largest farming operation, James Rankin. The wheel tracks head west along a man-made creek that accepts the runoff from drain tiles buried in the fields on either side of the creek. In mid-July, the corn rising from the dirt of those vast fields is usually waist high. If you go into the fields on a silent summer night, you can hear the corn growing. I do not kid. The leaves make a squeaking sound.

The track goes arrow straight to where the fields end, then it curves first left, then right around a small hill to where you might be surprised to find a body of crystal blue water, maybe four or five acres. A hundred and fifty years ago, the back of that small hill was excavated by the Chicago and Northwestern Railroad for gravel and stone that contributed to railway roadbed connecting the Windy City to the iron mines in upper Michigan. Long since abandoned, the quarry did what quarries do. It filled with fresh spring water. A limestone rim surrounds most of the water. At its highest, at the back of the gouged-out hill, the wall is probably thirty feet. High enough to prompt countless dares between boys sneaking a skinny dip. I've gone off it twice, vowing both times never to do so again. Head first or feet first, either way you hit the water hard.

The day I accepted the keys to the farmhouse from James Rankin, he drove me around the property in his new Chevy Silverado pickup truck. The quarry isn't on the plot of land under the farmhouse I rent, but he gave me a tour just the same. We parked on the flat remnant of a small gravel pit adjacent the quarry. I detected a note of boyish pride in Rankin's narrative.

"This might be the best swimming hole in the county," he said. We climbed out of the pickup cab. The day was sunny and clear. The blue on the surface of the water matched the blue in the sky. "Great place to bring a girl at night if the mosquitos aren't out in force."

"You sound like you don't mind visitors."

He shrugged. "Not so much. Prob'ly two, three times a week in summer the cops chase kids out of here. Doesn't bother me as long as they don't leave their empties. I brought a few girls here back in the day, although if Claire asks you, she was the only one."

"How long have you been married?"

"Forty-eight this summer."

I squinted at the man. "What? Were you twelve?"

He laughed. "Eighteen. She was nineteen and quite the worldly woman."

We walked up the slope to the top of the hill, the high point of the wall surrounding the quarry. On weathered limestone, we over-looked a drop that seemed much higher from above. I made my first of numerous vows never to go off this edge.

"It's deep. Forty feet at the low spot, which is over there." He pointed. "Twenty to thirty for the rest of it. There's a ledge on the far side, but the buckthorn has filled in right to the water line. You can wade out waist deep almost thirty feet before the drop-off. I had notions of putting a beach there, but never got to it. You'd have to swim across to it now."

"You're okay with kids coming here? Not worried about liability?"

"You can spend your life worrying about lawyers and liability, and if that's how you live, you ought never get outta bed. I can no more stop kids from coming in here than I can stop boys from wanting to get in girls' pants. Like I said, the local PD makes this a regular stop and clears it out sometimes. Parties and such. But that doesn't stop 'em. Somebody actually brought in a picnic table."

A sturdy table with bench seats occupied a scenic overlook position under the broad black boughs of a mature maple tree. Surprisingly, the wooden surfaces wore a nice coat of paint with almost no carved graffiti.

"I sometimes have my lunch here," Rankin said. "Anyway, I thought I'd give you the tour and tell you you're welcome here. If you bring some girl, turn off down there." He pointed at where the two-wheel track first met the hill. "Go right, around the back side. There's a box elder thicket where you can park out of sight. And if the cops still find you, just use my name and they'll leave you be. The swimming is great in the summer, although the water doesn't really warm up until the Fourth of July. And it's clean water. I have it tested regularly. It's spring-fed." He stepped to the edge and gazed down. Had we both been twelve-year-olds, I would have pretended to shove him over as a joke. Looking down at the serene surface, he might have been thinking about being twelve. "Been a while since I've been in the water, but it was always sweet and refreshing, 'specially on a hot summer night. You're welcome to it."

THE FARM I worked on as a teenager had a pond. More than a few times at the end of a hot summer day, after coating my skin with sweat and dust and hay, I drove to that pond and dove in. Nothing in my life was ever—or I think ever will be—as instantly rejuvenating. The memory drew me back to Rankin's waterhole often the first summer I lived in his old farmhouse, and each summer since. When Andy and I had dated long enough to know we never wanted to date anyone else, I brought her to the quarry several times for a picnic and swim, finally realizing my teen fantasy of being in a secluded swimming hole with a beautiful woman.

One evening, after we dined extravagantly at the Mexican restaurant at the other bowling alley in Essex, I drove her to Rankin's Quarry. My unannounced turn into the farm lane prompted mild tension in the car. I think she expected me to suggest a swim or a little fun in the grass, neither of which comported with the beautiful summer dress she wore, the added touch of makeup she had given her eyes, and the pretty twists and braids she had applied to her hair. By that time, I knew the woman well enough to know when she was looking for a polite way to say no to something. To my relief, she didn't protest when I parked in Rankin's hidden thicket and took her hand for a walk to the top of the hill above water barely rippled by a light evening breeze. The sun had set, igniting high cloud bellies with shades of crimson and orange.

Those sunset colors gave the tiny diamond I could barely afford something extra when I dropped to one knee, but both the sunset and the diamond faded beside the brilliant smile she paid me when she accepted my proposal.

The spot remains special for Andy and me. We visit it from time to time, but generally not for a swim. I've come to realize that the times she joined me in the water indicated her commitment to pursuit of me. Having exchanged wedding vows and rings, she no longer feels a need to show her affection by leaping into a quarry. I still like to swim, but I don't leave her sitting alone while I splash around. When we revisit the spot these days, it's often with a bottle of wine, a picnic basket, a blanket, and a front-row seat for a sunset. And for such other activities as the mood and mosquitos allow. The swimming, when I do it, I usually do alone.

THE DAY HAD BEEN a hot one. The temperature in Essex topped ninety degrees, but my flight schedule had taken me to Columbia, Missouri, which is 87 nautical miles from and six degrees hotter than St. Louis, and that's saying something. The FBO at Columbia Regional had air conditioning, and the flight home at nine thousand feet offered its own cooling, but at the end of the day I still had to taxi in, park on a hot airport ramp, and secure the airplane in the heat. The sun touched the horizon by the time the hangar door touched the floor. Andy had taken a late shift at the office and wouldn't be home until after eleven. A side trip to the Rankin Waterhole required no debate.

I almost didn't park in the hidden thicket. I didn't expect to be long. If any local kids intended to party at the quarry tonight, they probably wouldn't show up until after dark. I planned to be long gone. At the last second, however, I turned right and followed James Rankin's instructions to park where my car would be hidden. Habit, I told myself.

I left my phone, my Ray Bans, and my wallet in the car and locked it, then tucked my keys behind the left rear tire. Another habit. I should have undressed and locked up my clothes, too. Lesson learned. Instead, I walked to the top of the hill, to the cliff edge, and stripped down on the weathered limestone overlooking the water. I was long past wanting to take the high dive. I had something entirely different in mind.

Naked, I had nowhere to put the BLASTER that I had sealed in a Ziploc bag, so I held it in my hand when I took four steps toward the cliff's edge.

Fwooomp!

I vanished on the fourth step and glided over glass-smooth water. Forward momentum carried me toward the center of the quarry on a downward vector. I descended to about six feet above the water. Using the core muscle that manifests when I vanish, I rotated my body until my feet aimed at the sky.

Fwooomp!

I reappeared and instantly plunged into the glorious, refreshing water. The top layer had warmed nicely, but my dive took me into darker realms that retained a permanent chill. A little stark, it nevertheless felt good after having sun and sweat on my skin most of the day.

In the vanished state I still displace water. Absent gravity's grip and the properties of weight, vanishing underwater causes me to shoot up like a balloon. I can't lie. It's fun. Someone watching might see what looks like a geyser of spray over an inexplicable splash and ripple. I burst from the surface, reappear, and drop back in.

For the next twenty minutes I indulged in frivolous use of *the other thing* to pop out of the water and plunge in again, alternating between sleek dives and boyish cannonballs. After a particularly nice peg-leg, I popped out and spotted a crew cab pickup truck as it pulled into the flat gravel pit beside the hill. The truck looked new, suggesting James Rankin, who swaps out his truck annually. But I'd just seen him at the Silver Spoon Diner with a candy-apple red Silverado, and this truck was gunmetal gray with a Ford badge, something Rankin swears he would only ride in if it was a hearse and he didn't have a say.

The ripples from my last pop-up died before half a dozen teens tumbled out of the crew cab. Propelled by hormonal energy, they raced to the top of the hill. I extracted my BLASTER from the waterproof bag. Time to go ashore.

Using a low power setting for stealth, I initiated a glide toward the limestone wall. I thought I might attach myself to the wall out of sight, reappear, and then climb to the rim and ask everyone to go find something else to do while I dressed.

Laughter and shouts carried across the water. Not half a dozen, but five; the visitors numbered three girls and two boys. Or, it quickly became obvious, two couples and a fifth wheel. The fifth wheel wandered off and seated herself at the picnic table. She shifted a cloth satchel off her shoulder and pulled out a sketch pad. The two couples clung to each, explaining why Fifth Wheel had come prepared to occupy herself while her friends occupied each other.

"Hey! Check it out!" A tall boy sporting a nearly bald buzz cut pranced to where I had left my clothes. "Somebody's here."

All five kids searched the water's surface, perhaps thinking I was submerged and might pop up at any second. The two boys stood at the very edge, which threw a wrench in my plan to appear on the limestone wall.

"Must'a left his shit," the second boy said.

"Right. Sure. And he drove home naked," the girl at the table muttered.

"Ew. On a hot car seat?" the girl attached to the first boy cringed. "What if he got stopped by the cops?"

"*But officer, it's a stick shift!*" the tall kid joked. His pal laughed. His girl giggled and simultaneously pretended to be offended.

Without looking up, the artist at the table said, "Probably got busy with some girl in his car. The cops came. Neither one wanted to get out of the car, so they left his clothes." A droll but tidy hypothesis.

"Dude, check it." The first boy scooped up one of my black

Lucchese western boots. Before I could even think about shouting, he performed a softball windup and underhand launch of the boot on a high arc that came damn near to my flight path. I veered for it, reached, and missed. The boot splash prompted a triumphant hoot.

Son of a bitch!

Not that it mattered. Had I caught it, the visible boot would have dragged me down. The second kid peeled himself from his girlfriend and grabbed my other boot. His toss exceeded that of his buddy in height but lacked distance. I watched it plop and float briefly before disappearing. He whooped and performed a victory dance while my three-hundred-plus-dollar boots sank near the spot that Rankin had identified as the deepest in the quarry.

"Jace, don't be such an ass," the girl at the picnic table said.

Jace, the original boot-thrower, ignored her buzz-kill commentary and picked up my jeans. He thoughtfully patted them down before scrounging up a rock, which he dropped into one leg. He then balled them up and heaved them over the side. The rock contributed a satisfying *plunk!* My pants went the way of the Titanic.

Jace's pal picked up a stick and lifted my boxers off the ground. He waved them at Jace's face.

"Eat it! Eat it raw!"

"Fuck you, Theo!" Jace swatted at the underwear and dodged away.

Theo turned and threw the stick like a javelin carrying skewered underwear. The javelin pierced the water and the boxers sank out of sight. The stick returned to the surface.

My t-shirt got the rock treatment.

The girlfriends giggled and stroked their prancing companion's egos.

"Let's get a beer," Jace suggested. "Want one Rosie?"

"I'll take a Coke," the girl with the sketch pad said without looking up.

"Then get it yourself," Jace called over his shoulder. The others laughed.

The couples descended the hill and returned to the truck where they flipped open the lid of a cooler in the truck bed. They pulled beer cans from a mound of ice and climbed back aboard their manly land yacht. Jace started the engine, I presume to run the air conditioning.

I hung in empty space at the cliff rim nurturing molten anger. The instant my first boot became an artillery shell, my options dropped to few and none. Reappearing over the water would have dropped me into the quarry where I might have shouted at the kids to leave my shit alone. I didn't see indignation gaining much traction, not among boys pumped full of adrenaline and lust. Flying to the top of the stone wall and reappearing in front of all five kids wasn't practical because it meant revealing myself, in more ways than one.

Anger boiled into a stew of vengeful ideas. I considered deflating their tires, then calling the cops. That morphed into a quick flight home for some clothes, then returning with the cops so I could demand payment. The boots weren't cheap. For that matter, neither were the jeans. The two ideas merged, but then I ditched the deflated tire idea because that would make me the aggressor.

A round trip home wouldn't take long, and these clowns looked like they planned to stay a while. I'd make the dash home, get dressed, return, and interrupt their little party. And then take up a collection as an alternative to calling the cops.

Pay up or get busted.

Simple.

Yet not terribly satisfying.

While I hung in deepening twilight adjacent the cliff edge and stared bullets into the Ford's cab, the girl who remained at the top of the hill set aside her sketch pad. She rummaged through her big bag until she produced a bottle of nail polish and set about touching up cherry-red toenails.

An idea clawed its way out of the devious mists in my head.

I MADE a quick stop at the car and extracted a blanket Andy and I keep on the back seat. I wrapped it, skirt-like around my waist, then hiked up to the table. I approached the girl called Rosie from her blind side. She sat at the far end of the table. I figured she would hear me coming or catch sight of me with her peripheral vision, but she didn't. She diligently painted her toenails, an artist focused on each brush stroke, perhaps unaware that she hummed as she worked, deep in concentration. I startled her when I slid onto the bench on the opposite side and opposite end of the table. A tremor transmitted through the table alerted her. She glanced back, then shrieked.

"Please don't get up," I said. "If you won't, I won't."

I held the blanket tight around my legs and lap, covering up the essentials and concealing the BLASTER.

She looked like she might run.

"Seriously, don't get up. I'm at a bit of a disadvantage here."

"Then don't sneak up on people, perv!"

"Perv?"

"I'm not the one running around naked."

"I'm not the one who threw my clothes in the drink. I'm not the one trespassing. The 'perv' thing is on you guys."

She opened her mouth to reply but stopped, conceding the point.

She had a round face with a soft, creamy complexion. Her eyes were slightly oversized for her face. Lashes that looked both real and like they belonged in a cosmetic commercial exaggerated each blink. She didn't seem to know where to look or what to look at, so she twisted to face away from me. She held the nail polish brush in one hand, but the paint job had been suspended. Long, dark hair hung down her back. I guessed her to be fifteen or sixteen, which added an element of statutory danger to this encounter and demanded extreme caution on my part.

Going home might have been the better idea.

On the other hand, what would someone who wasn't me have done? Someone without the ability to vanish and fly away?

"I'm sorry about that," she said. "That was my brother and his idiot friend, Theo. Really. I'm sorry."

"Those boots cost north of three-fifty. The jeans, probably another fifty. The socks, t-shirt and underwear I don't really care about."

She reached back and blindly groped the tabletop until she found her cloth bag. She dug inside. After a moment, she reached toward me with folded currency between her fingers, stretching a little as if to get close without getting anywhere near me.

"Here." She wiggled her fingers. "Here's two hundred. That's all I have."

I didn't take it. She stole a glance to see why not.

"Take it."

"You didn't throw my stuff in the water."

"No, but I will definitely rat out my brother to my parents for doing that. Besides, it's their money. Mom gave it to be me because she thinks we went for pizza."

"Ah. Your cover story for coming here. Plus, you pocket the two hundred. Nice."

"Judgmental much?" She wiggled the currency. "Just take it."

"It would be better if your brother paid."

She laughed. "Jace? He never pays for anything he does. Please take it. I'll get you the rest. Take it."

I leaned forward and carefully plucked the bills from between her fingers. She pulled her hand back quickly. I counted ten twenties. I refolded the bills and dropped them in the Ziploc bag with my blaster.

"Well…thank you, Rosie."

"Wait! You know my name?"

"I heard your brother call you that. I was coming out of the water over by those trees when you all arrived." I pointed to our right, but then realized she was studiously not looking in my direction. "I didn't have time to run up here and get my stuff before— well, you know. And since I am most certainly *not a perv*, I wasn't about to run up here exposing myself to a bunch of kids."

"Yeah, well, like I'm really, really, sorry. Jace can be such an ass. He's down there now getting stoned with my best friend, and then he's going to be all over her, and she'll get mad at me for it, like it's my fault, and he won't even give a shit, and Madeline will blame me and then I lose a friend."

"That sucks."

"Won't be the first time." She twisted the brush cap back onto the nail polish bottle and threw it into her bag. "I wish just once he'd get—I dunno."

"Payback?"

She laughed. "Is this really happening? Am I sitting here talking about my asshole brother with Naked Guy? WTF?"

"Again. Not my idea. And for the record, not naked."

She reached back and waved her hand.

"Go ahead if you want to leave. I won't turn around. I won't look. Hey! Where's your car, anyway?"

"Don't worry about it."

"Here!" She dug into her bag. She pulled out a pair of white shorts and tossed them down the table to me. They had embroidered daisies down each side. An elastic waist band guaranteed a fit, if not a proper fashion statement.

"You always carry a spare?"

"You ever been a teenaged girl?" She ladled the teen attitude in dollops. "Just go. I'll tell Jason you looked like Dwayne Johnson and I talked you out of beating the shit out of him. Like you were all tattoos and a biker or something like that."

This time I laughed. She joined in, letting a little tension deflate.

"I wasn't going to stop and talk to you. My plan was to simply leave. Wouldn't be the first time I drove home naked."

"Really?"

"Not a story for your young ears."

"Said the Naked Guy talking to an underaged girl. Oh. Sorry. I didn't mean it like—I wasn't trying to say—"

"Thank you. I appreciate us both being crystal clear on what is and what *is not* happening here. This is not a situation I volunteered for. I…look, I appreciate you stepping up and paying for the clothes, and giving me these shorts, which I am sure will look great on me. The thing is…I really was about to just leave and call the cops—" mention of it made her stiffen "—but now I'm thinking that what your brother did demands a bit more…creative justice, wouldn't you say?"

"Like beating him up?" She remained tense.

"God, no! But the money—again, thank you—won't mean anything to him. He gets off without having to pay a cent. Does he skate like this all the time?"

"Pretty much."

"What would you say to giving your brother some payback? Something a bit…theatrical?"

She turned and looked straight at me. I tightened the blanket across my lap.

"Really?"

"Really. But I need that red nail polish. And a black pen or marker."

I EXPLAINED what I had in mind. The girl grinned, then turned her back while I slipped into her donated shorts. Except for the daisies, they looked like a pair of white boxers on me. I re-wrapped the blanket and gave her the all-clear. She slid to sit directly across from me at my end of the table. She produced a black Sharpie from her bag.

"Seriously, do you carry everything in that satchel?"

"I once calculated that I could live for two weeks from this bag, assuming I had access to drinking water. C'mere. Lean forward."

I turned my head and leaned across the tabletop. She went to work in the waning twilight.

"Don't take forever. They're not going to stay in the truck all night."

"Huh." She delivered it as a sour note. "Last week they made me sit in the back for two hours. Turn your head."

She touched the right side of my neck with the Sharpie. It tickled.

"Make it a little toward the back. I want them to see it, but not my face, okay?"

"I did all the makeup last semester for Sweeney Todd. I got this." She exchanged the Sharpie for the nail polish. It felt cold on my skin. She took her time, humming again. I wondered if she knew she did that. "There. Don't move around too much. And don't touch it."

I leaned back and automatically glanced to my right, but of course could not see her handiwork. The smile on her face told me it looked good.

We talked for a minute about what I would do, what she should do, when she should do it and where she should go. She made a couple suggestions, expanding the plan, which I rejected. I told her to keep it simple. She gathered her bag and headed down the back side of the hill toward the box elder thicket. It wouldn't matter if she saw my car. What mattered is that she would be out of sight of the truck and vice versa.

I pretended to sneak toward the truck, but as soon as she slipped from my line of sight, I balled up the blanket, held it tight, and vanished. My feet lost contact with the ground. I kept my BLASTER but dropped the Ziploc bag with the cash. It tumbled onto the grass and reappeared.

Free from worry about being seen, I motored behind the BLASTER to where the pickup truck faced away from the quarry. The interior showed no light. All four side windows were cracked. Pale smoke rose through the openings carrying marijuana's unmistakable scent.

I heard laughter and low chatter. The windows were not yet fogged, telling me that more intimate activities had not begun. I could not make out the words, but the conversation pattern seemed to be boys making creative comments about the quality and effect of the weed, with girls either laughing or commenting on the comments.

I glided slowly. Speed required stopping, which meant using BLASTER power, which meant noise. An occasional pulse of the device adjusted my flight path until I drifted slowly over the truck cab's roof. At the last second, I realized my plan didn't account for the possibility of the truck having a sunroof. Thankfully, it didn't. I flicked slow turns of the prop until all motion stopped and my feet kissed the glossy top of the cab.

Fwooomp!

I reappeared and settled onto the roof, careful to spread my stance to avoid loudly denting the metal. I tucked the BLASTER under one arm. I leaned toward the driver's side and unfurled and flapped the blanket. Once. Like someone shaking out laundry to fold. The move produced a deep *thwomp!* sound.

"Shhhhh! Quiet! *Quiet!*" Jace's voice. "Did you guys hear that?"

"Hear what?"

Someone giggled.

I flapped the blanket again. Twice.

"That! That! Did you hear that?"

"*What was that?*"

"Sounded like a bird," Theo offered. "Like an owl maybe?"

"That's one big fucking owl," Jace marveled.

I did it again, this time half a dozen times working from left to right.

One of the girls shrieked, tight and jittery.

"Close the windows!" Jace ordered. "*Close the fucking windows!*"

I balled up the blanket and heaved it into darkness. It spread out and fell a few feet forward of the right front quarter panel. One of the girls saw the cape-like movement.

"*It's there! There!*"

"Where?"

"RIGHT IN FRONT OF US!"

I jumped slightly and brought a hundred and eighty pounds down on the roof. The cab shook to a bass drum beat. A satisfying dent formed in the metal.

Screams erupted inside the cab.

I jumped again. More screams.

"*It's on the roof! Close the fucking windows!*"

The truck was still running, so I knew it was only a matter of a few more seconds before Jace would use the big V-8 to escape. Time for the grand finale.

Fwooomp! I vanished and deployed the BLASTER and the core muscle inside me. I maneuvered to a horizontal position just forward of the windshield, about a foot above the long truck hood with my back to the frantic occupants. I steadied myself as best I could, then curled the power unit in one hand and my delicate parts in the other. This next stunt might hurt.

Fwooomp!

I reappeared. My back and butt filled the windshield. Gravity slammed me into the truck hood where I flopped and froze with my right shoulder twisted back and my right leg slung forward. I faced away from the windshield with a slight up angle, just enough to show off Rosie's artwork on my neck.

Two black puncture wounds at the side of my neck oozed trails of blood red nail polish. Enough twilight remained to give the streaks deep color against my pale skin. I felt confident that my audience would fixate on the vampire wounds and ignore the daisies on my shorts.

Everyone in the cab screamed. After that, things happened fast.

Jace threw the truck in reverse and floored it. All four wheels bit the gravel. I slid forward off the front of the truck and dropped. I tried to vanish before hitting the ground. Not quite quick enough, I picked up some road rash on my left arm and left leg before I disappeared.

The truck shot backward then ground to a hard stop. Headlights flashed on, lighting up empty space where I had vanished. Screams from inside the cab mixed with muted *Where did he go?* and *Get us out of here!* and *Go! Go! Go!* Jace jerked the shifter into Drive and again stomped on the gas, spinning the wheels and throwing gravel.

A few yards into their escape, one of the girls screamed at Jace to stop. A window cracked open. Both girls cried out Rosie's name.

I deployed the BLASTER and powered myself into position above the cab.

All four occupants shouted.

"ROSIE! ROSIE! FUCKING GET DOWN HERE! WE'RE LEAVING! NOW!"

From the back side of the hill, Rosie played her part perfectly. She let loose a series of blood-curdling screams, which she deftly cut off as if something horrible severed her last terrified shriek. She put enough into her performance that goose flesh erupted on my arms.

I bent my knees. I gave the roof one more solid stomp without reappearing because Jace did exactly what I expected. He floored the accelerator. The truck shot out from under me. Jace must have hit fifty miles an hour on the twin tracks leading back to the road. I feared he might lose control making the turn, but a moment later he shot up the road chasing his own headlight glow, driving like the Devil rode his rear bumper.

By the time Rosie trotted down the hill, I had reappeared. I stashed my BLASTER behind a clump of grass.

Rosie came out of the darkness laughing.

"That was the best damn thing I have ever done!" she cried. "Ohmigod! That was insane! Did they see you? Did you get up on the hood?"

"First the roof. Then the hood. Like a dead body dropped out of the sky."

"I can't believe that!"

"Your brother is a bit of a jerk for leaving you to be ravaged by the flying vampire."

She grinned and regained her breath. "Oh, I don't know. We've seen every teen slasher movie there is. You always get killed when you go to rescue your sister or brother or friend. Plus, I'm set up to be a perfect Final Girl."

I didn't know what that was. My ignorance showed on my face.

"Survivor? Victim in the first reel? Comes back—never mind. *God, that was just AWESOME!"*

"It was." I gave in to a grin of my own. "Look, I actually *do* have a car back there. But I gotta be honest—don't take this wrong —but I'd rather not offer you a ride if it's all the same to you. Strangers and all." In my head that played as *Nearly Naked Guy gives underaged girl a ride.*

"No, no, no, no! Don't worry!" She waved her hands at me. "I can walk. It's only a couple miles to town. I can call somebody."

I shook my head.

"No. You get started for the road. My phone is in my car. By the time you get there, a nice lady detective from the police department will be waiting to pick you up—*don't worry*—she's my wife. I'll explain everything to her. She won't ask hard questions or make any trouble for you. Just a safe ride home. Okay?"

I waved my wedding band in the air between us.

"You're married to a cop? Jesus. We really are in deep shit."

"You're not. Trust me. And call it even on the money."

"You sure?"

"Oh, hell yes. This was worth way more than those old boots." Old, but broken in. I bit my tongue. We stood in the deepening darkness for an awkward moment until I said, "You better get moving."

"Again. Really sorry about the boots."

She gave me an apologetic wave and turned. A few paces into her journey, she turned again and waved. I waved back.

"Hey!" I called out. She stopped. "When you get home, don't let your brother see you. Put a little makeup on your neck and sneak around to his bedroom window. Pretend you're floating."

She laughed, then said, "You look really dumb in those shorts."

She wasn't wrong.

NAKED GUY
April 21, 2020 to April 24, 2022

Payment In Kind

7

PAYMENT IN KIND

The gyros in the cockpit hummed their way toward silence. The hot exhaust manifolds on the twin engines ticked as they cooled. I secured my headset, iPad and knee board. I watched the small caravan carrying Sandy and Arun depart, then slid out of the pilot's seat, climbed out of the aircraft, and closed the cabin door.

I took a moment to appreciate the scent of fresh-cut Iowa hay coming from an adjacent field. Second or third cutting of the season. My teen years as a farmhand taught me to favor any cutting after the first. The smaller yield per acre meant fewer bales, which meant finishing faster—the salient objective of any teenaged farmhand.

Except for a light breeze carrying the alfalfa perfume, the small-town airport lay still under a high blue sky. Crows carried on a debate in the distance. A confused cricket chirped in the grass at the edge of the ramp, apparently unaware that the sun had risen and the ladies looking for mates had retired from the field.

I took my time fueling the airplane. As I poured 100LL Avgas into the last of four tanks, I examined the ramp. A shallow downslope flowed away from the gas pumps. I decided to see if I could simply push the airplane a few fuselage lengths away from the pumps, rather than start the engines and taxi clear. Courtesy demanded that I leave enough room for the next guy to gas up, but beyond that, the ramp had plenty of space and this little one-runway airport wasn't exactly O'Hare Field. Shoving the Navajo aside would suffice. A benign weather forecast negated the need for a tiedown.

After turning the nose wheel to scribe a curved path away from the pumps, I leaned into the wing root to push.

"You want a hand with that?"

The voice startled me. I looked over the engine nacelle. The young man walked with purpose toward me. Jeans, denim shirt, and a cap with a farm implement dealer's patch on coordinated with the sun-colored, corn-fed face and friendly grin.

"I won't turn it down," I said.

He picked up the pace and hurried to the other side of the nose. He leaned into the right-side wing root at the correct spot. We rolled the airplane back, careful not to build up too much speed or momentum.

"That's good," I said, letting it go and watching it roll to a stop. "Thanks."

"Nice airplane," he said, backing away and looking it over.

"It is that. You fly?"

"We keep a Citation in that hangar over there." He pointed.

You win. He gave me a crooked smile that said he knew it.

"That'll get you where you're going. What business are you in?"

"Farming." He gestured at the sprawl of agricultural land all around us. I wondered if he meant the gesture as an example, or in the possessive sense. "How about you?"

"I just fly it. The airplane belongs to—"

"That Education outfit?"

"You're familiar?"

"My daddy's on the school board. I heard they were in town. How come you're not taking the tour?"

"I just fly the airplane."

"I love flying. The Citation's great, but we keep a 310 for short hops. So, what…are you just hanging around here all day?"

I confessed a plan to take the airport crew car into the small town for breakfast, having grabbed a solitary piece of toast on the way out the door before dawn.

"That crew car's a wreck. Lemme drive you into town. If you don't mind some company, I haven't had breakfast and I haven't had another pilot to talk to in forever."

Hard to argue with that.

* * * * *

"Baron's nice, but Beechcraft parts are pricey."

"310's nice, but I've got fifteen knots on you and a ride like a Mercedes S-Class."

Jason Redman put on a skeptical look. "What model?"

"E. The IO-520 engines."

The look evaporated. "The C, D and E were the best Fifty-fives before they went to the Fifty-eights. I'll grant you that much." He looked around, waved at the woman behind the counter and lifted his coffee mug. When she approached, I put my hand over mine.

"I'm fine," I said. The woman looked offended. "I've got a long flight home and there's no restroom on the plane." Her coffee also tasted like asphalt.

Redman took a refill.

Breakfast was good. Standard refueling fare. Bacon. Eggs. Hash browns. The conversation had been pleasant. I estimated Redman to be in his mid-twenties, a little entitled and something resembling farm royalty if the greetings he got when he entered the storefront diner on Main Street were any indication. He didn't brag about flying a Cessna Citation jet, which stood fine by me. The bigger, better, and more exciting the aircraft, the more I like a little humility in the pilot.

"Separate checks, please," I told the woman as she headed back for the counter.

"Maggie, put it all on mine," Redman said. He intercepted my protest. "Visiting aviators don't come along that often. My pleasure."

"Well, if you ever divert that Citation into Essex County, the Jet-A is about the lowest you'll find, and the Silver Spoon Diner is every bit as good as this was. On me."

Redman rotated his mug in his hands for a moment.

"So, this woman that runs the Foundation you work for... what's her deal?"

The way he asked, I jumped to the conclusion that he'd seen Sandy when she disembarked. Sandy Stone is a blonde knockout at any distance. She's one of the few women I know who can enter a room with my wife and make men short-circuit trying to figure out which one to stare at.

I formulated a polite way of telling Redman that Sandy's receptors to amorous advances might as well be on Mars. Sandy is all business, entirely focused on spreading Bargo Litton's hundred million dollars—for which she nearly paid with her life—among as many underfunded public schools as possible.

Before I could answer, Redman continued. "She the sole decision-maker?"

"You mean for a grant?"

"Yeah," Redman said. The conversational landscape shifted.

"She and her executive director," I replied.

"Right. The little Indian guy."

My senses tightened. Something about the way he said it ignited warning lights in the back of my mind.

"Mr. Dewar's input carries weight on every application," I said. Arun's detailed analysis of each grant application guides Sandy's decision. In truth, he has the final say. He just makes Sandy think it was her decision.

"What about you?"

"What about me?"

"You must have some influence."

I leaned back from the small table, a gesture designed to put some distance between myself and someone I began to wish I had not met.

"Look, uh…I don't know where you're headed with this. The conversation about airplanes was great, but if you're looking for me to—"

"To what?" Redman stared at me. He meant the challenge to hold my attention, because at that moment two men, both larger than either Redman or me, slid off their stools at the counter and pulled back the chairs on either side of our small table. They dropped onto the chairs and planted elbows mounting thick forearms on the table. There was nothing friendly about it, and introductions were not forthcoming. Redman's tone grew mildly belligerent. "To what?"

I glanced from face to face. The man on my right shared DNA with Redman. They seemed close in age. A brother, possibly a cousin. The man on my left had dark features, possibly Latino. I doubted a blood tie to Redman but did not doubt loyalty. He folded one hand over a clenched fist.

"You fellas might not understand my role in all this. I drive the airplane. That's it. If you're looking to sway the Foundation's decision, you're about as far off the mark as you can get."

"Oh, I don't know about that," Redman cocked his head to one side. "Make it worthwhile and a man will put his mind to anything."

"What kind of *anything* are you talking about?"

Redman leaned forward. "Look. Cards on the table, okay? You seem like a smart guy. Got a good gig flying. Build some time, hook up with a regional carrier and fly jets, right? That Navajo's nice, but you're probably sick of hauling people a couple hundred miles and sitting around all day while the passengers get wined and dined, right? A year from now you see yourself flying right seat in an A320 for Delta, right?"

I said nothing.

"And…maybe you got something going on with that blonde hottie." He smirked. On cue, his two companions smirked. "Maybe you have more leverage over things than you let on."

I used a long pause to suppress my immediate response.

Arun and Sandy don't make trips to visit applicant schools unless the pen is poised on the check. I was not up to speed on why we had come to this small Iowa town, but I knew for certain that the school district was about to benefit from a sizable grant from the Christine and Paulette Paulesky Education Foundation.

Which made me wonder why this yahoo felt a need to twist my arm.

"I'll answer this in two ways, Jason. First, like I told you, I just fly the airplane. Whatever decision the Foundation makes has already been made. Second, you would do well to check your tone regarding Miss Stone."

Redman's flat palms rose. "Meant no harm. That gal is a lotta woman, and I know how it is with some women around pilots. And some pilots around women. But here's the thing, Will. Your Foundation is stroking a fat check for our little county school system— Lord knows, they need it. We're all grateful for the Christian charity that has fallen from the sky. But I'd like to propose to you that some significant gratitude might come your way if you were to help us with a minor technicality in this transaction."

"I don't suppose if I told you I had no interest it would stop you from telling me about that minor technicality."

"Your, uh, *passenger*..." The smarmy way he said it made me want to smack him. "She's up there at the district office right now chatting about a check for seven hundred thousand dollars."

"If you say so."

"Two percent." He tented his fingers, making me think he'd seen too many cheesy spy villains on whatever giant screen he had in his home media room.

"Two percent...what, milk?"

"Two percent of what they're discussing comes to fourteen grand."

"See. Now maybe I should go tell them to call the whole thing off, seeing as how this community has a good grasp of math already."

Redman pasted a grin on his face. "Fourteen grand in your pocket if you help us out here."

"Help you do what?"

"Nothing illegal." The fact that he said it out loud eliminated any doubt in my mind. I offered no comment, prompting him to continue. "That money will go to the school district, minus a nice commission for you. Guaranteed. We just prefer that the funds be channeled through our own education foundation. All on the up and up. I told you, my daddy is on the school board. He also runs a foundation a lot like yours, dedicated to uplifting education in our county."

"Seems like a lot of extra paperwork and fourteen grand that could've been put to better use."

"Better use? Man, you could score a nice type rating for that."

"I got a wallet full of type ratings," I lied. I don't know why.

Redman's grin faded. "And here I took you for a smart guy."

"Smartass is more my speed."

The grin disappeared. "I don't think you understand the down-side. I told you the upside. The downside of not accepting my proposal could be painful."

Redman's two silent partners literally flexed their muscles. If I hadn't seen them do it, I wouldn't have believed it.

I reached over my empty plate and picked up the pepper shaker. As I spoke, I unscrewed the cap.

"You know, I don't think I've ever heard a grown man call his father 'daddy' outside of a *Dukes of Hazard* episode."

Redman stiffened. The grin disappeared. I set the pepper shaker cap on the table and cupped my left hand.

"While your offer is generous at face value, I suspect that running that money through a bogus foundation opens the door to all sorts of financial mischief. Not to mention the legal ramifications of me taking a kickback from a grant recipient. But most of all, I get the feeling the schools would not see much of that six hundred eighty-six grand , if any. And I'm dead certain I wouldn't see a penny of that 'commission.' Afraid I have to pass."

I poured a mound of pepper into my left palm, then closed it. Switching hands, I repeated the move in my right.

All three men stared at me.

"Okay, smartass. I gotta ask," the big man on my right spoke. "What the fuck is that all about?"

I stood up, both hands forming fists.

"Well, since you boys joined up with a pretty clear intention to intimidate me, I naturally assumed that me getting up and walking out on you wouldn't go over well. I figured we three might wind up on the sidewalk outside, carrying this conversation a little further."

Both big men sat frozen.

Redman restored his shitty grin. "It doesn't have to go that way."

"Good to know. I wouldn't want anybody to wind up on their knees coughing up their lungs and clawing their eyes out." I held up my hands to make the point about the pepper. "I'm leaving. Thank you for breakfast."

Brother-cousin made a move to follow, but Redman's hand on his arm stopped him. He spoke to my back.

"That's a shame, Will. This could have been a nice chunk of change."

I cleared the front door without looking back. Outside, I turned a sharp left to avoid the diner's windows. I set a casual pace on the sidewalk. The back of my neck tingled. I expected to hear following footsteps. A real estate office, a nail salon and two unmarked doors passed on my left. The second unmarked door occupied a recessed brick entryway. I glanced up and down the street, counted only two moving cars and zero foot traffic.

I ducked into the doorway.

Fwooomp!

The cool sensation that wraps around me when I vanish came with an extra dose of relief. The doorway had tall dimensions. I pushed off and rose until I floated level with a window above the door. Pressing my fists against the bricks on each side, I fixed myself in place and watched the street and sidewalk.

No one followed.

* * * * *

Earl Jackson once told me that if a fist fight became inevitable, filling his palms with pepper gave him an edge. I have no idea if that works. I thanked Heaven I did not have to find out.

I kept the pepper in my left palm and used a battery-powered propeller unit in my right to navigate back to the airport, which lay roughly two miles outside of town. I watched to see if Redman intended to renew negotiations at the airport. If so, I planned to use the pepper while still in the vanished state. The three of them would know what hit them, they just wouldn't know how. Those plans, however, did not ease my mind about the Navajo. An airplane on a ramp is vulnerable and hard to move quickly out of harm's way. A pickup truck can easily deny movement by simply parking in front of the nose; there's no reverse gear for a reciprocating engine prop plane. Damaging a parked airplane is not difficult, either. A flat tire puts to rest any question of movement. A minor dent to any control surface renders the aircraft unairworthy.

I had no idea how far Redman intended to go to make his point. I decided to board the airplane and depart. Better to roost at an airport thirty or forty miles away than remain exposed. Parked safely elsewhere, I could connect with Arun and Sandy. I had questions. Did they encounter 'Daddy' Redman? Did anyone suggest shifting the foundation grant to a local foundation? Many communities have education foundations that supplement strained school budgets with bake sales, charity runs and other sources of funding. It wasn't hard to imagine that someone might use one for less than legitimate purposes when close to a million dollars appears on the horizon.

Not being well-versed in tax fraud, embezzlement and other financial games, I didn't think about what Redman intended or how he planned to do it. Dewey Larmond, the Foundation's accountant, could fill me in later on what Redman's scheme might yield.

I focused on departing. The airport windsock suggested a northwest takeoff on the small airport's sole runway. The ramp joined the takeoff end of the runway not far from the gas pumps. Fuel was no issue, having already topped the tanks. Nothing blocked my way. Neither Redman's oversized pickup nor any other vehicle appeared.

The urge to act diminished slightly. The same summer breeze sent sweet hay scent drifting across the ramp. The same silence that surrounded me when I gassed up dominated the empty ramp.

Was I overreacting?

I flew a circuit around the ramp and then around the airport's single row of hangars. No vehicles. No lurkers. No ambushes.

Redman and his companions had been heavy-handed and

mildly absurd in a B-movie villain way. What were they going to do? Beat me up in a diner during the breakfast rush? Assault and battery would hardly advance a white-collar criminal scheme; it only calls attention to it. Redman appeared to wield power in his little community, but that did not lift him above the law. On the other hand, pressing charges from a hospital bed lacked appeal.

I finished my reconnaissance and reappeared at the Navajo cabin door. The urgency had diminished slightly, but I stuck to my plan to leave.

Mild OCD stopped me cold.

I can't help myself. I favor straight lines and symmetry. I take pride in pulling into a tiedown spot perfectly centered.

The Navajo did not occupy a tiedown spot, and it was not squared with the perimeter edge of the ramp. The aircraft sat at a slight angle, on the curved line I scribed when Redman and I pushed it back. It wasn't subject to my obsession for perfect parking. It wasn't aligned with a row of other aircraft.

But there had been a vein of asphalt sealant running on a line from the gas pumps to the edge of the ramp, and I couldn't help but notice when I pushed the airplane away from the pumps that the nosewheel came to rest on that vein of gooey filler.

Now it sat four feet to the left.

I looked around, feeling the weight of watchful eyes. The airport shack appeared deserted, but it would not be hard for someone to lurk in the dark interior. The windows reflected a bright summer day. The row of hangars had no windows, but that did not mean someone couldn't crack a door to watch.

I looked for unsealed hangar doors and found none.

Redman's hangar, home to a Cessna Citation jet and a Cessna 310 piston twin, dominated the hangar row at twice the size of other structures. It lacked windows and showed no sign of a cracked door.

Still, the emptiness of this small-town airport bore weight.

Why move the airplane?

The tires looked healthy. The aluminum skin appeared undamaged. I checked the oil in both engines and pushed my face against the intakes to study the engines in the cowlings. Nothing amiss.

I dropped to a crouch and scanned the belly, the bottoms of the wings, the landing gear wells. If someone engaged in sabotage, it didn't show.

Why move the airplane?

A small stain on the asphalt beneath the right wing caught my eye. Stains on aircraft ramps are not unusual and this ramp had its share. This stain looked fresh.

I knelt for closer inspection. I touched it. My finger came up clean, but it failed to pass the sniff test.

Avgas.

I checked the bottom of the wing. The oil streaks behind the engine breather tubes appeared normal. No dents. No damage.

A glittering droplet on the central fuel strainer drain flashed tiny light at me. I scooted over and studied it. A single drop of fuel, wet and round. Not enough weight to drop to the ground. More importantly, the ramp below the drain plug showed no wet stain. This was not a leak.

Fuel strainer drains exist at various low points along the fuel system. Their purpose is to trap water or foreign particles. Part of a preflight inspection for any airplane is to open the drain, allowing a small quantity of fuel into a clear tube to be examined for color, scent, and to see if bulbs of water, which are heavier than fuel, wiggle at the bottom. Sometimes the drains don't seal properly. I've seen airplanes with chronic leaks, most often exhibited by blue streaks where fuel drops fly back along the wing and the fuel dye leaves a trail.

This Navajo had no such issue. All the fuel drains on this bird were tight and reliable. During a preflight test, a drop might linger on the bottom of the plug after draining, but I always wick it off using the test tube.

Except I had not yet performed the drain test, saving it as the last step in my preflight walkaround. No single drip would have survived an engine start, let alone a flight.

I stood up and opened the fuel cap on the inboard tank. Liquid showed just below the filler opening. Full. I gave it the sniff test. Avgas.

I opened the outboard tank. Also full. I leaned over to sniff.

Jet fuel.

"Are you shitting me?" I cried out to the empty airport.

* * * * *

"Both the outboard tanks have been filled with Jet fuel." I led the deputy sheriff to the left wing and opened the inboard and outboard caps. I invited him to lean over and take a whiff from each. He noticed the difference.

"Smells like kerosene," he said.

"No shit." He gave me a hard look. "Sorry. But somebody drained the outboard tanks, then moved the airplane over to the pumps and filled them with Jet-A."

"And you know this how?" The deputy asked, pulling a notebook from his shirt pocket.

My wife has shared much with me about her days as a patrol sergeant on the City of Essex Police Department, and about the 'he said, she said' situations that inevitably arise. People often think their story is enough to draw an officer in and get them to take sides. Good officers, she explained, don't take sides; they investigate, determine if violation of a law requires them to act, but then leave judgment up to judges. An accusation, to hear Andy tell it, rarely lives in the same neighborhood as a fact.

My purpose in calling 9-1-1 was not to point a finger and

demand an arrest. I had a fair idea who had done this, and an equally fair idea that they were well out of reach of any proof or justice. My purpose in calling law enforcement was to get someone out here to protect the airplane and prevent something worse from happening.

"Did you gas up when you got here?"

"Yes."

"Did you gas it up from the wrong hose?" he asked, glancing at the fuel pumps. The 100LL Avgas box was less than eight feet from the Jet-A box.

With his pen poised above his notebook page, this officer was about to jot down that the pilot gassed up his airplane after arrival, recording that this was more than likely his own damned fault.

I chose my next words carefully.

"On takeoff, this aircraft always draws from the main tanks—the inboards." I pointed. "That one. The one currently topped off with Avgas. On this flight, I drew from the inboard main tanks for approximately twenty minutes at a flow rate of almost twenty gallons per hour. That significantly reduces the fuel in the tank. Then, for the bulk of the enroute portion, I switched to and drained the outboard tanks."

"Okay." He made a few notes, not nearly matching the detail of what I had just given him.

"On descent for landing, the checklist calls for returning to the inboard tanks. More fuel gets drained from those. Now here's the part that's important, Deputy. Yes. Yes, I did refuel the airplane after landing. From that pump right over there. All four tanks had been used, so all four tanks were down. I topped off all four from the Avgas hose. *Just the Avgas hose.* But now, the inboards contain Avgas. The outboards contain Jet-A. For me to have made an error, I would have had to fuel the inboards. Stop. Reel in the hose. Run my credit card a second time and switch hoses. A call to my credit card company will prove that my card has been run only once. And that the quantity of Avgas on my credit card purchase matches the quantity of fuel that would have been used on a flight from Essex County to here—a number I can provide. Do you see what I'm saying?"

"I think I get the picture," he said.

"Yes, I fueled the aircraft, but only with Avgas. Someone came here after I left, drained the outboard tanks, then moved the aircraft to fill the outboard tanks with Jet fuel."

"Maybe somebody was stealing fuel."

"Then why fill it up again?"

He sighed. "Who would do something like that? Did you see anybody?"

"Nope. I accepted an invitation from a local gentleman named Jason Redman for a ride into town and breakfast at the diner. We had breakfast. I hitched a ride back out here and found this. I'm guessing you know Mr. Redman?"

"I do. I'll chat with him to confirm all this." He lowered his chin and looked over the top of his Ray Bans. "Are you suggesting Mr. Redman was involved?"

I knew better than to make an accusation. "I don't see how that's possible, since I was with him at breakfast when this happened."

I studied his reaction. The way he pursed his lips and raised his face again hinted that finding out Redman was behind this would not give anyone a stroke.

"Do you wish to file a formal report?"

"I'm afraid you will be doing that."

He paid me a look that suggested I rethink telling him what to do.

"Deputy, this is a Homeland Security issue. If I were to take off like this, I would climb to cruise altitude on the main tanks. About twenty minutes into the flight, I would switch to the auxiliary outboard tanks. About twenty seconds after that both engines would be destroyed by ignition detonation. Even if I correctly analyzed the problem within seconds, it would take too long for the fuel in the lines to switch back. Both engines would be ruined. And unless I happened to have a nice long runway within gliding distance, landing an airplane of this kind at close to one hundred miles per hour in a field or woods would go very badly. Which means that you're standing at the scene of a federal crime. Interference with a flight. Aircraft sabotage. Not to mention the likelihood that the crash would have been fatal."

I might have exaggerated the last point. Iowa and Wisconsin are carpeted with big open fields, and an off-airport landing stands a good chance of success.

Judging by the look on his face, he got the message.

"What do you want to do?"

"Well," I said, "while you're taking samples from all four tanks, filing a report, and getting some help out here to put a watch on the airplane, I'll get on the phone with my maintenance base and find out what we have to do to fix this. All of the fuel has to be drained because I can't be sure the main tanks weren't contaminated, too. The lines have to be drained. The fuel pumps. I'll put together a field repair and have the work done here on this ramp."

The deputy looked around. "Isn't there a shop here? Maybe in one of these hangars?"

"No shop. Even if there was, I can't be sure that someone from one of these hangars isn't behind this. Whoever did this, knew what they were doing."

He took a fresh look at the hangars.

"One thing for certain, we need to drain a hundred and eighty-three gallons of contaminated fuel, so we're going to need some paper cups."

He cracked a smile. Something else Andy taught me. Treat the cop like a person. Make a connection if you can. You won't sway them or lower their guard, but you will provide evidence that you're not the asshole in the story.

"I think we can do better."

I glanced at the big hangar, at the ramp, and at the parking lot behind the FBO office. No sign of Redman's big pickup truck or Redman. He had the good sense not to return to the scene of his crime.

"There's something else you could do for me, Deputy," I said. "This...this was a lot of trouble to go to and the most likely outcome would have been an accident. The people I flew in here are from a foundation that has a lot of money, some of which they planned to give to the local school district. I can't help but wonder if they weren't the targets here. Maybe you could get someone to provide them with an escort? Just to be safe?"

"I think we can arrange that," he said.

"Much appreciated."

* * * * *

"Whatever you do, do NOT start up the engines," Earl shouted at me through the phone.

"I figured that much. We're draining everything, but the engines haven't been run so more than likely it didn't reach the fuel pumps."

I could almost hear him scratching his scalp over the phone. "Maybe. Gotta clear 'em anyway. It's all gotta come out. The sumps. The fuel lines. The pumps. All of it."

"I know. I'm on it. Can you spring Doc and maybe get Rosemary II to juggle the schedule and fly him out here? There's no shop here. I can have the tanks drained, but I need him to clear the lines and pumps."

"It'll cause havoc. Ain't gonna happen until morning, earliest. Who the hell did this?"

I decided not to elevate Earl's standard level of rage.

"Not sure. Call me back and let me know."

The line fell silent. I miss dial tones. Earl, I assumed, had ended the call. He's not much for goodbyes.

* * * * *

"Mr. Stewart? Hello!" The voice outside the aircraft belong to the fresh-faced young deputy who pulled up and parked off the left wing. I watched him dismount his squad car and adjust his belt, which looked heavier than he did. This kid had drawn the short straw, it appeared.

"In here," I called out from within the cabin where I had been killing time with the latest edition of *AOPA Pilot*. The first deputy had promised to contact a service station in town and have them drive out with barrels and a funnel. That was two hours ago.

I called Arun while the first deputy was still in sight on the long, flat county road that bordered the airport. He and Sandy were at lunch with the local school district's superintendent and most of the school principals. The restaurant sounded noisy. I wondered if it was the same one Redman had selected for our breakfast.

I shared an abbreviated version of events. Someone had messed with the airplane. Didn't know who. Working on fixing it. Meant we would be spending the night. I explained that I asked the deputy to send someone to keep an eye on them, which prompted an uptick in worry. Just a precaution, I assured him. Yes, a report was filed. No, we had no idea why this happened or if it had anything to do with the purpose of their visit.

Arun flexed from worried to angry. Who would do such a thing? Who would want to interfere with us coming to this community to give away money? It made no sense.

I let him rant for a minute, then asked him to stick close to

Sandy. He asked what I was planning. I told him I intended to stay with the airplane.

We agreed to connect after the afternoon meetings concluded.

"How're you doing, sir?" The deputy looked like he had been recruited out of high school. I met him at the cabin door and climbed out.

"I've had better days. Any word on that service station that was sending out something for us to drain the fuel?"

"Oh, yes! I saw them loading up fifty-five-gallon drums on my way out here. They should be along right quick. How much is there?"

"A hundred and eighty gallons." The kid seemed impressed. "Hey, what do you have for hotels around here?"

"Oh, there's no hotels. Or motels. You might drive down to Sioux City, I suppose, but that's a hefty drive. But we do have a couple gay ladies who run a bed and breakfast. Nice place, I hear."

I smiled at him. "I'm not sure you want to describe folks as a couple of 'gay ladies.' Just saying."

"Oh, no," he laughed, "they do it all the time. Nice ladies. I bet they could put you up for the night. It's you and two others, right?"

"Affirmative. And you'll stay here to watch the airplane?"

"'Til my shift ends at eleven. Then someone from the night shift will cover it. Nothing to worry about."

"Alright, then. I'll hitch a ride into town with that service station truck if they ever get here."

The kid pointed. "That's them now."

* * * * *

Draining the contaminated fuel took three hours. The drums they brought did not fit under the wing with a funnel so the fuel had to be drained into a five-gallon jerry can, then dumped in the drums. The drain sumps are meant for fuel testing, not off-loading.

Fully opened, they ran at the speed of a leaky kitchen faucet. The duration of the operation made me realize that whoever drained my tanks went to work on it the instant I drove off with Redman. I wondered if all or only some of the outboard tanks had been replaced. Choosing the outboards guaranteed that the engine failure would happen at high altitude. Did they mean for both engines to fail? Or did they want to set me up with a single engine failure, only to have the second engine fail at an even more critical time such as during a single-engine approach to landing? How much thought went into this act of sabotage?

What came out of the outboard tanks was unquestionably Jet-A. Kerosene smell hung thick in the air as it drained. The kid deputy had been sent with a handful of evidence kits. He took samples in what looked like urine cups, marked them, and stored them in the cruiser's trunk. Unless he planned to pull fingerprints off the Jet-A pump and hose, I did not expect the evidence to serve any real purpose.

At around four p.m. the last of the fuel went into the drums—no good to anyone. The deputy said something about a county hazardous materials disposal site and told me they charge by the gallon. Great.

I hooked a ride into town with the service station guy. He talked nonstop about flying into Canada on a pontoon plane—boy what a ride. He swore the pontoon took the top off a tree when they came in for landing on a tiny lake, but it was the best fishing of his life and he'd do it again in a minute. He asked if I flew pontoon planes. I said no. I asked him about the B&B. He knew right away which gay ladies I meant and offered to drop me off.

* * * * *

"I'm Sally." The woman greeted me at the front door of a huge old house occupying a corner lot on one of the half-dozen blocks that made up the small town. A stone pedestal on the lawn mounted a wooden sign that said Lilly House. I shifted my flight bag to my left hand and climbed the porch steps. We traded warm hand-shakes. She waved at the tow truck driver. "Thanks, Robbie!"

"What a beautiful house," I said. The curled and carved wood-work invited my eyes to linger. A pedimented porch surrounded three sides. Leaded windows nestled in detailed wood frames. Gables so numerous they nearly obscured the roof were topped with ornate spindles and cast-iron weathervanes. Gray with white trim, the house looked like it belonged in a dollhouse museum. "Queen Anne?"

The woman tipped me an impressed expression. "You know your Victorian architecture."

"Not really. The tow truck driver told me the history. Built by a man who owned a string of dry goods stores."

"The Sam Walton of his day. You get points for honesty. Did he tell you we were the gay ladies in town?"

"It seems to be a local highlight. Are you listed on the Chamber of Commerce website?"

She laughed. "I wouldn't be surprised. Come in!"

The interior surpassed the exterior. I have never seen so much varnished wood.

"Thanks for taking the last-minute reservation," I said. I glanced at my watch. "My associates will be here soon. That's what I'm told."

Sally topped out at somewhere around five feet, had short blonde hair and an open, welcoming face. Her edges suggested an age that got the blonde from a bottle, but she had a youthful energy and a lineless face that made it work.

"No trouble," she assured me. "We have five rooms, all empty, so you have your pick. Breakfast is included, as advertised, but Bernice and I have a big batch of chicken tikka masala simmering, about five times what we can eat. We would be delighted if you would join us for dinner, also included. I can tell you without boasting it beats anything you find at the diner or the McDonalds out by the highway."

"Sounds great."

"Let me show you the rooms."

* * * * *

I waited for Sandy and Arun on the porch. Sally offered iced tea but followed the offer with sly mention that she and Bernice kept a stock of Spotted Cow in the 'fridge. The surreptitious way she said it made me wonder if the neighbors were members of a Baptist temperance league.

"I will say yes to a Spotted Cow if you promise to include it on the bill."

"I have no problem lying to you and saying I will. Be right back."

"Will you join me?"

"If you don't tell Bernice." She hustled away. She returned with a tray, two brown bottles of cold beer and two glasses. She poured like a pro then took the next wicker rocker down the line.

"New friends," I said, raising the glass.

"The best kind."

We traded small talk about the town. She asked about the Foundation, about flying and about the circumstances that turned this trip into an overnight. I held back the story of the contaminated fuel but watched a flash of darkness cross her brow at the mention of meeting Jason Redman. I decided to probe it.

"Tell me about the Redman family. I take it they're a big ag operation around here."

"If owning half the county counts as big, then yes," she replied. "Are you doing business with Mr. Redman?"

"I think I came close to a fist fight with him."

"Then that beer definitely will not go on the bill, Mr. Stewart."

"You're not a fan?"

She looked me over. Finding me worthy of trust, she said, "I would be a fan of seeing them tarred and run out of the county. I don't mean to stick my nose in your business, but if you can avoid dealing with the Redmans, you will save yourself headaches and money."

"Noted," I said.

"Jason Redman has been a snot since he was a boy. Bernice taught in the district here for thirty-seven years. She had him off and on. He only got worse as he got older. But he's a shadow of his father. Buck Redman—"

"Jesus, he's not really called 'Buck' is he?"

"His name is Edward, but he has called himself Buck since he came back from Vietnam and took over—or I should say *took* the farm from his father. And there is not a single lie or underhanded trick he has not used to expand that operation to what it is today. Buck Redman treats this county like his fiefdom. He's on the county board, the school board, and the town select committee. He runs every one of them by pushing his incompetent friends and sycophants to fill all the seats. He will lie to your face, then call you a liar for producing evidence of his falsehood." She stopped abruptly, realizing that she had moved to the edge of her seat. "Goodness, that man gets me worked up. He fought us for ten years on our renovation and permits. He jacks up fuel oil prices every winter because he owns the oil company, and when we tried to switch to LP gas, he rammed through ordinances against having tanks bigger than a barbecue grille. I could go on and on. I shouldn't."

I wondered if any of this had surfaced when Arun vetted the school district, but the application would have come from the school administration, the educators working on a shoestring, not the board holding that string.

Sally continued.

"That man has had whole tracts of his own land condemned by the county board to reduce his tax bill—while he's out on that same land with his new combines and equipment harvesting. He devalues his property for taxes, then inflates the values for bank loans. If there's a scheme, he's behind it or in on it."

"Sounds like a gem of a human being." I started to ask if she knew anything about a Redman education foundation, but Sally slid to the edge of her seat again, scanning the yard and lowering her voice.

"The true tragedy of that family is his poor daughter. She was such a sweetie, I used to swear she was adopted. That girl never had a chance after her mother passed." Sally shook her head over the memory.

"What happened?"

"Girl trouble. You know. Girl-in-trouble trouble. That old bastard never forgave her for the shame of it. He drove her away, then fought her for the baby. It broke her. Drinking and drugs. Oh. Now I'm truly speaking out of turn."

She put her fingers to her lips and mimed the turning of a key. I wanted to know more.

"Do you happen to know—?"

"It's all come home to roost!" she blurted. "Karma. Or whatever you want to call justice. It is all coming back to roost on that man, and I am ashamed to say Good Deal. I never want to wish ill on any living creature, but God gives us leave to stray and on Buck Redman, my Christian charity doth stray."

"How do you mean?"

She leaned closer. "They say he's in trouble. Trouble with the banks. Trouble with the IRS. Money trouble. Word is the largest implement dealer in the state is deep into Redman, and not getting paid."

"Broke?"

She put up a hand. "Too much. I've said too much. There's straying and there's bolting off into the blue."

"The kid says his old man runs an education foundation."

She scoffed. "Well, if he does, Bernice and I have never heard of it. That old skinflint never gave a dime to the district. Probably another one of his scams. You're not doing business with Redman, are you?"

"No. Not the way you might imagine. But I think they've already done some business with me. Or to me."

We circled back to the reason for the trip. Without revealing the amount, I told her that a legitimate education foundation was about to give the school district a big grant.

Her eyes watered. To my surprise, she choked up. "Well, now. Bless your heart."

"Not me. Sandy Stone. Giving away money is her deal. I just fly the airplane."

"Doesn't matter. You're staying here for free tonight."

"No, you can't—"

"Don't you dare argue with me. Oh, if you only knew what little bits and shreds of funding our district has to scratch for year after year. Bernice worked and slaved away for next to nothing, doing with nothing, making do with old books and used up buildings, and any time a referendum was proposed, that old son of a bitch shot it down—excuse my French. Bernice will be over the moon when she hears this." She stood up abruptly. "You promise me that you will not give that money to Redman! Promise me!"

At that moment I would no more have refused that five-foot-tall tower of determination than I would have wrestled King Kong.

"There's zero chance of it."

"Good," she said. "I'm going to tell Bernice to make a pie."

With that, she hurried off.

* * * * *

Bernice made *three* pies. Cherry, apple, and rhubarb, which shocked me by being the tastiest of the three. Half an inch taller than me, with dark hair, dark eyes and a crushing hug, Bernice joined her partner in treating Arun, Sandy, and me like royalty. The ladies served dinner in a stunning dining room, on china adorned with gold leaf, with wine served in Steuben crystal glassware. I tried my best to fade into the scenery and let Sandy hold court. Sally and Bernice treated her like a goddess, and her mission to give money to deserving school districts like the Second Coming. Bernice bonded with Sandy over teaching. They shared stories and complaints and wishes while Arun and I quietly ate some of the finest food I have ever been served. Conversation sailed effortlessly around the room, and more than an hour passed between the time dessert appeared and I finally begged to be excused, claiming a need to be at the airport early. Earl had called back to tell me that Pidge would deliver Doc by nine, along with all the tools and supplies required to restore the Navajo to flying condition. I told the ladies that I didn't need an early breakfast, but they threatened to kill me in my sleep if I didn't accept a plate before leaving the house. We agreed that I would show myself in the dining room at seven a.m.

Arun and I excused ourselves. We left the three women entangled in conversation. At the top of the stairs, I stopped him and asked if anyone had suggested routing the grant money through a local foundation.

"How did you know?" he asked. "The superintendent brought it up."

I explained what happened at breakfast.

"You think they sabotaged the plane to force us to give them the money? That's—well, it's stupid!"

"It was done at the same time they tried to get me to line my own pockets. Hedging their bets. How did the superintendent approach you?"

Arun squinted. "Looking back on it, he seemed squeamish. When he brought it up, he treated it as an afterthought, a simple paperwork issue. That it would be easier to make the grant to their local foundation, which isn't unusual, except they never brought up having a foundation before."

"Make sure Sandy doesn't get hooked in by it, okay?"

"There is no question about that." I turned for my room. "Will, tell me. What would have happened if we had taken off with the fuel contaminated?"

"Nothing good." His face lost a little color. "Good night."

* * * * *

When Sally showed me the rooms, I selected the one with a door that opened on a tiny second-story balcony. I wanted a way out of the house without drawing attention. A few minutes after midnight I stepped onto that balcony with a power unit and propeller in hand. The power unit had fresh batteries.

Quaint lights up and down the streets cast pools of illumination on empty sidewalks. The streets lay silent. Cars whispered by on a distant highway. Few vehicles rolled the tree-lined town avenues. None were of concern to me.

Fwooomp!

I vanished and flexed my ankles, immediately rising from the balcony. I gripped a gable overhang and used it to heave myself up and away from the house. Light warmed the first-floor windows and an upstairs hall window, but I attributed that to the ladies making sure that guests wandering about in the night didn't fall down a stairway. The exterior of the house wore the glow of a pair of spotlights, making it look magical.

A bat fluttered past me as I got my bearings and found the landmarks that would guide me.

Fifteen minutes and a few miles west of town, I found the

Redman farm set a quarter mile back from a two-lane county road. Four tall pole lights illuminated the farmyard, a sprawl of buildings, and a row of silos. Metal sheds and stock buildings formed a U shape at the back of a vast lawn. On the lawn, a two-story farmhouse sat beneath towering cottonwood trees. A traditional red wooden barn, twice the size of the one in my yard in Essex, dominated the property. The farmhouse had been added onto over the years. An original rectangle squared up to the road, but an annex crossed the T at one end. No effort had been made to preserve the original building's architecture. The annex looked like a duplex shoved up against the wall of the farmhouse. It had first floor and second floor entrances, with wooden stairs rising to the latter.

The farmhouse had a front porch across the entirety of the building. It might have been a pleasant place to enjoy an evening, except it had no furniture to extend a welcome.

I aimed for the front porch. Less than fifty yards from landing, a set of headlights swept across the face of the building.

Jason Redman's silver pickup rolled up the long gravel driveway. I altered course and went high over the house to the back yard. The pickup rolled past the house and parked in front of a metal shed. The headlights winked out. The vehicle remained closed and motionless.

I eased closer, pulsing the power unit to slow down until I hovered a few feet above the cargo bed. From inside the cab, I heard laughter. Two dark heads bobbed in the front seats.

The driver's door popped open, illuminating the cab. Jason Redman leaned out and fell to the gravel. He shrieked and laughed. Whiskey smell billowed from the cab.

"Dude! I think I fell out!"

"Are we still moving?"

The inquiry struck both men as the funniest thing yet. They laughed until they couldn't breathe.

A light came on at the back of the house. A dark figure moved behind one of the windows.

"Shutup! Shutup! You'll wake the old man!" Jason whispered.

Cousin-Brother in the cab threw his hand over his mouth, but his laughter came through his fingers along with flying spittle.

"I can't find the door handle."

Jason Redman tried to lift himself on his elbows. He collapsed and flopped back to the ground.

"Whoa. We're not moving. Everything else is moving." He spread his arms and extended his fingers for a grip on planet Earth.

You ain't seen nothing yet.

I pulsed the power unit and dropped to the side of the cab. Gripping the open door for leverage, I leaned down and grabbed Redman by the ankle.

"Watch this, asshole," I said.

FWOOOMP!

I pushed and he vanished, along with the weight I felt when I lifted his leg. I aimed the power unit straight up and took off with a tight left-handed grip on his ankle. I expected panic and flailing, but apparently the sensation of disappearing and going weightless didn't conflict all that much with what he was already experiencing.

I lifted him above the pickup and aimed for a barn at the center of the property. The building had a traditional four-panel roof with a cupola at the top. I maneuvered to the cupola at the center, then rotated until I had my drunken passenger face down over the peak of the roof. I let go. He dropped. Hard. His torso lined up with the center of the roof. His arms and legs splayed downward on both sides of the peak. His face bounced off the asphalt shingles.

"Ow!"

I eased closer and reached for his collar. Planting both feet on either side of his neck, I lifted his head.

"Look around." I twisted his collar to turn his head. "Do you see where you are?"

He huffed out a pair of deep breaths. More whiskey odor.

"Whuh?"

I released his collar. His face smacked the asphalt shingles again. He turned his head and vomited. Coughed. Heaved again. And again.

I let him go and pushed off to get away from the nauseating cloud.

"I wouldn't try to move if I were you. It's a long way down."

I left him clutching the roof. The power unit issued a low growl. I maneuvered back to the parked pickup truck. The driver's door remained open. The dome light showed Cousin-Brother slouched against the passenger-side window, passed out. Steady snoring rose from the cab.

I eased the door shut until the light faded out.

A screen door opened at the back of the house. A stout figure filled the frame, dark and hunched. I drew a bead on him but kept the power low and the prop spin inaudible. A glide across the grass took me to where the figure stood on a concrete stoop outside a screened porch. A shotgun hung in the crook of his right arm.

"Boys! Izz'at you?" The voice was deep and gravel laden. Thinning white hair topped his head. Drawing nearer, the features of a hard-edged face took form. His prominent nose showed signs of having been broken a lifetime ago. His eyes hauled heavy baggage. Gray stubble spread on his cheeks and neck. Folds of loose chin and neck flesh suggested that shaving might be a challenge. "Goddammit! If you're both drunk again I will kick your asses from here to Kingdom Come!"

I thought Jason might answer from the barn roof, but the night air remained still. The old man froze in the doorway, listening.

Grabbing a loaded weapon is as foolish as it gets. I harbor no illusions about being an action hero, and I readily recognize that the smooth moves I see in movies belong to carefully choreo-graphed stunt men. In real life, things go bad quickly. I settled on a different approach.

I eased up beside Buck Redman and closed a grip on the open screen door. He had the sense not to stand with his finger on the trigger. Poking my own finger into the trigger guard was easy. I jerked.

BANG!

The noise and flash startled both of us. I jumped. He jerked backward, tripped on the threshold, and tumbled through the door. He landed on his ass emitting a loud grunt before winding up on his back.

The shotgun dropped from his grip and clattered on the concrete. I reached down and picked it up by the warm barrel. The weight pulled me down until my feet planted on the concrete. With a wide outside swing, I flipped the weapon up and over my head. It whistled through the air for a moment, then thudded onto the farm-house roof. I heard it scrape on the shingles and realized how stupid I was going to feel when it came sliding off and hit me on the head. An aluminum clatter told me it ended up in the gutter.

Fwooomp!

I flashed into sight and stepped through the door. The old man, now huffing on his back on the mudroom floor, glared up at me.

"Who the fuck are you?"

A substantial table with a pair of wooden chairs sat below the windows to my right. I grabbed one of the chairs, spun it around and dropped it over his broad chest and belly. Two of the legs landed above his shoulders. He reached up to fight it off, but I dropped onto the chair, pinning him down.

"You owe me for a hundred and eighty gallons of Avgas."

He grabbed the chair and fought but had no chance. His face reddened and his breath grew short.

"Fuck you! Get offa me!"

"No."

He struggled, eyes bulging. I waited. He gave up lifting the chair and tried to pound my legs with balled fists. The angle was bad. The best he could muster were weak punches, easily ignored. The effort left him breathless.

"Are you done yet?" I asked.

Another curse mounted his lips, but he began coughing.

"I cuh-cuh-can't—breathe!" It was a bad acting job. I checked. The chair put no pressure on his chest or lungs. I didn't move. "Whaddya want, asshole?"

"I'm the asshole?" I asked, incredulous. "You know, your type is easy to spot but a real bitch to deal with. You're a liar so you think everyone else is a liar. You'll stoop to anything, so you think everyone around you is just as foul. Behavioral norms are for suckers. You can't be shamed. You can't be corrected. When you're caught, you deny and deflect. I suppose it might matter to you if I spent the night damaging your equipment the way you tried to damage mine. But that would just reaffirm for you that everyone else is just like you—something I truly hope never to be."

"What do you want?" His voice had the tonal quality of ground glass.

"I want you to give me a credit card. I'll use it to fill up my airplane with gas in the morning, then I'll toss it in the weeds. You can either go find it or call and have it cancelled."

He chuckled. "Go ahead. Take my wallet. I'll just cancel it the minute you leave here."

"Uh-huh. You can surely do that. And I can just as surely come back here for another visit."

"And I'll be waiting for you, shithead."

"Not if I put you in the hospital first."

"Then I'll have the cops waiting for you. What are you going to do about that?"

He had a point.

I let out a sigh and took a minute to look around the inside of the farmhouse. The place had a shabbiness I didn't expect. Not from one of the richest men in the county. Sally's rumors of financial trouble echoed in my mind.

"You wanted the Foundation to put the money in your hands. For what?"

The look on his face said that if he could have mustered the saliva, he would have spit at me.

"What do you care? If you think you're still getting a cut, you can go fuck yourself."

The mudroom had the usual coats hanging from wooden pegs, boots lined up against a wall, a hutch stuffed with pairs of gloves and dirty hats. A pile of mail littered the table. Discarded cardboard piled up in a green recycling carton.

I recognized labels on the boxes.

I leaned over and picked up a handful of the mail on the table.

"Leave that be!"

Ignoring him, I flipped through half a dozen unopened letters.

"You're in deep financial trouble. How's that possible?"

"You ain't no farmer, that's for sure. Goddamned city pussy, probably never got your hands dirty."

"I was picking stones when I was ten. What's this?" I held up one of the envelopes.

He squinted to read it. I held it in front of his face. He made out the lettering on the label, clamped his mouth shut and turned his head away.

"Are you sick?" The return address read Stanwick Medical Laboratories. I looked at the discarded boxes.

"Why don't you get the fuck outta my house. Take the goddamned credit card. Probably won't work anyway. Most of 'em are maxed out or cancelled already."

"You got any health insurance?" I asked, a little astonished by the turn of the conversation I was having with an old man I had pinned down with a chair.

He laughed. "What fucking country do you live in? Those vultures will take your money for a lifetime but turn around and ask them for dime one and you get a form letter full of diddly squat."

"Is that what the money is for? Cancer?"

"Says who?"

"Says that empty Bleomycin box over there."

He glared at me. "What do you know about it?"

"Bleomycin is a Glycopeptide antibiotic. I've seen it on charts in cancer treatment hospitals." I had. It was crazy that I remembered it, but my visits to such places came with abundant down time and waiting around, looking at charts and whiteboard notes and maybe trying not to look too closely at the patient in the room. Most often, I poked around while I waited for small children to fall asleep. I almost never visited rooms with men or women Redman's age.

"You don't know shit! Get offa me and get outta here!"

Wild eyes and a clot of foam at the corner of his mouth told me I had hit a nerve. I started to worry that much more of this might cause a sick old man more harm than I intended. I had come to make a point, and maybe do a little damage. Now I began to map a route off him and out the door. Chances were good he meant what he said about his credit cards and taking one wouldn't be worth the effort.

I was about to ease up and hop clear when I heard a child's voice.

"Grampa! Grampa!" Boy or girl, I couldn't tell. The voice young.

Redman's eyes filled with rage.

"Fucking get offa me right now! Right now!" The child's calls renewed Redman's strength. He grabbed the chair legs and tried to lift me. Lack of leverage stifled the effort, which only fueled his anger—a desperate, protective anger.

"Hey!" I flat-hand slapped him across the side of his face. "Knock it off."

"You hurt that kid and I will skin you alive. I will find you. I will take a week to do it," he threatened through clenched teeth.

"It's not you. It's the child."

He ceased struggling. The rage remained, but his eyes lost some fire.

From another room, the child called out. "Grampa! I heard a noise!"

"Lemme up," Redman pleaded. "Godammit, lemme up!"

"On two conditions."

"What?"

"You answer my questions. And you swear on the head of that child you won't fight me. I didn't come here to hurt anyone, not even a worthless shitbag like you."

"Fine. Lemme up!"

I reached down and grabbed him by the chin. "See. Now that's what I'm talking about. You think because you just said, 'Fine' you didn't actually swear to anything, so you've got a loophole, which becomes justification in your wormy head to betray your word."

The rage boiled up again, cut off by more cries from the other room.

"Okay! I swear."

"On the head..."

"I swear on the head of my grandson! Dammit!"

I let his chin go. The child called out again.

"I'm coming Leo!" the old man shouted. To me, he said, "Are you going to get your ass offa me?"

"First condition. You answer my questions. Are you broke?"

I didn't expect truth. He surprised me.

"The kid's medicine is forty grand a month. Everything is gone. Everything."

"Sell the damned jet or the 310."

He laughed without humor. "Gone last winter. Both of 'em."

"That's why you wanted the Foundation grant money. You were going to steal it."

"Borrow it. I'd'a paid it back."

"Then why the sabotage? That jet fuel might have killed us."

He clamped his jaw and looked away.

"On the head of that child…" I reminded him.

"Jack Snell has the paperwork. From blondie." I assumed he meant someone from the school district, someone under his thumb. "Something happens to you all on the way home…he changes the deposit information, okay? That's all. No big deal. It just goes from one foundation to another. No big deal."

"Except the part where we all die." I wanted to raise the chair and bring it down on his face.

"*Grampa, I'm scared!*"

"For the love of God, let me up! You want me to beg? I'll beg!"

I didn't want him to beg. I didn't want him to utter another word. I'm too aware that murder hides somewhere deep in my heart, testing its restraints, looking for a way out. I've felt it before. I felt it now.

"*Grampa! Please!*" Genuine fear cut deep in the tiny voice calling from the other room. The child began to cry.

"You're a monster!" Redman snarled at me.

I reached for the table beside me. I grabbed a leg and pulled it. A good farm table, probably a hundred years old, made of old hardwood you probably couldn't drive a nail into today. I heaved it toward me, swung it sideways. It took some twisting, but I moved it to parallel Redman's body.

In one swift move, I rose from the chair, kicked the chair aside, then reached for the opposite lip of the table and tipped it over onto him. He let out a harsh *oomph!* The weight landed on his chest. He grabbed and lifted to relieve the pressure. Using the same grip, he tried to slide it away. It moved in fractions of an inch. He would work it free eventually, but it would take time and effort.

"What are you doing? Stop! Leave him alone!" he wheezed at me as I walked into the house. "*Leave him alone!*"

Like nearly all old farmhouses, the mudroom opened into the kitchen, which opened into a dining room and eventually the front or living room. Antiseptic scent met my nostrils in the kitchen where I should have smelled bakery or meatloaf. I followed the scent to the dining room where a hospital bed replaced the family dining table—the table now resting on Buck Redman.

The boy sat up in bed clutching an oversized stuffed bear, one member of a menagerie that guarded the bed and the room. An IV stand dangled plastic tubes near the head of the bed. An expensive-looking and complex monitor blinked relentless data in one corner of the room. On a dark old chest of drawers where family photos should have honored family and ancestors, rows of prescription bottles and boxes of medical supplies told a sad story, but none so sad as the boy himself.

He cried. Tears glittered down his shallow cheeks. His bald head glowed as if illumination came from within and not from the Winnie the Pooh nightlight plugged into the wall above the chest of drawers.

He looked at me with a mix of relief and dread.

"*I wuh-wuh-want my g-g-grampa!*" He clutched the bear tighter. His arms were small, his knees knobby under thin pajamas adorned with flying superheroes.

Six. Maybe seven years old. I've learned to account for disease that makes a child appear years younger, smaller. I'd seen all this before, but it never stopped cutting a slice out of my guts.

"Grampa's moving some furniture," I said. I sat down on the

side of the bed. "He'll be along in a minute. Who are these guys?" I pointed at his shirt.

He looked where my finger pointed at cartoon characters with capes, but he said nothing.

"Can they fly?"

He nodded. Sobs made his shoulders bounce up and down.

"Would you like to fly?"

He nodded again.

"I promise this won't hurt. You're going to love it. Will you take my hand?"

He shook his head, firmly.

"Okay, but if you want to fly you have to hold on." I held out my hand. In the mudroom I heard a thud and the sound of wood scraping on wood. Redman wouldn't be long.

One tiny hand released its grip on the bear. Full of hesitation, he held it out for me. I gently closed my hand around his.

"Here we go!" I whispered.

Fwooomp!

* * * * *

Doc helped me fit the cowling over the engine. It took a little wiggling, but eventually the corners clicked into place. He adjusted the glasses on the end of his nose and went to work on the dzus fasteners, snapping them one by one with a stubby flathead screwdriver. The original deputy I spoke to sat in his cruiser, parked at the other side of the ramp, working his phone. The Navajo rested near the gas pumps, shining in the morning light. After clearing every possible drop of fuel from the system, Doc had me pour a few gallons into each tank. We drained it and then repeated.

With the cowls back in place, I thought we might be ready to fire up the engines. I wanted to be gone. Pidge, who had flown Doc in to perform the maintenance, had already loaded Arun and Sandy into the Essex County Air Service Piper Mojave. Sandy carried her valise, and in it the signed grant authorizations that directed one point seven million dollars into accounts belonging to the school district. The increased grant came as no surprise. Sandy's conversation with Bernice had gone well into the night, Arun informed me. When Pidge lifted the Mojave skyward, I watched them until my eyes lost their lock on the shrinking spec in the eastern sky.

"We're gonna flood her," Doc told me. "I want you to prime the shit outta both engines, then we'll crank 'em without ignition."

It made sense. The last of any possible contamination would be washed clean. I started to climb aboard when a familiar silver pickup rolled around the airport shack and past the parked deputy. Jason Redman, looking pale behind his dark plastic sunglasses, pulled up to a stop but made no move to leave the cab.

The passenger door opened. Buck Redman lowered himself from the pickup cab. In daylight he looked even older, but no less formidable. I glanced at the deputy to see if this development suspended whatever game he was playing on his phone. To his credit, he eased himself out of his cruiser.

I checked Redman's hands for weapons. They were empty. I examined his face for rage. That, he carried in abundance.

"I oughta knock you on your ass," he said. He closed the door to the pickup and balled his fists.

"You got enough pull in this county to do that in front of an on-duty deputy?" I asked.

He glanced at the uniformed officer approaching across the ramp.

"I do," Redman said. He waited for the deputy to arrive. "Morning, Darryl."

"Buck." The deputy said it laden with reserved judgment. "Something we can do for you?"

"I need a word with this..." *asshole* danced on his tongue "...fella."

"A civil word?" Darryl the Deputy asked.

"Unless he makes it otherwise," Redman said.

I held up both hands, palms out. "I'm good."

Doc, who had been gaping at this exchange, quickly said, "I'll crank it over, Will." He beat a path for the cabin door. I strolled toward the open ramp. Redman followed. The deputy leaned against the grill of the pickup and watched from a distance.

We stopped and faced each other at arm's length. I studied Redman. Fury. Hate. Pain. He seemed to do battle with himself.

"Before you knock me on my ass, you might take into account that I have not yet suggested to that deputy that somebody see whose credit card bought a load of jet fuel yesterday."

Redman glanced back at the figure slouched behind the wheel of the pickup. "If that boy had shit for brains it would be an improvement. I found him on the barn roof this morning, drunk as a skunk."

He turned back to face me. I waited.

The battle beneath Redman's skin played out. His mouth moved, chewing and tasting words before spitting them out.

"Leo asked for breakfast this morning." The hesitant words ran counter to the fury on his face. "A week ago, a doctor told me if the child didn't start eating, we would have to feed him with a tube." The alfalfa breeze slipped between us. I waited. "He asked for bacon and eggs. Then he asked for more."

I said nothing. The effect of *the other thing*, the thing that makes me vanish, on cancer cells in children is a stone-cold mystery to me. I don't know how it works. I only know that some-times—most of the time—making a child vanish makes the cancer cells vanish, too.

"He says he got to fly last night, all around the yard, like a bird."

I said nothing.

"I told him he had a dream. Funny thing about that dream—he

said he saw me stuck under a table when he flew out of the house and back in again. You know anything about that?"

My silence stoked his anger. He leaned at me with clenched teeth.

"I ever find out you hurt that boy…"

"Whatever you find out, Mr. Redman, you feel free to pay it in kind." I walked toward him until we were close enough to feel each other's breath on our faces. He clenched his fists. I didn't. "I got a plane to catch."

PAYMENT IN KIND
August 28, 2020 – September 4, 2020

Earl Jackson's
Last Mission

8

EARL JACKSON'S LAST MISSION

"Hey!" Earl Jackson's growl bounced off the walls of the big Education Foundation hangar and jarred me out of deep contemplation. I sat cross-legged under the left wing of the Piper Navajo, staring at the left main landing gear, specifically at the brake pads.

Earl pounded across the concrete ramp between the Essex County Air Service office and the Foundation hangar. He marched as he always did, bowlegged and determined, like someone looking to find out who just shot his dog—which made the case of beer in his hands slightly incongruous. That and the fact that Earl doesn't drink.

"You think these pads will make it to the annual?" I asked.

He dropped his leathery bald head beneath the leading edge of the wing.

"Nope." Another person would have had to duck under the wing and kneel in front of the landing gear for a closer examination. Not Earl. He could spot a loose rivet on the belly of a DC-3 flying a low pass.

"I was afraid of that. Did you bring me some cold beer?

Because it's only nine in the morning, so I'd have to take the rest of the day off to work on it. You can't approach day drinking half-heartedly."

"This ain't beer. Rosemary II says you're sitting around with your thumb up your ass until Thursday."

"I doubt she put it that way, but she's right about the schedule. What's up?"

"I need a favor." He dropped the box on the concrete floor. The absence of bottles clinking dashed my hopes of breaking Andy's general rule (a guideline, really) of not drinking before four in the afternoon.

I scooted forward and pulled myself upright.

"I want you to run this out to Montana for me." He tapped the box with one foot.

"What's in it? Or should I not ask?"

"Books."

"Okay…" I gauged the terrain ahead carefully, knowing there was more to the story. "You do know there's a whole worldwide apparatus for delivering packages to just about anywhere you want. They have airplanes and everything."

"I want to get 'em there today. This afternoon."

"Must be some pretty good books," I said, wondering if we were really talking about books or if the word was a euphemism for exotic snakes or stolen treasury bonds.

"I wouldn't know. I don't read this stuff. The author was in here with his Baron, getting an oil change. He left a set, signed and everything. I want to get 'em out to Montana."

"Signed, eh? You're not keeping them?"

"Why would I want 'em?"

"I don't know. What are they about?"

He looked at me the way he looks at anyone who asks him a question, except I had enough experience to know that despite the glare, I had not asked a dumb question. I didn't flinch.

"Beats the shit outta me. A couple of 'em got airplanes on the cover so they can't be half bad. I hear people like 'em."

Like many conversations with Earl, the deeper this one went, the more mystery enveloped it.

"Sure."

"Sure what? People like 'em? I just told you."

"Sure, I'll take 'em out to Montana. Can't say I'm thrilled. Last time I was there I wound up in an orange jumpsuit."

"Oh, for the love of Christ, please don't remind me. Every time I look sideways at the girl, Pidge tells me that story of how she saved your silly ass with a feat of aviating that would make Lindbergh's heart go pitter-patter." He squinted at me. "Come to think of it, though, I never did hear how you wound up on your ass in the middle of the road like that."

"Where in Montana?"

"Ekalaka."

"Jesus," I said, "it's a gigantic state full of legendary western towns, and it seems like that's the only name that ever comes up. Pidge subbed a flight for me and took Sandy and Arun there."

"Good. Then you know how to find it."

Rosemary II had the schedule right. I was free all day. The run to Ekalaka in the Navajo would take just shy of four hours. I could make it out and back in plenty of time before Andy finished her shift at eleven.

I looked at the beer case. Spotted Cow.

"Books, huh?" I let the question hang. It had the desired effect. I've known Earl Jackson for a while and come to know a few of his quirks and triggers. Not all. But a few that help turn a conversational minefield into a startling journey through the man's checkered past.

He shifted his stance slightly, turning to gaze out the hangar door at the light blue morning sky. Beyond the clear air and a first wisp of cirrus, he saw something distant.

"Well, I only been there once, and not voluntarily," he said. I remained silent. "I was in a Comanche. The one with the big engine. Fast little mother. I flew it outta TJ loaded to the roof with bales and boxes and plastic bags."

I gaped at him. "Jesus, Earl! You ran drugs?" This I never knew.

"I told you. Not voluntarily. There was this girl."

As so many stories begin.

"She owed this guy and I didn't like the guy, but I liked her and he had his hooks in her and I decided to do something about it— oh, hell, the details don't matter. What matters is that the sono-fabitch knew I was a pilot and he had just lost one of his pilots."

"Accident?"

"Mexican prison. He was short-handed with a load that needed to get up to Canada. And he had this Comanche set up with a big fuel tank where the front passenger seat was—you had to slide over the top of it to get to the pilot's seat. I don't know why they didn't do it the other way around, fer chrissakes! The thing had dual controls. Anyway, he had it rigged up so you could make it all the way from TJ up to Saskatchewan non-stop, with the cargo stuffed in the back. I agreed to make the trip if he let the girl off. As much as you can trust a slimy bastard like that, we had a deal. Plus, he didn't want the airplane back when it was done. I was a little broke at the time, having spent a few nights in a poker game that might not'a been on the up and up. Figured I could salvage out the plane once I got the stink of weed outta it. One trip. That was it."

"How does Ekalaka figure in all this?"

"Well, I run into some weather. One of those winter storms they give names to these days. Wouldn't'a been so bad but about the time I cut that eastern corner of Montana, the whole 'lectrical system blew. The windshield iced up and I had about an inch and a half on the leading edges. But that Comanche, it's such a sweet, clean bird, it just kept on flying. Only I had no idea where I was or how long it would stay in the air, and the notion of crashing that thing with a big fuel tank between me and the door didn't have much appeal."

"Understandable."

He scratched his scalp and shuffled his feet on the floor. "Guess I was also lost about that time. I mean—I knew I was over Montana—so that's not entirely lost. But I was at the point of thinking a runway would be nice to have under the wheels. There's a whole lot of nothin' up that way."

"I've seen it. Close up."

"Well, it was getting' dark, and the visibility was down to about a mile, which in that Comanche going a hunnerd'n eighty something, gave me about twenty seconds of visibility—and I was down below five hundred feet. So, I started looking at roads and I had this one road picked out, lookin' pretty good. I heaved that thing around to circle it and while I'm scoping out the road, I look straight down and what do I see? A friggin' runway! Middle of nowhere. I figured it might be a private strip or something, but I was beyond caring. The snow was coming down in sheets, so I dropped the gear, chopped the power and planted it."

"Miracles happen."

"A miracle would'a been stopping that overloaded bird before I slid off the end. I bounced it a couple times and when it settled down, I found out that the surface was slicker'n baby oil. Rode that thing right off the end into the weeds. Didn't seem like I broke anything, or so I thought. I was in a bit of a hurry to get out over that dumb fuel tank, but once I got outside it didn't look all that bad. I figured I could walk up to the other end of the strip and maybe find somebody to pull it back onto the runway. Couldn't see any buildings from where I was. It was really comin' down at that point.

"Well, just as I'm gettin' ready to strike out across the wilderness, this set of lights come bouncing across the terrain. Here comes this old GMC pickup, rolling through the snow in four-wheel drive. Outta nowhere. I don't know how, but they must'a been on the highway and seen me sledding through the weeds. This guy and his wife drive up and he rolls down the window and says, 'Need a hand?' like this sort of thing happens every day. And that's how I met Terry and Deb."

"That's who the books are for?" I was still curious as to why he didn't just ship them. And something else. "Didn't you say this was all years ago? Seems like a long-term debt."

"Yeah, well as I'm standing there explaining myself to these nice folks who probably shouldn't get mixed up with an airplane full of contraband, I caught a wiff of hunnerd low lead avgas. And by wiff, I mean to tell you, my first instinct was to run. I looked back and the fuel is flowing outta the aft baggage door. The fella, Terry, looks at me and says, 'You might not want to smoke around that thing.' Cool as can be. That stupid extra fuel tank had split—the damned thing was made from some kinda plastic—and was spraying all over the back of the cabin.

"Now aside from the obvious issue of blowing my ass to kingdom come, there was the side problem of contaminating the cargo, on which a couple of lives were depending. Mine being one of them. That Mexican cutie being the other. The owner of that cargo was waiting to hear from his clients that it had been delivered. How was I supposed to explain that it had been soaked through with high octane? Anybody lighting up that shit was going to get high in a hurry. Plus, I had a couple of what I assumed to be law-abiding strangers looking to tap the goodness of their hearts and drag my sad ass out of a jam. I couldn't be sure they wouldn't turn right around and fetch the local fuzz. I was getting' close to tossing a match on the whole shebang when ol' Terry says, 'I got some duct tape in the back if you want it.' And his wife says, 'He's real handy. He does a lot of work around town.' And those folks were just so forthright and sincere that right then and there I realized there might be a new lease on my life."

"So, he fixed you up, towed you outta the weeds and got you on your way?"

"That he did," Earl nodded to himself. "That he did."

"That's neighborly and all, but what about the cargo? The crappy fuel tank wasn't your fault, but I don't think of people like that much caring whose fault is what."

"Yeah, that might'a been a problem. I had a delivery schedule to meet, and that load was pure and simple ruined." Earl chuckled. "To this day I can't believe those folks didn't just wheel outta there and drive to the sheriff's office."

I waited a moment, watching Earl's face. The permanent scowl shifted slightly, assuming the contours of a self-contained argument. He struggled for a moment with the unsolved mystery embodied in the kindness of two strangers, then seemed to simply take it on faith once again, as he had that night in the heart of a winter storm.

"Anyway," he abruptly terminated his reverie. "Run this box out to Ekalaka. Nine seven mike. I'll call and let 'em know you're coming. Put the gas on the Essex card." He turned to begin his march back to his office.

"Whoa! You can't just leave me hanging like that!"

He stopped. He slowly turned back to me. A curl at the end of his lips told me I'd been had.

"You want to know how I avoided a Mexican neck tourniquet?"

"Damn, boss. I know you can get yourself outta just about anything, but it's the *how* that makes the story interesting."

He shrugged.

"Wasn't me. Was Terry and Deb. Oh, he was handy, alright. They towed me back outta the weeds and all the way up the runway back onto that little airport ramp. Ekalaka. You've been there."

"Not me. Pidge."

"Terry helped me patch up that tank and drain the gas outta the fuselage. He got right down on the ramp with a portable drill and cleared out all the drain holes. I thought we'd blow ourselves up any second, but he was as calm as lazy river about it. Then they helped me unload the cargo. Soaked through, it was. We put it all in the back of their pickup and drove it over to the airport perimeter and dumped it out. Terry took an old rag and sopped some of it up, then lit the rag and tossed it from a safe distance. Even so, that pile went up with a whoosh that liked to take off a person's eyebrows.

"And there we stood, warming ourselves in the middle of a blizzard as that heap of weed went up in smoke. We all stood upwind, of course."

"Of course. But what did you do about the customer waiting at the other end?"

Earl slipped a sly look over the granite crags of his face. "See, now that's the thing about folks like Deb and Terry. She being a teacher, she's as smart as he is handy. I was looking a little down-hearted, thinking about my predicament, and without really notic-ing, they sorta dragged the whole story outta me. Down to the Mexican cutie—although I left out some of the details pertaining to her special skills. Before I know it, Deb's making plans and giving orders. She gave ol' Terry a shopping list. Plastic bags. Clear tape. Rolls of aluminum foil. A stop at some horse farm near where they live. And a stop at home to bring back a meat grinder. Off he goes while she called up somebody running an ag operation on the field. Next thing I know, we're set up in that ag hangar."

"A meat grinder?"

"Yup." He said it like I was an idiot not to realize every good story should have a meat grinder.

I folded my arms and planted my feet. "C'mon, boss. A meat grinder?"

That curl of the lip showed again. He was enjoying this.

"Terry showed up half an hour later, around the time I started warming up and could feel my hands and feet again. He rolled into that hangar with all the shopping list items and two bales of hay from the horse farm."

"And?"

This time Earl let loose the whole grin.

"And those kind folks spent the next six hours in that freezing hangar with me grinding up second-cutting alfalfa and packing it in plastic bags and aluminum foil until I had a load of weed the DEA would have given an eye to confiscate. Pure, one-hundred percent alfalfa. By dawn they had me gassed up and loaded up, and that storm thinned out and off I went."

"You can't be serious," I protested. "The customer had to know."

"Oh, those guys were dumb as a box of rocks. Amateur hour. They loaded it all up and took off like the Mounties were going to show up at any second. Eventually they figured it out—and weren't too happy. They expressed their displeasure by putting the supplier out of business. Permanently. Which let that little girl off the hook once and for all."

"Which made you her knight in shining armor," I said. "You never mentioned her. What happened?"

"She went to Mexico City and became a doctor. Seems appropriate. That girl knew a lot about anatomy."

I gave Earl a minute to enjoy a memory that I dearly hoped he wouldn't share.

"And you stayed in touch with the folks that helped you? Terry and Deb?"

"Nope. Never saw 'em again."

I blinked. "Now you're confusing me. What about the books?"

"Oh, those. Yeah, I told you. The guy who writes them brought his Baron in for an oil change. We got to talking, round about. Turns out his sister lives out that way with her husband. Got some kinda dude ranch or something. Ekalaka. You don't forget a name like that. I asked outta the blue if he thought his sister might know a couple named Terry and Deb. The guy laughed. He said everybody out there knows Terry and Deb—and he even knew about them because his sister mentioned that they like his books. And here I thought I was something special."

I looked down at the box. "So, you bought them some books? From the guy who wrote them?"

"Oh, hell no. He gave them to me. Kinda full of himself—handing out books he's written. Signed 'em, too. Like that might make them worth something someday. I figured this was as good a way as any to get rid of the damned things. Eight of them, fer chrissakes. What'm I gonna do with 'em?"

"Right," I said, thinking Earl was about to burn a few hundred gallons of expensive aviation fuel hand-delivering signed copies of a set of books to someone he'd met once just so he didn't have to buy a bookshelf.

"You make sure they get there safe." He turned and marched off. Without looking back, he said, "If you happen to see those folks, tell 'em Thanks!"

EARL JACKSON'S LAST MISSION
July 16, 2020

Pidge

9

PIDGE

We had something like ten straight days of high winds starting in early March and ending after St. Patrick's Day. The parade in Essex caught the last of it but the revelers soldiered on despite green crepe paper shamrocks flying off farm wagon floats. Essex County does not have a strong Irish contingent. The ethnic makeup leans toward central Europe. Lots of people of German, Polish and Baltic descent. But on that special day in March, everybody musters a little green in the bloodline, largely for the excuse to drink and welcome spring, even if nature kicks up a snowstorm or two before winter is said and done.

The winds plagued me in their own special way, making each flight I piloted for the Christine and Paulette Paulesky Education Foundation a rough ride. On two separate occasions, ATC issued a hold at the destination. Neither hold lasted very long, but even after just one circuit, Arun turned a little green around the gills. When we landed, he concentrated on his breathing and said almost nothing. I felt bad for the guy. He powered through his day of meetings and school tours both times.

The day of the second incident Pidge walked over to the Foundation hangar after punching the clock at Essex County Air. She wore her white uniform shirt and black tie under her leather flight jacket. She found me at my old desk in the hangar.

"Your main squeeze took off already," I told her. "We had a rough ride to and from Bloomington and he did not do well."

She slid onto the corner of my desk. "Did he blow chunks?"

"Nope."

I expected the conversation to end quickly, and Pidge to take off after Arun for an evening of solicitous nursing. She remained planted on my desk.

"Why are you out in the hangar? It's fucking cold out here."

"I like the atmosphere. I wasn't planning on spending the night." I had finished my logbook entry just as she arrived. I slapped the cover shut. "See? All done."

She didn't move.

"Something I can do for you?"

Pidge found fascination in the seam of her black pants. She ran an unpainted fingernail up and down the stitch line. Locks of her short golden blonde hair draped her cute twenty-something face. Pidge has blue eyes that resemble cut crystal and she is not afraid to aim them at friend or foe with equal intensity, but at this moment she fixed them on her fingernail.

"I've got a thing…"

"There's an ointment for that."

Instead of the four-letter response that my comment deserved, she said nothing.

Pidge speechless. The condition alarmed me.

I leaned back in my chair. "What's going on?"

"It's a family thing."

"Jesus. You're pregnant?"

This brought out the f-bomb I expected. "Fuck no. I'm not pregnant. Are you?"

"Do I look pregnant?"

"Now that you mention it, you do have a certain glow about you," she said.

"That's my luminous personality. I use it to guide ships at sea. Spit it out, Pidge. What's on your mind?"

She slid off the desk and took a few steps to the open airstair door of the parked Piper Navajo. She turned and sat on the second step and clasped her hands together between her knees.

"My dad died."

"Jesus."

One word was as far as I got. In an instant, she transformed. She became a little under five feet of blonde girl, someone's daughter, looking lost inside the cracked shell of her hotshot pilot persona and her signature toughness. It was like seeing one of those images that are two things at the same time, the kind that flash back and forth as you stare. I felt a nearly overwhelming urge to give her a hug, for which she was equally likely to punch me or hug me back.

"I'm so sorry. What happened?"

She released a single huffed laugh. "Fucking chemistry, is what. My dad's been dying for years. I guess taking his last breath made it official."

I found myself tallying up what I knew about Pidge.

In the eight-plus years I'd known her, I never heard her mention family. She started flying at Essex County Air when she was sixteen. She graduated early from high school—something about skipping a grade. I knew she had her own apartment. She lived and breathed aviation. I never thought about her having a home and family.

I felt bad for not showing more interest. I gave her a moment to fill in the blanks or leave it lie.

"I need a favor."

"Anything."

"You might not want to say that so fast. There's some legal bullshit. I was wondering if you'd go with me."

"Absolutely. Tell me where and when. I'll meet you there."

She shook her head. "My folks live—lived—up in a nowhere junction northwest of Spooner. That's where I grew up."

"Okay. I completely thought you were from Essex."

"No. I just finished high school here." A dozen questions came to mind. I held them at bay when she did not elaborate.

"You want me to go up to Spooner with you?"

"Burnett County. That's closest. Yeah. Will you?"

"Of course. When?"

"The funeral's on Saturday."

"I'm open Friday, if you prefer to get there sooner."

"Christ, you work fucking banker's hours. Nah. I got a trip on Friday. We'll leave Saturday morning."

"We can take this if you like." I gestured at the Foundation's Navajo. "Sandy doesn't care. In fact, for you, she'd insist."

"Works for me."

"Are you asking Arun to come along?"

"Fuck, no." She shook her head. "Fuck. I can't imagine."

"You're not, uh, at that stage yet? The 'meet the family' stage?"

"We will never be at that stage," she declared. Pidge has a vigorous and colorful sexual history. Since becoming enthralled by Arun last summer, she seemed to reign in her lascivious leanings. Arun was head over heels for her, but now I wondered if she did not reciprocate his serious and somewhat formal intent.

"Okay. Have you told Arun that?"

Pidge looked at me like I'd just said something stupid. "What? No. Oh—you got it wrong. It's not about Arun. Well—I guess it is, in a way. But no. It's my mother. I'll never take him anywhere near her. She's a raging racist bitch. See you Saturday."

She jammed her hands in her flight jacket pockets and walked off.

* * * * *

"I don't know," I told Andy when she dropped beside me on the sofa. The lights were low. I hit the mute button on the television remote. Dinner warmed in the oven, something with a curry accent. I took a guilty sip of Corona because Andy declared she would wait to have hers with dinner. "I don't know why she wants me there. What the heck do I know about wills or estates or legal crap? She'd be far better off taking Arun. That guy's a lawyer in everything but license."

"Do you think she really meant it? About her mother?" Andy has a long and contentious history with her own mother. It was not a stretch for her to nurture empathy with Pidge.

"She called her a 'raging racist bitch.' That doesn't sound like a healthy mother-daughter relationship to me. Showing up with a British gentleman of Indian descent might put the family pot on boil. Especially with Arun's permanent suntan."

"That doesn't seem like something she should hide," Andy said. "Not if she's serious about the relationship."

"It's crazy, but in that ten-minute conversation I learned just how much I don't know about that girl."

"Woman."

"What?"

"You always call her a girl. She's a woman. You need to catch up. You met her when she was in high school and she is short and she looks like she's fifteen, but she's not a girl, she's a woman."

Another mine in the marital minefield mapped.

"You should come along." I instantly warmed to the idea of Andy insulating me from Pidge's family drama.

"She didn't ask me. Besides, I have choir practice on Saturday afternoon." Andy had recently caved to the church choir director's long-running campaign to get her to join. My wife has a beautiful singing voice and regularly attends the small Presbyterian church near us, but her attendance is not out of religious fervor. Church, she once told me, is a bubble in which people at least pretend to care for one another, a salve to the darker side of humanity she finds in her job. I tend to see more pretending than caring, but I keep my mouth shut.

"Are you okay with me going?"

Andy shrugged. "Of course. She needs you. When do you think you'll be back?"

"God willing, Saturday night. But..."

"Oh, I know, I know. Don't make any plans for Sunday." I felt an impulse to apologize. She read it and patted me on the thigh. "It's fine. Go. I'll take your suit to the cleaners tomorrow."

"I gotta wear a suit?"

"It's a funeral, Will."

"Crap."

* * * * *

Pidge made me plan, file and fly the trip to Burnett County Airport. She kept me waiting on the ramp for twenty minutes past our anticipated departure time of ten a.m. As soon as I started the engines, she curled up in the back under a blanket. I suspected her of administering alcohol to her grief the previous night. My suspicions were confirmed when she tapped into one of the onboard oxygen bottles, taking a few strong hits while I taxied for takeoff.

Despite hints of a late night, she had applied some extra effort to her appearance. I detected more than her usual absence of makeup. Nothing overtly enticing, but enough to give accent to her eye color. Her lips carried a shade of gloss that approached red without putting on dancing shoes. She wore all black—neatly creased pants under a black turtleneck sweater covered by a black raincoat. The combination turned her blonde hair into a beacon.

I had questions, but we exchanged zero conversation during the flight. She didn't put on headphones and either fell asleep shortly after lifting off Runway 31 or she pretended to.

She didn't stir until I shut down the engines on the small ramp at Burnett County Airport.

"What time is it?"

"Eleven forty-five. Are we on a schedule?"

She sat up and stretched. I try not to notice these things, especially around my wife, but whatever Pidge decided to wear under that sweater nicely enhanced her figure, something she doesn't do when dressed for her job. Between that, the makeup, and the outfit, I put myself on notice that Pidge had returned to her roots with something to prove.

"We have to be at the lawyer's office at one-thirty."

"Is that when the whole family is meeting?"

"No. They got the bad news about an hour ago." She opened the cabin door. "I'll go get us a car and then let's get some lunch." She popped the door and stepped down to the ramp before I could ask the question.

What bad news?

* * * * *

Pidge obtained the use of one of two courtesy cars maintained by the airport manager. I secured the airplane. Pidge waited for me in the FBO office with keys in hand. I used the restroom, then followed her out to a silver Ford Crown Victoria.

"You didn't bring an overnight bag, so I assume we're not staying overnight." I climbed in the passenger seat.

"God forbid," she said. She cranked the car over and we set off. I settled in for the scenery.

Pidge turned onto State Highway 35. We rolled north into Webster where I thought she might stop for lunch at The Tap Bar & Grill on Main Street. When that didn't catch her eye, I figured we'd be eating Italian at a place called Zia's on the north end of the five-block town. Pidge kept rolling.

We cruised out of Webster into open country. I lowered my expectations of eating anytime soon until she abruptly turned into the parking lot of the Yellow River Saloon & Eatery. Half a dozen cars populated the lot, which spoke well of the place. A small patio joined the one-story building. The outdoor furniture had been retired for winter.

I followed Pidge into a cozy Wisconsin bar and, as the sign promised, eatery. The bar lined two walls of one room, sharing space with high top tables. An adjoining room featured seating for dining with simple, functional tables and wooden chairs. Roughly half of the available seating was taken. Another good sign.

Pidge chose a table along one wall. She pulled off her coat and tossed it on the chair beside her. I wore my flight jacket over my suit jacket, which looked stupid but kept me warm. My flight jacket went over the back of my chair.

"Andy made me wear a suit," I said, seating myself.

"I see that. And you wore your other tie."

"Only the best for you."

She handed me a laminated menu card from a rack between the salt and pepper and the ketchup and mustard.

A young woman appeared beside the table. She wore jeans and a Green Bay Packers sweatshirt but the order pad and pen in her hand conveyed her official standing. I guessed her to be around Pidge's age, at least six inches taller, and double Pidge's weight.

"Is that—?" She threw her hands to her hips. "Is that you, Cassie? Omigod! Omigod! I can't believe it's you!"

"Hi, Brenda," Pidge said, not smiling. Pidge wasn't wrong. The tag above the woman's left breast confirmed Brenda's name.

"Omigod omigod omigod! How are you? I haven't seen you— oh, God, I can't believe how long it's been. Like, since junior year, right?" Brenda's round face lit up with a wide grin that immediately winked out. "Oh! I'm so sorry to hear about your dad!"

"Thank you."

"Are you staying with your mom?"

"I'm just here for the day. For the funeral."

"You should come by here later," Brenda said. "Some of Cindy's friends are usually here on Saturday nights."

"I don't think we'll be staying." Brenda turned a steady gaze on me. Without missing a beat, Pidge added, "This is my husband, James Patterson. He's a writer."

Brenda put out her hand, which I shook.

"Nice to meet you," Brenda smiled. "Where do you two live now?"

I let Pidge answer.

"New York most of the time."

"Wow. New York. Nice. Cassie, what are you doing? Did you ever go fly airplanes?"

"I'm a training captain for Delta Airlines. I teach the new first officers on the 757 routes to Europe. Heathrow. Le Bourget. That sort."

"That sounds cool," Brenda said, blinking to signal that she had no idea what that meant. "So, what can I get you two?"

* * * * *

"Is that what this is?" I asked after Brenda had taken our order. "The cliché prodigal daughter returns to stick it in the face of the people she left behind?"

Pidge shrugged. "How was I supposed to know she'd be there?"

"Bullshit," I said. "You passed a couple other places to pick this one. We're here because you knew."

"I didn't *know* she'd be here. Not for sure. She worked here when I was in high school. Hung out with my sister. Christ, that was eight years ago."

"I'm sure she's Instagramming all her friends what you just said."

"Maybe."

"Maybe, my ass. That was the point. Well, you better hope she doesn't whip out her phone for a selfie with us, because I don't look anything like James Patterson."

"Really?" Pidge squinted at me. "I don't know. Is your hair getting thinner?" She gave up the first wispy smile of the trip.

"Funny. Not here, but when we get back in the car, it's time for you to fill me in."

"Fine."

* * * * *

"What did you mean when you said 'chemistry' caused your dad's passing?"

"Death. Chemistry caused his death."

Pidge drove. I sat and wished I hadn't ordered the onion rings. They were good. I just shouldn't have ordered them.

"Okay. Death."

"My dad worked for Ontonagon Mining & Mineral. He was a chemical applications engineer. A fancy way of saying he helped big mining companies poison the earth using chemicals to extract certain types of minerals. You know, like the way arsenic was used in gold mining. But, along the way, he managed to poison himself as well as the earth. He was a loyal soldier, however, and he would have gone quietly into disability, but some environmental lawyers from Washington, D.C. took up the case."

"His case?"

"Shit, no. The lawyers were after Ontonagon. My dad just got carried along. They needed a poster child. I don't know much about it. The whole thing started ages ago. I was, like five. About ten years ago, the company settled. By that time, dad was fully disabled. The lawyers did everything. By the end, they had him in their top category for damages. Don't ask me how it worked, but it got him a fat payout. Which was the nail in the coffin for this family."

"The settlement?"

"Yeah." She glanced at me from the driver's seat. "Money. My mother wanted it. My sister wanted it. My dad wanted me to take my share, which I didn't give a shit about, and I never asked for. Dad pissed everybody off because he didn't choose to take a lump sum payout, like seven figures. Instead, he opted for a fifty-year payout. Holy shit, did that go over like a lead balloon."

"Fifty years. How old was he when all this happened?"

"About your age when he first got sick, but that's not the point. He didn't have fifty years left. They gave him ten. He lasted nineteen. Surprised everybody."

"He was kinda screwed on that payout decision."

"Not the way he did it. The benefit went to him or his heirs, whichever he designated. He set it up for fifty percent to be divided between my mother and my older sister, Cynthia. And fifty percent to go to me."

"Ah. I begin to see the issue."

"I had nothing to do with it. This all happened when I was fourteen. Dad sent me to live with his sister in Essex. The money went into a trust for living expenses, and for flying lessons. Dad knew flying was my dream since I was a little girl. As soon as I turned eighteen, I filed for emancipation from my parents. My mother fought it because she knew it would put my part of the settlement money completely out of reach. And that's where good ol' Brenda and her friends come into the picture. Bitch."

"Pray tell."

"My mother hired a lawyer to fight the emancipation. My dad hired a lawyer to help me."

"Is that who we're seeing today?"

"Yup. So, to make a case against me, my sister convinced Brenda and her friends to trash me. How's that for a family?"

"Trash you? As in…'she takes twelve items to the ten-item checkout'?"

"As in I was whoring out of my dad's fishing cabin, doing drugs, all kinds of shit talk."

"Wow. I'm surprised you didn't punch her lights out."

"I did. Once. That only made things worse. All that happy-crappy back there, that was all bullshit. I fed her all that baloney because I knew she'd yap it all over town."

"Is this the first time you've been back here?"

"Affirmative."

"Holy crap. But you stayed in touch with your dad, right?"

She shook her head. "No. Dad sent me away and cut me off. Not from the money. I get a direct deposit every month. But he never spoke to me after that. My online bank statement is my loving family."

She knew the question I wasn't asking. I stayed quiet until she felt compelled to answer.

"Because he didn't want me to see him go that way. And he knew he would wind up in my mother's care, and he didn't want me to see that either. He knew my mother would try to guilt me into taking on that burden. He refused to have anything to do with me."

"Jesus."

"Jesus didn't pitch in, either."

I let her put another mile under the Crown Vic's tires before I asked, "So, I get the part about the lawyer and the funeral. Is that all we're doing here?"

Pidge didn't answer.

I thought about the intense, driven girl who showed up at Essex County Air asking how to become a professional pilot. Few students I ever taught had been so focused, so prepared for each lesson. Pidge scored ninety-eight percent on her private pilot written exam, the highest of any student I ever taught. Given the distractions available to a teenaged girl, I expected her interest to peak and wane at any time. Pidge never let up.

I had no idea what genuine distractions she had overcome.

* * * * *

The lawyer kept his office in a two-story Craftsman one block off Main Street in Danbury, an unincorporated town sporting a post office, a Dollar General, Amelia's Café & Bakery and a four by three grid of sparsely populated town blocks. Buttressing the main street, the St. Croix Casino stood where Highway 35 flowed into Highway 77, and the Yellow River flowed into the St. Croix. A well-shellacked hand-carved sign hanging in the lawyer's front yard advertised, *Robert Cheney, Attorney-at-Law.*

Attorney Cheney greeted Pidge with a warm and welcoming smile.

"Cassidy, so good to see you again!"

"Hi, Mr. Cheney," Pidge replied. "If you say, 'My, how you've grown!' I will turn right around and leave."

Cheney, a healthy-looking man with a rich and well-styled head of pure white hair, bowed slightly.

"I will utter no such cliché, Ms. Page. Please come in."

Pidge performed an introduction, this time giving my real name and the brief description of 'friend and colleague.'

"Do you fly, Will?"

"I do, sir," I replied. The sir attached itself automatically. Cheney had a formal and somewhat commanding presence. He did not object.

"Will was my flight instructor," Pidge added. "He still gets on my case when I don't do things his way."

"We never stop learning," Cheney ushered us into a tidy house full of antique furniture and well-maintained woodwork. He led us into an office that might have once been the dining room. He offered coffee or tea. I accepted a mug of coffee. Pidge passed on both. He fetched the coffee from a pot already brewed in his kitchen. I made a quick guess that he lived here alone.

Cheney gestured us into a pair of leather wingbacks facing a polished mahogany desk. He seated himself and folded his hands on an empty blotter with leather corners. We spent a few minutes trading pleasantries. Cheney inquired about Pidge's health and career, about where she lived. He seemed pleased with her successes. He did not mention her father's passing or express condolences.

"To business, then," he said. "I must first tell you, Cassidy, that you are not welcome at your mother's home today."

"Well, don't spare Pi—er, Cassidy's feelings, Mr. Cheney."

Cheney smiled at me, the equivalent of a patronizing pat on the head for jumping to Pidge's defense. "Please don't misunderstand. Mrs. Page instructed me to pass that along to her daughter—in not those words, precisely—after I met with the family this morning. The sentiment was considerably less cordial. Your father's will, as I forewarned Cassidy, was not well-received."

"I don't really give a flying fuck," Pidge said. "And I want to tell you, Mr. Cheney that I really don't care what my dad did with whatever he had left."

"Well, as I mentioned on the phone, the only item to which you are named is the lake property."

"And as I told you, I don't give a shit. Do I have to take it?"

"You do. You do not have to keep it if you are not inclined to do so. However you plan to proceed, there is a stipulation that you will have to deal with. The cabin was left to your mother and sister."

"Well, then, just give them the rest of it. I don't want it."

"It doesn't quite work that way."

"This is some bullshit. I wish Dad would have just sold it."

"I understand your feelings, Cassidy, but your father was fond of the property. He had good memories of you there with him. He said so when we wrote his will." Pidge didn't respond. I caught a damp glitter filling her eye. "Cassidy, you should know that this will was written when your father moved you to Essex. He told me at the time why he wouldn't see you and he never wavered. He never altered the will."

"Fuck." She sniffled loudly, then plucked a tissue from a box on Cheney's desk. She blew her nose. "Sorry."

"Don't be sorry. Your dad cared a great deal for you. I spoke to him often over the last few years. He always talked about you but made me promise never to speak to you about him. About how he had deteriorated."

Pidge spilled tears onto her cheeks. She wiped them away with her sleeve.

"Fuck this."

"If you don't mind my asking, sir, is this bequest the thing that has her mother's hair on end?"

"Among many things," Cheney said. Cheney picked up a fat envelope and handed it across the desk to Pidge. "Your father left the cabin to your mother and sister, but he left the land in your name, Cassidy. It's all in here."

"I still don't get how that's supposed to work."

"Simple. You own the land. Your mother and sister own the cabin and have a right to its use for as long as it remains standing."

"They hated that cabin."

"Perhaps that was the point. Regardless, they have no right to build, expand or rebuild it without your permission. You, however, can use or develop or sell the land as you wish. It's all in there, along with copies of the registered deed and a *pro forma* lease that applies to the cabin. And there are, of course, no changes to the settlement disbursement from Ontonagon."

"I get why you're not invited to the house for finger sandwiches," I said. "Can her mother fight any of this?"

Cheney shook his head. "She tried. A few years ago, your mother and sister hired a lawyer from Minneapolis to try and usurp your father's original agreement with Ontonagon Mining, but it was a costly effort that didn't go anywhere." Cheney did not hide his satisfaction.

"I didn't know that," Pidge said.

"Something else your father did not wish to share."

Pidge gathered herself. "Is that everything, Mr. Cheney? Because we should be going. The funeral starts at three."

Cheney's brow furrowed.

"I'm sorry, but—the funeral was this morning." Dawning awareness came from reading the bewildered look on Pidge's face. "They didn't tell you? Of course, they didn't. I'm so sorry. I only heard about it when they asked to move the reading to nine a.m."

"It doesn't matter," Pidge lied. "I do have one last question. Did my dad specify what he wanted done with his remains?"

"He did."

* * * * *

Maybe it was Pidge's stark comment about "whoring" that prompted the image, but her mother's house oozed the impression of a streetwalker clinging to her prime with heavy makeup and gaudy apparel. One of a cluster of homes that seemed to have randomly fallen around a highway junction, the Page home wore siding that looked new, but had not been precisely applied. The windows appeared new but were of cheap clad vinyl. The railings and posts supporting a wide front porch wore fresh paint, but the steps needed replacing. Despite the kind of lean that irritates my too linear eye, the garage had also received new siding. Thanks to the lean, the corners did not join squarely. On any other day, I would have looked for the customary abandoned vehicle in the yard, but on this day the driveway and parts of the road contained a parked parade of vehicles, most of them pickup trucks.

Confederate stars and bars hung limp from the eaves.

Against all better judgment, we departed the Crown Vic a hundred yards down the road and walked to the house on the pavement. I read the bumper stickers on the pickup trucks with growing unease.

"What no Nazi flag?" I muttered as I followed a determined Pidge up the driveway.

"They save that for tattoos."

"You serious?"

"As a heart attack. You'll see."

We made it as far as the porch steps before the front door opened. A woman dressed in black stepped onto the porch. She looked as if she had been made with the same bones as Pidge, but then stretched several inches taller which pulled the skin tighter on a sharp chin and stark eye sockets. The net effect removed any warmth and humor from her face.

"That's far enough."

Pidge stopped. "I'm here for dad's ashes, Cyn."

"Are you, now?" The words came from an equally thin man wearing black jeans and a black t-shirt who stepped up behind Pidge's sister. Pidge wasn't wrong about the tattoos. He had them on his neck, arms, and the backs of his hands. I didn't have to study beyond the swastikas above each collar bone to understand both his politics and his IQ. Nor did I need to guess his habits after one glimpse of his dental work. "Well, you can go fuck yourself."

"Nice to see you, too, Bruno."

"And take your snooty writer husband with you," Cynthia Page gestured at me. I caught Pidge fighting a smirk.

Two more t-shirt and tattoo models slipped out the front door and flanked Cynthia and the man I took for her husband, given the way he put his hand at the back of her neck and locked a possessive grip.

"Dad wanted his ashes spread at the lake," Pidge said calmly.

"That's not what he told Mom," Cynthia said. "Between the drooling and the incoherent babbling at the end, that is. 'Course, you wouldn't know anything about that, would you? Or his screaming fits. Or how he would poop and piss himself. 'Cuz you left all that to us, bitch."

I readied myself to grab Pidge before she flew up the steps with her claws out. The black-clad twins on either side of Pidge's sister and her husband flexed and folded their arms. I resisted the temptation to roll my eyes.

"Dad wanted his ashes spread at the lake," Pidge repeated. "I came to see that it's done."

An older version of Cynthia slipped out the front door. She had bright blonde hair, but not the natural golden color God had given her daughter. Her do radiated an off-the-shelf yellow hue. Like her older sister, Pidge's mother shared Pidge's features, but in a gaunt and lifeless way. She had the slightly fanatic look of a devout evangelical who is prepared to kill if that is what's necessary to spread God's love.

"Aren't you going to introduce us to your husband, Cassidy?" the woman asked.

"I'm not married," Pidge said. She held up her ringless left hand. "He is. I'm not. Whoever told you that is a fucking idiot."

"Running around with a married man?" Cynthia asked. "Oh, my."

"I am married," I said. "I'm accompanying your daughter because the jet she flies requires a first officer. It's a Gulfstream G-five. Belongs to Lonnie Penn. Ms. Page is the captain. I'm the FO, ma'am. Name's Lindberg. Chuck Lindberg."

"Izzat Jewish?" one of the two idiots asked.

"Proletarian."

"Your father's wishes were that his remains should be kept here, Cassidy," her mother said. "They're here. They're safe. Would you like to see?"

Mrs. Page pasted a smile on her lips and swept an extravagant gesture toward the front door. A cluster of faces watched from inside. More stood at the windows. I deeply and sincerely wished that Pidge would decline, and we would be on our way.

"Fuck yes," the petite tornado beside me said. She marched forward. I clenched my jaw and followed. Her mother led the way.

There were fewer people in the house than I expected. Five or six men and only two women that I could see. The home had a thick atmosphere that was not helped by cigarette smoke and the scent of half a dozen open pizza boxes on a dining room table to the right of the front door. A tapped beer keg occupied one corner of the same room.

Mrs. Page led us into a large sitting room with a fireplace. She stopped at the fireplace and performed a Vanna White hand gesture at a small cardboard box tied with a string. The box sat on the mantle.

I might have stared at what looked like a takeout carton full of human remains if not for the portrait hanging behind it.

The Standard Bearer.

I knew the name. I don't recall how. The artist signed his work in the lower right corner. Hubert something; I ignored the last name. The painting, not particularly good, showed a man in knight's armor on the back of a horse. The man held a flag I'd seen far too much of recently—red with a white circle and a black swastika in the center. The bad hair. The silly moustache. And the ghastly meaning behind it all stunned me. Here it was, framed above a mantle in an American home. I wondered how many boys of military age from this part of Wisconsin died trying to rid the world of the plague this print represented. I wondered what those boys would say about their neighbors today.

"Isn't that guy dead?" I said, wondering why in hell I could not keep my mouth shut.

"He will rise again!" someone barked at me. I didn't look for the shouter.

I turned and closed a grip on Pidge's upper arm. "I think that your mother is not wrong about your dad's remains being safe. It's time for us to go."

Please don't fight me on this.

I tried to meet Pidge's eyes and convey to her that we weren't the only two people in that room. Her sister and a squad of hillbilly stormtroopers surrounded us. A few of them took a step closer.

Under my grip, Pidge tensed, ready to pull away.

"Cassidy," I said, "you don't need to be concerned about *things you cannot see.*"

"This is bullshit," Pidge said. "This has always been bullshit."

"That kind of talk is not welcome in this house," Mrs. Page said stiffly.

"Oh, fuck that, Mother, as if that *thing* over the fireplace isn't an obscenity."

Mrs. Page's face reddened.

"We were just going," I said loudly, pulling Pidge by the arm.

"Don't come back," Mrs. Page told her daughter.

"Fuck you, Mother!" She jerked her arm free. I braced for disaster, but Pidge abruptly turned and marched out the door.

"Nice poster, ma'am." I squeezed past the two idiots and followed Pidge into cold March air with my heart pounding.

* * * * *

"Jesus. And I thought Andy's family had issues."

Pidge drove without speaking. Her face was flushed. Her grip on the steering wheel rendered her knuckles in pale contrast to her hands.

We retraced our path down the country roads that had taken us to her childhood home. I glanced back any number of times. The road we left behind remained clear. Had it not, I would have considered pulling over and making us both disappear.

As if reading my thoughts, Pidge braked and steered the Crown Vic onto the shoulder.

"She can't fucking have him."

"She doesn't have him. Your dad is gone. That's not your dad in that box."

Pidge released the wheel and turned her head. I have both weight and size on her. She barely reached the pedals from the fully-forward front seat of that Crown Vic. Yet she deployed power and determination I could not fight.

"I am not leaving him. I'm going back for him, and then I'm taking him to the lake where he wanted to be. That was his wish. Not to sit on a mantle under that fucking abomination."

"I thought you might say that."

* * * * *

I told Pidge to drive us back to the airport. I explained why and she agreed. On the way, I opened my iPad and reviewed the Airport Facility Directory listing for Burnett County. Finding the crucial piece of information I needed, I checked my watch. The timing wasn't quite right, so we killed a little time by finding a gas station and filling the car's tank. After parking the courtesy car in the airport lot, we had a nice chat with the airport manager. We traded a few stories and I made a point of asking what time it was. He told us it was just past four-thirty. He said he had to close the office and I told Pidge we had to get moving. I plucked a copy of his business card from the FBO counter in case we needed a witness to our time of departure. We thanked him for his courtesy and conversation and loaded up the Navajo. I started the engines, ran them up on the ramp, then taxied for takeoff and lifted the airplane into the sky with a turn southeast. Ten minutes later, I rolled into a one-hundred-eighty-degree turn and soon after that touched the wheels once again to the runway at Burnett County. We taxied to the ramp where Pidge pointed to the empty parking space where the airport manager's car had been. To be on the safe side, we taxied to a row of hangars and parked beyond the last hangar on a patch of exposed frozen grass. Not entirely out of sight, but it would have to do.

I pulled two BLASTER power units from my flight bag. One went in my pocket. I gave the other a quick test. We climbed out of the cabin. I held out my left hand for Pidge.

"Fuck. I haven't done this since you threw me out of that building."

"Carried you out of that building." I grasped her right hand in my left.

"Whatev—"

Fwooomp! We vanished.

"Dammit! Warn me next time!"

* * * * *

Pidge guided us on a direct route to her mother's house. The collection of vehicles remained in the driveway and on the road. Growing darkness made the interior lights brighter by contrast. Thumping loud music covered the sound of the BLASTER bringing us to a halt on the front porch. I maneuvered to the window that looked in on the sitting room.

Empty. Good.

We moved across the front door to the window that looked in on the dining room. Bruno's pals milled around the table and the decimated pizza boxes. The keg remained in business—that or a replacement had joined the fight. One of the two idiots that flanked Cynthia and her husband vigorously pumped the tap to fill a Solo cup. Beyond the dining room, Pidge's mother held court in the kitchen. She leaned against a countertop with a smoldering cigarette pinched between two fingers. Pidge's sister sat at a sway-backed kitchen table with her tattooed husband.

"Front door," I said.

I pushed off the window frame. We glided until I felt Pidge grab and turn the front doorknob. She pushed. All that accomplished was to move us away from the door.

"Hang on." I turned around and propped one foot against the porch rail. "Now try."

Pidge gently pushed the front door open far enough to let us slip inside using the jamb as a grip. No one seemed to notice, and if they did, I didn't care. Doors open all the time. A latch doesn't catch. A breeze pushes. Sometimes a door opening on the other side of the house creates a pressure drop, pulling the opposite door open.

Pidge tried to close it behind us.

"Leave it," I whispered. I pushed against the door to propel us into the house. The move produced a nice glide across the foyer. I contacted the arched entrance to the sitting room and used a grip to send us to the mantle. I felt Pidge move to take the cardboard box of remains.

"Let me," I whispered.

I wasn't sure she could make it disappear the way I can. I reached up and lifted the small box, which had the immediate effect of pressing my feet to the floor. My plan was to draw the box close to my belly and slide it up under my jacket.

"What the fucking shit!"

Cynthia's husband Bruno stood in the foyer with one hand on the open door. He stared at the box floating off the mantle.

Crap!

I calculated that we had only seconds before others would emerge from their beer and pizza fog to see what had startled Bruno the Tattooed Man. I rotated us to face him. Pidge's grip tightened.

"Take the box!" I whispered. I felt her grip the box of ashes. *"Point it at him."*

Pidge extended her father's ashes in Bruno's general direction. I planted one foot on the hearth of the fireplace.

I reached back for the framed poster. The frame was cheap plastic, but the overall weight told me the cover was glass. The picture came off its hooks with one swipe. I followed through and hurled the portrait at Bruno. He threw up his arms to ward it off and simultaneously staggered away from the door.

I gave the hearth a kick. The box, albeit light, still weighed more than we did, and it forced my feet to the floor. I used flat-footed steps to charge the door. Bruno let out a shriek and batted at the frame, which hit him in the chest edgewise, then dropped to the floor. Glass shattered and sprayed everywhere. Bruno tumbled onto his butt against the wall beside the door.

Despite the attack of the obscene portrait, Bruno could not take his eyes from the box of ashes floating toward him. Pidge aimed it directly at his pale, stunned face. Bruno issued a girlish shriek.

Passing Bruno, I summoned the deepest, coarsest half-whisper, half-growl I could manage.

"You will never have me! Hitler burns in Hell!"

Pidge added her own harsh whisper, *"He can't wait to meet you, asshole!"*

We crossed the threshold onto the porch. I grabbed the box from Pidge and shoved it up under my jacket, which caused it to vanish and ended gravity's influence over us.

I kicked off and we sailed into the twilight.

* * * * *

Pidge laughed until she cried. Getting directions out of her wasn't easy, but eventually she told me the way.

This part of Wisconsin is dotted with small lakes, some not much larger than a mill pond. The property Pidge inherited contained a larger-than-pond but smaller-than-lake body of water that she called No Name Lake for the obvious reason. Less than five miles from the Page home by air, we covered the distance quickly using the BLASTER to drone just above the treetops.

I came in low over the water. No Name Lake reminded me of a biology class diagram of a human stomach, including a creek that entered at one end and exited at the other. A single wooden structure populated the lake, the cabin where Pidge stored her childhood memories. I swerved right and took the long way around the lake's perimeter. Pidge slipped into silence beside me, which I took as a sign of appreciation for the tour.

We approached the cabin from the water, easing to a landing on a slender pier that invited belly flops and cannonballs to break the glass-smooth surface.

I made sure both our feet contacted the pier, then—

Fwooomp!

—we reappeared and settled. Pidge shook off the grip she had maintained since we left the airport. I flexed my fingers to regain blood flow.

We faced the lake and watched the last light bleed away. Stars poked bright holes in the night sky above us and floated in reflection on the water.

I handed Pidge the box. She took it in both hands but made no move to untie the string. She gazed across and around the small lake. She looked at the old pier and at the yard surrounding the cabin.

"We were up here all the time, me and Dad. Cyn and Mom never liked it. I couldn't live without it. Fishing. Catching frogs. Chasing fireflies. A fucking Norman Rockwell eternal summer."

"What happened to your mom? Was she always…you know?"

Pidge shrugged. "What do you ever know about your parents as a kid? You have this image in your head, and you have reality, and then you find out the reality of your life isn't what everyone else considers normal. My mother threw around the N-word all the time. I grew up thinking it was just how you describe certain people, but I guess even as a little kid, I knew there was something potent about it. She always seemed mad when she said it. Eventually you learn. And you decide to accept or reject."

"And your dad?"

"I guess he loved her. Or the idea of her, what she was…once. There are some old pictures somewhere. She was pretty. Before. Then she got the way she is and…not so much. I think when Dad saw Cyn go down the same path, he decided to give me another choice. He knew what I wanted. You know what it's like with airplanes. I wouldn't shut up about them."

"Yeah. Not everybody gets it."

"My dad did."

We didn't speak for a few minutes. Pidge lost herself in the scenery. I wondered how she wanted to handle the ashes. She didn't seem anxious to get the job done.

"The property is twelve acres. It encompasses the lake. I guess it's mine, now."

"It's pretty."

She shrugged. "I don't know if I can keep this. I don't think I ever want to come back again. Not if they're here." She pointed at the cabin. "I'd like to take a last look inside."

I followed her to the small structure. Nothing fancy. Not a log cabin. A peaked roof and stone chimney over what looked from the outside to be one room, although I couldn't be sure there weren't bedrooms at the back. Facing the water, a flat porch fronted the building. I pictured Andy and me at a spot like this, sipping cold ones and watching the sunset color the water.

Pidge ducked down and reached under the porch. She patted her hand around and found an old Fanta can. It rattled. She shook it until she was able to pinch a key from the pop-top hole.

"That's been there forever. Let's see if they changed the locks."

They hadn't. She opened the door and flipped on a light switch. A pair of lamps flooded the wooden interior with warm light. Pidge stopped in her tracks.

"Holy crap," I muttered.

Flags. Banners. Portraits. Posters. Shelves with military memorabilia. A collection of bayonets. What looked like a potato-masher hand grenade. The cabin interior was a museum—and not the good kind. A duplicate of *The Standard Bearer* hung on one wall. Squared up around it were framed black and white photos that my eye begged not to translate for my brain. I saw what I didn't want to see. The striped convict uniforms, the concentration camp wire, the huts, the ovens.

I could not speak.

"This is sick," she whispered. Her face went pale. "I knew it was bad, but this…"

"I'm sorry you saw this," I said.

"It was never like this. Bastards. They took out everything my dad had here. He had board games. Puzzles. In that nook over there, he always had something new for us to do. He built model cars. He had stupid old beer signs. He had a fucking deer head that he put a red nose on at Christmas. Jesus! Look what they've done! Fucking Nazi clubhouse."

"We should go."

She pointed at the dormant fireplace.

"Fucking idiots use a space heater. Dad never allowed a space heater in here. Goddamn fools are too stupid to turn off the water to keep the pipes from freezing."

An old metal-cased heater sat on the hearth, plugged into a wall socket. I walked over to it. The dial had a rudimentary temperature selector—Off, Low, and High. The knob pointed at Low, accounting for the warmth inside the cabin.

"Hold this," Pidge handed me the box.

She stepped onto the stone hearth. A huge red, white, and black flag hung above the fireplace. With two hands, she jerked it down, tearing through the fabric.

"Oops."

She reached down and turned the setting on the space heater to High. She watched the coils glow red. Satisfied, she stepped back and billowed the flag like someone spreading a sheet over a mattress. The stark colors settled over the heater. Hot coils glowed through the swastika embedded in the fabric.

"Now we can go."

She locked the door behind us. A few minutes later, she stood on the pier and flicked the key into the water. She watched the ripples until they reached the shore. Unable to put it off any longer, she opened the box. She hesitated. I understood. Simply dumping them in the water seemed insufficient.

I pulled out a BLASTER.

"Here." I hooked one arm in hers. "Cover it with your hands."

She did. I folded my hand over hers.

Fwooomp! We vanished. The open box went with us.

The circuit I flew around the lake was easy to see. A trail of light ash marked our passage, slowly settling onto the serene waters.

* * * * *

Pidge insisted on piloting the Navajo. After takeoff, she banked north instead of southeast. She leveled off a thousand feet above the dark landscape. Small clusters of light marked Webster and Danbury. The casino cast a gaudy glow toward the sky near the St. Croix River. The lakes, glittering flat spots within the endless woodland, reflected the stars and our flashing navigation lights.

Beside one of the lakes, a bright yellow glow spread to the surrounding trees and reflected off the snow and the water. Pidge pulled a tight turn. She stared down over the left engine. From altitude the blaze looked more like a warm, inviting campfire than a burning cabin.

Pidge broke the silence on the intercom.

"If you ever tell anyone about this, I'll cut your nuts off."

"I love you, too."

PIDGE

February 10, 2022 to February 11, 2022

WATER LANDING

10

WATER LANDING

"Something you want to tell me?"

Rosemary II fidgeted with her computer mouse. Her dark-eyed gaze landed on a point somewhere in the next county. She absently clicked one of the mouse buttons. The screen pointer danced harmlessly on a wallpaper image of her daughter Lane smiling brightly enough to shame a sunny summer day.

I wasn't certain she heard my question.

I finished the flight manifest paperwork and pushed the clipboard across the office countertop. She made no move to pick it up. Instead, she shifted her attention down the hall to where our paying passenger waited, having arrived an hour and forty minutes earlier than expected.

Mr. Rowan Dunland occupied a corner chair in the pilot's lounge when I poked my head in to apologize for being late. The apology was *pro forma*. The charter wasn't scheduled until two p.m. and I wasn't supposed to be the pilot. The Sacred Schedule listed Dave Peterson as pilot for the flight. Dave wasn't due back until one p.m. Ordinarily, there would be no reason to juggle the schedule for an unplanned early arrival. This time, Rosemary II called me. My reaction was to mutter (to myself) that she assumes I have nothing better to do than hop when she snaps her fingers. It doesn't help that, as a rule, that would be correct.

When she called, Rosemary II told me the client's name in a way that made me think I was supposed to know him.

"He was a high school teacher," she prompted.

"Okay."

"Can you take this?"

"I guess."

"Good."

She broke the connection. Fifteen minutes later, I presented myself at my old employer's office in a crisp white uniform shirt and slightly wrinkled black tie that I planned to iron if I ever learned how to use an iron. Ten minutes after that, I finished the requisite paperwork.

"Something you want to tell me?" I repeated, waving a hand between Rosemary II and whatever distracted her. She blinked. As if fearing our passenger had superhuman hearing, she waved me to lean closer.

"You know who that is, don't you?"

"Uh, you told me. Teacher, right? Must have been after my time."

"He's not teaching anymore. Will, don't you read the newspaper?"

"Does anybody? Wait. I did clip a coupon for a lawn mower tune-up. Well, actually Andy did."

Rosemary II gave me the look she paints on all her children, biological and otherwise, who disappoint her by being such dunces. She backed away, reached down, and pulled open the desk drawer.

"He paid in cash." A loosely organized pile of bills lay in the drawer. I spotted denominations starting with one. The cash looked like it had been dumped out of a piggy bank.

"For a charter flight?" I shrugged. "Why not?" The response

failed to satisfy the Goddess of The Schedule. She frowned at me, so I decided I better play. "Is that a problem?"

She pushed the manifest clipboard back across the countertop and planted a wicked, varnished nail on the Destination box.

"N3G," I said. "I'm aware. So?"

"Northport, Michigan. It's on the peninsula at Grand Traverse Bay."

"Yup. Just did the flight plan." Ten thousand airports serve cities and towns of every size in the United States. Charter flying can reach nearly all of them. The flight had been booked in one of Essex County Air's twin-engine Beechcraft Barons, the 58 model. When the N3G airport identifier brought up Peninsula Township Airport, I checked the runway length against the Baron's accelerate/stop distance. The single asphalt runway of 4,300 feet ensured safe margins for both landing and takeoff. "Is this a drop off or an out-and-back?"

"I asked if there would be pilot wait time. He said, no."

I glanced at my watch. Takeoff in about fifteen minutes. Forty-five minutes of flying, give or take. A quick drop-off, then home with plenty of time to spare. This didn't even warrant a call to Andy.

A glance at Rosemary II prompted me to ask the question once more.

"Something you want to tell me?"

She huffed a loud sigh and gestured for me to follow her to the inner office. She closed the door behind us.

"Rowan Dunland doesn't teach anymore because last summer he lost his daughter in a boating accident." She lifted her eyebrows at me. My blank stare did nothing to alter my dunce status. "In Northport, Michigan. Northport *is where his daughter died*. Or was killed. How did you not hear about this?"

Last summer had been busy, what with the broken pelvis and

all. On top of that, I pay little attention to the local newspaper and less to local gossip.

"It was ruled an accident, but her father blamed the boyfriend." She gestured in the direction of the lounge. "The girl was his only child..."

"Huh."

Rosemary II's emotional trigger was obvious if nothing else about this was. She didn't have to remind me that Lane was her only child. And I didn't have to dig too deep to feel my guts twist over the memory of nearly losing her.

"Not really seeing where you're going with this."

"Why would he go there?"

"Closure?"

"That's the problem."

"What's the problem?"

"That," she gestured again in the direction of the pilot lounge on the other side of two walls and a hallway, "is a man at peace. Don't you feel it?"

"We didn't exactly chat."

Wrong answer. Rosemary II put a firm hand on my arm.

"Promise me you will be careful."

"Let me check my calendar and see if today is a 'be careful' day."

"Will!"

"I'll be careful. Promise." Rosemary II's perturbed glare made me think I should add a promise to floss and eat my vegetables.

* * * * *

Failure to fully understand Rosemary II's intuitions did not mean I didn't trust them. I decided to pass on inviting the passenger to sit up front with me. Not that I had visions of him making a suicidal grab for the controls or anything so dramatic. Dunland had a vibe about him, I was willing to admit, but all that told me was that he wouldn't be much for conversation on the short flight across Lake Michigan.

Air charter services like Essex County Air don't get many walk-ins. The business relies on steady corporate customers. People occasionally find us on the web and assume we offer an alternative to the cattle car experience of commercial airline flight, but the price tag sobers their thinking. Sometimes a crisis renders money irrelevant, but those flights are usually silent, with passengers too absorbed in worry or tragedy to pay attention to the flight or the flight crew.

Was this a crisis? I had no idea.

Physically small, Rowan Dunland wore bifocal glasses and dressed the part of a high school science teacher. He layered a gray blazer over a blue chambray shirt topping faded blue jeans. I'm bad at guessing age and would have pegged him as qualifying for Social Security, but I reminded myself of his loss. The sunburst of lines at the corners of his eyes, the receding hairline, the pale skin suggesting a vitamin D deficiency may have been products of grief. Dunland's loss embossed a sadness on the gray irises and cloudy whites of his eyes that I doubted time would fade.

When I fetched Dunland from the pilot's lounge, he greeted me with a skin-deep smile and quiet pleasantries.

"Any bags?" I asked.

"Oh, no. Just this." He patted a weathered briefcase, a cliché accessory that matched the patches guarding the elbows of his sport jacket.

"Traveling light. Very well. Let's go commit aviation."

* * * * *

My passenger obeyed the boarding instructions without question. I placed him in the forward-facing right rear seat, helped him with his seatbelt and explained the location of the airplane's flotation gear, the pins for removing the rear windows, and the latch for the cabin door, which I made him demonstrate. I told him the flight would be smooth, but that I'd prefer he keep his seatbelt on for the duration. He offered no resistance, asked no questions. He rode with his head turned to the window. When we left the Wisconsin shoreline behind, he gazed down at the endless water.

The flight across Lake Michigan took four minutes less than I anticipated. Cruising at seven thousand feet, the Baron rode as smooth as the blue/silver lake stretching in all four directions below. Mare's tail cirrus clouds made of ice crystals floated twenty thousand feet above us, tattooed by white contrails from airliners. Faint sun dogs tried and failed to appear; the pale blue lacked enough ice to generate the luminous phenomenon.

I landed in the first thousand feet of the runway at Peninsula Airport and spared the brakes by allowing the Baron to roll to the end of the asphalt. A turnoff accessed the field's small ramp. There was no fuel service, which didn't concern me, having departed Essex with all four tanks topped. Three old hangars nudged one end of the ramp, the only structures on the field. Nothing resembling a fixed base office or pilot's shack invited me to disembark my passenger. I rolled to where a path led from the ramp to a gravel parking lot. One vehicle, a dark decade-old Lexus, collected dust in the lot.

I shut down, hopped out the front cabin door and off the wing. I opened the aft doors for Dunland, who tried to get out of his seat without unbuckling his belt. I helped him release the belt, for which he thanked me.

He stepped from the plane clutching his briefcase to his chest.

"Is someone meeting you?"

"Uh...no."

Technically, my job had ended. *Thanks for flying Essex County*

Air Service. Hope you had a pleasant ride. Think of us next time for the ease and speed of direct point-to-point flying. Have a great day.

Dunland took a hesitant step, turned, offered a shallow smile, and half-waved. My cue to go. I nodded at him and wished him a good day. He walked to the dirt path, then stopped. He examined the empty lot and the hangars. He dug a phone from his pocket, gazed at the screen, then pocketed the phone again.

Clearly, this was not what he had expected.

I had no obligation to the man. All I had to do was secure the rear doors, hop on the wing, hot start two engines and blast off. Andy's dinner plan promised spaghetti with a Sicilian sauce recipe she claimed had been carved in secret stones on Mount Etna by Calogero Vizzini himself. Leave now, and I'd be home in time to help stir the pot.

Sometimes there's no explaining the dumb impulses I follow.

"If you don't mind my asking, Mr. Dunland, what are your plans?"

"I suppose I will call a taxi."

"Right. Um, I sincerely doubt there's a taxi service here. Maybe Uber. Do you have an Uber account? Lyft?"

He shook his head.

"I don't need to get far," he said. "I can walk. It's a beautiful day."

There it was. Serenity. Unless I imagined it.

"No argument there, but you may have a longer walk than you think. Are you headed into Northport? It's about five miles from here."

"No. I'm visiting…someone." He dug in the pocket that held his phone and produced a slip of paper. "I have an address."

"Hang on," I said. I strolled to the parked Lexus which, despite its luxury nameplate, had seen better days. Deep blue paint had faded in the sun. A section of chrome molding on the driver's side had gone missing. I tried the door handle. It opened. I dropped onto the driver's seat. The car smelled musty. I found an envelope on the dash. Inside, a set of keys jangled against a pair of singles and a five. The note on the front of the envelope answered my question.

Gas or cash. Leave it clean. Thanks!

"Mr. Dunland," I called to him from the car interior. "I think you've got your ride."

* * * * *

I would not have driven the car had Dunland walked to the driver's side expecting me to hop out. Instead, he stepped to the passenger door, opened it, and sat down beside me with his hands folded on the briefcase.

He looked mildly bewildered.

"Crew car." I dangled the keys. "People park cars like this at airports for the convenience of anyone who comes along."

"What a wonderful idea." He picked up the envelope, read the note, and extracted his wallet from his back pocket. He found a twenty and tucked it into the envelope.

"Uh, that's a bit much."

"Live simply, love generously, care deeply, speak kindly, and leave the rest to God."

"Shakespeare?"

"Ronald Reagan." He produced the slip of paper and read the address.

"Hold on." I jumped out and ran to the Baron. I grabbed my iPad, locked the airplane and rejoined Dunland. I flipped open the iPad and typed the address into Google Maps. GPS magic produced a short blue line on zigzag rural roads. "Got it. Not very far."

"I can walk, then."

"Nope. You already paid the fare."

* * * * *

"This is fine. Pull over here."

"It's no problem. I can drive in—"

"No. Please. Here." A flash of something stern came out of nowhere. A hint of the teacher, commanding his class. Dunland pointed. I stopped the old Lexus under an arch of overhanging tree boughs. Off the right front fender, an unpaved driveway penetrated dense green woods. We'd seen glimpses of the bay through the trees for the last half mile, so the assumption that the narrow gravel lane led to a waterfront property was a safe one.

Dunland stared as if watching someone stroll down the overgrown lane. I waited nearly a full minute for his reverie to dissipate.

He turned and extended his hand to me.

"I apologize. I didn't get your name."

"Will Stewart." I clasped fine-boned fingers and a traded a light grip.

"Very nice to meet you, Will Stewart," he said. "Your flying is, in my judgment, exceptional. I enjoyed the ride."

"Thank you, sir. Likewise. Are you sure you don't want me to wait?"

"Quite sure." He placed his hand on his briefcase.

"It's just, well, if you don't mind me saying, you don't have any luggage, so I assumed you'd be flying back with me after... whatever this is."

He shook his head. "No. No, I have all I need." His hand lightly patted the briefcase. "You have a good flight home, now."

He opened the door and climbed out. Bending slightly, he waved at me through the passenger window. I watched him stroll down the lane between arches of thick green vegetation. A man entering a cave.

Here there be dragons.

I turned the key and started the Lexus V6 engine. I dropped the gearshift in Drive. The old girl rolled smoothly ahead.

I drove ten feet beyond the driveway before I planted my foot on the brake pedal.

"Dammit."

I craned my neck to see down the driveway, but Dunland had slipped out of sight.

Just drive back to the airport. Fly a magnificent airplane across a Great Lake enjoying a view few humans have the good fortune to witness. Hug your beautiful wife and open that Door County cherry wine that Pidge brought back from her Memorial Day weekend getaway. Sip the wine and fuss over the spaghetti sauce with Andy.

Simple.

Not so simple.

A man at peace.

What constitutes peace for a man who knows grief beyond words?

Northport is where his daughter died. Or was killed.

Crap.

* * * * *

I drove the Lexus another forty yards and found a flat spot to pull over, leaving only the left side tires on the pavement. Traffic was no factor. A sign a mile back warned of No Outlet. I hadn't seen a single car since leaving the airport.

I killed the engine and pocketed the keys. From a cargo pocket in my pants, I pulled out a device resembling a flashlight along with a six-inch carbon fiber propeller, the kind meant for radio-controlled model airplanes.

My trusty power unit. Basic Linear Aerial System for Transport, Electric Rechargeable.

BLASTER.

I attached the propeller and tested the device using a slide control. The prop whined. I stepped out of the car but didn't lock it. Old crew cars like this can ambush you with unreliable locks. Better to leave it.

I shoved the imaginary levers in my head to the stops.

Fwooomp!

My body vanished along with the BLASTER. My feet lost contact with the pavement. I held out the unseen power unit and pushed the slide control forward. The prop blew a cool breeze over my arm and pulled me forward. I skimmed inches above the pavement. At the driveway, I veered left and followed Dunland's trail down the sloped, wooded lane.

It was, as I expected, a lake property. The driveway ended in a single-car garage bay attached to a one-story house that overlooked the vast, glass-smooth Grand Traverse Bay. There didn't appear to be a front door. I guess the designer did not expect callers from the local church auxiliary. A plastic bin leaned against the siding with "Packages" spray painted across the front. A narrow walk made of flat stones skirted the garage.

My glide path traversed the side of the building. Passing the corner of the house, I floated forward over a sharply descending embankment. The land sloped to the water where a pier extended into the bay. A deck at the back of the house offered the money view. Concrete steps connected the house-wide wooden deck to the pier. A riot of weeds and vines spread in either direction on the slope.

Dunland descended the steps toward the beach. He watched his footing carefully.

On the pier, a man carried a plastic cooler onto a large, moored power boat, a cabin cruiser. A tackle box and several fishing rods waited for loading. After depositing the cooler in the boat cabin, he returned and bent over for the fishing gear. Dunland stepped onto the pier. Alerted, the man loading the boat lifted his attention to the visitor.

I glided over the water's edge twenty feet above a narrow gravel beach kissed by lapping, unhurried waves. Deft application of reverse thrust brought me to a halt between Dunland and the boater.

Recognition bloomed on the boater's face. He drew himself upright.

"Mr. Dunland. Ah…this is a surprise. What do you want?"

Dunland closed half the distance to the boater. He said nothing. Careful not to drop it over the side of the pier, Dunland cupped the bottom of the briefcase in his left hand while he released the snap latches with his right. The case split narrowly open. He reached in with his right hand like a lawyer digging for a writ or a professor groping for his day planner.

Neither filled his hand.

Dunland swept a handgun from the case and pointed it at the boater. I recognized the Beretta M.92 semi-automatic pistol. Andy has one; she and most of the American military.

Despite the short range, I gave Dunland little chance of hitting his target. His hand shook and the weapon weighed on his outstretched arm.

If this development worried the boater, he didn't show it. I guessed him to be in his twenties. His muscled physique strained a tight t-shirt made of shimmering material; probably expensive, probably meant for but never actually worn for sports. He had long hair on top, swept back above the sides and a rear that had been buzz cut. It's not my favorite look. The three-day beard stubble that's been popular for too long shaded his square jaw. I suspected that his perfectly proportioned nose and blue eyes spiced his visits to a mirror. From his good looks sprang confidence. I detected a law enforcement vibe, the kind I see in some of the younger offi-cers who work with Andy at the City of Essex Police Department.

A little cockiness. A little aggressiveness. But Andy's fellow offi-cers would have the good sense to recognize the danger in this moment. This man did not.

"Is that a gun, Mr. Dunland?" Boater spoke politely. He took a step toward Dunland. I didn't think that was smart. I calculated my options which are always complicated by and weighed against the question of revealing myself.

What would Andy do?

Grabbing a gun from someone is as foolish as it gets. Letting this play out ran a close second.

Boater took another step closer.

"Stop." Dunland jerked the weapon. It was a wonder it didn't go off. His target threw up his hands submissively.

"Sir, I know what you're feeling. I feel it, too. My heart is broken. She was everything to me. But don't do this. Don't let this tragedy consume you."

"Shut up."

Boater took another step toward Dunland. Then another. I adjusted my position above them. A dive down on Dunland might knock his aim off but could just as easily startle him into pulling the trigger. In my head and in her voice, I heard my wife's favorite question regarding heroics.

And then what?

"You think you're the only one in pain?" Boater pleaded. "I don't sleep. I don't eat. I can't focus. Nothing in the world matters to me anymore."

Apparently, that didn't include fishing.

Boater kept coming. Dunland's hand quivered. Ten feet. Eight feet. Boater approached with his hands held high. I wished he would stop.

"Have you seen anyone? Talked to anyone? Grief is hard, sir. You can't go it alone. I know. I'm getting counseling." Six feet. "I shouldn't admit this to you, sir, but I've wanted to hurt myself.

There. I said it. I wanted to hurt myself for what happened. I had no idea Abbey was so drunk. I had no idea she left the cabin that night. I could have stopped her. I play it over and over in my head. *But I had no idea.*"

"You lie." Dunland's voice cracked. He cleared his throat. "You lie."

"I told the police. The Coast Guard. I searched. I screamed for her, over and over. I couldn't believe she had gone. We were so happy."

"Liar."

"Sir, did she…did she give you any indication that she was—you know—depressed? That she would hurt herself?"

Boater halted his advance at four feet.

"I get it. I don't want to admit it to myself, either. I don't want to face the truth. But Abbey left no room for doubt."

"Don't say her name! Don't you dare say her name!"

"I loved her. I don't know if I can ever love again."

That's when I stopped giving Boater the benefit of the doubt.

A split second later his left hand flashed forward and closed a grip on both the pistol and Dunland's hand. Boater's oversized palm encompassed both. He pushed the pistol away and down. If Dunland fired, only the fish need worry.

That should have been enough. Boater had the advantage of size and strength. He had command of the weapon. The grieving former teacher posed no threat against this body builder.

I felt relieved, not least for worrying that I'd nearly contributed to a murder by bringing Dunland here.

Boater balled his right hand into a fist and drove it into Dunland's diaphragm.

Dunland doubled over and dropped backward onto the pier. He landed on his butt, clutching his chest. He gasped for air.

The pistol hung in Boater's hand.

* * * * *

There's a good reason that airships like the Goodyear Blimp maneuver slowly and carefully. Directing and positioning an object in the air with dynamic thrust requires planning. Every acceleration demands a deceleration, and vice versa. The same applies to me. Unless I have a grip on a fixed object, or unless *the other thing* performs one of its impulsive moves on its own, something I have yet to control, I am not quick. As much as I wished I'd done something, hanging twenty feet above this scene left me all but helpless.

I pulsed the power unit and descended on a path toward the edge of the pier near the two men. I had no idea what I might do, but at least I'd be close enough to do it.

Boater dropped to a knee. Dunland heaved and wheezed. His face reddened. His fingers clawed at his chest.

"Mr. Dunland, are you alright? Sir? Are you okay?" Boater continued his sticky-sweet patter while his rough hands patted and searched Dunland. He jerked open Dunland's shirt. Buttons plinked into the water. "Sir, are you having a panic attack? Should I call someone?" The words rang discordant with his actions. He dug through Dunland's pockets. He stopped when he found what he was looking for.

He lifted Dunland's phone, looked at the screen, then reversed it and held it up to Dunland's face. Boater grinned and lifted his finger to his lips.

He spoke to the phone.

"Sir, you better sit down. I'll get you some water." He touched the screen and laid the phone on the planks just as I rotated and grabbed the pier's edge. I stopped short of breaking the surface of the water. From my vantage point and within reach, I saw what ignited Boater's look of triumph.

Dunland's phone displayed a voice recording app.

Boater's performance suddenly made sense. So did Dunland's.

Boater stood up and walked to the moored cabin cruiser. He tossed the Beretta onto a cushion at the rear.

Dunland struggled to draw air into his lungs. Utter defeat washed over his face, his posture.

He had not come to murder. He'd come for truth. Whatever happened to his daughter, Dunland apparently believed it happened at the hands of this man. Dunland was a father who failed to protect his daughter. And he had failed again.

Boater returned and dropped to a knee. The polite, solicitous cohort in grief was gone. He double-checked the phone screen.

"Fuck, old man. You came here to record me? What did you think? That I'd take one look at that gun in your hand, wet my pants, and confess everything to you? Huh?" He slapped Dunland hard enough to turn his head 90 degrees.

Heat built up behind my eyes. My muscles developed an electric tension. Options flashed through my mind. Disappear Dunland and make a getaway. Grab Boater and make him vanish. Lift him thirty feet straight up and let go. He'd hit the pier hard, maybe survive, maybe never walk again.

Something cold stirred in my heart.

"Hey, asshole! I'm talking to you!" Boater grabbed Dunland's shirt and shook him. "You've been a pain in my ass since day one. Jesus. You had the fucking cops and Coast Guard all up in my shit. They fucking believed you. Do you know how many times they questioned me? Shit."

I reached for the phone, which lay close to the edge of the pier. I touched the screen. The little triangle icon changed to two bars. The recording app's digital counter resumed counting.

Boater slapped Dunland again. The blow knocked his glasses askew. Blood bubbled from his nose.

"Huh? You came to hear me confess? Think you can turn me in to the cops? Huh?" Another slap. "AM—I—RIGHT?"

Dunland nodded. Blood ran down his upper lip. Tears over-flowed his eyes.

"Fuck. Why not? Let's do this, old man. Lemme tell you what really fucking happened out there. Every daddy wants to know, secretly, how their little girl takes it, right? Wanna know? Wanna know what I did to your little bitch kitty all night long before I threw her pathetic ass over the side? Want details?"

I tightened every fiber of my body against the impulse to drive a fist into the side of Boater's head.

Digital tenths of a second mounted on the phone screen. A tiny VU meter assured me that Boater's voice registered.

For the next three minutes or three hours or three years Boater described in horrifying detail the final night of Dunland's daughter's life.

Boater described taking her on the boat.

Taking her to the middle of Grand Traverse Bay.

Taking her.

I hovered my free hand over the phone. If Boater reached for it, I would scoop it up. Make it vanish before his eyes.

Boater ground his words into broken glass and forced them into the poor man's ears. He grinned and reveled in the way he had perfectly crafted his story. He mocked his desperate call to a 9-1-1 operator and frantic radio call to the Coast Guard. He praised himself for his performance during the search, for his tears in front of the sheriff's deputies. An Oscar, Boater declared, is what he deserved for breaking down and crying three weeks later when the body of his beloved Abbey was found on a stretch of pebbled beach.

Abbey. Every time her name passed his lips, I sided with Dunland. Boater had no right to speak her name.

The cold black thing lurking deep inside me rose up.

"I should kill you, too," Boater said calmly. "I should take you out to where I took her. Throw you over. Watch you flounder, like I watched her. Funny. She was a good swimmer, you know. I let her pound those waves and get within inches of the boat, then I pulled away. Over and over. She never gave up. She kept coming until the hypothermia set in. And, oh did she beg."

Dunland sobbed. Boater grinned. I welcomed ice into my veins.

Boater ended the torment abruptly. He grabbed Dunland's lapels and jerked him to his feet.

"Get the fuck out of here, old man. Now you know. You fucking know. I hope it burns a hole in your brain." He shoved Dunland in the direction of the beach. Miraculously, the crushed, defeated man stayed on his feet.

Boater stroked his fingers through his top mop of hair.

I dropped my hand onto the phone, touched Pause, then closed my palm over the device. I felt an electric snap when it vanished. I lifted it from the pier and carefully tucked it in a zippered pocket. The phone belonged to Dunland, more now than ever. And I would return it to him.

First things first.

Boater started toward his cabin cruiser but stopped when he remembered the phone. He turned and saw that it was gone. He walked back, kneeled, and peered over the side of the pier into the murky water below.

"Shit."

I estimated the depth to be more than arm's length. For a moment, I thought Boater might go in after the phone, but then his attention shifted to Dunland looking back at him. Boater stood up and took a menacing step forward.

"Beat it, old man."

Dunland staggered toward the stone steps. He needed help, and I wanted to render it, but something else called to me.

* * * * *

Boater apparently wasn't interested in getting wet, or else he figured the phone wasn't going anywhere. He watched Dunland's painful climb up the steps. When the father of his former girlfriend finally staggered around the corner of the house and out of sight, he returned to his cruiser and fired up the engines. The noise covered an aggressive shot of BLASTER that took me to a railing at the stern quarter.

Boater didn't dawdle. He closed a grip on the twin throttles and goosed the engines. The bow lifted. Water boiled at the stern. The big cruiser shot forward on the serene waters of Grand Traverse Bay. Sunlight made the white Fiberglas hull luminous.

Boater posed at the wheel, letting the wind style his hair. Pleased. Seeing himself in his own movie, I assumed.

I gripped a chrome handrail above the transom and let my weightless body extend in the breeze like a pennant.

I don't know how long we cruised. At its widest, the bay spanned ten miles. When I could see both sides of the bay, I guessed we were five miles out. That's four point nine miles farther than I can swim.

Boater operated his craft from an enclosed cockpit. Above that, a flybridge offered a duplicate set of steering and throttle controls. With the wind tugging at my clothes, I moved hand over hand down a short rail that led from the aft cruising platform to the transom above the twin props. The wake raced out behind us, spreading its foam signature to mark our passage.

Above the transom, I planted a two-handed grip on the rail. I curled my legs forward and kicked the flat stern. The motors drowned the sound. I watched Boater. He remained fixed on his course across the water.

I kicked again. Again. Again.

He turned his head. He may not have heard me thumping the Fiberglas of his hull, but the vibration reached him.

I kicked. He cocked his head. I kicked again.

He eased the throttles back. I upped the tempo of the kicks as he powered down. He detected the change and tested it. He advanced the throttle briefly. I slowed the beat. He powered down again, and I resumed rapid pounding on the hull.

Bang bang bang bang.

He cut the throttles sharply. I stopped.

"What the…?" He stared at the stern. To my eye, he looked directly at me, and as always when that happens, my breath hitched.

He pushed the throttles forward, head turned, listening.

I resumed kicking.

He abruptly pulled the throttles to idle and started in my direction.

Using the railing, I jerked myself on an angle to the side rail. Boater crossed the aft deck. When he cleared, I heaved myself toward the cockpit. My aim was true. I caught the back of the captain's chair just as he hopped down from the cruising platform onto the transom.

He landed with both hands free. No grip. He bent over the water.

I yanked myself over the captain's chair and slapped both throttles. The motors growled. The bow lifted. The boat surged.

I heard him splash and turned in time to see him bob to the surface in the center of the vee wake, twenty feet back. I cut the throttles.

I performed a short glide back onto the cruising platform and fixed a grip on the railing above the transom platform. The boat drifted, opening the gap to nearly forty feet. Boater shook the water off his face, but not the shock. Wide, wild eyes signaled bald panic.

He launched a breaststroke through the chop. His panicked look subsided when he saw himself closing the distance by half.

"Nice water landing."

My voice stopped him in the water. He searched the deck, the cabin.

"Who's there?"

"Judgment, asshole."

He resumed his stroke.

"What are you doing on my boat?" he demanded. I wondered how he considered himself in a position to demand anything.

I let him close the distance. I reached in my pocket and pulled out Dunland's phone. I laid it on the cushion beside the Beretta. It snapped into view. I woke the screen, found the voice recording app and opened Dunland's saved recording. A semi-circular icon offered the option of rewinding in increments of thirty seconds. Much of what Boater had uttered to Dunland was something I never wanted to hear again. I tapped the rewind button. When I stopped tapping, the audio began to play. For a moment I feared that the recording didn't pick up Boater's cruel monologue. Then I remembered to touch the speaker button.

I heard Boater's voice and tapped the Pause button.

When Boater stroked within fifteen feet of the transom, I touched Play.

"*...you flounder, like I watched her. She was a good swimmer, you know. I let her pound those waves and get within inches of the boat, then I pulled away. She never gave up. She kept coming until the hypothermia set in...*"

Pause.

Boater stared up at the empty deck, still stroking. His eyes grew wider. His breath pumped hard. I pocketed the phone, which vanished. I lifted the Beretta off the seat cushion and tossed it into the waves where it issued a satisfying and final *plonk!*

"Who's there? Who are you?"

He drew closer. I shoved off the rail and floated into the cockpit where I reached around the chair to rest my hands on the throttles.

"You a good swimmer?" I asked.

He pumped hard for the transom. Salvation closed to just a few feet. I goosed the throttles. The motors growled. The wake foamed in his face. The boat heaved forward, quickly building up twenty or thirty yards of water between Boater and safety.

"C'mon, man!" he cried. "C'mon, I'm sorry! I didn't mean any of that!"

I quieted the engines.

"Feeling it? The hypothermia?"

He didn't answer. He pounded the waves, this time in a full Australian crawl. Head down, then up for breath, then down. He had good form.

I watched him cut through the light chop. He could have easily gone in the water to rescue his beloved Abbey. If he hadn't been standing on the deck, that is, playing with the throttles, letting her get within inches of the back of the boat, then goosing the power.

I wanted to treat him to the full experience.

But I wasn't him.

Once more I let him gain on the drifting cruiser. This time he reached for the transom when I hit the throttles. He managed to gain a grip. Foam from the dual props flew into his face. The cruiser dragged him several yards through the water before water pressure tore loose his grip. He screamed and slammed a fist into the water.

"Goddammit! I said I was sorry!"

Another forty feet spread between us. I cut the power and returned to the aft deck.

"How long did you tease her like this?"

"Please! Please don't do this!"

"Is that what she begged of you?"

He started to answer but mistimed his outcry. His mouth slipped under the surface. He came up spitting and swearing. He struggled to stay afloat. Maybe that dense muscle mass wasn't such a good thing when treading water.

He called out again. Swore. Started swimming again.

When he pulled himself to within thirty feet, I eased the throttles forward until the boat paced the swimmer. He gave it everything those muscles would buy. Boat and swimmer crawled across the light sunlit surface of the bay.

He had a fighting chance. More than he gave Abbey Dunland or her devastated father. He would have to dig deep into reserves of strength to catch up. Maybe he would.

I tapped my toes and left the deck. I floated straight up. The boat slid away beneath me with Boater punching his hands through the surface, stroking hard thirty feet behind.

I aimed my power unit for the beach without looking back.

* * * * *

Dunland wasn't at the car.

I arrived at the water's edge but stayed high and cruised above the house, above the trees shading the driveway. When I reached the road, I angled down between branches and eased up beside the trusty old Lexus.

Fwooomp! I reappeared with a grip on the car door handle. For a minute or two, I held on, heart hammering, arms threatening to shake. I thought about going back. I pictured Boater, pounding the surface of the bay, muscles tiring, cramping. Maybe he didn't deserve this.

I pictured a young woman I had never met, never seen. Terrified. Taunted. Feeling her body betray her as cold soaked cramping muscles while her tormentor laughed.

Any thought of returning to the bay evaporated.

A new horror sprang to mind. What if Dunland simply waded into the bay to join his daughter? If he had, I could not blame him, but I could certainly blame myself for leaving him alone.

Was he that far gone? I climbed in the Lexus, started the engine and did a Y-turn. I accelerated back the way we had come.

Half a mile down the road, I caught up. Dunland trudged the edge of the asphalt oblivious to the approaching car. I paced him and rolled down the window.

"Sir?"

He did not stop. He did not lift his tear-stained face.

I pulled ahead and parked. I climbed out and waited. He approached without breaking a defeated stride that dragged one step after the other.

I pulled the phone from my pocket.

"Mr. Dunland, I think you dropped this." I held it in front of his face. He had no choice but to halt. He lifted his shattered gaze to the phone.

I touched the little triangle icon, then the thirty-second rewind icon.

"*…She never gave up. She kept coming…*"

Pause.

Dunland's eyes shifted to me.

I handed him the phone.

WATER LANDING
October 9, 2021 to October 15, 2021

WHEN IT MATTERS

11

WHEN IT MATTERS

"Don't."

Earl Jackson's one-word admonition, barely above a whisper, landed like an engine block between us. His calloused hand fell on my shoulder with equal weight.

I dropped back onto my chair at the Silver Spoon Diner.

"Christ, Earl!"

He squeezed my shoulder to emphasize the point, then lowered his hand. A few of the Saturday morning regulars at our table pretended not to notice the exchange, or the cause.

"Look," Earl said. "You want to fix it. I want to fix it. But if you do anything about it right now, it lands back on her ten times over."

The young couple entered the diner around the time our high school-age waitress finished a circuit at our table collecting six different orders she probably has memorized. The woman coming through the door wasn't much older than the waitress, but the baby carrier hooked under one arm and the weight of a baby bag on the other added years. That and the worry etched in her face. The son of a bitch with her wore neck tattoos, a ratty leather jacket, a greasy

Dallas Cowboys hat and a pockmarked face that wanted to pick a fight. He sealed my negative first impression with two moves. First, he sucked in one last lungful of smoke from a stubby cigarette and tossed the butt over his shoulder like the world is his toilet. Second, he waited until he was halfway through the door before blowing out his second-hand smoke. Old diners like the Silver Spoon used to be thick with breakfast smokers, but that doesn't mean today's guests pine for carcinogens. I smelled it from across the room.

He ignored the young woman's struggle with the baby equipment. A couple of buddies in a booth by the window flagged him down. He stopped to talk a little too loudly with them and left her to find her own way to a table. She mounted the baby carrier on a chair and slid onto the seat beside it. She lifted a faded blue blanket to see if the passenger inside had any interest in the proceedings. She released a tense breath after confirming that the child slept.

Things might have gone differently if she hadn't placed the diaper bag on the table. The Silver Spoon is quick to bring coffee to its guests. The young mother waved the waitress away from her cup but hurried a nod for a cup to be poured for her man. It could have been my rush to judgment, but I thought I saw the waitress flick a sneer toward the back of that ratty leather jacket. The girls at the Silver Spoon know everybody in Essex.

He gassed with his buddies, then sauntered over to the table. The young mother watched for him, stealing a self-conscious glance or two around the room. Too late, she realized the bag remained on the table. Maybe they'd already had that discussion. Maybe he'd already meted out some domestic justice about leaving that baby shit all over hell. The way she moved when she realized her error, it struck me as Pavlovian.

She jerked the bag clear, intending to shove it under her chair, but she misjudged the arc. The corner of the bag caught the coffee mug and launched a brown fan of Silver Spoon's best off the table and onto his shoes.

"Clumsy bitch!" he snapped. He danced back a step and looked down at steel-toed work boots long past their prime. A little coffee on them wasn't the worst injury they'd suffered, not by a long shot. "All over my goddamn shoes!"

She scrambled. She found the napkin holder on the table and plucked half a dozen sheets. She was about to dive to the floor and sop it up on her hands and knees when he grabbed her wrist. She flinched and froze.

"Leave it! They got a mop here." He didn't so much release her arm as throw it at her. She sank obediently in her chair. The spill called out to her, but he directed her attention to a few drops on the table. "Clean up this shit. I'm not paying for that you dumb bitch. That's coming outta your pocket."

He wasn't loud. Not loud enough to turn heads. But between the movement of his thin, downturned lips and his menacing tone, I made out every word.

I might have let it go if he hadn't faked a lunge at her. She jerked against her chair, which barked out a tight screech on the linoleum. She'd seen that move before.

He curled up one lip, satisfied his point was made.

That did it for me.

Erica—the high school waitress working the Saturday morning shift, the one who seemed to know this guy—offered coffee refills at a nearby table. In my mind, I slipped the pot out of her hand and applied its scalding contents to the asshole's face before she could ask if I wanted regular or decaf.

That's when Earl prevailed on me to remain seated. He muttered one final comment. "You're gonna do something in a situation like that, you do it when it matters."

He was right, of course. Aside from the difficulty of explaining an assault charge to my police detective wife, I recognized the futility of influencing a bad domestic situation. A chivalrous act lasting a moment in a public place would do nothing to protect this young woman from the asshole's knuckles behind closed doors. I would have done her more harm than good.

I didn't have much appetite for my Mexican Skillet when it arrived, or for the standard Saturday morning bullshit that flew around the table.

The young couple remained hunched over their breakfasts in sullen silence when I excused myself and escaped into sharp October sunshine.

* * * * *

"You can't be serious," I told my wife. We sat at the kitchen table over remnants of a Thai chicken pizza. "You want me to help those weenies on the fire department?"

"Okay, I admit, it runs counter to all that is good and holy in this world, but I thought this might be perfect for you." She lifted her eyebrows at me. "Just don't get carried away."

Andy has a few tells. A slight underbite gives her lower lip prominence when her emotions are up. Too much, and you best run for your life; just a little and she's thinking on a path divergent from what she's saying. The lower lids of her eyes rise slightly when she's plotting. They frame her gold-flecked green irises in an exotic way—suggesting that she's looking at you and looking at something a mile over your shoulder at the same time.

She noted my stare.

"What?"

"I don't know…feels like I'm falling for something."

"Come on! It'll be fun! More fun than slinging beer at the cop tent."

Every year since we met, I've volunteered to help Andy and her colleagues at the Police and Fire Department Fall Festival—or the Fire and Police Department Fall Festival—depending on whose poster you were reading. But I contract my beer serving talents exclusively to the police beer tent, a venue far superior to the fire department brat fry or EMT haunted house.

Andy's proposal smacked of treason.

She rose and cleared her dishes. I snagged the last triangle of delicious Thai goodness and wolfed it.

"Al Thorson and his wife Rita run the haunted house every year. He's really into it. He goes more and more Hollywood all the time. He's always looking for people to put on makeup and hop out of the shadows. You would be perfect for it."

I swallowed quickly.

"I could use *the other thing* to scare people! Genius!"

"Absolutely not! It's dark in there. Just do what Al says and you can scare the daylights out of people without any *special effects*. You'll be a hit."

I hopped off the chair, stepped up to her and slid my arms around her slender waist. She tensed, suspicious.

I leaned in and pressed home a long kiss. She remained rigid for an instant before joining the effort. When it ended, I leaned back and smiled.

"Fine!" I said, thinly veiling the fact that I was thrilled by the idea. "I'll do it."

* * * * *

Approach Control cleared me for the visual approach to Essex County Airport. Fifteen miles out at five thousand feet, I spotted the X formed in asphalt by our two runways.

"Twenty-one Hotel Whiskey, I have the airport, cancel IFR."

"Roger Navajo One Hotel Whiskey, cancellation received, squawk VFR, frequency change approved."

"So long."

I rotated the transponder code to 1200 and thumbed the autopilot switch to the OFF position. Beyond the tip of my left wing a forest fire's worth of fall color ringed the cobalt blue surface of Leander Lake. Red, orange, yellow and tan sprawled away in all directions. Peak color, the TV weather guy had called it, proving his point with a graphic showing various bands of color across a map of Wisconsin.

"You should see it from here, pal," I said aloud to him.

I checked for traffic and rolled the big airplane left, putting the setting sun behind me and taking sole ownership of the color spectacular that is Fall in Wisconsin.

Twenty-five satisfying minutes later, after a side-trip tour of the countryside, dusk and the Navajo settled on Runway 31 at Essex County Airport.

Essex County Air Service's best pilot sat in a lawn chair near the open door to the Education Foundation's hangar. *My* lawn chair. Holding *my* beer in her hand. Pidge glanced up as I taxied toward the hangar. The Foundation's insurance guy wouldn't approve, but with a little deft energy management, I cut both engines on the roll and coasted across the ramp, then slowly into the wide-open hangar.

"Don't ever let Earl see you do that," Pidge commented when I stepped down the aircraft airstair.

"Holy Christ, no!"

Earl Jackson's idea of what is and is not proper procedure isn't so much good operating practice as it is law punishable by death.

I fixed a gaze on the bottle in her hand. "Help yourself to a beer."

"Don't mind if I do." She tipped the Corona my way and drew a healthy slug.

"What's wrong with this picture? You're off duty, yet you're still in uniform. You aren't flying, yet you're still at the airport. Do I owe you money?"

"You probably do. Go get a beer and a chair."

"You're in my chair."

"Get another one. I need to talk to you."

Like any man, I look for the Red Alert button when a woman says, 'I need to talk to you.' I checked my watch. Andy wouldn't be home for a couple hours. I had nothing better to do and no reasonable excuse to avoid this.

"Shoot," I said a few minutes later, propping open a second lawn chair with one hand and holding a cold bottle of Corona in the other. I sat down and savored both the drink and the way the orange October sunset contrasted with black silhouetted hangars and trees. There's a reason for those drugstore Halloween colors.

"I've got this friend," Pidge opened.

I looked sideways at her.

"No, dumbass, not me. Her name is Kelly. Kelly Pratt. We were friends in high school. Super nice girl, but with the worst luck. Her parents are shitty. Her taste in boys sucks. She's a sweetheart, but she gets—I don't know—blind and all girly around total losers. It's why I stopped hanging out with her." Pidge looked down at her hands. I listened for a note of guilt in her voice. "We stopped being friends—or rather I cut her off—because of the current abusive asshole in her life."

My interest meter dropped into the yellow. I wasn't sure what Pidge expected from me. My only curiosity sprang from the fact that Pidge normally didn't invest in this kind of soap opera.

"You might want to cut to the chase here," I said.

"The dirtbag she's with is planning on moving away with her."

"And?"

Pidge shook her head. "She can't. She can't go with this guy. He's the worst of the worst. He's living off her right now because he got fired from yet another job. He gets fired from every job. He can't get a regular paycheck or go on Unemployment because they'll garnish it for child support. He's run up her credit cards—"

"Wait. The guy has a kid with someone else? And now your friend is with him?"

Pidge heaved a sigh. "She dated the guy back in high school. Then he ran off, got some girl pregnant, then left that chick and called up Kelly to come get him. She did—poor stupid idiot. She actually drove to Texas and brought him back here."

I'm not sure what motivates women under ordinary circumstances. This baffled me entirely.

"And then he got her pregnant, too."

"Your friend is pregnant?"

"No. She had the kid two months ago."

I made a face.

"I know! I know! See what I mean? Dipshit's got no job. He drinks. He does drugs. I'm pretty sure he deals, too." Pidge paused. She debated something with herself, then she said, "He uses his fists on her. I saw her last spring. Once. Didn't say hi. Just saw her. She had bruises and a cast on her arm."

I wondered if Pidge planned to use her fists on this guy.

"Look, Pidge," I mustered a little of my flight instructor demeanor, "there are battles you can't win. If your friend is into this loser, you won't change her mind. Disaster is in her DNA."

"I thought the same thing. He's ruining her life and she doesn't see it. We had a couple fights over him, and then I just stopped seeing her. Now she has this baby."

I remembered Earl's admonition at the Silver Spoon. "Pidge, this is like rescuing a drowning person. More than likely, they'll take you down with them."

The night air cooled rapidly around us. I enjoyed the crisp air. There wouldn't be too many more Indian Summer days like today, what with Halloween on short final and winter holding just over the horizon.

Pidge shook her head. "She can't go with him. She has a cleaning job in Essex, but if she leaves, she'll lose the only income they have. Neither of them has any money. He wants to move them in with his father in New Jersey. The old man is worse than Eric—that's the asshole. It will be awful—for her, for the baby. No job. No money. A house full of idiots. Eric smokes like a Memphis barbecue. The baby's going to have asthma before he's two!"

"Let it go."

"Jesus, Will! I need to stop this from happening."

"But you can't. You said it yourself. She's blind. And maybe a little desperate. Or hopeless. Or damaged."

Pidge didn't like what she was hearing. "The thing is, she's a sweet thing. Really. She's funny, but he's killing that in her. She's smart, but he's pounding into her that she isn't."

"Her choice."

"No, Will! He's holding the kid hostage and she's practically a prisoner. He never lets her go anywhere except to work. She works for a cleaning service during the day, so he stays at home with the baby. He drinks. She said she came home one day, and the baby was in one of those mechanical swing things, dripping and crying, and he was passed out on the couch."

"Wait," I said, "how do you know all this?"

Pidge twisted the bottle in her hands, wringing its neck. "She reached out to me a couple days ago. She said it was to say good-bye because we were friends once. She said she was sorry. To me! Christ, I dumped her like old trash and she's apologizing to me! See what I mean? She's such a fucking sweetheart!"

"Dare I ask? What do you want me to do?"

Pidge leaned back in the lawn chair and cast a blue-eyed, blonde pixie spawn-of-the-devil look my way.

"I want you to make her disappear."

* * * * *

"Andy can't be involved," I told everyone. We congregated in a small lounge in the office portion of the Foundation hangar. "That has to be clear up front. What we're doing is straight-up kidnapping and if Shithead goes all legal on you," I pointed at Kelly, who sat with her eyes downcast and her hands folded in her lap like a scolded Sunday School girl, "he's got the law on his side."

She nodded.

It was her. The girl from the diner. A little taller than Pidge with long waves of red hair and an ivory complexion surrounding bright blue eyes. She had a thin but sweet face. She reminded me of every nice girl I'd ever known in school. The ones who always helped. The ones who never had a catty word. I could not, no matter how I tried, imagine how she wound up with the hawk-faced moron.

Pidge had filled me in on the loser. An early adopter of weed in his middle school days. In and out of juvenile court half a dozen times before he dropped out of high school. His out-of-state antics were shrouded in mystery, but when he called Kelly to renew their fiery relationship, he had more at stake than an unwanted ex-demanding child support. Kelly thought he had a warrant for his arrest in Texas.

After returning to Essex, he worked construction for cash under the table. Two weeks in he'd been fired. Then he got fired from a warehouse job. Then from a job with a landscape service.

"He parks his GMC pickup at a friend's house because Al Raymond pulled repo papers on it," Pidge had told me.

Despite all this, he had a brand new 65-inch HDTV and a PlayStation delivered to Kelly's apartment. It didn't take a genius to figure out he'd drained her credit cards. Worse, Kelly said their apartment manager came looking for two month's rent, which she had given Shithead to pay.

With another month coming due, he planned to run.

Pidge sat beside her friend. Earl Jackson occupied a corner of the small room, holding down a fat recliner and scaring the girl with his friendliest face. He hadn't spoken a word.

"You said he wants to leave Friday morning?" I asked.

Kelly nodded quickly.

"Any particular reason?"

"Um, he says Tony will give him his last pay on Thursday night," Kelly said in a small voice. "He says Tony owes him for three weeks."

I didn't know who Tony was, but I doubted he intended to pay Shithead anything. Nevertheless, I hoped the promise of cash would serve as an anchor. Losers love to believe their own bullshit.

"And you're sure about Thursday night?" Pidge asked. "You're sure he wants to go to the Fall Festival?"

Kelly nodded shyly. "We went last year. He spends all his time in the beer tent, but he says the fireworks will be his Goodbye Forever to Essex." Kelly looked at each of us, then added in a small voice, "I like the fireworks."

Earl said nothing.

"Then I guess it's Thursday night," I said.

Pidge looked at her watch. "We better get you back to work. You told your boss we were only going to Subway."

Kelly gathered herself obediently. "Jeanie and the other girls always take too long for lunch and Audrie gets really mad. Audrie also tells on me to Eric." Kelly reached for the cell phone she had placed on the coffee table. Twice during the short meeting, the device buzzed to alert Kelly to text messages from the Shithead. Each time, Kelly responded quickly. "If I don't answer him right away, he calls and calls until I pick up."

Earl rolled his eyes at that, so I knew he was listening.

I hadn't been sure about bringing Earl into this. Even after Pidge helped me put two and two together and I realized that Kelly was the unfortunate girl from the diner, I wasn't sure Earl would help. It surprised me when I hesitantly told him what I had in mind and he agreed to sit in on the meeting.

Yet so far, his presence only served to scare the poor girl.

Earl abruptly stood up and loomed over Kelly. The girl caught her breath. Pidge tightened her hand hold on her friend.

"Why haven't you left him?"

Kelly didn't lift her eyes to Earl when she replied. "He said if I ever left he would get a lawyer and take Seth away from me."

"Where would he get money for a lawyer?" I asked. Earl didn't budge.

"He said his dad would give him money for a lawyer and I could never afford one to fight him."

"Do you want to go with him?" Earl asked.

Kelly shook her head.

Earl balled his fists and planted them on his hips. "He shows up in your life six months from now, are you gonna wet your panties and run off with him again?"

Kelly shook her head emphatically.

"Why are you agreeing to this now? Why haven't you run before?"

"Where?" she asked, finally lifting her eyes to his.

Earl didn't answer. He reached for her. She flinched. Pidge steadied her. Earl's hands pass for potent claws, calloused and full of scars and knobs earned as badges of pain and misadventure. Kelly shrank from his touch—a sign of her training.

Earl gently pressed a finger to the corner of her jaw near her left ear and slowly turned her head. She winced.

"He hit you?"

Despite a thin layer of makeup, Earl's finger found the blue and yellow bruise under her skin.

She swallowed. Her eyes fell in shame.

"He break your arm last spring?"

I barely heard her reply. "He didn't mean to."

He dropped his hand.

"Thursday night," Earl said.

* * * * *

I love Fall. I love the atmospheric shift to cool, crystalline days. I love the mystery of leaves that dress in wild colors to celebrate dying. I love the way Halloween unleashes its whimsical mix of monsters and ballerinas, vampires and superheroes.

The Police and Fire Department Fall Festival spices the calendar with a last gasp of fun before November slips in on the turn of a page. Before darkness begins and ends short days.

The festival filled Library Park. Game and vendor tents lined the park paths. Families arrived early to spread blankets and stake out lawn space for the evening fireworks. Staging a festival this late in the season carries risks. Some years the dominant activity is finding a spot out of the rain. This year, for a solid week, the planners held their breath as a fat high pressure system floated across North America. Stark blue skies performed a spectral shift each evening, turning pink, then orange. Thursday night—Halloween Night, the start of the festival—the sunset put on a spectacular display. The City of Essex celebrated with citywide Trick or Treat from four p.m. to seven p.m. Fireworks at nine-fifteen topped the evening, although the police tent continued serving beer and live music until eleven.

Andy deployed an extra bounce in her step when we arrived. She enjoys working the police department beer tent. This year marked our fourth Festival and our first year apart. I should have been unhappy with the separation, but I was energized by my new job as a ghoul lurking in the haunted house. Or zombie. Or zombie ghoul.

"You need to go put on your makeup," Andy pecked me on the cheek and pointed across the park grounds at the haunted house.

"Words I never thought I'd hear you say. Will you visit my scary lair later? Maybe make out with the resident monster?"

"Oh, hell no!" she declared. "I'm not having you jump out at me and I'm not making out with some monster and getting all full of grease paint. Stop over here later, though. I want pictures. I'll pour you a free beer. Now go!"

I found Al and Rita Thorson hustling around a fold-out camper behind the haunted house—a full-blown carnival rig that Al claimed he found on eBay. I suspected him of being related to a carny. Either way, I gave him the Boy with The Best Toy Award. Roughly the size of an eighteen-wheeler's trailer, the rig unfolds to three times that dimension. An electric tram system carries thrill-seeking guests through a maze of dark rooms. Al added home-town touches, renaming the bloodstained marquee *The Essex House of Horrors* and slipping in references to local sights and cemeteries. Two- to three-person tram carts wind and jerk their way through a honeycomb of small rooms filled with flashing lights, leaning skeletons, and dangling spiderwebs. Some of the chambers remain completely dark as water drips on riders or cold air blows down their necks. Others offer tableaus of horror. Al adds live actors in some of the scenes. Trained werewolves and prancing monsters extract screams during the five-minute ride. I've long admired his work.

"Where do you want me?" I asked, reporting for duty.

Al wore the classic Count Dracula outfit. The cape. The high collar. The slicked back hair and pasty white complexion. He stood beside a werewolf with a set of teeth that looked capable of taking down a rhino.

"Hey, Bob," I said.

"Hey, Will," the werewolf replied. "Great night for this!"

"Amen. A little later I'll find a stick and we can play fetch."

"Fetch this," he replied, holding up a huge, hairy paw. I tried to guess what gesture he displayed beneath the fur.

"You! Come with me!" A tall woman with stacked hair, a stark white face and black lips grabbed my arm. I followed Al's wife Rita. She maneuvered me to a stool beside a small table. She popped open a toolbox containing dozens of small tubes and vials.

"Jesus, Rita, you know there are kids here tonight, right?"

Rita Thorson stopped and grabbed both sides of the filmy gown barely covering her abundant bosom. "Ugh! This thing keeps riding down. I'll pin it or something, but let's get you made up!"

"What are you supposed to be?"

"One of Dracula's vampire babes. I feel more like a hooker."

"Stop staring at my wife's boobs, Stewart," Count Dracula scolded me. "As soon as she's done with you, I'll show you where to go and what to do."

I had come prepared. I wore a ripped old gray sweatshirt over a black t-shirt and black jeans. Rita Thorson swabbed me in sweet-smelling gray makeup, then darkened my eyes and lips to lend my head the look of a skull. She deftly applied colors to create cracks and gouges in my skin, and what looked like open, oozing sores. After an eternity in her chair, she handed me a mirror.

"Holy shit!" I exclaimed. "I wouldn't want me jumping out of the dark at me!"

Rita wasn't as impressed. "Your hair is wrong. Too nice." She disappeared into the trailer and came back holding what looked like a dead animal. With some tugging and adjusting she added a black and gray wig that itched but which frosted the cake with wild spikes of hair.

I looked awesome.

Al left me no time to admire myself. The moment he saw that Rita's work was done, he grabbed me and ushered me up a short ladder through the back entrance of the Essex House of Horrors.

"This is the rear exit. Or you can follow the tram track out to the front. There's a footpath beside the track but watch your head. Also, that ladder won't be there once we get started. Last year some kids climbed up and snuck in the back door. If there's an emergency, you can go out that way but it's a five-foot drop."

"What's this room?"

Al produced a small flashlight and flicked it on. A seven-foot-tall reptile man appeared on the other side of the tram track.

"Gator Man." The reptile statue wore a chipped green plastic sheen. "He needs some work, but he still has it in the dark."

"You sound like my wife."

"Come on. You're in here. Near the end." Al stepped along the tram track through a curtained opening. "You're not epileptic, are you? I should have asked sooner."

"No. Why?"

"This is your station." He pointed at the corner of a narrow space where the tram track curved tightly. "When the tram gets about halfway through, the light starts to strobe. You'll be over in the corner. Stand really still. They'll think you're a mannequin. The light starts off yellow, then turns greenish. When that happens, move toward the cart. You don't have to lunge or anything. Just moving in the strobe light will scare the shit outta them. Trust me."

This was the last scream stop before the tram carts swung through the exit.

"So, I'm the grand finale?"

Al shrugged. "More of an after-thought. Next year I'm thinking creepy clown. Like, with an ax or something. But you'll do." He patted me on the back. "Couple things. Here's the emergency light switch." He aimed his flashlight at a round plastic button mounted on an electrical box on the wall. "And down here, by your feet, there's a pedal that will stop the tram. Anything goes wrong, anything at all, step on that. I'll come running."

"Got it."

He moved toward the path where the tram ran through another curtain into darkness. "One more thing."

"What?"

He pulled a phone from his pocket and held it up. The flash caught me by surprise. He grinned at me.

"This'll be your program picture for next year's Fire and Police Softball Tournament," he said. He issued a maniacal laugh and ducked through the curtains in a cloud of cape. From the darkness next door, I heard him call out, "Showtime in ten minutes! We go until nine and shut down for the fireworks, then another hour after!"

I backed into my corner thinking about the plan Pidge, Earl and I had hatched, and how the timing of it slotted into Al's schedule. I reached in my pocket and pulled out a Bluetooth earpiece. After slipping the wig out of the way, I inserted the device. I pulled out my phone, swiped the screen and touched the contact for Pidge.

"You all set?" she asked by way of answering.

"Ready. Remember. Eyes closed. All the way. Eyes closed."

"I'll tell her. Again."

I tapped the screen and ended the call.

Total darkness closed around me. I heard a mechanical whine and felt distant thumping and bumping. The tram chain rattled in its channel.

For the next hour and a half, I scared the living daylights out of men, women, and children—many in costumes of their own. I made teenagers too cool for all this silliness jump and shriek. I made grown men cry out. The strobe light revealed me slowly, but I enhanced my act by moving out of the corner, crouching beside the tram track and vanishing. When the tram rolled through, and the strobe flashed, it seemed as if this tiny room had nothing to offer. After a few seconds of flashing lights—

Fwooomp!

—I reappeared inches from the tram riders.

Freaking hilarious.

A teenaged girl dumped her soft drink all over her boyfriend. A kid sitting between his parents whipped his cotton candy up into his father's face, coating a pair of glasses in strands of pink. The young and old shrieked and screamed. I nearly took a punch to the face from a boy in an Essex High letter jacket who tried to convert his girlish scream to bravado. From that point on, I gripped a pipe running parallel to the tram track so that I could dodge reactionary fists.

Disappearing again seconds later when the lights went out was almost as shocking as appearing out of nowhere. People grabbed the safety bar, grabbed each other, and spun their heads around looking for the zombie ghoul. As the evening wore on, I perfected my timing and often reappeared just as the cart reached the exit curtains. The last-second shrieks were gratifying.

As nine p.m. approached, I anticipated Pidge's call.

The plan directed Pidge to "run into" Kelly and the Shithead in the police beer tent. Kelly assured us that Shithead would install himself there, fanning out singles for beer after beer, but keeping his woman and her baby close. Kelly was instructed to beg him to take her to the haunted house. She assured us he would refuse. She was to keep asking until Pidge showed up, by which time Shithead would have a comfortable buzz on and be only too happy to let Pidge field the nagging request. Shithead's stool in the beer tent would serve as perch for him to watch them enter and exit the haunted house, keeping the leash short. Except they wouldn't exit. Pidge pre-positioned her car. Earl waited at the airport. I manned the escape hatch.

At eleven minutes to nine, my phone rang as a cart exited my chamber of terror. I touched the earpiece.

"You're cutting it close," I said.

"No, we're fucked!" Pidge said breathlessly. "He's taking her on the ride. Not me. Fucker jumped up at the last second and butted in. He's not letting her out of his sight. They're on their way to you now!"

Voices mocked Gator Man in the next room. The next cart approached.

"Shit!" I tried to think. "Screw it! Get to your car and be ready. Did you tell her—"

"YES, I fucking told her! Eyes closed!" Plan B.

The call ended. My heart thumped in my chest.

The next cart burst through the curtains and rumbled toward me in the dark. I stood frozen for too long—completely out of character—as the strobes lit up. They flickered and flashed and the two kids sitting in the cart stared at me.

"Lame," one of them commented blandly as the cart jostled them out of my space.

"Crap! Crap! Crap!" I muttered to myself. "What's the one thing we know about plans, Stewart?"

They change.

I jumped back into my routine for the next cart. And the next after that. And six more after that, thinking about my options, thinking about the dimensions of the room and the location of its equipment.

I kept my position near the track. After each cycle of strobe lights ceased, I had roughly twenty seconds between carts to see through a slit in the curtain into the Gator Man chamber.

Dammit! I should have told Kelly to sit on the right side. Riding with Pidge, it didn't matter. With Shithead in the picture a sinking feeling told me that if she wasn't on the right, she would be out of my reach.

He's all about controlling her.

He'll make her get in first.

That puts her on the wrong side!

A cart entered my chamber. I dropped my routine and stood like a statue, using the strobe lights to study the small room. Directly above the cart, a black framework channeled electrical wires across the ceiling and provided support to the inner wall. People riding on that side—Kelly's side—could easily reach out and touch the wall. It left no room for me.

The strobe show ended. I crouched to my former position and vanished, fixing a grip on the pipe beside the track. I reached behind my back and found the floor pedal that stops the tram. I focused on the slit in the curtain.

A flash of red hair caught my eye. *Kelly.*

Then a stubbled face. Shithead.

The cart rumbled through the curtain. Kelly sat on the inside —*the wrong side*—her eyes squeezed shut. She cooed softly to the baby in her arms.

The cart jerked and rolled closer. I counted down the seconds. By now I had a firm sense of the timing. Three. Two. One. The strobes fired on schedule. Caught in yellow flashes, Kelly clutched the bundle in her arms, her mouth moving as she hummed and spoke to the infant. Shithead sat arrogantly beside her, an unlit cigarette in his mouth, working hard to look bored.

Fwooomp!

I appeared. I lunged at Shithead and howled. He shrieked. The cigarette flew from his mouth. His hands flew up to ward me off. I pulled back, closed a fist and punched him in the chest.

"What the fuck!" He flailed at me and jerked on the safety bar at the same time. I extended my left foot and found the pedal.

A switch snapped.

Clunk! The tram stopped. Strobe lights captured my movements as jerky flash photos. Shithead fought the safety bar and shouted at me.

"Motherfucker! I'm gonna kick your fuckin' ass!" Spittle rode his words. He twisted himself against the safety bar. I reached behind the seat and pulled the safety release lever. The bar flew up and Shithead jumped to his feet to keep his ass-kicking promise.

Fwooomp! I vanished on a beat of the strobes, leaving him to cock his arms for a swing at—

—nothing. He jerked his head back and forth, searching.

"COME ON ASSHOLE!" he shouted.

I tapped my toes and rose ten or fifteen inches until I could reach the two-by-four framework on the ceiling. I pulled myself across the tram track above the cart. Shithead spun and jumped, looking for me in the narrow open space beside the cart.

I reached down. Kelly huddled over her child, protecting the bundle from the fury and confusion beside her. Her soon-to-be-ex-boyfriend shouted and cursed. She leaned as far away as she could, eyes squeezed tightly shut. I grabbed the cart and pulled myself down until my face touched her red hair beside one ear.

"Don't open your eyes, sweetie. I've got you!" She shivered. "No matter what, don't open your eyes!"

I clamped one hand on her left forearm, near her wrist. I pushed the imaginary levers in my head.

FWOOOMP!

She vanished along with the child in her arms. Kelly issued a muted cry. I felt her body tense against the sensation of weightlessness.

"No matter what! No matter what!" I repeated, keeping close to her ear as I pulled her upward. She floated free of the cart with me. "Curl up! Keep it tight! I got you!"

"MOTHERFUCKER! WHERE ARE YOU?!" Shithead screamed in the dark.

The strobe cycle began again. He spun around and spotted the empty cart. For a moment he stood staring blankly, not comprehending. "Kelly? Kelly! KELLY! BITCH, WHERE ARE YOU?!"

Shithead dominated half of the available space in the small chamber, swinging his arms and jabbing at the darkness. The cart and track occupied the other half. I pulled myself along the framework above the track to the curtain separating my chamber from Gator Man's.

"Easy, Kelly, easy," I whispered. "I got you. Keep yourself in a ball. Curl up in a ball so I can carry you."

She complied. I pulled her against my chest. She hugged the

child to hers. I used my free hand to pull us through the curtain. The humanoid plastic lizard leered over a stopped cart containing a middle-aged couple. Genuine fear painted their faces as they listened to the curses coming from the room ahead. Things grew worse when they saw the curtains part, then fall back in place.

"GET BACK HERE YOU BITCH!" Shithead lunged at the curtain, tripped on the edge of the plank path beside the track, and dropped hard, pulling the curtain down with him.

Both faces in the cart flashed wide-eyed fear. Shithead writhed on the floor in a tangle of curtain.

I aimed for the rear entrance. The strobing lights from my zombie ghoul chamber ceased, but the bottom-lit face of Gator Man showed me the black door and its simple knob. I rotated, stretched my legs against the cart containing the couple watching Shithead have his meltdown, and turned the doorknob. The cart gave me a launch platform. I kicked and shoved open the door—a little too hard. It slammed against the outside wall.

The woman in the cart shrieked.

I floated through the frame gripping a shivering ball of Kelly against my chest.

"You're okay. You're okay," I repeated over and over. Kelly held her knees up and her infant to her chest.

The glide took me to Al's camper. Earlier, the camper had been a chaotic scene. Now nothing and no one moved below me as I touched the awning over the makeup table. I gripped and pulled us over the canvas roof.

From my hip pocket I extracted a power unit and propeller combination. One-handed, I snapped a prop onto the unit and thumbed the slide. The prop spun, producing thrust. With my left arm around Kelly and my right hand on the power unit, I eased into controlled flight.

Pidge's Honda idled among rows of vehicles parked in the main lot adjacent to the softball field behind the festival grounds.

I curved left around a small tree, crossed the right field chain link fence, and made a run down the first base line. I maneuvered around the backstop fence, then lined up on the space between two rows of cars. I landed yards from where Pidge stood.

"Honey keep your eyes closed and put your feet down now. All the way down," I said softly. I couldn't just reappear with Kelly balled up in my arms. We'd both go down hard. Not good with the baby between us.

Kelly unwound herself. I hoped for the best.

Fwooomp!

We reappeared and dropped onto the gravel parking lot. Kelly wobbled but remained standing.

Pidge hurried to my side and grabbed Kelly by the upper arms.

"Open your eyes, girl!"

Kelly blinked at Pidge and broke into a breathless laugh. She shifted her wide eyes in my direction. I thought the makeup might frighten her, but she simply stared at me in wonder.

"What was—?"

"We gotta go!" Pidge pulled Kelly around the front of the car. She hurried her to the passenger door and ushered her in. Returning to the driver's door, Pidge threw me a disapproving glance.

I was about to defend my appearance when a chilling cry cut the night air.

"BITCH I'M GONNA KILL YOU!"

Shithead rounded the corner of Al's camper and sprinted toward the parking lot.

"Go!" I snapped at Pidge. "GO! GO! GO!"

Pidge didn't need encouragement. She slammed the car door and shoved the Honda in gear. Her front tires kicked gravel at my legs.

I glanced around. Clear.

Fwooomp!

I vanished, tapped the ground, and shot upward. Pidge raced between rows of parked cars toward the lot exit.

Shithead had no chance. I anticipated the satisfaction of seeing him stagger to a halt while the Honda's taillights disappeared with Pidge flashing the finger from an open window.

I was wrong.

He didn't draw up, frustrated and out of breath. He didn't stop. Nor did he pursue Pidge. Instead, he broke left and retreated toward *The Essex House of Horrors* at a dead run.

"What now?" I asked aloud.

I thumbed the power unit slide control and cruised back onto the festival grounds. Lights from the rides, food tents and beer tent lifted a glow into the remaining leaves of tall trees. A sizable crowd dotted the channels between tents and clustered near a bandstand where a local group covered "Bad Moon Rising."

Shithead ran through the crowd like a sinner with the devil at his heels.

Where do you think you're going?

He shot past the entrance, then angled right toward Park Street. Park ran north and south and eventually joined Main. The street ends with the library, the fire station, and Library Park with its soft-ball fields on the far side. The softball fields have their own parking lot—a lot with its own access road that curved around the fields and joined—

Shit! Park Street!

Pidge had to go the long way around to get to Park Street. Shithead knew that. By slicing through the festival grounds, he cut her off.

Just as the realization hit me, Pidge's Honda broke into view to my left, tracking up the access road to join Park Street. Shithead bolted ahead of her, on Park, still running. I wondered, why doesn't he stop? He's got her. But then, what could he do? Stand in front of her car? Pidge would leave him in a broken-boned heap.

Either way, it wasn't good.

Pidge made the turn onto Park. I aimed the power unit on a flight path that intersected the street, thinking I could dive down and shout a warning to her.

All available parallel parking had been taken up hours ago. Foot traffic on the sidewalks was light to nil since most people were already in position for the fireworks. I looked for one of the auxiliary cops Tom Ceeves pulls in for the festival, but none of the reflective-vest volunteers stood in sight.

Shithead pounded the pavement, racing ahead in Pidge's headlight beams. The Honda accelerated briskly. If Shithead tried to barricade her, Pidge stood an excellent chance of committing vehicular manslaughter.

He veered left abruptly and cut between a parked car and a black pickup truck with a canvas tarp over a substantial load in its bed.

A truck loaded for moving.

His truck.

As Pidge darted past, he jerked open the driver's door and jumped in. The pickup roared to life. He slammed it in reverse and smacked the pickup's high steel rear bumper into the front end of the car behind him. He twisted the front wheels sharply and shot forward, not quite clearing the car ahead, shattering its taillight with his brush bar as he shot into the street in a squealing U-turn.

Pidge accelerated rapidly up Park Street. Shithead roared after her. I pumped up the power on my propulsion unit and joined the chase. I aimed high to clear the trees that arched over the street and to ensure that I wouldn't tangle with wires.

This enterprise had jumped the express elevator to Hell. No outcome now seemed viable. Unless Pidge lost him, he would simply follow her to the airport and put himself between Kelly and her baby and their escape. No part of the role Pidge or Earl or I played in this would stand up to legal scrutiny. It didn't matter that he might beat her senseless behind closed doors. Even a mediocre lawyer could make Kelly out to be the criminal here.

He might be a deadbeat, a loser, and a violent domestic partner, but he had rights and Kelly, along with her co-conspirators, trampled those rights tonight. This game could only be won if Kelly disappeared, the last hope for a woman when the police and the law can't stop the fists from flying.

I saw only one chance of that now.

Shithead peeled down the street after Pidge.

Where Park met Main the light flashed from yellow to red. Pidge braked long enough to make the turn and then blew through the red onto Main over squealing tires.

Shithead followed.

Main Street is also State Highway 34, which heads east out of town past the airport. If he didn't catch her in town, he would catch her on the open highway. And for all I knew, he already had his cell phone in hand, reporting a kidnapping to the police.

Andy's voice snapped in my head. *What on earth were you thinking?*

Pidge widened the gap, catching Essex's few traffic lights on green. Judging by the power I needed to keep pace and the relative wind tearing at me, I estimated her speed at over fifty miles per hour through town.

He drove faster. The V-8 under his pickup's hood roared. At Main and Second Street, traffic slowed to stop for a red she squeaked past. He veered into the open oncoming lane and blew through the intersection as cross traffic rolled forward. Multiple near-miss horns blasted.

No question now. Pidge stepped on it in vain as she passed the last gas station on the east side of town and accelerated into open country. A quarter mile behind her, Shithead drove with nothing ahead but Pidge's taillights.

I dove for the pavement. I had a small lead on the pickup, but he came on fast.

I checked for wires. Power lines ran parallel to the north side of the highway on my left. To my right, open fields. The airport perimeter approached.

I dropped to the height of a car roof. I held the power unit forward and let my body follow, thinking not for the first time that it would be damned cool if someone could actually see me doing this.

It wasn't easy, but I ducked my head to see Shithead approaching rapidly behind me. He carried more speed. I was maxed out. What I had in mind would depend on luck and would probably knock me senseless when I hit his windshield like a bug.

His engine howled. He surged toward me. I gauged angle and distance to the brush bar on the front of his pickup.

It happened too fast for me to think. One moment we both shot down the right lane of Highway 34, catching up to Pidge who began braking for the turn into the Essex County Air Services lot. The next moment his hood slid under me.

I flipped the power unit free and hooked both hands on his brush bar. The steel jerked me forward, but my grip held. I became a human hood ornament with the wind tearing past me. I pulled myself up to the brush bar. My feet and knees banged on the hood of the pickup.

A glance at the face behind the windshield showed me a rictus of fury, blind and deaf to anything, utterly without reason. Whatever he had consumed in the beer tent now fueled the mean side of drunk. I had to stop him before he reached within striking distance of Kelly or Pidge.

I heaved myself over the brush bar. I reached down and grabbed the bumper, then pulled myself toward the streaking pavement. I twisted. My legs came down. My entire body pressed against the grille. The headlights blazed in my face.

I curled up and repositioned myself directly in front of the enraged face behind the wheel.

FWOOOMP!

I reappeared and popped up over the brush bar screaming at the top of my lungs.

Zombie ghoul attack!

He screamed. I screamed.

He slammed on the brakes.

The overloaded pickup shimmied and slewed unevenly until one set of tires left the pavement. Once that happened, it was all over. The brakeforce distribution system tried to compensate, but it didn't account for the panicked driver, who threw the wheel wildly from side to side in a vain attempt to avoid the zombie ghoul crawling toward him over the hood of his truck.

The truck left the road and ground across the shoulder, then down a shallow embankment. I might have been in some deep shit if I had held on, but the first sharp bounce threw me like a cowboy leaving the back of a bucking horse.

Fwooomp! I jammed my levers forward and vanished. The upward shot sent me skyward. I had no second power unit. Unchecked upward trajectory threatened to shoot me straight into space.

The truck passed beneath me, shaking loose its load as it dove into the ditch. The tarp flapped and boxes tumbled through the air. A cloud of dust rose where the tires gouged the gravel shoulder. I heard a loud bang; an axle or part of the suspension snapping. Shithead's truck continued through the ditch, shedding parts and load. It rumbled to a halt upright and in one piece.

STOP!

The billboard-sized subconscious thought filled my head.

The core muscle that runs down my center when I vanish clenched.

I stopped.

I stabilized thirty feet above the ditch. Shithead's pickup rattled to a jarring metallic halt on a steep angle beside Highway 34.

I hung in the still air as the engine shuddered and died and a dust cloud caught up with the wreckage.

An Essex PD squad car pulled up with its red and blue light bar painting the scene. Shithead tumbled out of the pickup cab.

A light breeze, barely a breath of air, pushed me toward the airport. A second squad car arrived, this one containing Bill Morgan and Thor, the police K-9 unit's drug-sniffing star performer. Thor waited patiently in the back of the unit while Bill and the first officer on the scene handcuffed Shithead and moved him to the back of the first cruiser. The two officers interrogated their prisoner, then stepped away and discussed the probability that the driver left the road under the influence—probable cause for a search of the vehicle.

That's not good news for you, Shithead.

I slowly drifted out of earshot. Fireworks began to burst over Essex Library Park, tentative at first, then rapidly multiplying to fill the sky with flying stars and flaming flowers. Aerial bombs sent rolling thunder across the landscape to compete with my hammering heartbeat.

Simultaneous to the pyrotechnic celebration, strobe and flashing navigation lights rose on Runway 31 at Essex County Airport. I recognized the throbbing Continental engines of Essex County Air Service's Beechcraft Baron. It soared rapidly skyward, but then dipped and swung over Essex. I watched it swing a wide circle around the fireworks.

That would be Earl Jackson, playing his part, winging a scared young woman and her infant child into the night sky. A little more than an hour away, Candice Hammond Stubowsky Day Jackson O'Connor Thorpe—one of Earl's ex-wives—waited at her hunting resort near the Canadian border for the chance to add a sweet young woman to her live-in staff where seclusion would give Kelly and her child all the safety and security they needed.

Earl dipped a wing at the bright display marking Kelly's freedom, then climbed into the night sky.

The breeze sent me across the airport perimeter. I drifted closer to the earth until the fall caused by reappearing and submitting to gravity wouldn't kill me.

I popped into view and dropped on the grass near the t-hangars on the north side of the field. Dew painted my boots while I weighed my options. Pidge might still be at the airport office. I could hit her up for a ride.

Or I could walk to the road and try thumbing my way back into town.

Maybe see if anyone would pick up a zombie ghoul on a dark Halloween night.

WHEN IT MATTERS
July 12, 2019

A Way In A Manger

12

A WAY IN A MANGER

"Don't forget to stop at the hardware store and pick up an outdoor timer," Andy said.

"Digital or mechanical?"

"What's the difference?"

"Never mind. I'll take care of it. What time does the service start?"

"Six. And please don't be late."

"I won't. Love you," I said.

"You, too."

I ended the call and pocketed my phone.

"What service?" Arun asked. I had stopped in his office to tell him that I closed and locked the main hangar and to hint that he should go home. The desktop pile of grant applications to the Christine and Paulette Paulesky Education Foundation seemed to grow at his touch, rather than diminish.

"Christmas Eve Eve."

He cocked a skeptical eye in my direction. "Is that a thing?"

"Andy's church likes to put on a Christmas Eve service and potluck dinner, but attendance has been dropping off. Too much competition with family travel plans. This year they bumped it up one day. 'Tis the night before the night before Christmas."

"I did not take you for a religious man, Will."

"What are you talking about? I pray every time we take off. *Please, God, don't let me screw up.*" I winked to head off the blossoming look of horror on Arun's face. "Church is Andy's thing. I go along for the major holidays because they have food." I zipped my jacket and waved to him. "Thus, I bid you a Merry Christmas Eve Eve! I'm off to purchase a replacement timer for the Nativity scene. Baby Jesus needs a nightlight!"

Outside, light snow quilted the silent airport. The green and white rotating beacon swung around and around. Falling flakes solidified the beams of light against the night sky.

I brushed fresh snow from my car and made the run to Ace Hardware where I confronted a dizzying array of indoor and outdoor timers. I settled on a mechanical type that used green and red plastic pins to map the hours of darkness and light.

A line formed at the single open register. I checked my watch and calculated the time needed to reach the church, install the timer, and seat myself with Andy for the service. The line moved slowly. I might have to slip into the pew during the first hymn.

A young woman ahead of me laid a coil of garden hose on the counter, then added a candy cane from a countertop jar. She dug into her pockets, pulling out crushed bills and a fistful of change. I caught a whiff of body odor and noticed greasy hair tucked into her stocking hat. She wore an old letter jacket over sagging workout pants and blown-out sandals over wet socks. Her attire contrasted sharply with that of the church full of worshipers I would soon be joining—good Christians decked out in their holiday best.

"Seventy-five, eighty, eighty-one-two-three." The teenaged clerk counted out the last pennies from the spill of pocket change. "Uh…looks like you're twenty cents short."

The woman stared at the coins, willing them to reproduce.

I laid the timer on the counter.

"Put the candy cane on mine," I said.

The kid looked at the woman for confirmation. She did not raise her head, but rather lifted the hose off the counter and scooped up the candy cane. She turned abruptly and hurried out the double doors.

"Merry Christmas to you, too," I muttered, instantly wishing I hadn't.

"Yeah, really," the kid at the register agreed, doubling my regret. "Who needs a garden hose at Christmas?"

He waved his scanner over the bar code on the timer box.

I fished my wallet for my rewards card. The unpleasant scent lingered.

* * * * *

I caught up to the woman in the parking lot. She crouched beside a rusted Dodge minivan, struggling with a clutter of clothing, toys and unidentified objects that had spilled into the new snow from the van's open side door.

"What were you doing, Casey?" she demanded, kneeling to gather up the debris.

A small girl leaned out. "I was building a fort! Please don't be mad, Mommy!"

"Shush! You'll wake the baby!"

I tossed the timer in my car and turned to lend her a hand, but she was too fast. She scooped up the laundry and shoved the pile behind the front passenger seat. She picked up bits of plastic, a flat cereal box and a few other items, shook the snow off, and tossed them in. Her mountain of possessions threatened a fresh avalanche. She avoided disaster by yanking the sliding door forward. It groaned on a rusted track. She put her shoulder into it and forced the door to latch, then hurried around the van. The Dodge cranked reluctantly to life, and she wheeled out of the lot. Watching her go, I thought her night stood a good chance of getting worse. She drove with one taillight out.

* * * * *

The Essex United Presbyterian Church is a country church, founded by the farmers who settled Essex County when President Tyler doled out land grants. The church dominates the northwest corner of the intersection of a county road and a narrow town road. The pastor's manse faces the church from the opposite corner. The congregational cemetery takes up the northeast corner. Cornfields and hayfields abut all borders of the church property, isolating it. The white steeple, when lighted, is visible for miles in each direction, especially in winter.

Tonight, Christmas lights in the windows and the spotlighted Nativity scene on the front lawn supplemented the holy spirit with holiday spirit. At a distance, the white wooden church looked like a decorative miniature in a snow globe.

I pushed the speed limit on the empty county road. My watch said that the organist was warming up and Andy was taking her seat with the rest of the congregation. If installing the timer gave me any trouble, my arrival might not be covered by the first hymn.

Two miles from the church, a single brake light flashed ahead. A right turn signal flickered. The lights disappeared quickly. Between the snow charging into my headlights and my preoccupation with the looming task of finding the extension cord running from the church to the Nativity scene, I hardly took note.

Except to wonder.

Who needs a garden hose at Christmas?

When I reached the intersection where the vehicle turned, I glanced east, down the side road. A puff of exhaust bloomed red around a solo taillight.

A small park sits between two cornfields, donated to the county by the farmer and billed as a meditation spot in memory of his mother. It's not much more than a three-car gravel lot, a picnic table and a half acre of mowed grass that ends where a stream passes at the back of the property.

The red light glowed briefly before turning into the tiny park.

I lifted my foot off the gas and pumped the brake. My car slid to a stop. The engine and I sat idling.

Wondering.

My built-in time sense warned that Andy's beautiful eyes would judge me harshly for showing up late, but my hand closed on the shifter and threw it in reverse. I retraced my path through the intersection. I stopped, shoved the car in gear, spun the tires and turned east.

Approaching the park entrance, I slowed to a crawl. I squinted through my wet side window. The dark boxy shape of the minivan crouched on the snowy lot. The park entrance sloped and had not been plowed. Deep tracks suggested that turning around and driving back out again might be challenging, especially in an old front-wheel drive minivan.

I eased my car to the side of the road.

I killed the engine and climbed out for a better look.

Winter landscapes, especially under falling snow, bear a signature silence. Or should. This silent night was broken by the steady hum and occasional wheezing of the old Dodge's engine. A cloud of exhaust billowed from the rear of the van.

I walked back to where her wheel tracks left the road.

You're going to scare the poor girl, I warned myself. She probably had a perfectly good reason for stopping.

I wasn't crazy about hiking down the snow-covered slope in my freshly polished and buffed boots. The footing on leather soles can be slick. I considered vanishing and floating across the snow. A BLASTER power unit and propeller nestled at the ready in the pocket of my leather jacket. Yet disappearing carried with it the complication of reappearing beside her vehicle—or creating cause to question why I left no tracks.

I trotted down the slope and trudged up behind the one-eyed rear of the minivan. Snow and moisture glossed the dark, fogged windows. Dashboard lights lent an interior glitter to wet drops accumulating and freezing on the glass.

I stopped.

A curved line in the snow began just below the tailpipe. The indentation snaked around the left rear of the van and then forward, parallel to recent tracks. I followed the line until it reached the driver's door. There, the newly purchased garden hose rose out of the snow. It hung from the driver's window, which had been nudged up to secure the hose end. Clothing had been stuffed in the gaps on either side of the hose.

I retraced my steps to the rear of the vehicle, to the exhaust pipe. The garden hose had been inserted in the pipe, but it must have been a poor fit. The hose end lay in the snow.

Shit.

I thought of the little voice that begged, *"Please don't be mad, Mommy!"*

Mommy wasn't mad. Mommy was *Done.*

Mommy found the end of a road I could hardly imagine. I thought about the mountain of possessions, the odor, the scramble for change and surrender of what must have been her last dollar for a last resort.

I thought about the candy cane she couldn't afford but couldn't do without.

The snow falling on my shoulders suddenly acquired weight.

I walked back to the driver's door and closed my left hand on the handle.

Fwooomp!

Vanished, I put my right hand on the minivan for leverage and pulled open the driver's door. It creaked angrily. I let it swing to the stops and held on.

She startled.

She lay across the front seats with her back to the passenger-side door. A golden-haired bundle of mismatched snow pants and oversized winter jacket curled up against her shoulder. She clutched a smaller bundle in a blue blanket against her chest. The van smelled sour and dank, but with a hint of peppermint. I've smelled better barns.

Red-rimmed eyes flared on the woman's elfish face. She had been pretty before the road leading her to this final parking spot drained her face of softness and light. Glaring into the darkness, a mix of fear and guilt embossed her expression.

"Who's there?!" she cried, tightening her grip on the children. "Who are you?"

"The name's Gabriel," I replied.

She jerked the children closer and sat up. Her head shot from side to side, searching the windows.

"Where are you? What do you want?"

"I'm right here." I reached for her feet and tapped her ankle. She jolted and pulled her foot back. "Hey, relax. You're the one who called me."

"I didn't call anyone!"

I reached up and wiggled the hose end dangling through the cracked-open window. "Uh, you kinda did. This is what you wanted, right? To end it all?"

She blinked.

"Fast acting. Painless. I'm here to take you the rest of the way."

She swallowed.

"Mommy, who's there?"

"The name's...uh...Gabriel, Casey. Sorry you can't see me. I'm an angel."

"How do you know my name?"

"Come," I said. "Come outside."

The little girl obediently shifted to crawl out, but her mother pulled her tighter. "No! Go away! We're not—done yet!"

"If you weren't done, would you be talking to me?"

She said nothing.

"Okay look, I may have intervened here. The truth is, if you finish *this*—you're technically committing a couple of crimes I'd rather not name in front of Casey. And that might send you off in... let's just say another direction."

She stared at the empty open doorway.

"It's okay. You're going to be okay. Trust me. Come."

Trust came slowly. She let the little girl go first, then slid across the front seats and eased out of the van. Sinking her sandaled feet into the snow, she pulled the small girl close and frantically searched the empty lot.

"I'm right here," I said. I gripped the steering wheel and leaned in to turn the key in the ignition and kill the engine. "No point in wasting gas."

She whirled around and stood wide-eyed. "Are we...?"

"Going someplace warm? Where there's food? Yup."

"I'm hungry, Mommy. Are you really an angel? Why can't I see you?"

"You can't see me because—well, because it doesn't work that way—because if I appear, I'll get my wings all full of snow. And then I can't fly. Here. Do you feel that?" I reached out and touched the little girl's cheek. She broke into a bright smile.

"It's magic! Mommy feel it!"

The mother blinked at her daughter. I didn't want to touch the mother's cheek, so I squeezed her shoulder instead. She shivered and jerked away.

"Okay, here's the deal," I said. "We need to travel. And what's one thing angels love to do?" I directed the question at the little girl.

"Angels can fly!"

"And you can, too," I said. "I'm going to give you all a hug. Ready?" I pulled out the BLASTER power unit and snapped the prop in place.

The young woman's lips quivered. Wet drops ran down her cheeks. She scooped the little girl off her feet. The move split between defensive and compliant.

"Are you ready?" I asked again.

She dipped her chin twice.

I closed my left arm around them. The woman stiffened, but I pulled the collective bundle into a hug. I gripped the levers in my head and pushed.

FWOOOMP!

They vanished in my arms.

The woman shrieked. She tightened her grip on the small girl and baby. *The other thing's* cool sensation replaced the biting cold that seeped under my coat and through my clothes. Gravity let go. The woman sucked in a harsh breath.

"It's okay," I said softly. "You're gonna love this."

I flexed my ankles and pushed gently. We broke contact with the ground and rose, which ignited a gasp.

"Mommy, look!"

I held the three of them against me with my left arm. I rotated us and extended my right hand, aiming the BLASTER unit.

"Get ready! Here we go!" I pushed the power unit slide control. The prop hummed. We eased forward across the fresh snow, rising slowly.

"MOMMY! MOMMY! Look! We're flying! We're angels, Mommy!"

The woman whispered, "We are, honey! We are!" A choked sob shook her against my grip.

"Do you know Santa?" Casey asked.

"We're best friends," I replied. I aimed higher. The snowscape fell away. The minivan, a dark blot on virginal white, receded. My own car sat by the road in puddles of parking light illumination. I hoped the young mother wouldn't notice; if she did, she might question Gabriel's arrival via worn out Toyota Corolla.

"You know Santa? Really?"

"Angels can't lie," I lied.

"Mommy! He knows Santa!" The young woman squeezed her daughter in reply.

We glided across the small park, over a fence and across corn stubble smothered in fresh snow. I navigated under a set of power lines and veered right to follow the road, skimming six feet above the pavement. I set a course for the beacon at the next intersection, the white steeple towering over fields of snow. The illumination cast to the four corners of the compass gave the winter scene a ghostly serenity.

"Mommy, the angel knows Santa!"

"That's right, I do," I said when the woman didn't answer. "If you tell me what you want for Christmas, I can tell him myself."

"Mommy!"

I steered to the front of the church and eased to a landing on the concrete stoop beneath big double doors that wore twin evergreen wreaths. On the lawn, the Nativity diorama glowed, turning the falling snow into a cascade of sparkles. Spotlights aimed at the steeple filled the sky with glitter.

"Easy now," I said, ensuring that the woman had her feet firmly under her. "Get ready."

Fwooomp! I let her go. She snapped into view and wobbled on the salted concrete. I kept my hands close, ready to catch her, but she found her footing. For the first time, the baby cooed and squeaked. She quickly adjusted the blanket over the infant's face.

"Go inside," I said. "They're waiting for you." She didn't move. She looked for my voice in the air. "Go on."

I fixed a grip on both handles of the big doors. Using one for leverage, I opened the other.

No question. I missed the first hymn. The pastor's voice carried, amplified by speakers in the small church lobby.

"...so Joseph went up from the town of Nazareth in Galilee to Judea, to Bethlehem, the town of David..."

"Go ahead. It's okay."

Bewildered, she stepped into the candle-lit church. I pushed her gently.

"Wait! Wait!" the little girl cried out. In the church congregation, heads turned. "Where are you? You have to tell Santa!"

I pulsed the power unit to lower myself. I bent my knees, dropping to face her. I reached out and put a hand behind the child's head, then kissed her cheek and whispered in her ear, "You can tell me."

She lifted a hand and found my chest, then traced my neck and cheek. She leaned closer, cupped my ear, and whispered loudly, "Tell Santa I want a house for Mommy."

"I will," I whispered back.

The woman fought off a sob and gently tugged her daughter forward. I let the door close behind them. Alone outside—

Fwooomp!

—I reappeared. Silent snow fell, dusting my shoulders and hair. A trio of wise men, a camel and a cow loitered on the lawn, ignoring me, enchanted by an infant under a rundown shelter.

At least they had a barn.

I'm not sure why, but it kinda pissed me off.

I gave it a long minute, then opened the door and hurried into the church. The scent of fresh-cut pine boughs and green bean casserole warming in the basement kitchen greeted me. The pastor continued his Christmas story.

"...but the angel said to them, 'Do not be afraid, for I bring you good news that will cause great joy for all the people...'"

She hadn't moved. If anything, the young mother stood more frozen with fear than when I'd found her. I stomped the snow off my boots, which caught her attention.

"Hi!" I whispered loudly. "Merry Christmas!"

She didn't answer. She dropped her eyes and pulled her daughter out of the path of the stranger, making way for me to pass her by. It occurred to me that I wasn't the only one able to exist unseen.

Andy, seated on the aisle four rows from the front, leaned out and turned her head. She fixed a questioning look on me, then shifted it to the woman with the small children.

"Why don't you come and sit with me and my wife? And then we'll eat."

She examined her shabby clothes and shook her head vigorously.

"No way!"

I smiled. I held out my hand for Casey, who took it without hesitation.

"Way," I said.

A WAY IN A MANGER
28 November 2019

ABOUT THE AUTHOR

Howard Seaborne began writing novels in spiral notebooks at age ten. He began flying airplanes at age sixteen. He is a former flight instructor and commercial charter pilot. Today he flies a Beechcraft Bonanza, Beechcraft Baron and a Rotorway experimental helicopter he built in his garage. He lives with his wife and writes and flies during all four seasons in Wisconsin, never far from Essex County Airport.

Visit www.HowardSeaborne.com to join the Email List and get a FREE DOWNLOAD.

DIVISIBLE MAN

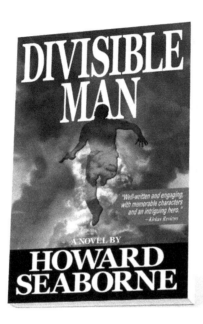

The media calls it a "miracle" when air charter pilot Will Stewart survives an aircraft in-flight breakup, but Will's miracle pales beside the stunning after-effect of the crash. Barely on his feet again, Will and his police sergeant wife Andy race to rescue an innocent child from a heinous abduction—*if Will's new ability doesn't kill him first.*

Available in print, digital and audio.

Learn more at **HowardSeaborne.com**

DIVISIBLE MAN: THE SIXTH PAWN

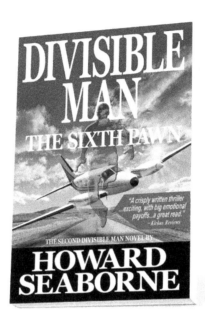

When the Essex County "Wedding of the Century" erupts in gunfire, Will and Andy Stewart confront a criminal element no one could have foreseen. Will tests the extraordinary after-effect of surviving a devastating airplane crash while Andy works a case obstructed by powerful people wielding the sinister influence of unlimited money in politics.

Available in print, digital and audio.

Learn more at **HowardSeaborne.com**

DIVISIBLE MAN: THE SECOND GHOST

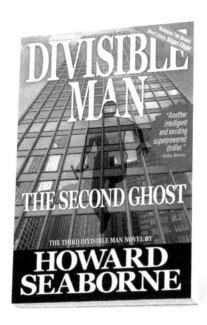

Tormented by a cyber stalker, Lane Franklin's best friend turns to suicide. Lane's frantic call to Will and Andy Stewart launches them on a desperate rescue. When it all goes bad, Will must adapt his extraordinary ability to survive the dangerous high steel and glass of Chicago as Andy and Pidge encounter the edge of disaster. **Includes the short story, "Angel Flight,"a bridge to the fourth DIVISIBLE MAN novel that follows.**

Available in print, digital and audio.

Learn more at **HowardSeaborne.com**

DIVISIBLE MAN: THE SEVENTH STAR

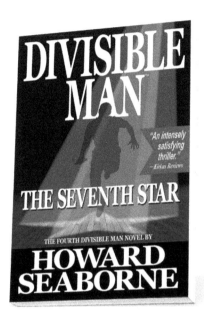

A horrifying message turns a holiday gathering tragic. An unsolved murder hangs a death threat over Detective Andy Stewart's head. And internet-fueled hatred targets Will and Andy's friend Lane. Will and Andy struggle to keep the ones they love safe, while hunting a dead murderer before he can kill again. As the tension tightens, Will confronts a troubling revelation about the extraordinary after-effect of his midair collision.

Available in print, digital and audio.

Learn more at **HowardSeaborne.com**

DIVISIBLE MAN: TEN MAN CREW

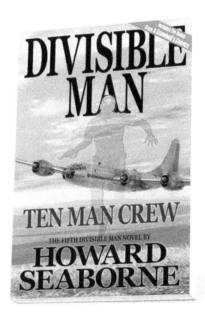

An unexpected visit from the FBI threatens Will Stewart's secret and sends Detective Andy Stewart on a collision course with her darkest impulses. A twisted road reveals how a long-buried Cold War secret has been weaponized. And Pidge shows a daring side of herself that could cost her dearly.

Available in print, digital and audio.

Learn more at **HowardSeaborne.com**

DIVISIBLE MAN: THE THIRD LIE

Caught up in a series of hideous crimes that generate national headlines, Will faces the critical question of whether to reveal himself or allow innocent lives to be lost. The stakes go higher than ever when Andy uncovers the real reason behind a celebrity athlete's assault on an underaged girl. And Will discovers that the limits of his ability can lead to disaster.

A Kirkus Starred Review.

A Kirkus Star is awarded to "books of exceptional merit."

Available in print, digital and audio.

Learn more at **HowardSeaborne.com**

DIVISIBLE MAN: THREE NINES FINE

A mysterious mission request from Earl Jackson sends Will into the sphere of a troubled celebrity. A meeting with the Deputy Director of the FBI that goes terribly wrong. Will and Andy find themselves on the run from Federal authorities, infiltrating a notorious cartel, and racing to prevent what might prove to be the crime of the century.

Available in print, digital and audio.

Learn more at **HowardSeaborne.com**

DIVISIBLE MAN: EIGHT BALL

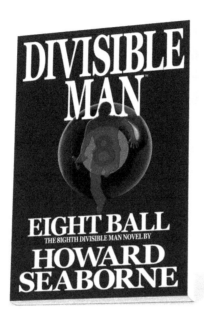

Will's encounter with a deadly sniper on a serial killing rampage sends him deeper into the FBI's hands with costly consequences for Andy. And when billionaire Spiro Lewko makes an appearance, Will and Andy's future takes a dark turn. The stakes could not be higher when the sniper's ultimate target is revealed.

Available in print, digital and audio.

Learn more at **HowardSeaborne.com**

ENGINE OUT AND OTHER SHORT FLIGHTS

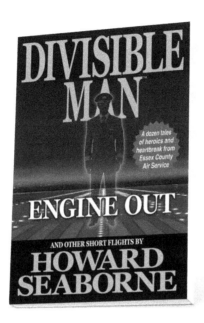

AVAILABLE: JUNE 2022

Things just have a way of happening around Will and Andy Stewart. In this collection of twelve tales from Essex County, boy meets girl, a mercy flight goes badly wrong, and Will crashes and burns when he tries dating again. Engines fail. Shots are fired. A rash of the unexpected breaks loose —from bank jobs to zombies.

Available in print, digital and audio.

Learn more at **HowardSeaborne.com**

DIVISIBLE MAN: NINE LIVES LOST

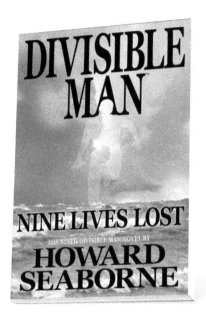

AVAILABLE: JUNE 2022

A simple request from Earl Jackson sends Will on a desperate cross-country chase ultimately looking for answers to a mystery that literally landed at Will and Andy's mailbox. At the same time, a threat to Andy's career takes a deadly turn. Before it all ends, Will confronts answers in a deep, dark place he never imagined.

Available in print, digital and audio.

Learn more at **HowardSeaborne.com**

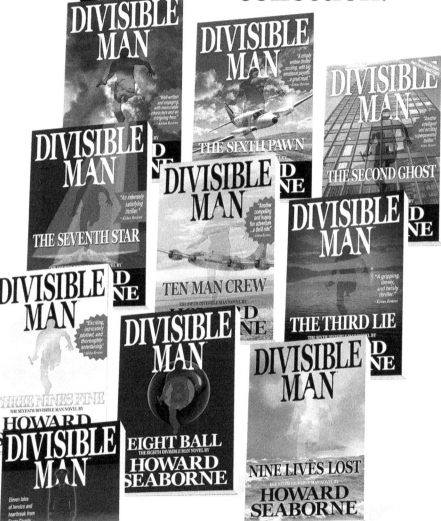

CPSIA information can be obtained
at www.ICGtesting.com
Printed in the USA
LVHW081652171122
733426LV00025B/582/J